**MAYBE TOMORROW
I'LL KNOW**

MAYBE TOMORROW I'LL KNOW

ALEX RITANY

A Novel

Norton Young Readers

An Imprint of W. W. Norton & Company

Independent Publishers Since 1923

Copyright © 2026 by Alex Ritany

All rights reserved
Printed in the United States of America
First Edition

For information about permission to reproduce selections from this book, write to
Permissions, W. W. Norton & Company, Inc., 500 Fifth Avenue, New York, NY 10110

For information about special discounts for bulk purchases, please contact
W. W. Norton Special Sales at specialsales@wwnorton.com or 800-233-4830

Manufacturing by Lakeside Book Company
Book design by Hana Anouk Nakamura
Production manager: Delaney Adams

ISBN 978-1-324-08363-4

W. W. Norton & Company, Inc., 500 Fifth Avenue, New York, NY 10110
www.wwnorton.com

W. W. Norton & Company Ltd., 15 Carlisle Street, London W1D 3BS

Authorized EU representative: EAS, Mustamäe tee 50, 10621 Tallinn, Estonia

10 9 8 7 6 5 4 3 2 1

For Abby

AUTHOR'S NOTE

As I wrote this book, the world was gearing up for a campaign of hatred against transgender people. As much as this book is an ode to the process of self-discovery, it is also a response to the notion that being trans is the worst-case scenario. My hope is that you reach the end of this book with a determination to honor the life you were given, whatever that may look like. But in order to illustrate why that determination is so important, I had to explore the harmful rhetoric that challenges it. As such, be aware this book contains on-page transphobia through a religious lens and allusions to suicidal ideation that may be disturbing to some readers. Take caution, be well, and as always, have hope.

MAYBE TOMORROW I'LL KNOW

1:00

ONE.

When the nightmare ends and I open my eyes, I know three things only: first, freckles spatter the backs of my hands where they rest on the steering wheel; second, the radio is blowing static; and third, I'm going a hundred and twenty clicks on a highway I've never seen before in my life.

The fourth thought comes late, like the sting after a slap: *I love the hell out of this car*, which is a strange thought to have, because it's not mine, and I have no idea who it belongs to.

My heartbeat rattles.

Maybe it's the nightmare, but adrenaline sings through my veins as I hit a pothole so hard my teeth clack together, and it hits me that everything I know in the world is what I can see in this car and through the windshield. Bright morning sun pours across my knuckles and spills over the gray leather seats. Green fields stretch into oblivion on my left while a layer of blue hazy mountains bracket the rolling foothills on my right, and I don't know my own name.

I don't know my own name.

I don't know my own name, and this is not my car, and these are not my hands. I take them off the wheel, flexing the long spindly fingers I don't recognize, brown sugar freckles disappearing under the long sleeves of a gray plaid flannel shirt that isn't mine either.

The clock on the dashboard says it's exactly one o'clock.

One hundred and thirty clicks. My heart leaps, beating light and fluttery like a hummingbird's wings as I snatch the wheel again and ease off the gas, down to one hundred, to eighty, sixty, too slow for a highway, drifting into the other lane. I overcorrect to get out of the way, careening off the side of the road before I even realize I'm in danger.

The impact slams me forward against the wheel, a crack of fracturing glass—a headlight, I think.

I groan.

The radio is still blowing static.

Five seconds too late to be useful, the airbag deploys, pushing me back so I slump in my seat. Long, light brown hair falls into my face, fanning around me and obscuring my vision.

Slowly, I take stock.

Nothing's broken, but my neck is sore. Other than that—

Where the *hell* am I?

I flip the sun visor down.

A set of shocking blue eyes stare back at me through the dusty rectangular mirror. Blue eyes, those same brown-sugar freckles scattered over a long, large Roman nose set over a pointed chin, cheeks narrow and angular. Mascara—*mascara?*—clings to my lower lashes, smudging under my eyes like I left it on overnight, or like I was just crying.

I'm in the middle of thinking that I hate wearing mascara when it occurs to me: it's the first thing I'm sure is true about myself.

No. The car.

My stomach twists.

The car is the first thing I'm sure is true about myself. I just crashed the car that I love so much, and I can't even remember—

Trying to discern *why* I love it triggers a throbbing ache in my temple.

Fumbling, I turn the keys in the ignition. The radio cuts out as the low roar of the engine stops, and because the sharp sting of gasoline makes me nervous, I open the driver's-side door and shimmy out from under the airbag onto the dry, prickly, bone-white grass on the side of the highway, falling to my knees and scrambling back to my feet, coughing from the sudden smack of hot air.

"Hey!"

I whirl.

A green John Deere tractor idles at the mouth of a side road across the highway from me. A figure hangs out the side, waving an arm.

Shielding my eyes from the glare of the sun, I watch the figure drop from the tractor onto the dusty road and jog across all four lanes.

It's a guy, probably in his late teens, with sun-bronzed skin and high cheekbones, long black hair tied back, tendrils escaping and clinging to his face in the rasping heat. Once he gets closer, I see the aftermath of what must have been a nasty hit to the face: a dark-purple bruise ripples under his eye and over the bridge of his nose.

"Hey!" he repeats as he crosses the last of the painted-on lines and slows to a walk. "I saw you crash. Are you okay?"

His voice is a deep bass, a little hoarse, like he's been shouting.

"I—" I stammer, and then choke on the sound of my own voice, high and airy. Even though this face looks like a girl's, it's still startling, disorienting like I missed a step going downstairs. I blink rapidly to make the sudden stinging go away. "I'm okay, thank you."

"What happened?" He rounds the front of the car to take stock, screwing up his nose.

"I don't know," I tell him, because that's pretty much all I've got.

"Looked like you lost control. You were going pretty fast. Something spook you?"

"You could say that," I mutter, following him to the front of the car.

It could be worse.

The headlight *is* busted, but I could probably fix—

Wait. Do I know how to fix car stuff? Trying to hold the idea in my head feels like trying to hold water in my cupped palms.

"Probably need a tow," the guy says, mostly to himself, scratching his head. His exposed shoulders gleam in the sun, muscles rippling. "Do you live around here?"

I open my mouth, then hesitate. My instinct is to say no, but I don't know if I can trust myself with any details, and even if I could, I don't have a frame of reference for where I am to begin with.

I've waited too long to answer him.

Squinting, he walks toward me, rubbing his hand on the front of his black tank top. "Do you remember if you hit your head?"

Up close, he's kind of a lot. Flyaway hairs catch the light and glow blown-glass orange, and when he turns, his eyes in the sun are amber and honey-warm under straight dark eyebrows.

My mouth goes dry. "I don't—" I stammer. "I don't think so. Just some whiplash."

He nods, lips pressed together. "What's your name?"

Ah, fuck.

Floundering, I give him the first name that pops into my head. "Uh, Laurie."

And, like, it doesn't feel *wrong*.

It just doesn't feel like *anything*.

"Okay, Laurie." He frowns down at the front of my car once more.

It's an old car. Silver, slick like a little beetle, kind of like a James Bond car—

Cool. I know about James Bond, but can't remember my own name.

"I'm Gideon." He touches a hand to his chest, an assortment of beaded leather bracelets clacking together on his wrist. "I doubt we can get your car out of the ditch by ourselves."

I nod, looking down at my knobby knees. Whoever this body belongs to, I don't imagine she does much lifting. And even though this Gideon guy looks plenty strong, I don't think he can haul a whole car back onto the road, no matter how much I'd like to see him try it.

I pat down my pockets, hopeful.

Nothing. Completely empty, except for a gum wrapper in the front pocket of my shorts. So, whoever this body belongs to, she also hates me.

"Do you have anyone nearby?" Gideon asks, scratching his head.

This, at least, is easy to answer. I shake my head, but I don't want him to feel like this is *his* problem to solve. "Maybe I could..."

But I don't know how to finish that. I have no context for where I am, or why, or where I was going, or where I've come from. Nausea rises with rolling déjà vu, and I snap my mouth shut.

All I know in the world wraps into a neat little package: I crashed a car I apparently love, I can't remember a single thing from before five minutes ago, and I'm on the side of the road with a stranger in a body that isn't mine.

TWO.

"So. Laurie." Gideon cuts me a glance from the driver's side as the tractor rolls slowly down the highway. "Where are you from?"

Swallowing hard, I fiddle with the elastic hair tie around my wrist, leather of the passenger seat sticking to my thighs.

A thin layer of dust and grime coats the front windshield, tinting the world sepia. All I can see for ages to my right are prairie fields, and to my left, those rolling hills leading to the mountains. Then, because the town we're headed for doesn't look like much more than a dark scuff on the near horizon, I take a gamble and tell him, "The city."

He nods like this makes sense. "Just taking a joyride, then?"

"Something like that."

About every ten seconds, I reconsider telling him the truth, but every time, I chicken out. After all, I know nothing about *him*. He could be an awful person, or a serial killer or something.

But I doubt it. Unless his MO is making sure strangers on the side of the road are okay and then driving them into town to peel their skin off.

Cautiously, I ask, "Where are we? I was sort of zoned out while driving. I must have missed the sign."

There it is, that frustrating looming feeling. I know about serial killers and highway road signs, like somewhere in my head there's a file folder full of information locked behind a firewall. See? File folders. Firewalls. I know stuff.

Just nothing helpful.

"Nanton," Gideon tells me, guiding the tractor around a curve with his grass-stained knee. "We're about an hour south of Calgary."

Something in my head lights up with a little *ping!* like a homing beacon.

Hell, maybe I *am* from the city.

"Cool."

"Where were you headed anyway?" he asks.

This time, I risk just not answering at all, instead countering with a question of my own. "What happened to your eye?"

His hand flies to brush the edges of the bruise, brows pulling inward, but then he just smiles, this devilish thing that makes his cheeks dimple and makes my stomach lurch a bit. "You should see the other guy."

I flex my fingers. "Ah."

"Don't worry," he assures me. "I don't bite. Too hard."

The little wink he shoots my way does not do a spectacular job of either reassuring me or settling my stomach.

My cheeks tighten with heat. "Right. Okay."

Up ahead, the town of Nanton sprawls. I scan everything I can, taking in the splash of green trees huddling around the rows of houses, hoping something will spark any flicker of recognition.

But it's just a collection of houses.

Gideon steers the tractor toward a large shed just off the highway, the silence spreading between us like thick honey. Mouth dry, my mind races as I consider my options. Do I even *have* options? Once we get into town, I don't have any money, and I don't have a phone, even if I did have someone to call.

It's just me. And this body, whoever it belongs to.

Close to the shed—which contains two other identical tractors—a young guy slouches against a weathered, lichen-eaten fence, shirtless except for a lime-green safety vest. As Gideon pulls up next to him, he pushes off the fence, spitting a stalk of grass onto the ground and shaking out a mess of brown curls. "Who's the chick?"

Gideon rolls his eyes and chucks the tractor keys at him.

Catching them against his chest, he tilts his head. Under the vest, his hunched shoulders look patchy, like he's sunburnt badly one too many times.

"This is Laurie," Gideon tells him, climbing down from the tractor with a little groan, like it hurts, and there's something *immediately* different in his demeanor—he's gone all surly. But also deferential somehow. "Bit of car trouble, s'all."

I pat my shorts pocket once more to make sure the keys are still there.

They are.

Slowly, I climb down out of the tractor.

"And you really don't have anything else with you?" Gideon asks me, just like he had before he offered me a ride.

Again, I shake my head, though now I'm regretting that I didn't at least pop the trunk to double-check.

"No phone, no wallet." Gideon eyes me.

"Shit." The other boy chews on the corner of his thumbnail. "Are you being trafficked or something?"

"Shut up, Ricky." Gideon rolls his eyes. To me, he says, "Ignore him."

"Or, if you want, I can take over." Ricky gives me a wicked flash of a grin. "You're taking her to Tenley, right?"

"What's Tenley?" I ask.

"She's—" Ricky cuts off with a squawk, stumbling backward as Gideon steps toward him, eyes flashing. "*Fuck*, man, seriously? There's nobody here. Not like she—fine, I mean, *they*—would hear me."

"You're a piece of shit, Ricky," Gideon snaps, and it sounds like he really means it: brows low, straight lines, expression drained of mirth, leaving me fighting the urge to step back and away, dread rippling up my spine.

Ricky surrenders, both hands held aloft. He cuts me a strange, nearly conspiratorial glance—as if to say *Get a load of this guy*—before he turns, tone loud enough that we both hear it when he mutters, "Good fucking riddance, Norris."

Gideon's nostrils flare. As soon as Ricky's out of earshot, voice flat, he tells me, "And that's Ricky."

I cough a little into my hand. "He seems . . . nice."

He just snorts, shaking his head. "We're gonna have to walk the rest of the way. Sorry."

"To Tenley?" I fall into step behind him. When he nods, I urge, "Who is . . . ?"

"Oh, shit, yeah." Gideon glances over his shoulder at where

Ricky's watching us. "Tenley's like . . . I don't know. Dad, I guess. You'll know what I mean."

That clarifies absolutely nothing, but I don't bother pointing that out.

Late-morning sun beats down on us as I follow him along the shoulder, the back of my neck prickling. It *must* be summer. There's something about the way it smells that makes me think of a sprinkler arcing low, the ice-cold raspberry punch of a popsicle melting on my tongue, like—

Shit.

Was that a memory?

I stop walking.

So does Gideon, pivoting on his heel. I must not be doing an outstanding job of hiding my expression, because he frowns. "What?"

I shake my head, blinking. If that *was* a memory, it's useless trying to hold on to it, because it's swirling away. "Nothing."

He starts walking again, faster now. "Tenley will know if you have a concussion."

Maybe this Tenley will know what's wrong with me too. Or at least help me figure out who this body belongs to, if I can muster up the courage to tell the truth.

"Why'd Ricky say 'good riddance' like that?" I ask.

Gideon laughs. It's not a pleasant laugh. "Don't worry about it. It's just Ricky. He's always saying dumb shit. It's not a big deal."

The dark edge to his tone does nothing to convince me. "How do you guys know each other, then?"

At that, Gideon laughs again, a yelp of surprise this time,

broken glass. "What a question," he muses, leading me past the first house and off the side of the highway, onto a little well-beaten dirt path lined with dozens of tiny white daisies. To himself, he echoes, "How *do* we know each other?"

I just wait.

So far, I'm getting the impression that Gideon is not the most open of books, so it surprises me when he heaves a sigh.

"Ricky . . ." His voice slides away, uncertain. "He's sort of my brother."

I blink.

"Or, he used to be."

THREE.

We find Tenley almost ten blocks into town. By the time we're approaching the flickering neon Open sign that hangs in the window of a nondescript gas-station convenience store, sweat drips down my spine in a wavering line.

Gideon shoves open the glass front door—inside, a bell goes off, crackling with electronic static—and gestures me in.

Inside it's crammed with shelves overflowing with color, lines of chips and boxes of candy and packages of nuts alongside fluorescent bottles of soda and energy drinks.

"Tenley!" Gideon announces, walking in like he owns the place. "I found another one!"

My stomach drops. Another what? What does *he* think is going on?

At the counter, a figure—Tenley, I assume—looks up at us over thick tortoiseshell glasses. Long gray hair cascades over their shoulders in an unruly cloud, and deep grooves carve into their warm brown skin, crow's feet and deep dimples, dark eyes glittering. They do not smile. They look at Gideon. "What's the matter?"

He walks right up to the counter and leans an elbow on

the plexiglass surface. "Saw this girl drive into the ditch just out of town."

This girl sends discomfort crawling along my skin, a hundred invisible insects.

"No stuff, no phone," he continues. "Car'll need a tow, for sure."

At *no stuff, no phone*, Tenley's eyebrows lift and they turn back to me. "What's your name?"

Their voice is low and gravelly, a rich bass beaten to a scraping crackle.

"Laurie," I tell them, because what the hell. It might as well be my name. And then, because it's been a persistent itch in the back of my head, cheeks flushing hot as my voice cracks, I add, "And I don't have money for a tow truck."

But Tenley just nods. "Don't worry about that. Gideon will take care of it."

If this is a surprise to him, Gideon doesn't let on. Turning to Tenley, he asks, "You'll be okay to take care of her for me?"

And I *object* to that sentiment. "I'm—"

"Not that you need to be taken care of," he assures me with a careless wink.

My cheeks flare and I snap my mouth shut.

Tenley comes out from behind the counter, leaning heavily on a cane covered completely in brightly-colored Pokémon stickers, which, okay, I recognize Squirtle, apparently. They squint up at Gideon—he's a good head taller than they are—and barrel straight on to a new question without answering his original one. "Have they changed their minds?"

Gideon's smile wavers and then slips. "You think this was gonna do it?" He gestures to his eye, which looks ghastly under the fluorescent lighting. When he laughs, it's that unpleasant sound again, all sandpaper and serrated edges. "No. And they won't, so don't you go after them."

Tenley shakes their head and reaches up to take Gideon's arm.

Gideon winces a bit, though by the looks of Tenley's swollen, reddened knuckles, it's the deadly serious expression on their face that's getting to him, not their grip.

"You're not going to run off on me, are you?"

"I'll find you tonight," Gideon assures them. "Swear."

They release him with a glower and a low, gravelly "You'd better."

Then, waving him off, Tenley turns to me. "Now. Laurie. What do you need?"

"I—" I stammer, taken aback. "I don't—"

"I'll be back later," Gideon tells me, still serious and unsmiling. "Gonna go find someone with a truck."

Tenley lifts a finger. "Try R—"

"Not him." Gideon shakes his head. "Come *on*, Tenley."

They shut their mouth and lean on their cane with a heavy sigh.

Gideon turns to me. "You trust me?"

And, like, I don't really have much of a choice. But I *do* trust him, as much as I trust anybody in my life, which so far is the two of them and Ricky. So I nod, even though I don't know where this is going.

"Can I have your keys?" he asks. "Won't even run off with them, promise."

I fish them out of my pocket, and my chest only twinges a little when they hit his palm. Softly, I tell him, "Thank you."

With a swift nod, he turns to leave.

My eyes prickle and I turn away, cheeks and ears flushed. I don't need Gideon to see me getting all emotional just because he's helping me when he has no good reason to. But Tenley notices, and that's almost worse.

The bell sounds again as Gideon walks out. I cross my arms as Tenley watches me intently. For a moment, we're both quiet.

Then they ask, "So. What's going on, Laurie?"

The base of my throat hardens into a knot.

"No stuff, no phone." Slowly, they migrate back to their post behind the counter. "Such an unusual set of circumstances."

Wordless, I nod.

"You don't have to tell me anything." They gesture to the door. "And nobody is trapping you here. You can go whenever you want. But it'll be an awful lot easier for me to help you if you stay and tell me what's going on."

Longingly, I gaze through the dusty glass to the parking lot beyond. Common sense begs me to get the hell out of here so I can figure everything out on my own, but even if my head isn't sure, the rest of me trusts Tenley. Anyway, Gideon has my keys now, so it's a moot point.

Tenley surveys me, both hands resting on their cane, waiting.

I remember Ricky—*You're taking her to Tenley, right?*—and the pit in my stomach releases. Then I remember Gideon—*I found another one!*—and it contracts again just as quickly.

Either Tenley *is* the person they go to when someone needs help, or that joke about trafficking wasn't a joke.

I gesture to the door. "I could go?"

"If you want," Tenley says, and then laughs at the look on

my face. "What, do you think *I* could stop you? Honey, I had hip surgery six weeks ago. You're a free woman. Do what you want."

Jerkily, I nod.

"You need help," Tenley tells me when I don't make a move to leave, not like it's a question.

I nod. "I just—I don't really know . . . what I need help with yet, is the thing."

Tenley just laughs. "What a puzzle you are, Laurie. Sit down."

When they pat a little stool next to them behind the counter, I go, if a bit hesitantly.

"I do have some questions," Tenley says. "Just the basics, if you're all right with that."

Clearing my throat and tugging the plaid flannel around me—which keeps falling off my shoulder—I nod.

They heave a sigh. "Are you in danger?"

What a question. I almost laugh. Then I decide right there that if I don't know, I'm just going to go with my best guess, because I don't think Tenley would be very patient with endless *I-don't-knows* from me, and telling the truth is a capital B Bad Idea and out of the question.

So I shake my head. "No."

"Is there anyone coming after you?"

Shit. I hadn't even thought of that. Slowly, I shake my head.

"Is that the truth, Laurie?"

"It's the truth." *As far as I know.*

"Okay." They nod. "Lastly, do you need a place to stay tonight?"

Finally, a question I actually know the answer to, and I'd rather die than answer it.

Heat tightens my cheeks, and I squeeze my hands into fists in my lap before I nod. "But I don't—like I said, I don't have any money, so—"

"Nonsense." Tenley waves me off. "I don't make a habit of charging people who need my help."

Gratitude wells up in me again, pooling in the back of my throat and behind my ears, too warm for comfort.

"Here's what's going to happen," Tenley says. "Gideon's going to get your car off the side of the road and bring it somewhere to see if it needs any fixing, okay? He's good people; he'll take care of it. And then, if you want to, you can drive off to wherever you were going."

Just the fact that it's an option makes relief burn.

Their smile makes their eyes crinkle. "But if you'd rather, I have a spare room with your name on it."

Now tears really threaten to bloom. I swipe at my eyes. "Why are you being so kind to me?"

Tenley says nothing for a long time, mercifully not commenting when a tear wells and spills down my cheek. Then, like it's that simple, they tell me, "Because you need it."

FOUR.

In the convenience store, hours stretch on like days.

I realize by the clock on the wall that my dashboard clock was off by nearly two and a half hours—it's not even noon yet—and as the second hand crawls along, Tenley fills the quiet, seemingly content to talk enough for the both of us. I hear all about the surgery on their hip—partial replacement—and the cancer scare last year that made them give up smoking. They tell me about their grandchildren, all surrogate, since they had no children of their own, although some girls in their book club do very much feel like daughters, and *act* like it too, if I'll believe it. Apparently, they've lived in Nanton their whole life, and they saved for years to have enough to own this store, though they hope that soon they'll get to retire.

Every so often, we're interrupted by the bell, and almost always, whoever it is knows Tenley and wants to talk for five to twenty-five minutes. They navigate questions about me with a deftness that would be shocking if I wasn't already getting the impression that they're deceptively clever, which means I mostly sit on the sidelines and listen as they talk to a mother of four about school while said four children tear up the chip aisle and have to be corralled into putting it back in order. A boy with a shock of white hair and eyelashes slouches up to the counter to buy seven SD cards, fielding Tenley's questions about a school project by shooting back several of his own about their garden until they're distracted enough he can slip out without being rude.

On the tail end of a flash rainstorm, a grizzled man in beat-up light-wash jeans with a scruff of salt-and-pepper beard stomps into the store, raindrops spattering his broad shoulders, scowling at us from under a Calgary Flames cap.

I recognize the logo with a jolt, and suddenly, it's like I can almost smell—it's like—

"You a hockey fan?" Tenley asks me as the man leaves, eyebrows raised.

"Yes," I tell them, breathless. Abruptly, I realize I've stood up, and I sink back down onto my stool. "I—I play."

Which is news to me, but, hey. I'm *certain* it's true, somehow, like I can feel it in my legs and lungs and where my heart is racing.

Tenley raises their eyebrows even higher. "Really?"

I nod. Technically, this is the first piece of information I've volunteered about myself. I know about ten times more about them than I know about myself, but I *know* this.

"What position?"

"Center," I whisper, and that's *also* true.

But no matter how hard I try, I can't conjure any more information than that, even when Tenley asks. The rules of the game feel blurry and ambiguous, like I wouldn't be able to explain them, when I *know* I know them, inside and out.

"Gideon plays too," Tenley tells me, and I come back down to earth with a clunk. "Only for fun, s'far as I know, but he's a pretty damn good goalkeeper, last I saw."

Idle curiosity gnaws. "Do you know Gideon well?"

"About as well as I know anyone," they tell me. "Him and his sister have lived here a long time now."

I turn this information over in my head. "Do you know . . . Ricky said something like *good riddance* when we left him behind earlier. What would that mean?"

At the mention of Ricky, Tenley's lips tighten into a frown, and they shake their head. "Ricky's not known for tact."

"You wanted to make sure Gideon didn't run off," I continue cautiously. "Why?"

"Just a spot of bad luck." Their shoulders slump and weariness carves the lines of their face into deep fissures.

And I may not know much, but I recognize a *not your business* when I hear it. So I shut up and stay quiet when Tenley changes the subject.

The sun slides over the far wall while they tell me all about the drama surrounding the high school's attempt at a theatre program, and I listen and nod when it feels appropriate. My legs are buzzing with pins and needles and I'm nearly faint with hunger by two o'clock when Tenley pulls out their lunch and offers me half of a ham sandwich.

After that, we're quiet, but I don't mind. Tenley turns on the radio and I don't have to think of what to say as we listen to classical music that crackles over the hum of the refrigerators.

It's nearly four by the time Gideon returns, shouldering the door open with a scowl at something behind him outside. Dust billows in the wake of a truck pulling out of the parking lot, whirling into the store behind him on a gasp of hot air.

I'd forgotten how bad his bruise was, or maybe it's just gotten worse since earlier, but I still wince at the sight of him. Honestly, it might not even be the bruise itself. I'd forgotten how *much* he is in general: all long legs, loose jeans slung low on his hips, planes of muscle on display as he lifts his shirt to wipe at the sweat beading his brow.

"So?" Tenley asks as they rise, with an amused shake of their head that's lost on me.

Gideon tosses me my keys—I catch them against my chest—as he approaches the counter. "Good news. Car's fine, except for the busted headlight, but DeMarco said he could fix it if he can have it overnight."

"I don't have—"

"Yeah, yeah." He waves me off. "DeMarco owes me. And I sure as shit might cash in now, eh?"

By the intensity of his tone and the way Tenley's expression darkens, I get the impression I'm missing something. I worry at my bottom lip, then fold my arms. "Are you sure—"

Gideon cuts me off with a look. "Knock it off. It's fine."

His expression doesn't leave much room to argue, so I don't. I just nod. "Thanks."

"Don't mention it," Gideon tells me. Then, "Seriously. Don't."

I have no idea what that means, but, like, what the hell else is new, right?

"Can we talk for a second?" he asks me. Then, when I nod, he jerks his head toward the door. "Outside."

Tenley raises their eyebrows but shuffles over to let me aside.

I follow Gideon out of the store and into the soupy heat of the afternoon. On the sidewalk, Gideon kicks at a pebble. It skitters down the concrete and lands in a patch of grass sprouting from a crack in the pavement.

The hum of insects nearly masks his voice when he says, "So. Laurie."

My stomach plummets. Here comes the interrogation. "Uh-huh?"

"Tenley's not gonna ask, because they're too polite. I'm not, though. Are you in deep shit here?"

I swallow hard.

"Like, you gotta know why I'm asking." He tugs the bracelets around and around his wrist. "It's just, turning up with no phone and no money . . . you *are* in some kind of trouble, aren't you?"

The silence stretches for so long, I almost worry he's going to walk away from me.

Then I nod. "Some kind of trouble. You could say that."

"And you're not gonna tell me what kind, I'm guessing," Gideon says, sounding almost amused.

"I—" My voice falters. "I wish I could."

"I won't make you tell me," he says. "So long as it's not gonna get Tenley in trouble. And you seem like a decent person, so I can only hope that if it *was* that kind of trouble, you'd say so."

It's not a threat. And even though he's saying I seem like a decent person, I don't think it's meant to be a kindness, either.

"Why do you think I'm decent?" I ask, before I can stop myself. Something in my rib cage constricts tight, a snake's coils around me.

"Somethin' in your eyes, I guess," Gideon says with a lilt in his tone. "Though I've been fooled by pretty girls before, so I guess there's no way of knowing."

I can't breathe, I realize all at once. My hands are shaking, palms sweating, and I can't get air in, or make myself move, or anything. My view of Gideon tunnels, hazy at the edges, a dancing constellation of bright spots spinning across my field of vision.

"Oh, shit. Hey. Laurie?" Gideon touches my bare elbow, where my flannel's fallen again, and I feel it as though through layers and layers of fabric. He repeats, more urgently, "Laurie?"

I manage only a mumble in response.

A sharp pinch at the skin inside my wrist makes me gasp and wince, and the sounds around me crash in again, bright and clear. The rush of cars in the distance, a bird chirping high. Gideon's shoe on the pavement.

"Sorry," he says, backing away, both hands up. "Just, you know. Looked like you were having a bit of a freakout."

"A bit," I echo, chest heaving, then, "sorry."

He waves me off. "Look, you're going through some shit, obviously. And like I said, Tenley's too nice to make you talk about it, and clearly you don't want to, so all I'll say is this."

I stare.

Gideon holds up one finger, flyaways catching the sunlight. "First, no one can help you if you don't tell us what's happening."

"You already helped," I say, but he just gives me a stern look.

"Second, if you hurt Tenley, directly or indirectly, there will be some serious hell to pay, and not just from me, okay? Got it?"

And all I can do is croak, "Got it."

FIVE.

Tenley lives in a small stucco house on the edge of town, close to the gas station.

"It's not much," they tell me as they lead me up the path that cuts through their unkempt lawn, long grasses bowing to brush at our ankles as the sky dips toward pale purple in the dusk behind us. "But it's home for me, and there'll be a place to sleep for you, and besides that, she's all we have."

"I like it," I tell them. "Thank you, again."

Tenley gives me a sharp look. Granted, it's the most words I've said in a row since Gideon left, numbed into quiet shock.

I haven't remembered *anything* new. And I have no idea where to start on who this girl is. This body belongs to someone, and it's not me. Is she out there somewhere too? Stuck in my body with no memories, just as lost and confused as I am?

Rows and rows of boxes line the entryway to their house, so cramped that we have to turn sideways to fit. Even though I'm pretty sure this isn't normal, Tenley seems completely unselfconscious about the mess. Maybe the baseline for *normal* in my apparently useless brain is just wrong.

How would I know?

In their cramped kitchen, we make dinner. Or—Tenley makes dinner, and I help as best as I can, discovering that I know how to cut vegetables, and that I'm probably not *totally* useless in the kitchen, because when they tell me to sauté an onion, I know how to do that too.

Gideon was right: Tenley doesn't make me talk. Not then, not during dinner when they listen to CBC radio, not while we're doing dishes, and somewhere along the way, I get the sense that they've done this before, maybe many times.

Am I the first one like me, though? As Tenley's busy getting the bedroom sorted—I've been banished to the living room, where there's nowhere to sit except a squashy La-Z-Boy that is so clearly theirs that I don't dare sit in it—I stare at my hands. Freckled. Long, narrow fingers. Maybe this girl is a pianist.

A stranger's hands. The pit in my stomach tightens, and nausea burns.

"I'm going to let you rest for tonight, all right?" Tenley's voice is gentle as they lead me into the room, which is a long, narrow box of a space, barely big enough for the double bed jammed against the wall. Light-pink floral wallpaper stretches to a popcorn ceiling, where a recessed light casts a dim yellow glow across the quilted bedspread.

"Thank you," I mumble, for what feels like the thousandth time.

"Oh honey, it's nothing." Tenley leans on their cane. "Tonight, you just rest. Tomorrow, though, we'll need to have a real talk, all right?"

My stomach turns as I nod.

Tenley hands me a toothbrush in fluorescent green packaging.

I get ready for bed, numb. Those wide, shocked blue eyes stare at me in the tiny oval mirror over the sink.

A girl.

Very few things make sense right now, and nothing feels right, but at least I can navigate in the dark by what feels *wrong*, and the skin-crawling dread I feel looking at this reflection is enough to know at least that I'm definitely not a girl.

It's not that I don't like the way she looks. Whoever she is, this girl is mostly pretty. Like, most-of-the-way pretty, I think, and then promptly feel bad for it. Her eyes are too wide-set in her narrow face, and there's a bump in her slightly crooked nose, like it's been broken.

It's a fine face. The slope of her waist is *fine*. I just know *my* body—wherever it is—feels different.

I touch my fingertips to the bump in her nose, self-conscious all at once. How did it happen?

She has a birthmark. A little splotch on her forehead, just above her eyebrow. The rest of her is narrow, lithe and sinewy, like maybe she's a runner.

Back in the little bedroom, Tenley's left a large T-shirt on the bed. I change into it, averting my eyes from the mirror on the wall—her body isn't my business—keeping my shorts on. Then I lock the door and window before sliding into bed.

The sheets are cool against my skin, and for a while, I just lie there, shivering.

Tomorrow.

By tomorrow, I need to have an explanation. Or at least a really, *really* good lie. Will Tenley buy it, though? Somehow, I get the sense that if I straight-up lie to their face, they'll know.

I lie there for a long time, not sleeping, trying to figure out an alternative to telling the truth, but I can't think of a single thing that won't get me sent to an institution, or worse.

But in the end, there's no point in worrying, because tomorrow never comes.

SIX.

VAL

Last day.

The first thought I have when my alarm blares at half-past six is this: *Today is the last day of this shit.*

Well.

Second-last, technically. But tomorrow is going to be a joke, so after my quiz today, I'm counting high school as officially *done*.

My last day starts with possibly the most ominous text message I've ever received.

Stomach turning over, I sit bolt upright in bed, rubbing at my eyes.

My best friend Bri, 12:13 a.m.: What's wrong with you?

Thumbing open to the messages, I scour our last conversation to see if I missed something, but it's the same collection of casual back-and-forth as always. My last message to her is about meeting up after school yesterday, which we did, and everything was *fine* then.

I text back a string of question marks and wait.

Nothing.

Naturally.

I'm used to that question, weirdly enough. God knows I've heard it enough times by now.

It's just that usually it's not Bri asking it.

Mom is downstairs trying to cajole Kiki into taking her medication, which is going about as well as you can expect when the patient is a ball of vitriolic fluff that hates everything, including being conscious and having to breathe.

I take my seat at the kitchen island, tugging a bowl close to me and dragging a hand through my hair.

Mom eventually gets the meds into Kiki, who promptly skitters down the hallway to go try to throw it up or possibly exorcise herself on the guest bed. Straightening, Mom puts her hand to her forehead and then leans her hip against the island with a sigh, surveying me.

Bright morning light glistens off the marble countertop and the chrome fixtures.

"You look puffy."

I dig into my grapefruit and don't look up. "Thanks, Mom."

"No, don't be like that." She waves a hand. "I just mean—are you keeping up with your training regimen?"

"*Yes*," I tell her.

"Just because it's the off season and you've already got a spot on the team at school doesn't mean you can afford to slack off."

"I know." I nod, only halfway paying attention as I text Bri again: What are you talking about?

When I look up, Mom is watching me.

Something about the weight of her gaze raises the hairs on the back of my neck. Tentatively, I ask, "You okay?"

"Fine," she says, clipped.

So, not fine.

"Did I do something?"

"Did I say you did?"

Okay, cool. I flip through the last few days in my head. Bri, school, Brett, youth group, more school, practice, school. Is she still mad that I didn't choose the dress she liked best for grad this weekend?

I can't think of anything else, and the dress incident was low on the Richter scale of patented Cheryl Eaton Bad Moods™.

Still, the hold of her mouth makes me uneasy.

"Seriously." I turn my grapefruit spoon around in my fingers. "Did I do something?"

"No," she says, and gives me a tight little smile that does *absolutely* nothing to assure me she's telling the truth.

But if she's denied it twice, she's not going to tell me, so I drop it. "Dad's already gone?"

"It's Thursday," she says, like she's considering whether the private school education was worth all that money. "Prayer meeting with the elders."

"Oh, right."

"Did you and Brett sign up for the War Room yet?"

"No? I didn't think I had to." Biting into the grapefruit, I grimace at the sour tang. I like mine with sugar sprinkled on top, but since Mom's watching, I have to stick it out plain. "Aren't I automatically supposed to be there?"

"Names on paper," Mom says, tapping the counter, French tips clicking. "Optics are important, you know."

I fight the urge to roll my eyes as I take a sip of orange juice. Not that I'd *ever* roll my eyes at Mom—I wouldn't dare. I know optics are important. She's been saying so for as long as I can remember, long enough that it's permanently imprinted into my gray matter. We're always being watched. Always being looked up to. There's a lot of responsibility that comes with being a pastor's kid.

"Speaking of," she says, "when Elijah comes home for the summer—"

I choke on my juice, spluttering and coughing as I thump the dead center of my chest.

She is *delusional* if she thinks he's coming home for the summer. Like, he didn't come home for Christmas, and I know for a fact that he hasn't called once since September, because Mom brings it up at least once a week in this wistful tone, like I'm supposed to fix it somehow.

"Sorry," I croak when the last of the coughing dies down. "Choked."

When I look up, she's watching me intently, like she's trying to solve a puzzle.

A shiver runs up my spine.

"What were you saying?" I ask, carefully picking up my glass again.

"When Elijah comes home, I was thinking it might be nice to take a family holiday," she says.

Optics.

I set the glass down just as carefully, willing my face not to betray anything. "So you've heard from him?"

"Well, not yet, but what else is he going to do? Does he think he can support himself alone?"

He is, I think. If anyone knows how to start over, it's my brother. I stare down at my juice and wonder idly if it's possible to drown myself in that small an amount of liquid.

"Have you heard from him?" she asks.

Discomfort wriggles through me. Could she *know*? It feels like I'm always seeing it in her face. Invisible proof. Can she smell it on me?

"No," I tell her, and give her my best reassuring smile. "I haven't."

She just looks at me for a long time. Then she clears her throat and nods. "It won't be like this when you go off to school, will it?"

I go still. "How do you mean?"

"I mean, you'll come home for Christmas, won't you?" she asks, and she sounds *genuinely* hurt at the idea that I wouldn't. "You'll call?"

"Sure I will," I say, back to turning my spoon around and wishing I were instead, perhaps, suffocating to death.

"Family doesn't do this," she says sadly, pulling out her phone and looking at it like it's done her a very real grievance. "And we're *family*."

I swallow, hard. Then I tell her what I know she wants to hear, even if I'm not sure it's true. "Don't worry. We'll always be family."

00:99

SEVEN.

When the nightmare ends and I open my eyes, I know two things with sudden and vivid clarity: first, freckles spatter the backs of my hands where they rest on the steering wheel, and second, I've been here before.

The third thought comes late, like the groan after a punch: *What in the ever-loving fuck?*

Morning light streams through the windshield and across the gray leather seats and I smash the button for my hazard lights and slow down to a reasonable speed, heart slamming in my throat.

The slow fizz of the radio crackles, and the memory of the nightmare drains away until it's merely a vague impression, a fog in my peripherals, and then gone.

I pull off the road and park, hazards still flashing, hands trembling. Slowly, I suck in a breath and squeeze my eyes shut. The softness of Tenley's pillow is still so real I can almost feel it against my cheek, and the sudden brightness of the sun makes my eyelids glow red.

I stay there for several long seconds, breathing deep.

Maybe *this* is the dream.

But when I open my eyes, I'm still in the car. The leather

under my thighs is soft and warm, and very, very real. The digital dashboard display gives me a number I've never seen on any clock in my life: 00:99.

As I kill the engine, a green tractor pulls onto the highway. At the last second, I do a double-take, and my breath catches.

It's Gideon.

It's Gideon *again*.

Gideon, driving a tractor into town again, the same way we went yesterday.

Except this time, he doesn't stop.

I watch the tractor pass, jolting when Gideon turns to look at my car. If he recognizes me through the window, I can't tell. He offers me a hesitant little thumbs-up, like he's asking if everything is all good.

It is *not* all good.

But I don't even know what's wrong to be able to tell him, so instead, numb and shaky, I return the thumbs-up.

And then he's passed me. Slowly, the tractor gets smaller and smaller in my rearview mirror until it vanishes.

Legs trembling, I get out of the car, leaning against the hood, metal hot against the backs of my thighs and my palms.

I'm wearing the same thing I was wearing yesterday. Those black shorts, the gray plaid flannel over a black tank, gray slip-on shoes. My pockets are still empty, except for the gum wrapper.

This time, though, I don't have anyone looking over my shoulder, and my car isn't in the ditch.

Because I don't know what else to do, I round the car to the back, keys jangling in my hand. For a moment, I pause, listening to the hum of insects around me before I fling the trunk open.

To my surprise, it's full—stuffed to bursting with bags, two hockey sticks jammed diagonally, barely fitting in the tight space, a jersey tossed over everything, like it was a last-second addition.

I pick up the jersey—white and green—and shake it out. Number 7. A good number, I think, with no basis whatsoever for why I feel so strongly about it.

So this girl plays hockey too.

The bags are all full of gear. I find skates, a helmet, all varieties of padding, a mouth guard, like she either packed *just* hockey gear for her adventure, or like it's always in her car and she didn't unload it first.

I'm betting on the latter.

There's nothing *useful* in the trunk, though. I close it, letting out a low breath, and I'm not really expecting anything when I look into the backseat, which is why I gasp loud enough that I disturb a magpie when I see a backpack.

It's wedged under the driver's seat, like this girl either stuffed it there for safekeeping, or it fell. I snatch at it, yanking it up onto the seat, hesitating for a moment.

Is it still snooping if I'm technically piloting the body of the person who presumably packed it?

I decide that desperate times call for desperate measures.

In the main compartment, I find a green-and-orange bottle, and I instinctively squeeze a stream of water into my mouth before thinking about it, gasping with relief and then shock.

It's not mine, I think, staring down at it in my hand.

But, like, it sort of is, and anyway, the next discovery is too important to dwell on anything else.

A wallet.

My heart skips a beat. A shimmering driver's license peers through the clear plastic window, and—that's this face. *My* face, for the time being.

And a name.

The tiny print next to the picture reads EATON, Valerie Lauren.

I suck in a breath, pulling the license out from the pocket. "Okay, Valerie Eaton. Who are you?"

The important thing is this: I have a home address.

My heart skips as I stare down at it: 14 Spruce Vista. It doesn't ring any bells, not that I expected it to. *Valerie's* home address means nothing to *me*, whoever I am.

A flash of green in the main pouch of the wallet catches my eye.

Cash, and lots of it.

Carefully, I slide the license back into its pocket and count the bills out, fingers shaking. Two hundred dollars.

So now I have the license, a *name*, a home address, two hundred dollars in cash, a debit card, a Calgary Public Library card, a half-filled stamp card for a shawarma place, and a black-and-white Polaroid.

The tiny image is blurry, like whoever took it had shaky hands, but I recognize my face—or rather, Valerie's face—pressed up against the cheek of another girl with light curls, who has her eyes squeezed shut, her wide smile overexposed with glowing teeth.

I turn the Polaroid over, but there's nothing written on the back.

The contents of the rest of the backpack are . . . concerning. A phone in a sage-green rubber case, which *would* be as exciting as the wallet except that it's dead, rendering it a useless brick. That's not what concerns me, though. The rest of the main compartment is full of socks and underwear, rolled up tight. Two T-shirts, both plain slate gray with large sleeves. A fleece burgundy quarter-zip sits wedged at the bottom of the backpack, and as I pull it out, a small navy-blue booklet goes flying.

It's her passport.

"Where the hell were you going, Valerie?" I murmur, running my fingers over the smooth photo, her expression solemn and serious, peaky in harsh lighting.

Whatever was happening, it looks like she was prepared to *go*.

No phone charger, though. That snags something in the back of my head. Those socks are folded *precisely*, but she doesn't have a phone charger?

A pit forms in my stomach. Something about the creases in the T-shirts tells me that this backpack has been ready to go for a *while*.

A teenager on the run, no matter what the reason, can't bode well. At least the car looks too clean to be properly lived in, so Valerie probably isn't homeless.

At least, not yet.

Carefully, I put everything back the way I found it, except for the wallet and the phone, both of which I pocket before I get back behind the wheel.

Slowly, I turn around and drive into town. I can't follow the route Gideon and I took to Tenley's store, because that had been a footpath, so it takes a bit of aimless circling before the streets become familiar. The sun slinks behind a curtain of heavy, ominous clouds.

At last, I catch sight of the orange sign I spent all afternoon staring at yesterday, and then I pull into the gas station.

Hope only lasts as long as it takes for the bell to sound.

Tenley looks up from the register when I enter, and it's a little chilling the way there's *no* recognition in their eyes, like we've never met, when to me, less than two hours ago, I was *in their house*. I was standing at their kitchen window tossing scraps into the yard for the chickens.

But their expression is pleasant enough, and I've got a reason to be here besides testing to see if they remember me.

I clear my throat. "Hi. How are you?"

They blink, clearly thrown off, the way it always feels in retail when a customer acknowledges you like you're a real person, a sensation I just *know* is from experience.

Cool. I've *definitely* worked retail. One more piece of Laurie trivia.

"I'm well, thank you," Tenley says, with a nod. "And you?"

"I've certainly had less complicated days," I tell them, which is probably true, unless—the thought drops into my head like an ice cube, frigid—I just spawned out of nowhere yesterday. I hope my voice doesn't sound *too* wobbly when I ask, "Do you sell iPhone chargers?"

They give me a little smile and gesture to a row of cords literally *immediately* to my right.

I flush hot.

"What kind of phone have you got?" they ask.

My mouth goes dry. If I say I don't know, are they going to think I *stole* this phone? But when I fish the phone out of my pocket and glance at the base, instinct has me saying, "I'll need a lightning cord."

Tenley picks up a long ruler—covered in Pokémon stickers, like their cane—and points at the right charger, just as I'm reaching for it. They smile as the ruler connects with my knuckles. "Sorry. Looks like you've got it figured out."

Fortunately, I already know from yesterday that they take cash. I pay for the charger, feeling a twinge of guilt as they hand me my change.

Sorry, Valerie.

I'm all the way back to the car before I realize it doesn't have an outlet to plug in the charger, which renders it as effectively useless to me as the dead phone.

Heaving a sigh, I get right back out of the car. I'm almost tempted to ask Tenley if I can charge my phone in there, but I'm about a thousand percent certain that if I have to make small talk with someone I'm supposed to have never met before right now, I'll combust on the spot and *die*.

So I set off down the sidewalk, so distracted that I walk straight into a boy with a shock of white hair and translucent eyelashes.

He stumbles back as I gasp an apology.

It's the same boy.

It's the same boy from yesterday who came in for SD cards, wearing the same slouching hoodie, at the same time. He doesn't give me a second glance as he disappears into the store.

Overhead, thunder rumbles.

EIGHT.

Some part of me knew already, but it still draws an icy cold finger down my spine to think about it.

It's not that a raindrop hits my nose today while I'm crossing the street at the same time it rained yesterday.

It's not that the kid in the hoodie turned up at the gas station today at the same time he did yesterday.

It's not that Tenley has the same shift today as they had yesterday.

It's not even that Gideon was driving the same route he drove yesterday.

It's that today *is* yesterday.

The air around me chills all at once.

If Gideon had seen the same car in the same spot on the side of the road after he'd gone to all the trouble of getting it towed yesterday, he would have stopped. He *would* have. I just know it, even if I don't know *how* I know.

A group of younger teenage girls huddled at the window of a drive-in shriek as the rain hits, crashing down in sheets that force me to duck under the awning and into the nearest building.

Fortuitously, the building in question appears to be a café.

A *weird* café. Even though my prior life experiences amount to a fat question mark, I'm quite certain I've never been to a café that also functions as a place of worship to possibly every model plane ever manufactured.

An old man behind a rickety little hostess stand peers up at me through glasses so thick they make his eyes enormous. Frizzy white hair rings his head, a bald spot reflecting the overhead lights. His name tag reads VERN in handwritten capital letters. A yawn swallows the first half of his question. " . . . yourself, today?"

The door swings shut behind me, letting in a gust of wind that curls around my calves. I clear my throat. "Um."

Pushing his glasses up on his forehead, he squints down at something behind the register. "Seat yourself, and one of us will be right over."

"Do you have a table by an outlet?"

He points me toward the corner, where a booth next to the window sits under a display of a dozen hanging Boeing 747s.

I slide into the booth, tearing open the packaging for the cord. The outlet sparks when I stick the prongs into it, and I shift away nervously before plugging in the dead phone.

At least it lights up with a charging symbol.

It's the little things, I guess.

Outside, lightning flashes as rain rattles the windowpane.

When I look over my shoulder, Vern isn't at the hostess stand anymore.

The café is empty, and I'm alone.

A crack of thunder rumbles.

While the phone is charging, I examine the space. It honestly leans more toward shrine than coffee shop. Tall shelves line the walls, and model planes swallow up every inch of shelf real estate. At a glance, it seems like the planes are organized by type, but I don't know enough about aircraft to know for sure. A tiny bar in the corner features an espresso machine crammed next to dozens of syrup pumps, and a workbench against the opposite wall displays neatly arranged rows of small metallic bottles of paint and tubes of glue, an enormous magnifying glass, and a half dozen sets of tiny tweezers.

I'm about to get up and inspect closer when the phone pings to life.

I snatch at it, fingers trembling.

The first fact is that it is 1:21 p.m. on Friday, June 26.

The second is that Valerie has four missed calls.

The third—and most unfortunate—fact is that she has notification previews turned off while the phone is locked. Of *course* it's locked, and face ID doesn't even work because of the little notice that reads: Passcode required when iPhone restarts.

Naturally.

I try 1–2–3–4–5–6.

Nothing.

I yank out the wallet, flipping to Valerie's birthday on her driver's license, and I try that.

Incorrect.

I try another combination of the same numbers, then another one, and then the phone vibrates unhappily in my hand, and I've officially gone and gotten myself locked out of it for sixty seconds.

I slump forward with a little groan, and because this is all starting to be a bit much, I just stay there.

A voice above me startles me so badly, I jolt. "Are you . . . okay?"

My head snaps up, and then my mouth drops open.

Yeah, it's a small town.

Still.

Gideon cocks his head when I don't answer. He's changed out of the black tank and jeans in favor of a clean black T-shirt and cargo pants, still-damp hair tied back. The bruise under his eye is just as awful as it was yesterday.

"You work here?" I blurt out.

Unease ripples across his face, and then he raises an eyebrow. "Sorry, have we met?"

"No," I say, because if Gideon doesn't remember yesterday, and today is yesterday all over again, then I suppose technically we *haven't*.

"New in town?" Gideon's hand hovers over a notepad.

I give him a tight smile and lift a shoulder. "Sort of. Just passing through."

"Wait." He snaps his fingers and points at me. "You were the one on the side of the road earlier."

"Yup."

"You survived whatever that was, I take it?"

"Just had to stop for some directions," I lie, and then immediately justify it in my head: it's not *really* a lie.

"Did you get them?" he asks, and there's something new in his tone. Lighter, more flippant, like he's—like he might be—

Is Gideon *flirting* with me? Mouth dry, I tell him, "More or less."

"How elusive," he says with a grin. "What's your name?"

"Do you need that for the order?"

"No," he admits, then smiles wider. "I need it for me."

"Valerie," I tell him, testing it out. My stomach lurches and yanks, like someone's pulled a ripcord and turned my insides to liquid.

At once, I wish I could take it back. That's *not* my name. But I've already said it, and he's already nodding.

"I'm Gideon." He sticks out a hand.

I take it, startled by how warm his skin is, trying to ignore the calluses and firm grip as we shake hands. Blinking away the surrealness of it, I tell him, "Good to meet you."

"Likewise."

"You don't have school?"

Gideon's smile goes lopsided. "Nope."

"Nice gig." I gesture at the shelves. "Are you into all this plane stuff?"

"Sort of. It's mostly good volunteer experience. Someone has to make sure the place doesn't burn down during Vern's inevitable nap in the back, so I turn up whenever I'm free, and it's usually quiet enough I get to mind my business."

"Oops." I lift both shoulders. "Sorry."

"No, no." He shakes his head. "This beats my plans by a long shot."

"What *were* your plans?"

He doesn't answer the question, just smiles good-naturedly. "Don't *you* have school?"

"Maybe I ditched."

"*Maybe*," he echoes. "You sure don't like to give up much about yourself, do you?"

"There's not that much to give up," I counter, because it seems like he might like it, and he doesn't have to know that it is *completely* true.

He shakes his head, smiling lightly. "Is there anything I can get you, food-wise?"

"Not food-wise," I tell him as an idea strikes. Gideon helped me once before—went *significantly* out of his way to help me, I'm realizing—so maybe he'll do it again. "You wouldn't happen to have spare paper maps lying around, would you?"

"I . . . maps?"

"I didn't actually get those directions yet, so I need a map. And I need help finding an address."

"Okay," he says cautiously. "What about your phone?"

"It's broken," I tell him, which is not technically true, but, you know.

"I can look it up for you." Gideon reaches for his back pocket.

I double-check the license while he's not looking. "14 Spruce Vista."

"Okay." His fingers fly over the keyboard as he leans his hip against the booth. "Yeah, that's about an hour away. In the northwest of the city, looks like."

"Thank you."

An hour away from home. *Valerie, what were you doing?*

"I'll still need a paper map, if you know where I can find one," I say.

He smiles. "Can I ask why?"

"Broken phone," I remind him.

"Give me a second." He holds a finger up and pushes off the booth, frowning down at his phone. "I can probably print one in the back."

"Oh, you don't have to—"

"Give me a second," he repeats, tossing me this smile over his shoulder that I honestly might start a war for, if pressed. Then he disappears into the back.

I rest my chin on my hands. Outside, the rain slows to a spatter. Valerie's phone tells me it's just before two—at least it gives me that much, even if unlocking it was a dead end. The dark clouds are lifting already, and a sunbeam breaks through to illuminate the squat brick building across the street, raindrops glittering on the windows and in the square of grass next to the front door.

What am I doing? I can't just hang around here all day looking at model planes. I should focus on trying to find Valerie, right?

Yes. That makes sense.

Who am I kidding? *Nothing* makes sense.

I press the heels of my palms against my forehead, breathing deep. If I could just remember something about myself—where I live, what I look like—but trying to summon an image only brings on the same throbbing ache in my temples, and I just—I don't *know*. Frustrated, I heave a sigh.

"You good?" Gideon asks, back at the table somehow. When I jolt violently, he laughs. "Sorry, I didn't mean to startle you."

"No, no." I wave him off, pressing a hand to my heart where it races. "Not your fault. I'm just on edge."

Gideon sinks into the booth with a little groan, like he's stiff. He has a sheet of paper with him, and he sets it on the table, puts his phone down next to it—screen on and still displaying a map of his own—and uncaps a black felt-tip marker. Then he pauses, hand hovering over the paper. "Do you mind?"

I shake my head.

Carefully, Gideon traces a long line on the paper, stopping occasionally to circle a highway sign. He snaps the cap back on the marker once he's traced the route down and pushes the map across the table.

"Thank you," I say, struck for the second time in two days—technically—that Gideon's gone out of his way to be helpful *again*. Swallowing down a lump in my throat, I add, "That's very kind of you."

"It's nothing," he says. "You sure I can't get anything for you?"

I feel bad coming in and not buying anything, so I follow him up to the counter and let him sell me a bran muffin, which I pay for, and then promptly realize I don't know if Valerie has allergies. Last night, the pure shock of my situation dissolved most of my common sense, but now my hackles raise. I mean, accidentally killing Valerie *would* presumably be one way out of this, but as far as experiments go, death by anaphylaxis isn't high on my list.

So I just stand there staring at the raisins dotting the top of this potential murder weapon, feeling a bit stupid.

"Anything else I can help you with?" Gideon asks after a moment.

"Yeah, actually," I say slowly. "Last question."

He lifts his eyebrows. "Yes?"

"Do you know any guys named Laurie around here?"

Slowly, he shakes his head. "Off the top of my head? No."

I grimace. "Okay. Worth a shot."

"Some kind of Missed Connections thing?" he asks.

My mouth drops open. "Oh, you're *brilliant*."

His eyebrows arch. "Sorry?"

Face flushing warm, I shake my head. "No, I just—that's a great idea. Missed Connections. I'm going to try that."

"You're . . . welcome," he says uncertainly. "I think."

I flash him a smile while I'm turning to go. "Thanks for everything. Seriously."

"Good luck, Valerie." He shakes his head as I push the door open. "Sounds like you might need it."

NINE.

The rain has stopped by the time I get back to the car, paper folded and held carefully under my shirt.

The dashboard clock still reads 00:99.

Which, okay. I have a little sinking feeling about what that means, but I decide that's a crisis for later. One at a *fucking* time. Christ.

As I get back onto the highway, I relish the feeling of the steering wheel under my hands. I enjoy driving, I realize, one of the few pieces of trivia I have about myself: Driving. Hockey. Retail.

Gideon's map is a reassuring presence on the passenger seat, neat lines in bold, the engine a steady rumble underneath me.

On the drive into the city, the euphoria of the Missed Connections idea fades. If Valerie and I truly swapped places, there's no guarantee she remembers anything other than her own first name. It's still worth a shot—I'll do it as soon as I can get my hands on a computer, but it feels like certainty is draining out from between my fingers.

At least I have something to do.

Except that once I make it into the city, I get . . . *very* lost.

What should be an hour's drive takes me two, because I get turned around and then somehow get stuck downtown, trying to navigate the maze of one-way streets and traffic lights with turn-lane specifications. I have to stop once I'm out of the city to get my bearings, and then I wish I'd gotten my hands on a *real* paper map, with more information on it than this printout, so I go into a gas station to buy one, and the man behind the counter looks at me like I've grown a second head when I ask him to help me figure out where we are on it.

But at least he helps.

By the time I actually find the house, it's almost four p.m. Wildwood is a tidy little neighborhood, with houses that look like they belong to normal people, right up until I turn onto Spruce Vista.

And then . . . yikes.

The houses that line this looping street are *enormous*.

14 Spruce Vista is no exception. Built with sleek, minimalist grays and dark blues, the house must be at least three stories tall. Vaulting gables form impressive arches over the front door and a little balcony above it, with wide windows reflecting the sun.

Trepidation churns as I pull into the driveway next to a large black SUV. To be sure, I check Valerie's license one more time.

Yup.

Oh boy.

The yard is *pristine*, with a lush green lawn rolling right up to the edge of the property, where the brittle yellow grass of the park next door forms a stark dividing line. Even rows of flowers line the walkway, continuing in planter barrels on either side of the steps as I make my way up to the front door.

Cautiously, I peer through the rippling glass of the door, looking for movement.

Nothing.

No lights on, at least not that I can see from here, and the door is unlocked, so I take a risk and go in.

Valerie's house is obnoxiously large, with tall doorways and a high ceiling, so open that it feels a bit like the space was built for giants. Gleaming hardwood reflects the light streaming in through the west windows, and straight down the center, I can see the view out the back. The house is set on a ridge overlooking a valley. Lush green trees border a winding blue river in the distance.

Warily, I take it all in, abruptly uncomfortable and out of place.

The *moment* the door shuts behind me, I run into a problem.

Around the corner and down the hall, a woman's voice calls out, "How was school, honey?"

I freeze.

Well, shit.

Carefully, I peer around the corner.

A woman with honey-blond hair stands in the dining room with her back to me, hands on her hips. As if she can *smell* me, or something, she turns around, and because I'm due a small mercy, she doesn't look surprised to see me standing in her entryway, so this must be the right place.

The woman wears light-purple exercise gear with a puffy silver vest. I'm not sure if it's meant to make a statement other than *I have a lot of money* or *I probably do Pilates*, but if it is, it's missing the mark. She has narrow wrists and ankles, skin glowing and radiant. I'd put her in her late forties, probably, but she's clearly been putting a lot of effort into looking young.

I'm trying to figure out what the hell to say when I'm spared the effort by a rabid ball of lint coming out of nowhere and attacking my ankles. When I look down, a thieving snarl of fur has its teeth in the rubber border of my shoe and is trying to run off with it, which would probably be more effective if the thief in question weighed more than a quarter pound.

"Kiki, stop it!" The woman—Valerie's mother, I can only guess—sighs as she comes down the hall, scooping up the demonic toilet brush, which turns out to be the tiniest Pomeranian that's probably ever existed. Then, as she straightens, she grimaces, eyeshadow shimmering on her lids. "Oh dear. Did you look in the mirror before you left this morning?"

"I overslept," I lie, because, what the hell. Rude.

"Did you?" She frowns. "It's your last day, Val."

The dog—Kiki—wriggles so violently that Valerie's mother is forced to put it back down, which is fine until it makes a dive for my ankles and *bites*. Hard.

"Ow—*hey*." I scramble away, resisting the urge to punt it across the room.

"Kiki!" Valerie's mom objects.

Fucking *Kiki*. That's way too cute a name for a creature that is so clearly full of nothing but evil intent. Bent at the waist, hand clenched around a collar covered in rhinestones, I rechristen the dog the Devil in my head.

"She's been cranky all day," Valerie's mom says with a sigh. "I might have to put her in the crate this evening."

At the word "crate," the Devil goes still and growls, a sound that's neither intimidating nor cute, but *does* give me the sense that I should let go, like, *right* now.

"How was it today?" Valerie's mom asks me as I release the collar. "Did you and Brett get to talk?"

Who the hell is *Brett*?

I hesitate before I nod, and the Devil yaps at me.

"You're all sorted out?" Valerie's mom asks, bending down to stroke her between the ears.

I nod again, helplessly.

"Well, brush your hair before dinner, at least," she says with a little sigh as she straightens. "And about last night . . ."

I look up, barely managing not to flinch when she reaches for me.

"Who you let yourself believe you are is going to impact everything about the next few years," she says, gently resting a hand against my cheek. "How about we just put it behind us? No further consequences. And we can talk about Elijah after grad."

Obviously, I have not a single clue what she's talking about, so I just nod and try not to look stupid.

"I'm going to finish working on this banner," she tells me. "You'll be all right until dinner?"

"I'll just be . . ." I trail off, because I have no idea where I'll be, because *this isn't my house, and this isn't my mother*. "Yeah, I'll be all right."

She pats my cheek and turns away, clicking for the Devil to follow her.

I slip away down the hall. The first two rooms I find—some kind of spare bedroom and a bathroom—are decorated in the same grays and blues as the rest of the house, but I don't spend more than a second glancing through doors before I find what I'm looking for.

An office. And in the office, there's a computer.

I slam down into the spinning chair so fast it nearly slides away from me. There are three users—one for Cheryl, who I can only assume is Valerie's mother, another for Jeff, and one that just says Family. The last one isn't password-protected.

At least *someone* in the universe loves me.

After some quick searches, I find a missed-connections website that looks legitimate, except then they want an email, so I have to go make one, and then once I've made the email account and registered for the site, I have to verify the email, and by the time I hit the big Verify button, I'm about ready to tear my hair out.

Actually, I've been ready to tear my hair out for hours. Every time it brushes against my collarbones I cringe into myself, but putting it up doesn't help, because then it brushes against my neck, and I feel it every time I move, to the point I'm eyeing the letter opener in the jar next to the keyboard with more than a little temptation.

Then my eyes snag on the framed photo, tucked just behind the monitor.

It's of me.

Or—it's of Valerie. It's this face I'm stuck with, but younger. Softer. She has her arms around a tall, narrow-looking man with salt-and-pepper hair and a megawatt smile. Jeff, I guess. He's wearing a suit, and she has on a light pink dress with a gathered waist.

There are several other frames scattered around the office, now that I'm looking. Some are photos of Valerie alone, younger and younger the farther down the wall they get, missing teeth, and some are of Cheryl and Jeff together, and some have all three of them.

Several of the frames along the wall are filled with cute stock nature photos, which feel weird interspersed with family photos like that, and there's a certificate of ordination for Jeffrey Eaton in a gilded frame hanging offset to the analog clock on the wall, but by that point I have a verification email, which means I have better things to think about.

Carefully, I type out the post for the Missed Connections website.

```
Subject: Laurie looking for Valerie

Your name is Valerie Eaton, and I think
I'm trapped in your body. If this is
really you, you'll know what I mean. I
wake up just outside of Nanton. Email me
at laurieisstuckinatimeloop@gmail.com,
PLEASE.
```

I read it over to make sure I'd know what it meant if it were me reading, without giving too many details. Then I hit Submit. And then, because I have internet access, I spend an hour reading everything I can find on time loops. Specifically, how to get *out* of them.

I don't really expect anything, but it's still maddening how most of the search results are creative-writing pieces. The poems are pretty but extremely unhelpful from a practical standpoint.

Even browsing forums doesn't help much, because they're all hypothetical. I'll have to do a proper deep dive if I'm going to find anything actually useful.

After a while, I lean back in the chair, listening to a YouTuber talking about time travel, though I end up sort of zoning out when it becomes obvious he's just rattling through conspiracy theories.

Spinning in the chair, I heft a paperweight in my hand, then frown at it. It's heavier than I feel like it should be. Is Valerie really that much weaker than I'm used to being?

I *hate* not knowing. Now that the shock is sort of fading--as much as it could, considering everything about this clusterfuck of a situation—the lack of information is *really* getting to me.

A surge of frustration rushes through me. I can't help but wonder: does Valerie hate being trapped in my body as much as I hate being trapped in hers?

TEN.

Dinner is exactly as excruciating as I thought it would be.

Valerie's dad is working late, so it's just me listening to Cheryl talk while I pick at my chicken casserole. An enormous canvas looms on the wall next to us, featuring swirling calligraphy that reads: *Commit to the Lord*. It's possible that there are no flavors in this dish, and also every texture the good Lord thought to create. Forget the Devil. This casserole is my new nemesis.

Cheryl talks even more than Tenley did. She tells me everything about this squabble two of the women in her book club are having, the details of the errands she ran this morning, all about this "tiff" she got into with a cashier at the dry cleaner, and I do a perfect job of resisting the urge to roll my eyes all the way back into my skull.

For one thing, her life sounds *exceptionally* boring. I feel like if I were in her position, I'd have pulled out my blond highlights *ages* ago. I'm about to start an attempt at rationalizing it, like, different strokes for different folks, do what makes you happy, or whatever, but then I realize I haven't seen her smile.

Not even once.

And she doesn't smile during the rest of dinner. When we're

cleaning up—I help, because I have no way of knowing what's normal in Valerie's house, and because I'm not an animal—I notice this little pinch on either side of her mouth, a wrinkle from a perpetual frown.

She invites me to watch TV with her after dinner. I think I'd rather be shot, so I say no, and she doesn't even look that disappointed, which I consider a win as I slink back down the hall, exploring as soundlessly as I can.

Probably, I'll have to sleep here tonight. If I'm going to monitor that Missed Connections post, I might as well. Plus, it's not like I *don't* belong here. Valerie belongs here, and I'm wearing her skin, so.

It takes me seven wrong doors—*seven*—to find Valerie's bedroom, up the stairs and down the hall. I know it's hers right away, because it's the only room that actually looks lived in, and because it's painted green, not the shades of gray and blue that dominate the rest of the house.

An unmade double bed sits in the corner with a desk next to it. Two bookcases stand guard on either side of a window overlooking the valley, now submerged in dusk. It's not a *messy* space, exactly, but there's a little pile of clothes on a chair next to the closet door, an overflowing hamper, crooked posters on the wall, and the unmade bed, all of which comes together to form a fuck-you to the rest of the house that truly delights me.

Over the course of an hour of thorough snooping, I learn several things about Valerie. First, the poster of Hayley Wickenheiser on her closet door confirms my theory that she's also a hockey enthusiast. The framed photos on the desk of who I can only assume to be her in uniform only solidify the idea.

Second, she's a *huge* nerd. The bookcase against the window is stuffed to overflowing with every kind of book I can think of.

She has severely ancient copies of a few Dickens titles, a battered collection of Penguin classics, and a whole shelf of biology and engineering textbooks—like, grown-ass adult textbooks, I note with begrudging admiration—all littered in brightly-colored sticky notes, so she's the type of person who reads textbooks like they're fiction narratives.

On my list of Valerie trivia, I add: *Probably not that fun at parties.*

There are other books too. It looks like she reads a lot of fantasy, and she owns four different Bibles, one of which has her full name embossed on it in curly gold lettering: *Valerie Lauren Eaton*. Another point for *not that fun at parties.*

A well-worn sage-green backpack hangs on her door handle, canvas fabric covered in little marks and scuffs. In the main compartment, there's a laptop, but it's password-locked too, so no dice.

At half past eight, a brisk knock at my door makes me jump.

Before I get the chance to respond, the door opens and Cheryl marches in, glaring at me. "You have got *some* nerve, you know."

Blanching, I slam the laptop lid shut. "What?"

"Why did I get a call from the school saying that you *never showed up* today?" Her voice takes on a shrill edge. "And you stole your phone back? What are you thinking? I know it's the last day of school, but you can't just *skip* and not tell anyone where you're going."

I have no idea what to say, but it doesn't matter, because I don't even get an opportunity to flounder.

"Is this about last night?" She heaves a sigh. "I know you were upset, but like I said, this isn't—this isn't the time to be thinking about things like that. You have graduation, and there's the internship at the church this summer, and you have Brett, and he's *lovely*. Why would you jeopardize everything?"

At once, I feel a rush of pity for Valerie. I don't know what this conversation they had was about, but I sympathize on a gut level with her.

"I can't believe you sometimes," she says with a little huff. "Your *last* day. Did you miss anything important?"

"How would I know?" I snap back before I can stop myself, leaning heavily on the sarcasm. "I wasn't *there*, remember?"

She stares at me like I just pulled my pants down and took a shit right on the carpet in front of her. "Valerie!"

Instinctively, I drop my eyes. "Sorry."

"This isn't over," she warns me. "Tomorrow, when your father's home, we're going to talk about this."

"Okay," I mumble, and I think I'd feel actually nauseous about the prospect if I had any certainty I'd be around tomorrow at all.

"He won't be happy," she tells me.

At that, I *do* roll my eyes.

"What's gotten *into* you tonight?"

For a single hysterical moment, I consider just telling her the truth.

I'm not your daughter. I'm some random guy stuck in your daughter's body, and I also *would like for this to not be the situation we're in, but here we are, so you'd better put on your big-girl pants and get on the making-the-best-of-it train too, or we're in for one helluva time.*

To my horror, Cheryl comes the rest of the way into the room and sinks down onto the bed. "What's going on, Val?"

"Nothing," I mutter. "Nothing's going on. I'm just tired, okay?"

She sighs.

"I don't really want to talk about it."

"We need to talk about it sometime," she tells me, and her voice is *almost* gentle, but it makes my skin crawl with a dread I can't begin to understand.

"Just not tonight, please." I don't even have to try that hard to sound choked up and miserable.

After what feels like an eternity, she gets up and leaves me be.

Slumping back onto the bed, I groan.

What the hell did Valerie tell them last night? Something that would jeopardize her church internship and whatever she has going on with Brett, that much is obvious. Is she flunking out? Is she *pregnant*? Dubiously, I pat my stomach, then close my eyes, waiting, but I don't feel anything. Maybe she's taken up drugs. The idea almost makes me laugh.

When I open my eyes, my gaze locks onto the Hayley Wickenheiser poster again.

Shit.

Shit.

I sit bolt upright.

Is *that* what Valerie and I have in common?

I get up, scouring the bookshelves again, but this time with an agenda, squinting at titles I don't recognize—most of them, honestly—and scouring the backs for any hint of what I'm looking for.

Nothing.

Frowning, I stand in the middle of the room. It just doesn't—it doesn't *feel* right. If Valerie is what I think she is, there *has* to be proof of it somewhere.

Fuck it, I've got time.

I whisper a swift apology to Valerie—like she's a saint or something, what am I, a Catholic now?—and start a complete and thorough exploration of her room. Her drawers are boring, all clothes. The desk drawers are even worse. What teenager uses file folders? She's *obsessively* organized, which would be annoying except that it's making it really easy to know that what I'm looking for isn't here.

Her closet is just as bad. Neatly hung clothing drapes over rows of shoes, and a pile of boxes in the corner looks intentionally placed. Nothing is haphazard.

Carefully, I pull out the boxes. The first is of old school projects, which I scan through with muted interest before setting aside.

The *second* box, though.

Ohoho.

Oh. Okay.

I sit back on my haunches, pressing a fist to my chest over my heart.

Books stare up at me, titles damning. *The Song of Achilles. The Color Purple. Annie on My Mind. Giovanni's Room.*

I've read every single one of these, I *know* it. Clearly, Valerie has too, and more than once, if the broken spines and well-worn edges are anything to go by.

Sitting there, my heart breaks a little for her. I have no idea what my own parents are like, but they must be cooler than hers are, because the *injustice* of it stings so badly my lungs ache.

I take *The Song of Achilles* out of the box. It's the most well-worn of the bunch, and I turn it over in my fingers, almost reverently. I can feel—I can almost *remember* the impact this book had on me when *I* read it for the first time, which is crazy, because I remember nothing about my life at all.

Opening the book to the first page, I walk with it back to the bed and sit down, sucked into the story so thoroughly and immediately that I've been engrossed for an hour and half by the time there's a second knock on the door.

"Honey?"

I freeze, shoving the book under the duvet.

A man's voice.

Jeff? Most likely.

Cautiously, I call back, "Yes?"

"Your mom told me about today," he says. "Is everything okay?"

Fuck. Shitballdickhole.

Hesitantly, I say, "Yeah."

"Listen, we can talk about it all a bit more tomorrow."

I blow out a breath. "Okay."

"Love you," he says.

And it feels like an *egregious* overstep to say it back. I've never even met Valerie's dad before. This isn't—I shouldn't, should I?

Indecision wins, which means I don't. But I still feel bad when, after a moment's silence, his footsteps recede down the hall.

Shit.

Sorry, Valerie.

I squeeze my eyes shut. Church internship. A guy named Brett. How repressed is Valerie? Obviously, if she has these books hidden away and was talking to her parents, she's probably pretty aware of who she is, right?

A fist of misery in my chest tightens with every passing second.

Poor Valerie.

To distract myself, I pull the book back out. I read until the house has gone quiet, and then I sneak back downstairs to the office. A floorboard creaks under my foot and I freeze, certain that the Devil is going to wake up and come for my ankles again.

But nothing happens.

I slip into the room silently, and carefully, I log back into the account, holding my breath.

Nothing.

No new notifications. No engagement, *nothing*.

Not that I expected anything, but still.

I sit in the desk chair, watching the clock on the wall tick closer and closer to midnight. Maybe that's when I reset.

But midnight comes and goes, and nothing happens.

Disappointed, I creep back upstairs to Valerie's room—avoiding the creaky floorboard this time—and close the door behind me with a soft click.

On her bed, her phone lights up as a dozen new text messages roll in. I stare down at the screen, wishing for the umpteenth time that Valerie didn't have her message previews turned off.

With a low groan, I flop back on the bed. Too many questions. *No* answers.

I lie there fully clothed for a long time, thoughts swirling, but even as the clock ticks toward one a.m. and sleep threatens to take me, I only have one thought clear enough to act on:

I've got to get the hell out of here.

00:98

ELEVEN.

When the nightmare ends and I open my eyes, the clock on my dashboard reads 00:98.

Well, shit.

Hey, I got my wish. I got the hell out of that bedroom. I just—back *here* wasn't what I was thinking, exactly.

00:98.

My heart sinks, a ripple of icy dread sending shockwaves through me. Even though I knew it—*I knew it*—the shock still means I almost crash the car for real this time, swerving back into my lane at the last second, heart hammering.

So, I was right.

I'm in a countdown.

This time, I don't pull over. I don't stop.

I flash past the green tractor, catching Gideon in the rearview mirror only for a moment, and I keep driving south.

Somewhere ahead of me lies wherever Valerie was going. I'm two days in, and for whatever reason, this thing is counting down from one hundred.

So I keep driving. I drive, and I drive and I drive, through the same scenery of rolling hills and mountains on my right, flat plains on my left.

Three hours in, I pass through a city called Lethbridge, and even though that pings something in my chest the same way Calgary did, I don't know why, and I don't have any urges to stop, so I don't, except to get gas before I leave the city.

Where was Valerie going? Clearly, her attempt at coming out didn't go well, but it's not like they kicked her out. What could have been so bad that she wanted to up and leave that cushy life? I mean, it definitely had to be serious, because leaving that kind of security would be impractical on all counts, and I'd think twice first, if it were me in her shoes.

But I don't know the details.

Eventually, in the midafternoon, I hit the U.S. border. Valerie packed a passport for a reason, I decide, after five minutes of nail-biting indecision in a Tim Horton's bathroom. And anyway, I've always wanted to go to the States—I have the distinct sense that I've never been, somehow—and maybe if I cross a border, something will trigger, like, cosmically, and I'll escape this cycle.

Maybe that's where she was going all along.

Except I can't cross. It's June 26—Valerie's birthday is July 9. She's not eighteen yet, which means the crossing agent wants a letter from her parents. As if Valerie would have a letter from Cheryl and Jeff granting her permission to cross the border on her own.

I search her backpack again, just in case.

And then I get turned away.

Driving back north only makes me feel horribly cranky and like

I've wasted my time, so I turn left the second I get the opportunity, heading west toward the mountains.

It's like the farther I drive, the more geography is rebuilding itself in my head. I know where we are on a map of North America, in a vague sense. Calgary is in Canada, and by this point, I'm pretty certain both Valerie and I live in the city, which makes me Canadian, or at the very least, a resident.

The Rocky Mountains stretch vaguely north–south to the west of the city, and somewhere beyond that, I know there's an ocean, and I'm going to drive until I either get there or reset, no matter how long it takes.

It takes *forever*.

Boy howdy, does it take forever.

Somehow I know it's supposed to take hours, but I'm wondering if I really mean *days* by the time the sun sets in front of me, right in my fucking eyes. It's only irritating for a second before the brightness dips behind a mountain. Dusk spreads a haze of blue across the horizon that fades in what feels like mere moments, plunging the highway into darkness.

I don't stop except for dinner. The money in Valerie's wallet has reset, which is a small mercy. I get a sandwich in a town called Osoyoos and sit on a bench in the mountains, and it's when I look up at the stars that it occurs to me to be afraid.

I am *alone*.

Like, completely and truly alone, and I have no answers, only infinite questions.

If I die in this time loop, is it just *over*? Or do I reset? My stomach turns at the thought, and I can't bring myself to finish the rest of the sandwich, so I bring it with me, and it sits on the passenger seat like it's made of ham and judgment instead of ham and provolone.

The dashboard clock is useless, and Valerie's dead phone isn't any more help, so I have no idea what time it is, but it's been dark for hours when my eyelids start to droop.

I've been changing the radio station all day, chasing frequencies, and now I turn the volume up, trying to stay awake, and when it gets truly unbearable, I stop in the middle of the night for gas and I buy a coffee.

"Long day?" the girl at the counter asks when I order a large. She has frizzy blue hair and pretty graphic eyeliner.

By the clock on the wall, it's ten to midnight.

I give her a wry little smile. "You have no idea."

"Where are you headed?"

At that, I pause. "I don't actually know."

"Ooh. An adventure."

"Yeah, I guess so," I muse, and decide that I like the sound of that. An adventure is the nicest way to frame this existential nightmare.

"Be safe," she calls when I'm on the way out, and I go still with my hand on the door.

Emotion rises, threatening to cut off my air supply. Before I leave, I tell her, "Thank you. I will."

The mountains drag on forever. I steadily make my way through the coffee, watching the road signs flash by, bright in the headlights, vanishing into darkness.

Gut instinct recognizes the names on these signs. Like maybe *I* lived here, at one point. Or at least like I've been here before.

At long last, the mountains recede. I keep them in the rearview and keep driving, out of the valley and into the city, where even now in the middle of the night the streets are busy. I'm not alone anymore, except that I am.

A digital display outside of a bank tells me it's a little before five in the morning. There are no stars, only the scattered lights of a city stretching in front of me down to the water.

There is no moon.

It's at least another hour before I hit the coast.

My legs feel like jelly from sitting for so long, and for a minute, I just lean against the hood and stretch, burying a cavernous yawn in my shoulder.

The ocean is vast in the dark. This enormous void could swallow me whole and no one would ever know what happened. Mildly, I wonder what would happen if I drowned. Would I just restart? Or would it be over?

I kick my shoes and socks off and leave them on the rocks, stepping gingerly to avoid sharp shells in the bleak night.

The blanketing warmth I left behind in Nanton is nowhere to be found. Brisk breeze rolls off the water and cuts through my thin flannel. When I step into the surf, the water is so cold I feel it in my bones immediately, feet aching, teeth chattering.

My eyes burn, and I don't even know if it's exhaustion or emotion or both this time.

"What do you want?" I ask the dark, surprised when my voice breaks. "What do you *want* from me? What am I supposed to do?"

The dark, predictably, doesn't answer.

I stand there trembling until I can't bear it, then scramble back up the beach, scooping my shoes and stumbling to the car, where I rip through the backpack and wrestle my arms into Valerie's fleece.

Then I crawl into the driver's seat, knees to my chest.

My heart doesn't slow for a long time.

It must be past six in the morning. The horizon stays dark, but in my rearview, the sky lightens gradually. The fleece is warm, and the fresh-laundry smell makes my heart ache.

Are her parents worried? Are *my* parents worried? What is the rest of me doing, right now, out there in the world?

It hits me all over again how *alone* I am.

Except here, like this, it's not fear I'm feeling as much as grief, somehow, big enough to curl up around. It's a familiar ache. A tear slips out over the bridge of my nose and drops onto the seat.

Whoever I am, I have a feeling that I'm used to being lonely.

I'm—

00:97

TWELVE.

I open my eyes and slam on the brakes.

The tires screech and I skid a little, but after a moment, the car comes to a full stop on the highway, and it doesn't even matter, because nobody's coming, and I know that before I even look in the rearview, because I've *done* this before.

00:97 on the dashboard. Bright morning sunlight drenches my hands on the steering wheel and I blink rapidly until my eyes adjust from the darkness of the ocean.

Goddammit.

The static from the radio sends a shiver up my spine, a frequency so invasive it buzzes in my bones.

I didn't fall asleep, but apparently that doesn't matter. I reset anyway.

"For *fuck's* sake." I yank the knob on the volume way down until the car is quiet.

My fingers tremble on the wheel, and just like the other times I've woken up here, my heart is racing.

Slowly, I pull off the highway and onto the sloping grass.

Going back to Valerie's only raised more questions. Driving didn't bring any epiphanies, and even though one hundred days—well, ninety-seven—feels like an eon, I have a nasty feeling that time is going to go by quickly.

I get out of the car and pace, restlessness eating at me. The low hum of machinery carries on the air. A gopher scampers into view, stopping in a patch of grass, staring up at me.

I stare right back, tilting my head at it. "What do *you* think I should do?"

"Hey!" Gideon shouts from across the road.

I jolt.

"You okay?" he asks, hanging out of the tractor, a hand raised to shield his eyes from the sun. "Need a hand?"

I hesitate. I do need help, but I don't know with *what*. And this time, my car is fine. No crash. Nothing broken. I don't even know what lie I would make up.

So I shout back, "I'm good, thanks!"

The gopher scuttles away into the long grass at the sound of my voice.

"Okay," Gideon calls back, giving me a little wave and ducking back into the tractor. The second it turns onto the highway, I regret waving him off.

The *only* constant so far in this whole mess is that Gideon's been helpful, and here he is again, offering help for no reason other than that it looks like I need it.

The tractor disappears down the road. Fists clenched, nails biting into my palms, I stand there waffling for long enough that the gopher returns and the sun beats down on my neck. When I decide, it's all at once. I get back behind the wheel and slam the door shut.

Fortunately, I remember the turnoff for the little shed where he'd left the tractor. I pull off the road, gravel crunching under the wheels.

The tractor is right where he parked it the first day, but it's empty.

I get out of the car, craning my neck, but Gideon is nowhere to be seen. Frustrated, I turn on my heel. I can't have been more than a minute behind him—where *is* he?

That's when I spot Ricky.

Just like last time, he's leaning against the fence, except this time he's watching me. The keys to the tractor sit next to what looks like a half dozen other sets on a carabiner hanging from one of his belt loops, and he's chewing on that stalk of grass again, arms folded over that offensively green safety vest.

His eyes are on me, one eyebrow raised.

So I take a risk, and I take a step toward him. "Hey, have you seen Gideon?"

Ricky eyes me up and down. "Who's asking?"

"Me," I tell him, hesitant to give any more information than that, cheeks warming.

Spitting out the piece of grass, he pushes off the fence. "You just missed him."

I suck my bottom lip under my front teeth and ball my fist. "Well, shit. Do you know where he's going?"

"Home, probably," Ricky says. "Why? For real, who's asking?"

I don't bother responding, craning my neck down the stretch of road.

No sign of Gideon, or which way he went, or where the hell *home* might be.

"Also, do I know you?" he asks, a frown in his voice as he shakes out that brown mop of hair. "I feel like I know you."

I cut him a sharp look, but his curiosity is mild. Nowhere close to *real* suspicion, and definitely not like he actually recognizes me. "No."

"What do you need Gideon for?"

"I need his help with something."

"Well, *I* could help you," Ricky points out. "Seeing as he isn't here. And anyway, if you already know Gideon, then you know today isn't the day to be asking favors."

Intrigued, I step closer. "Oh?"

"I mean . . ." Ricky gestures, a movement that's clearly meant to convey a single sentiment: *duh*. "I'd be happy to help you, unless what you need is Gideon-specific. Although, I gotta say, I can probably still help you, even if it *is* a Gideon-specific sort of thing. We've got a similar skill set."

"Do you really?" I muster all the skepticism I can.

"Uh-huh," he says, all sly. "Will you tell me your name, at least?"

I open my mouth, pivoting away from the technical truth at the last second. "Laurie."

Saying it just *feels* better than it had to give Valerie's name. It rolls off my tongue and out into the air, and today it feels right.

It feels like mine.

"Laurie," he muses. "Short for what?"

"What's Ricky short for?" I counter.

His eyes flash, and he tilts his head, a frown pinching his forehead. "Hang on."

Whoops.

Eyes narrowing further by the second, he asks, "How did you know my name?"

I scramble for an excuse. "Gideon told me about you."

"Oh." Ricky's expression flattens out. "Well. All right, then."

"*All right, then*," I echo. "What does that mean?"

"You should know Gideon's all talk." He kicks a patch of dry grass. "Whatever he told you, it's not true. Like, yeah, I'm not a saint, but that doesn't mean I'm a fucking snitch. I wasn't the one who told."

My eyebrows arch.

"He told you I'm a snitch, right?" Ricky asks. "He's always telling people that, but it *wasn't* me."

"Actually, he didn't mention it."

"Really." It's not quite a question, dripping with skepticism.

"Scout's honor." I hold up a hand.

There's a pronounced, heavy-bellied pause.

"It's short for Richard, by the way," he says, a little sourly, not answering my question. "But I'd think that was obvious. There's not a lot *Ricky* can be short for."

I nod, feeling uncertain and on the edge of doing something *seriously* stupid. After all, there's still one thing left I haven't tried. The mere thought makes my heartbeat spike, but maybe that's a sign. It's the only option left, really. I've tried seeking answers, and I've tried running from them, and neither of those things got me any closer to the truth.

Maybe now honesty is my only choice.

So I take a deep breath. "Gideon didn't actually tell me about you."

Ricky's whole posture shifts. He crosses his arms, turning toward me, confusion rippling across his expression. "Huh? Who did, then?"

Not where I'm going with this. I try again. "No, I mean, he didn't tell me your name, and neither did anybody else."

At that, he stops. "Oh?"

"I already knew it."

His eyebrows spike. "How?"

I take a deep breath. "I'm in a time loop."

Ricky stares at me. Then, strained, he laughs. "What?"

Even before I explain, I know this was a bad idea. "I'm serious. I'm stuck in this day. I've already lived it three times."

He just watches me warily, forehead pinched.

"Gideon was the first person I met," I tell him.

With a good deal of reluctance, Ricky says, "Right."

"Please, I don't care if you believe me. I just—can you help me find him or not?"

Ricky considers carefully, and it looks like he's *really* thinking about it until another tractor rolls off the road with a crunch of gravel. He says, slowly, "Or not. I think."

I heave a sigh, running a hand through my hair.

"Look, I gotta deal with this, okay?" With a tight smile, he jerks his head toward the second tractor. "Good luck with your . . . time loop, or whatever. Sorry I couldn't be more helpful."

"Can you at least tell me where Gideon lives?" I ask, a desperate last resort.

"Yeah, I think I'd better not do that. It was good to meet you," he says while he backs away, in a tone that does absolutely nothing to prove he means it.

"You too," I mutter, voice a little flat, watching him go down the sidewalk.

Well, *now* what?

I throw my hands in the air, frustrated. Then it occurs to me I *still* have one lead. I have no idea what time it is, or if he'll be there yet, but, hey. Worth a shot.

I get back in the car and drive slowly, scouring the roads, doubt creeping in. Naturally, he's not at Vern's yet. That would be too easy.

Gideon could be anywhere now, but at least I know where he's *going* to be.

It turns out, stakeouts are severely boring. I park across the street from the café and wait, which is easy for about two minutes, until I realize I have *nothing* to occupy myself with.

But I stick it out for what must be at least an hour. Then, when I spot Gideon walking along the sidewalk—to Vern's, I assume—I pull over onto the side of the road and throw the car into park.

By the time I get out, he's already halfway down the block, almost out of sight.

"Hey!" I call after him, clapping a hand over my mouth to stop his name from slipping out.

Gideon pivots on his heel. At the sight of me, he frowns and points at his chest, like he's not sure I'm addressing him.

"Yes, you!" I jog to catch up to him.

At least he waits.

"I need your help," I manage as soon as I'm close enough that he'll hear me.

Unsteadily, Gideon says, "Um."

"I'm stuck," I tell him, and then I take a deep breath. "Gideon, I'm in a time loop."

THIRTEEN.

Gideon's quiet for a long, long time.

He doesn't look surprised.

Hope surges.

"Did you say . . . a *time* loop?" Gideon tilts his head, almost like this is a fun experiment, and he's waiting to see what's going to happen. "You know, I thought Ricky was fucking with me."

I grimace. "Ricky *told* you?"

"Listen, if this is some kind of practical joke, I—"

"It's not!" Frustrated, I kick a rock and watch it skitter across the street. "Trust me, I wish it was. Here: I know you're about to go to Vern's. Right?"

"Is that supposed to be proof?" Gideon asks. "Everyone knows I volunteer at Vern's when I have the time."

I grind my teeth a little, grimacing. "Listen, it's *true*."

"How do you know Ricky?" He turns and walks away in the opposite direction.

It doesn't look like he's inviting me to join him, but it also doesn't look like he's trying to leave me behind on purpose, exactly, so I fall into step next to him while he pulls out his phone and starts tapping at the screen. "I met him with you." I ignore the way he shakes his head. "What did he say to you, anyway?"

"And I quote, 'crazy chick asking about you comma, thinks she's in a time loop. Watch out, knife emoji.'"

I roll my eyes, fighting the urge to wince at "crazy *chick*."

"And what do you mean you met Ricky with me?" Gideon asks. "Sorry, are we supposed to know each other?"

"No." With a breathy laugh, I correct, "Yes, actually. Sort of."

"Sort of," Gideon echoes. There's a closed-off, pinched cast to his expression I haven't seen before.

"You were the first person I met," I tell him. "You stopped to help me on the side of the road."

"Okay," he says, a little doubtfully.

"But you don't remember it."

"I'm pretty sure I would remember you." He raises an eyebrow. "It's not every day you meet someone who . . ."

Evidently, he can't figure out a polite way to phrase that he thinks I have well and truly lost my marbles, so he just doesn't finish the sentence at all.

"You're getting sent away tomorrow," I blurt out. "I don't know where to, but you've told me before, or—sort of. You and Tenley were talking, and I got the gist, and I don't know why, because you seem really nice, and . . ."

He blinks at me.

"I don't think you're *supposed* to be sent away, though," I tell him, and all at once it feels true. "I think maybe . . . that's part of why I'm stuck."

Gideon shakes his head slowly, then a little faster, like he's trying to rid his ears of water. "*What?*"

"And, I don't know, maybe Tenley knows more about this, but I've been afraid to ask, because—"

"Sorry, you know Tenley?" Brow furrowed, he rubs a hand along his forehead.

"Yes, because you introduced me. You called Ricky a piece of shit."

At that, it looks like I *almost* get a smile out of him, even if it fades almost instantly. "Well, I stand by that, but, like . . . I have no idea who you are."

"I know." Exasperated, I have to skip a little to keep up with him. "Like I said, I'm in a time loop. So I know you, but you don't know me."

"Uh-huh," Gideon says. "Sorry, do you have any way to prove this?"

I'm about to flounder my way through an answer when I realize where we're going.

"Oh, you've got to be kidding me," I mutter as we round the corner and the orange sign of the gas station comes into view.

Gideon keeps his lips pressed together the whole time we're approaching, shouldering open the door with all the grim determination of a man walking into a DMV.

Tenley looks up at the sight of us, with the same expression they'd worn the first day, when Gideon brought me here for help.

"Hey, Tenley." There's a note of wariness in Gideon's tone that wasn't present last time.

"Hello, Gideon," Tenley says agreeably.

"This is—sorry." He frowns. "I didn't catch your name."

Ouch. I smile weakly. "Laurie."

Tenley smiles back at me. "And Laurie, hello, nice to meet you."

I offer them a tentative little wave.

Gideon cuts right to the chase. "Do you know anything about time loops?"

"Is this the first time you're asking me this?" They give him a little wink, and when he doesn't laugh, the smile slides right off their face. "What's going on, Gideon?"

"Laurie believes she's in a time loop," Gideon says, and all the civil politeness in the world cannot mask that he does *not* share my belief.

"I *am*," I insist.

Tenley hums an acknowledgment, then turns to Gideon, voice lower. "Did they change their minds?"

"No," Gideon says sullenly, matching their tone, so quiet I almost can't hear him. "And they won't, so don't you go getting involved, okay?"

"You're not going to run off on me, are you?"

"Don't worry, I'll come find you later."

I listen, fascinated. Technically, because things are happening differently today, this is a divergence from my first day in the loop, but they're still playing out this same conversation, almost word for word.

Then Tenley turns back to me. "Time loop." Their voice is a soft scrape. "You know, that's on my bucket list."

I blink up at them. "Sorry. What?"

"It's fascinating stuff. But . . ."

My heart sinks. "But what?"

"But there are so many complications. What prompted the loop? What are you trying to fix?"

They sound almost infuriatingly on board with the concept. It would be a comfort if I had any idea whether they actually believe me or if they're just humoring me.

"I don't know if I'm trying to fix anything," I say. "I'm stuck in someone else's body."

"Maybe you're here to fix *their* problem," they point out, with no real degree of surprise at the idea that I've swapped bodies with someone.

"But that's not fair," I burst out. "Shouldn't she fix her own problem?"

Leaning against the counter, Gideon puts his face in his hands.

"What do you know so far?"

"I think she's running away," I tell them. "I think she's— maybe she tried to come out to her parents, and it went badly, so now she's making a run for it, but the problem is, I don't know where she is, or where my real body might be."

"That *is* a problem." Tenley rubs at their chin, and Gideon shoots them a sharp, disbelieving look.

"I went to her house," I explain. "The address on her license. I met her mom. I *sort* of get why she'd be running away, but I don't—"

"I don't have time for this," Gideon interrupts, and I realize at once exactly how antsy he looks, tension in the set of his jaw and the line of his shoulders. "Look, I'm sorry, you seem really nice, but I don't—I can't—"

I swallow, hard.

Helplessly, he gestures. "Sorry, okay?"

As if to prove his point, Gideon's phone rings. With a glance, his shoulders tighten. He tells Tenley, "It's Archer. I gotta go."

"We'll be okay," Tenley assures him. "Won't we, Laurie?"

FOURTEEN.

We will not, in fact, be okay.

"I'm going to be honest with you, Laurie." Tenley heaves a sigh and leans back in their armchair next to the fireplace. There's no fire in the grate—the whole thing is full of stacked plastic boxes. "I have never met someone who claims they were in a time loop."

"That you remember." I try for a joke, but it doesn't land.

Tenley just watches, expression layered with a solemnity I don't understand.

We're back at their place. It's been just like my first day all over again, hanging out at the gas station with Tenley until they close and following them back home, with one notable difference: *I've* been the one talking nonstop, explaining everything that's happened so far, down to the slightest detail. This time, I didn't go to bed right after dinner, and we're still talking, even though it's late enough the sky has gone dark.

"The first time," I open cautiously, "Gideon brought me to you and told you he'd found 'another one.' What did he mean by that?"

Tenley's mouth twitches into a smile. "Just that I'm the person to go to in situations like this."

"Well, I got that much," I say. "Do people get into trouble around here regularly?"

"More often than you'd think. I have a spare room, and I know what it's like to be in trouble with nowhere to go. If I can help someone else the way I wish I'd been helped, I will."

"That's very kind."

They just shake their head with a sigh, bracelets clacking together as they shift in their seat. "Walk me through it again," they say. "The loop."

So I do.

Tenley is a good listener. They don't interrupt, except to ask questions. By the time I've gotten through it all for a third time, it's late enough that my eyes burn.

We lapse into silence. In the distance, police sirens wail.

Tenley's lips purse, the wrinkles around their mouth deepening as they think.

Ten minutes pass before they break the quiet.

"It's interesting that the only thing you know about yourself is that you play hockey," they say. "Perhaps it's a good idea to get back on the ice."

"Yeah, maybe." I cross my hands in my lap.

"So, you believe that maybe you're here to stop Gideon from being sent away?"

"I don't know." Wearily, I rub at my forehead. "I don't know anything. That's the problem."

"And that bothers you?"

"Of *course* it does." I laugh helplessly. "Wouldn't it bother you?"

"I suppose it would." They rub at their chin.

"I just don't know what to do."

"Gideon's a skeptic at heart," they tell me, like that's somehow related in their head. "I'm not surprised this is the one time he was reluctant to help."

"But he did help," I rush to assure them. "He *did*. He just also thought I was totally nuts."

Their mouth quirks into a smile. "Well, to be fair, your story *is* pretty nuts."

I flush.

"Don't take that as a criticism. I just mean that you have to understand where he's coming from, right?"

The ancient rotary phone on the table under the window rings once, a shrill rattle ripping through the silence.

I jolt a little. It's just after midnight. Much later than I was awake last time I was here.

"Who on *earth* is calling this late?" Tenley sounds crankier about this than they have about anything else so far as they haul themselves to their feet. When they pick up, they don't speak. They just stand there, listening to whoever is on the other end of the line. "Yes," they say at last, voice low. "Yes, of course."

Something prickles along the length of my spine at the sudden shift in their tone.

"Oh, darling, you didn't." Tenley touches a hand to their mouth and listens, nodding. "Of course. Of *course*. I'm on my way. Don't say another word until I get there, all right? Okay. Good."

They hang up and then just stand there for several long seconds.

"What's going on?" I ask the moment they turn around.

"I have to go." They rub a tight circle into the skin between their eyebrows. "Gideon's been arrested."

FIFTEEN.

Bri is not waiting for me at our usual spot at school.

Not that I'm really expecting her. Radio silence all morning only tells a familiar tale. I'm used to the occasional Blanchette silent treatment. When Bri's annoyed, it can take her a little while to get over herself and remember that I've literally never not been on her side.

Still, I linger in the corridor where the science hallways intersect for a few extra minutes, just in case.

No dice. No Bri. Just me and the Trinity High bulletin board plastered with colorful end-of-year sentimental garbage and the nausea-inducing flicker of the fluorescent lights overhead.

I sit through first period with itching impatience, wishing she'd text me back. Around me, the rest of the grade buzzes with the same impatience. We're all thinking it: today is a waste of time. Exams are done. We walk across the stage on Saturday. Final quizzes are *dumb*. What the hell are we doing here?

At least second period is with Mr. Furaha. I've been obsessed with his class ever since our first day. Like, *obsessed*, to the point where Bri said it was creepy, and even Ibha "queen of parasocial relationships" Agarwal agreed.

But it's not creepy. It's not like I have a crush on him, or like I ever *would*. It's just rare that I meet an adult that I respect as much as I respect Mr. Furaha, and the fact that he got to be a teacher, let alone a teacher at our very private, very religious school, is inspiring.

Plus, he teaches biology, and I love biology.

Like always, Mr. Furaha is wearing a brightly colored button-up shirt, and like always, the little silver pin with the blue-pink-and-white striped flag sits on his collar, impossible to ignore.

"I'm going to miss this class," I confess as I approach his desk after the lunch bell rings. Then I duck my head a little and lower my voice. "Don't tell anyone else, but you've been my favorite teacher this year."

"Well, it's not over yet, is it?" he asks with a wide grin, white straight teeth standing out against his dark-brown skin. "Tell me you're not planning to *skip* on the last day."

I shake my head. "No, I'm not. I'll be here tomorrow, I just, you know. In case I didn't get the chance to say it."

"Well, don't tell anyone else," he says, tossing me a little wink as he passes a hand over his tight, coiling curls, "but you've been my favorite student."

I shouldn't feel so pleased. Even so, my cheeks flush.

"Where are you headed in the fall?" He tears the corner off a piece of paper on his memo pad and scribbles something with his ballpoint pen.

I lean my hip against his desk. "Lethbridge."

He nods. "You gonna play hockey?"

"That's the plan."

"You will excel, I'm sure."

My cheeks flush even hotter.

Mr. Furaha caps his pen and pushes the torn piece of paper across the desk toward me. "Here's my out-of-school email. Anything you want to talk about, just give me a shout."

At that, my throat goes tight. I always feel like he *knows*, somehow. Like how I feel when my mom's eyes cut me in half with laser precision. Except with him, it's a slow weep of relief to be seen instead of crackling dread.

"I mean it," he says with a pointed jab of his pen against the paper, pushing it the rest of the way.

I toss him a long, lingering look, and then I take the piece of paper. "Thank you."

He gives me a swift smile as one of my classmates approaches the desk, holding my gaze for a moment before he repeats, "Anything."

I'm still rubbing the piece of paper between my fingers when someone knocks their fist gently against the locker next to mine in greeting.

"Yo, Eaton." Brett's best friend Matty tosses me a wicked grin as he spins his combination lock, blond curls catching in the sickly hallway lighting and—somehow—glowing golden. "How's it going?"

"It's going." I trade out my books, slipping the torn bit of Mr. Furaha's paper between the pages of my beat-up day planner. "You?"

"I think Mrs. Engler hates me," he says with a little sigh, "but that's old news."

"Well, only one more day, and then we are *out* of here."

"Speaking of, I'm taking names and numbers. Summer team. Just for fun. Some scrimmages and whatnot, so we don't get rusty."

"As if you'd let us get rusty."

I'm—obviously—not on the boys hockey team, but some of us from the girls team elect to join Matty's conditioning sessions on the weekends, which are kickass and leave me feeling like every single muscle in my body is made of rubber. But it's worth it, because I want to be able to do what he does, even if it hurts like hell to get there.

Matty on ice is liquid talent. As captain of the hockey team, he's the only one of us who is *absolutely* one hundred percent going to continue on to professional hockey. He's that good. No one can out-skate him, except maybe my brother, but that doesn't count because he's a year older, anyway.

Off the rink, Matty's bright and funny, and I envy everything about him, from his skill to his confidence to his complete and utter freedom of spirit. Plus, it's hard to be openly out in any sports setting, let alone at a private Christian school, but he's never let it crush his spirit. It would be really easy to hate him, and lots of people do.

But I don't. Matty's easy to talk to.

Too easy, sometimes.

"It's a coed team?" I ask cautiously.

"Enough," he says with a smile that means *yes* and also a dozen other things that make my stomach flip with nerves. "You in?"

"Obviously."

"Fucking *excellent*." He shakes out his unruly sand-blond curls and leans closer, tone abruptly serious when he asks, "Did you tell him yet?"

A half dozen memories run through my head in swift succession: the dashboard clock of Matty's car reading half-past three in the morning, the soft fabric of his sweatshirt against my skin, my voice hoarse, the way I'd cried so hard after I'd almost made myself sick, the way he'd been so patient, how he'd rubbed my back and told me it would be all right when I knew it wouldn't.

I lean forward, rest my forehead against the locker, and groan. "*Matty*. Give it a rest, would you? I'll tell him when I'm good and ready."

"Tell who?" Brett asks just behind me, and I startle so badly I fumble with my books and drop my keys.

Matty catches them by the lanyard before they hit the ground, then hooks his index finger through the canvas loop to swing them in a slow circle, letting go at the last second so the keys arc through the air and drop neatly onto the book on the top of my stack. "Easy, there. How much coffee have you had today, Eaton?"

I scowl at him.

Matty raises a hand to Brett. "Hey, man."

"What's up, Lawrence?" Brett smacks his palm against Matty's and bumps his knuckles. "You're still coming tomorrow night, right?"

"Where the hell else would I be?" Matty grins.

"Anyway, tell who about what?" Brett loops an arm around

my waist and briefly rests his jaw against the side of my head in greeting.

My boyfriend is just about perfect. Brett's gentle, and kind, and sometimes funny, not to mention he's the only guy besides Matty who can reliably get the puck away from me on the ice. We've been together for almost three years, which makes us the longest-standing couple at Trinity.

And I have been lying to him for *months*.

"My dad." It's not even difficult anymore. I don't tell the truth, and Brett doesn't know, and I sleep like a fucking baby. Most of the time. "About the scratch on the car."

Brett frowns. "He doesn't know about that yet?"

He does. Dad had blown a gasket, which is to say, he'd sat down at the table and scratched his chin a lot and then told me he was disappointed in me.

"Thought you said you could buff it out." Brett's frown deepens.

"I probably can. I was just asking for advice."

"Why would you need advice?" he asks, and at least he sounds genuinely curious rather than suspicious.

I huff a sigh and try not to squirm away when Brett leans in and noses at my cheek. He's been extra handsy in the last few weeks leading up to tomorrow night. I swallow down the thought along with a sharp acidic burn at the back of my throat, and then I don't even have to answer his question.

"You know my brother Isaiah's a detailer, right?" Matty asks, the most casually placed deflection, and gratitude bursts in my chest. "He should start paying me for all the free business I give him."

It's not even a lie. I learned how to do that from Matty—how to lie without lying, using genuine statements in the right place so nobody suspects a thing.

Anyway, the car isn't even a big deal. I backed out of our driveway and scratched the length of my car on a rogue tree branch.

But Brett buys it. He's back to his easy, elastic smile in half a second, which loosens the knot in the pit of my stomach. If he's this relaxed, Bri can't be *that* mad at me. It's easy to use one as a temperature gauge for the other—they live under the same roof, and before that, they occupied the same womb at the same time.

When I catch Matty observing me, I shake my head. I've told him a hundred times: What Brett doesn't know won't hurt him. It's not like it's going to be a long-term problem.

I can see it in his face, though, that he disagrees.

Matty gives me a pointed look, knocks once on the locker, and walks away.

00:96

SIXTEEN.

When the nightmare ends, I open my eyes and peel off the road, kicking up dust and gravel in my wake, too distracted by whirling confusion to be properly annoyed that I'm here *again*.

I'd been reluctant to follow Tenley's suggestion and go to sleep after they left to find Gideon, right up until it occurred to me they weren't coming back. When I finally did, it took me ages, fitfully tossing and turning, the same questions spinning on a rinse cycle.

Gideon? Arrested? For what?

At least today I have a plan.

This time I can follow him.

Not in a creepy way. I'm not trying to interact. That's not what today is for. I'm just . . . tailing him. Observing.

Here's what Gideon does with his June 26:

When I wake up, he's driving the tractor into town. I don't know where he's coming from, but after he drops the tractor off with Ricky, he walks home, moving gingerly, like he's being cautious.

Home, apparently, is a farmhouse on the other side of town, offset from the rest of the neighborhood at the end of a long gravel road. I absolutely do not muster the courage to follow him all the way out there, and I don't really have an accurate timepiece, so

I don't know what happens while he's in there except that when he comes back, he's showered and changed.

I tail him to Vern's, following from a distance, idling close to the curb and waiting for him to get far enough ahead that he won't notice. Gideon spends *ages* at Vern's—probably close to two hours. Nobody comes in that whole time, especially not during the flash rainstorm, during which I stay in my car, and after he goes straight to the gas station.

Through the window, I can see him talking to Tenley for at least fifteen minutes. Gideon gets the world's biggest, tightest hug from them and leaves, looking like he'd like to be shot point-blank.

After that, he walks to somebody else's house a few blocks away, which is where he stays the rest of the night.

Or, that's what I *think*.

The thing about stakeouts is that the media really cannot possibly show you how boring they are. And another thing is, you *can't* conceivably sit and watch a building for nine and a half hours. You can try your best, and I do, but even so I *have* to leave twice, once to hunt down a public bathroom, again because at half-past seven, I am, like, *actually* starving.

But then I'm right back in the car, waiting. And watching as the sun goes down, as darkness submerges the neighborhood and streetlights flick on, even though I'm bored to tears. All I have to pass the time is the worst game ever: flicking through the mental Rolodex of songs I know by heart, most of which turn out to be religious songs for kids. I guess a childhood of *VeggieTales* is another thing Valerie and I have in common, though I can't imagine ever wanting to own four Bibles, so I'm probably less of a diehard.

I hope. When I reach out into the hopeful, foggy canyon and ask myself what I believe in, I twitch away like I've just touched an open flame.

It's past midnight when I hear the sirens.

Shitting *hell*.

How did that happen?

I start the engine, rolling my window down so I can follow the sound *all the way across town, what the hell, Gideon*.

The sirens cut out well before I get to them, which means I have nothing to go by for the last five minutes, driving around aimlessly in the dark until I finally glimpse flashing lights.

I arrive on the scene just as an ambulance pulls out onto the main road. I park two blocks down and walk in the cool night air to find a small crowd gathered around two police cruisers on a shabby street corner.

It's too dark to tell if Gideon's in the back of one of them, but I sure as hell don't see him anywhere *else*.

On the sidewalk, a girl with shoulder-length black hair sobs into her hands, hunched with her elbows on her knees. The flashing lights cast her shadow into sharp relief against the brick wall behind her, and when she wipes her eyes, I think I see a spattering of blood across her knuckles.

I'm not the only one drawn by the sirens. A dozen people have gathered, a fair few in pajamas.

When I catch someone saying Gideon's name, I whip around.

It's the boy from the gas station. The one with white hair who buys SD cards every day. He's standing next to a short, broad-shouldered boy with skin so dark he almost disappears into the night, the two of them looking like yin and yang in the flashing lights.

"What happened?" I ask the blond boy. "Was Gideon arrested?"

He blinks at me, slow like a cat, eyes glassy under the streetlight. "Not to be rude," he starts cautiously, "but who in the hell are you?"

"Never mind." I shake my head.

"He was, though," he says, at the last second, when I'm about to turn away. "Arrested."

I pivot. "Why?"

He and the other boy exchange a dark look.

"That bad, huh?" I ask weakly. "Listen, I'm sure it was a misunderstanding, or something, he—"

"It wasn't." The short boy's expression is solemn as he turns to me, wrenching his eyes away from one of the cruisers. His gaze is steady on mine when he adds, "He earned it."

00:95

SEVENTEEN.

He *earned* it?

I wake up with my hands on the wheel, confusion and intrigue blistering between my lungs.

What the hell is Gideon's deal? Kind enough to go out of his way to help a stranger for no reason. Bold enough to have earned himself a black eye like that. Comfortable enough in his own skin to flirt with strangers. Getting arrested. *Earning* it.

I decide that I'm going to tail him again. Not as closely this time, at least not at first. I'll pick a new vantage point to watch once he gets to that house, because he had to have gotten out *somehow*, and unless there's a secret tunnel system running through Nanton, which I *very* much doubt, chances are he left through the back.

So I do tail him. Sort of. I head straight to Vern's, and then I park across the street and wait for him.

Waiting in the car got boring *real* fast last time, so once I see Gideon coming up the road, I get out of the car and walk. Just slow loops around the block, since it's nice out, and I know approximately how long he spends there. I know where he's headed after, anyway. If I lose him here, it's not the end of the world.

At the first drop of rain, I duck under the nearest awning. I'd keep walking, except I know how heavy the rain gets, so after a moment of consideration, I tug the door open, glancing at the inscription on the door. *Thelma Fanning Memorial Library.*

Library.

A *library.*

Libraries have computers.

With one glance over my shoulder and another at the old photos lining the walls, I head inside. Then, when I catch sight of the person sitting at the front desk, I freeze in place.

It's the girl from last night.

The one who was crying at the scene of whatever crime Gideon committed to *earn* getting arrested.

Her name tag reads: JAYDA.

A new plan forms at once.

If she was *there*, I could tail *her* this time, right? I could observe her like I tried to observe Gideon, and maybe this time I'd have more luck.

"Hi," she says with a distracted smile, and then something about me must catch her attention, because she pauses, tilting her head. "You okay?"

Ah. Well. What a question. I touch a hand to my collarbone. "I . . . yes?"

"You look like you're having a shitty day, is all."

Running a hand through my hair, I grimace when it gets caught in a tangle. "Yeah, you could say that."

"What's up?"

I give her a little smile and shake my head. "Can I use the computer?"

"Sure." She jerks her head toward one of the monitors. "Any of those are fine. Just not the one towards the back. That's for exams only."

Taking the little slip of paper she gives me, I use it to log in to the computer, where I jump through the hoops of making an email address and using it to make another Missed Connections post, just in case.

Then I log off, retreating to the back of the library, picking up a book at random, settling in to observe her.

Of course, observing goes terribly right off the bat. I've hardly been sitting there for ten minutes when Jayda approaches, leaning her hip against a shelf, watching me.

I try to pretend like I haven't noticed her—after all, I'm trying not to interfere, if I want the day to go as it would if I weren't here—but that doesn't deter her.

After another five minutes, she says, "You're not even reading that."

It's true—I've been staring at the first page of this Dan Brown novel, trying to look as uninteresting as I can—but I don't like that she can tell. I close the book. "Maybe I was."

"You weren't," she says cheerfully. "You look miserable."

"Do I?"

"Excessively. How come?"

"Oh, I'm in a time loop," I tell her, because what the hell. Observing her without interfering is already out the window, and I might as well have fun with it.

She laughs, this bright and joyous sound that's both somehow familiar and makes me smile before I even realize I'm doing it, like we're in on some tremendous joke together.

"I'm Jayda." She pushes off the bookcase and extends a hand. I take her hand and shake. "Laurie."

"Have we ever met, in this time loop?" The way her eyes twinkle tells me she absolutely doesn't believe I'm being serious, so this is a game now.

"Not till now."

"Shame." She crosses her arms. "Wanna tell me about it?"

And honestly, I sort of do.

She collapses into the chair opposite mine, hooking her knee over the arm, which doesn't strike me as very professional, but I guess telling a patron they look miserable isn't either. "How'd it start?"

No holds barred. I tell her *everything*, starting with waking up on the side of the road. When I mention Gideon, she laughs.

"What?" I frown. "Do you know him?"

"Yeah, a little," she tells me, with this little grin that I don't know what to make of. "Keep going."

So I do. I explain the way I reset on the road, and about staying up late but resetting anyway. When I tell her about Cheryl, she rolls her eyes. "She sounds like my foster mom. Is she one of those uber-religious types?"

"She has Bible verses on the walls, she's married to a pastor, and Valerie has a summer internship with a church, so I'm gonna go with yes."

"Foul," Jayda says cheerfully. "So, what are you going to do?"

"I don't know. I keep thinking that it's smart to learn more about the girl whose skin I'm stuck inside of, but that's hard to do."

"Maybe learning about this Valerie girl is actually a *bad* idea," Jayda points out. "Like, you'll get stuck as her or something."

I shudder.

"So, it'd be in your best interest to just sort of chill out and do whatever," she says.

I don't quite think that argument holds water, but it's not like I have any *actual* ideas.

"You should do something crazy instead." She grins. "Why not, right?"

"Why not?" I echo with a significant layer of doubt. "What do you mean by crazy exactly?"

"Something you wouldn't ordinarily do. Like, buzz your hair. Get a tattoo. Something you'd only do because there aren't any consequences. Because if you really are in a time loop, there *are* no consequences, right?"

This, I think, is the first solid point Jayda's made.

It's not like Valerie will care—tomorrow, it won't even matter, because tomorrow, everything resets. I might as well do it, just to see. If only to feel a little more at home in this strange body.

"Yeah," I say, then again, with a little more confidence, "*yeah*. Why not?"

"*That's* what I like to hear!" she crows. "So. What are we thinking it's gonna be?"

"I don't know yet. Maybe you were onto something with the hair thing."

"I'm always onto something. Want to know a fun coincidence? *I* cut hair."

"I *see*," I respond, teasing. "I get what this is. You just looking for new clients?"

"Practice clients," she says. "I'll do it for free, I'm just saying. You in, or what?"

If there are *any* perks to being stuck in a time loop, zero lasting consequences has to be high on the list. So I grin. "Hey, I don't have anything to do until midnight."

"What's midnight?"

I give her a little smile. If she didn't know Gideon, I'd tell her. But I don't want her to do anything that might change it. "Guess you'll find out later."

"I *like* you," she says. "Come on. My shift ended five minutes ago. Let's go make you bald."

EIGHTEEN.

"Not bald," I tell Jayda for the fourth time as she points me down a back street behind the elementary school, gravel crunching under the tires.

"I know, I know." She waves me off. "I won't buzz it, if that's not what you want."

"It's not," I say. "I just want it shorter."

Then she points me over to a long gravel road, and I figure out where we're going all at once.

My mouth falls open.

I don't even know why I bother with surprise at this point.

Him and his sister, Tenley had said.

"Hang on," I say. "Is Gideon your brother?"

"Guilty as charged. Has he been a total asshole to you in this time loop?"

"Not at all."

"Figures." Jayda sighs deeply as I park where she directs me on the side of the road. "You're very pretty. It's his fatal flaw."

My cheeks flare with heat. "Thanks. I think."

Jayda and Gideon live in a squat white farmhouse, and even

though the floorboards under the porch creak under my feet and the paint is peeling, I'm thoroughly charmed.

She unlocks the front door and leads me inside. Battered hardwood floors stretch to high baseboards, walls painted a cheerful yellow, and I scan the living room as we pass by it down a narrow hallway, fascinated. It's almost difficult to picture Gideon in a place like this, and I pause on the landing as Jayda stomps up the stairs.

There are pictures on the walls, but none of either Gideon or Jayda. Instead, I see a family of five, two boys and one girl, all with the same brown curly hair and freckles, and—

Hey, wait a minute.

Staring at the familiar grinning face, years younger in this picture, I ask, "You live with Ricky?"

"God, no. Not anymore, anyway. He moved out." Jayda waits for me to catch up, then turns to me. "Do you want a water or anything?"

Wordlessly, I shake my head.

"Mine's that one," she says, pointing to a door at the end of the hall. "Go on in. I'll be right back."

I do, despite feeling awkward about it.

Jayda's room looks like her, up to a point. A line of tape divides the room in two—I didn't think people actually did that in real life—and on one side, band posters plaster the wall—Green Day, blink-182, Bikini Kill, Guttermouth—and a threadbare old patchwork quilt lies bunched at the foot of the bed, clothes flung haphazardly around exactly one half of the floor space. It looks as though someone has gone to great pains to toe the clothes back over the line. The other half of the room is hauntingly puritan: plain white sheets, plain white duvet, furniture painted—you guessed it—white. A shoe rack displays a magazine-ready row of barely worn boots, the wardrobe next to it displaying a gleaming, spotless mirror.

"Yeah, I share with the youngest girl," Jayda says as she returns with a cardboard box, catching me eyeing the tape on the floor. "At least until she gets committed." At my expression, she squawks. "That was a *joke*, dude."

I manage a tight laugh, though I don't see what's so funny about it.

Jayda drags a chair from the desk on the neat side of the room and sits me down. "Touch okay?"

"Sure."

Turning my head this way and that with her fingertips, she nods. "How do you know Ricky, anyway? I never asked—are you new in town or just passing through?"

"Passing through," I tell her, wincing as she runs a brush through my hair and it catches in the tangles. "You said your foster mom is religious, right?"

"Like, *uber*-Catholic." Jayda sighs, gentle fingers parting my hair. "Where do you want this to land?"

"Middle, I guess."

"You *guess*." She shakes her head. "I've never met a girl who's this chill about her hair."

"I'm not like other girls," I tell her, deadpan, and she barks a laugh.

"Anyway," she says, parting my hair down the center, "yeah, they're all super religious. Like, Patricia—the mom—caught

Gideon with these old journals from this guy who used to live here in the '30s, and apparently it was all about his old-timey gay sexual awakening or something, and you'd have thought she'd caught him with the manual for the apocalypse. I don't think I've ever heard the f-slur so many times in one evening."

"Jesus."

"Yeah. Anyway, now she thinks he's gay, so she's been making him go to church, which is hilarious."

I pause. "*Is* he gay?"

"Fuck if I know." She gathers my hair into a ponytail and wraps an elastic band around it. "I almost hope he's a *little* bisexual, just to stick it to them. But he doesn't talk to me about stuff like that."

Personally, I hope he's a *lot* bisexual, but I don't say so out loud. "Right."

"You sure you wanna do this?" Jayda hefts a sharp pair of shears.

"Sure as shit." I steel myself, squaring my shoulders. "Do it."

"You know what? You're a lot of fun, Laurie," Jayda says, and then she cuts off the ponytail.

We both jump at a creak just outside the room as my hair hits the floor with a dull thud.

"Jesus," Jayda says, voice a lot sharper, head turned away from me. "What the hell happened to your face?"

"Yeah, you'd like to know." Gideon's voice sounds sharper too, narrow like a blade.

I shiver.

"What do you want?" Jayda snaps, releasing my head.

Gideon leans against the doorframe, observing us with a little frown, gaze lingering on me. When I catch his eye, he tilts his head, and for a split second, I *swear* I see a flicker of recognition. But then it's gone. "I don't *want* anything," he says slowly. "I just came to say hi and see what you're doing."

Smile a little sardonic, a little *too* sweet to be genuine, Jayda makes a sweeping gesture. "Laurie, as you already know, this is my brother Gideon, aka, party pooper of all time."

He flips her off. "Are you—are you *cutting hair* in here?"

Jayda gestures with the scissors, as if to say, *duh*.

"Don't make a mess." Voice low, Gideon rolls out his shoulder with a wince. "Patricia will *freak*. And be quieter."

Then he turns away and walks down the hall.

Jayda rolls her eyes. "Ugh. Don't mind him. He's just butthurt."

"Butthurt about . . . what?"

"He's going to this camp to be a counselor for the summer or something." She waves a hand. "I don't really know the details. Honestly, he probably thinks it's going to be super lame and so he doesn't want to go, but they're making him anyway."

"Who's making him go?"

Jayda jabs down toward the floor with her pointer finger. "Our foster parents."

Several of the things Tenley said drop into context in my head. "What kind of camp?"

"Beats me. He won't talk about it."

It occurs to me that extrapolation may not be Jayda's strong suit. "You don't know what happened to his eye?"

"Do *you*?"

"Not really," I say, wishing I'd gotten up the courage to ask him. "I assume he got into a fight."

"Whatever happened, he probably deserved it." Jayda sighs. "Next thing you know, he's gonna get arrested or something."

The statement hangs in the air, weighted for me, drifting on a breeze for her.

"Okay. Forget Gideon." Jayda changes the subject as she turns on the clippers, oblivious to her own prophetic gift. "You seem excellent."

I raise both eyebrows. "Thank you?"

"There's a party tonight," she tells me. "And you're coming with me."

NINETEEN.

The hardest part of the haircut is not letting Jayda see my eyes well up with relieved tears when she holds up the mirror. It's not me—it's not my face—but it's closer, and it's a literal weight off my shoulders.

After some wheedling, I give her permission to buzz the back, and the rest of my hair falls in waves around my ears. Once we're done cleaning up hair off the floor—I pretend not to notice when Jayda sprinkles some of it over her roommate's dresser—we lounge in her room and I let her play me four whole albums from her favorite bands. I hope I'll recognize even a few of the songs, but if I've ever heard any of them before, I can't tell.

It's nice to kill time with Jayda. Under the relentless pounding of the drums as the early evening sun pours through the window and heats her room like a sweltering greenhouse, I almost forget that I don't know who I am.

But by the time she's dragging me across town to the party, it's impossible to forget.

The party is in an empty old barn. Bass thumps so loud I can almost feel it through my shoes when we step onto the grassy field off the road. I can't stop running my hand over the bristles at the base of my neck, marveling at how light my head feels.

"Just stick close to me." Jayda snags my hand as she leads me through the wide-open sliding doors and into the barn. Hay lines the ground, and the stalls are empty except for the kids perching on the stable walls, laughing loudly.

I know in my bones that I've been to my fair share of parties like this. Not necessarily the in-a-barn part, but the rest of it is familiar. Loud music, lots of bodies. Nobody who looks like they're here to talk. Glassy eyes, wide smiles.

I don't have fun, exactly, but I'm not *miserable*, and Jayda looks happy as she dances around the room and nurses the same can of beer for an hour, ghosting around different groups. It seems like she knows *everyone*, and she's at least well-liked enough to be greeted with smiles wherever she goes. I follow her up onto the second level, scanning the people for any faces that might be familiar.

Naturally, everyone here is a stranger, right up until half past ten.

I'm listening to Jayda talk to someone named William about his summer plans with his family out at Barrier Lake when someone walks past us and then stops.

A slender girl with warm brown skin and long, sleek black hair turns back to me and stares, glossed lips parted in surprise.

The hair at the back of my neck prickles.

"Val?" She sounds slightly out of breath.

"Wait. You know Ibha?" Jayda blinks over at us. "You should've said!"

Fuck. *Fuck.*

That's the problem. I *don't* know Ibha.

My mouth opens and closes, and then I'm nodding, because what *else* am I supposed to do?

"I like the hair." This Ibha girl smiles, a little tentatively. There's something strained about it, though. Wary, or maybe defensive, it's hard to tell.

"Thanks." I touch a finger to the back of my head.

"How have you been?" she asks, still hesitant, like she's afraid to ask, or like she doesn't think she's supposed to, as if we're—

Oh shit.

Are Valerie and Ibha *exes?*

I have to get the hell out of here.

"Good to see you," I blurt out, and then I turn on my heel.

She calls after me. "*Val!*"

But I don't stop, not until I've gotten outside.

I don't expect Jayda to follow me. I don't know why, really—we *have* been attached at the hip all day, and she brought me here in the first place—but I'm still touched when she trails behind me out into the night air.

"Jesus," I gasp, the second we're outside, bending over, hands on my knees.

"The hell was that?" Jayda asks amiably. "If you're going to be sick, please don't do it on my shoes."

"I won't be sick," I promise, even though I'm not sure that's true.

"Do you and Ibha have secret beef?" Jayda gasps. "*Wait.* Wait, hang on. Do you know what her deal is?"

"Her . . . deal?"

Evidently, my confusion means something to her, because she shakes her head. "I think she just left a lot of shit behind when she moved, if you know what I mean."

"I don't," I tell her hopelessly. "I don't know her."

"She knew your name." Jayda considers me. "Or, like, Val's name."

Even if she doesn't believe me about the time loop, it's nice that she's playing along.

I repeat, "I don't know her. I don't know anyone, remember?"

"Okay. Do you want to go back in?" Before I get the chance to answer, she shakes her head. "No. *No*, of course you wouldn't. It's time for something different."

At least by now I've caught my breath. I straighten. "Something different?"

"Total transformation part two." She pulls her phone out. "My boyfriend's working tonight. He'll do it for cheap."

"He'll do what for cheap?"

"Tattoo," Jayda says absently, texting furiously.

"Sorry—you were serious about that?"

"You don't have to." It's *all* Gideon from top to bottom: the innocuous delivery; the mild tone; and the devilish, nearly taunting grin she shoots me after. "I just thought you were in a time loop."

Jayda's boyfriend is tall. Even taller than Gideon. He has two eyebrow piercings, a lip ring, and a scuff of short-cropped blond hair over a pinched, narrow face. Actually, *all* of him is pinched and narrow, limbs too long like pulled taffy. He looks a bit sour, but Jayda beams at him like he personally discovered gravity.

He doesn't introduce himself, but it doesn't matter. Jayda's already told me everything I need to know on the way over: his name is Knox; he's already graduated; his parents are as Catholic as they come and hate Jayda; and that doesn't matter, because he and Jayda have been going steady for a grand spanking two and a half months.

Inside the tattoo parlor, Knox takes my two hundred dollars in cash, thumbing through it and then shrugging, loping away toward the back of the shop without a word. If he thinks it's bizarre that his girlfriend is bringing a stranger to get tattooed, I can't tell. I can't read *anything* on him, actually, which sends discomfort rippling up my spine.

"What are you going to get?" Jayda spins slowly on a leather stool.

"I didn't get that far." Honestly, I'm still not even sure if this is a good idea, but Jayda's right. It's not like there will be consequences, so I might as well. "What do you think I should get?"

"Something that would piss off your parents."

"A snake." I blink. The answer was *immediately* present in my thoughts, somehow.

"Fuck yeah. Snakes rule. Right, Knox?"

Knox grunts as he comes back to us, uncapping a marker with his teeth, mumbling around it, "We good with freehand or do you want a stencil?"

"I . . . don't know the difference."

"Stencil is art I draw and then *stencil* on you," he says, like I'm a little slow. Jayda takes the cap of the marker from between his teeth. "Freehand, I'll draw directly onto you. Sketch first, figure out the rest after."

"Oh," I say, and then because a stencil sounds like it would take longer, I mumble, "Freehand is good."

"Snake? That's what you want?"

"I've always wanted a snake tattoo."

He must take that as a yes, because he snatches my wrist and starts sketching in translucent yellow, grip loose, knuckles scuffed red.

Wait.

I stare at his hand. It might be just the lighting. Maybe I'm just looking for any dots to connect in this insane mess.

Or maybe Knox's knuckles are bruised.

"Tight coil, d'you think?" he asks.

"You're the artist," I tell him, because it's not like it's going to matter. And it's a snake—it's *going* to be cool. "What happened to your hand?"

He shoots me a sharp look and ignores the question, jerking his head toward my arm. "You know this shit is *permanent*, right?"

Permanent until tomorrow, I think, but I don't say so out loud. "Yeah. I know."

At first, I try to make small talk. But when Knox answers my questions only with grunting, I fall silent. So does Jayda, drawing her knees to her chest and watching Knox with stars in her eyes as he draws on my arm.

After a while, my hand falls asleep, numb and tingling with static. Knox gets the green light from me on the placement and then goes over the sketch in more detail with purple marker.

Jayda fiddles with the music playing over the speakers, then kicks back and keeps watching, gaze intense.

It turns out getting tattooed *does* hurt, but only a little. A safety-pin scratch against my skin, a *nearly* familiar sensation that sends little spiders of apprehension skittering up my spine. Knox makes the first mark down by my wrist and then looks up for approval before continuing, the low buzz of the machine cutting through the low funk synths.

I breathe deep through the first few minutes until I get used to the sensation, and then it's almost easy to ignore it, zoning in and out as he works.

We're halfway up my forearm when Jayda's phone vibrates on the counter. She looks at the caller ID and huffs, but still answers.

"What do you want, G? Aren't you getting shipped out at the ass crack of dawn?" Jayda snaps, tossing her hair over her shoulder. She pauses, then wiggles her eyebrows at me. "I'm at the shop. Yeah, Laurie's getting a tattoo."

Knox nudges my arm, so I shift a little bit.

Jayda gives me an apologetic look and then rolls her eyes, standing up. "Yeah, Laurie. The girl from earlier. *Yes*, I'm with Knox. No, I don't know how late he'll be. *No*, I will not *keep you updated*—you're such a dick, you know that? I'm not five."

Knox raises both eyebrows but says nothing.

She wrinkles her nose. "Gideon, *lay off*."

I raise my eyebrows too.

"Okay. Yeah. Okay. *Yes*, okay. Love you too. Whatever. Loser." Jayda hangs up and makes a face at her phone.

"What did he want?" I ask her as she slouches back into her seat.

"He was trying to tell me what to do."

Knox shakes his head.

"What do you think of Gideon?" I ask him.

He blinks up at me, startled. "Why?"

"I'm getting jabbed a billion times with a needle and trying to make conversation," I say.

He pauses, tattoo gun buzzing. Then, voice low, he says, "I think he's a self-righteous idiot."

If Jayda takes offense, she doesn't say so.

I know she wasn't being serious earlier, and maybe it's the adrenaline high of the tattoo, but I can't stop the question from slipping out. "Has Gideon ever been arrested?"

She laughs, a sharp bark of a sound. "Not yet. He hasn't done anything stupid enough *or* ballsy enough, but—"

Knox snorts, low and derisive. "I can think of a few things."

I have to fight to stay still. "Really? Like what?"

"You a cop, or something?" Knox asks, abruptly sharp.

"Yeah, I'm really overcommitting to going undercover and letting you tattoo me so I can ask questions about a guy I barely know."

Jayda laughs.

Even Knox gives me a begrudging smile. It's not a *nice* smile, though—too sharp, with a mean edge.

"Like what, though?" I prompt. "You said you could think of a few things."

"Knox thinks he's too protective," Jayda answers for him. "Though I'm not sure if that qualifies as a good reason to get *arrested*. And being a liar isn't enough to get you arrested either," she says lightly.

My eyebrows spike. "A liar? About what?"

"Well, he—"

"Jay," Knox interjects. "Shut up."

We lapse into another silence.

It's nearing midnight by the time we're finished. Knox wipes down my swollen tattoo with a disinfectant that immediately cools my raw skin and shows me the tattoo in the mirror.

The snake wraps around my forearm from the cap of my elbow to my wrist, sparse, tight lines, flickering tongue frozen in perpetuity.

"Thank you," I tell him as he's covering the tattoo in a plastic wrap that sticks to my skin.

He just grunts.

"Not a man of many words," I muse as he takes the equipment and disappears into the back of the shop.

"He's an artist." Jayda sounds a bit dreamy—not a tone I thought people took outside of movies.

When it becomes obvious that Knox isn't returning, Jayda leads me out the back entrance. Streetlights illuminate the exact intersection where I found Jayda last night, sobbing on the sidewalk.

Jayda narrows her eyes when I bark a surprised laugh. "What?"

"Nothing," I tell her, tipping my head back. The scattered stars above us feel brighter than they do in the city.

Something is bringing me back here.

Do I believe in fate? I'm not sure it's important. Still, I thank whoever is responsible for the prime-time view of whatever is about to go down.

"Why did Knox interrupt you back there?"

She waves a hand. "He was right to. I'm too impulsive, you know? I say and do things I regret when I'm mad."

"Why are you mad?"

After a moment, she just lifts a shoulder.

"What did Gideon lie about?"

At that, she gives me a sharp look.

I get the sense I *could* push her, but I don't think she'd tell me anything real. So I just sigh and ask, "You don't really believe I'm in a time loop, do you?"

"Absolutely not." She snorts as she lights a cigarette, then gestures with the box. "Want one?"

"No, thanks. Why'd you let me cut my hair and get a tattoo on impulse, then?"

"Carpe diem," she answers at once, pulling in a drag and exhaling sweet-smelling smoke. "Duh."

"Carpe diem," I repeat, touching my fingers to my mouth. I'm almost *certain* that whoever I really am, I'm not a *carpe diem* sort of person.

A soft, strangely serene silence stretches between us. Night air cools the back of my neck, soothing where I touch light fingers to the raised skin under the wrap. I watch the road, scanning the street for moving shapes in the dark, but nothing comes.

Jayda smokes her cigarette down to the filter and puts it out on the brick wall.

My watch ticks past midnight.

The sirens never come.

TWENTY.

When the nightmare ends, another begins.

I wake up hurtling down the highway, and when I go to brush my hair over my shoulder, it's *not there*.

I freeze, slamming on the brakes.

Oh my God.

Oh my *God*.

No consequences, my *ass*. I cut Valerie's hair off, and it's stayed short. And if that weren't enough, my arm burns as inky scabs stretch. Around the uncovered tattoo, the skin is red and raised, dark lines winding around my arm.

I peel off the road at the next turnoff to stop, and then I sink low in the seat, heart hammering.

Fuck. *Fuck*. I squeeze my eyes shut.

Sorry, Valerie.

At least I *like* the tattoo once I get up the courage to look at it. The line work is more intricate than I'd thought it would be now that I can inspect it without the bandage, twisting my arm this way and that.

Well. I hope Val likes tattoos, if it's still here at the end of all this, assuming I don't evaporate on the wind when this fucking countdown runs out.

I stare at the 94 where it taunts me from the dashboard, a sick pit in my stomach.

For a long time, all I can do is sit there. I mean, where the hell am I supposed to go from here? I've been trapped for six days, but it's only now that finally, between fight and flight, I'm slipping into *freeze*.

It feels like one helluva familiar skin.

Eventually I get back on the road, pulling a U-turn to go back into town, but my heart doesn't slow. All I can do is alternate watching the road and my arm. The implications are almost interesting enough to distract from the existential dread of it all: changes I make to my appearance stick in this time loop, apparently.

Even when I'm not looking for Gideon, I find him.

With no trouble, actually, because he walks in front of my car. Or maybe I'm just not watching where I'm going.

Either way, I slam on my brakes at the last second, swerving out of the way, and he still has to smack the hood so I don't hit him.

Palms flat against my car, Gideon gives me a sharp look, as if to say, *What the hell?*

I fling open the car door, a hand to the side of my cheek. "Oh my God, I'm so sorry. Are you okay?"

"I'm fine." He steps back onto the sidewalk, rolling out his shoulders. In the harsh daylight, his black eye looks worse, somehow. "Should have been paying more attention."

"No, that was completely my fault."

I just almost hit Gideon with my car. And now that I have proof that there can be permanent consequences within the loop, the thought is chilling. How horrific would it be if vehicular manslaughter was my ticket out of this hellscape?

My cheeks burn. "*Shit*. Can I do anything? Can I at least drive you wherever you're going?"

Gideon waves me off. "Don't worry about it."

"Seriously, I don't mind. It's no trouble, and I don't have anywhere else to be."

He opens his mouth as if he's going to protest again, but then just looks at me, deliberating. After a moment, he laughs. "You know, it's not every day that the person who just almost hit you immediately offers their driving skills for free."

My cheeks flush. "I swear I'm usually better behind the wheel."

"I'm going to take you at your word." He rounds the car to the passenger side. "If you're secretly on a murder spree and this becomes a documentary, this would be the part where they smash-cut to a detective saying, *Big mistake*."

I laugh as I climb back into the car. "I'd promise you I'm not, but I feel like anything I say would sound like empty words."

"Wise," he says sagely, nodding as he slides into the passenger seat. "I'm Gideon, by the way."

"Laurie. Nice to meet you."

"Likewise." He eyes my arm. "Nice tattoo. That shit looks *raw*. Is it new?"

"Got it last night." A little thrill runs through me at the approval in his eyes as they linger on the dark lines.

"Did it hurt much? I've always wondered."

I file that away with the information I've been collecting about him. Gideon Norris: No tattoos. "Nah. Stung a bit, I guess. Where are you headed?"

"Just to the school," he says, which surprises me, and then doesn't. If I were him, I wouldn't want to give out my home address either, and if I remember correctly, the school is close to the farm. "Do you know where that is?"

"You might need to direct me." When he nods, I start the engine and pull onto the road.

"New in town?" Gideon grimaces as he shifts in his seat, like he moved too quickly. "I don't think I've seen you around here before."

Something tiny deflates in my chest.

Like, yeah, I know. That's the whole deal. Every day, I'm a stranger. It's just that it's getting a bit old.

"I live in the city," I tell him, just like last time, except this time I know it's true. "Northwest. I'm just passing through. You're local?"

"Sure am. School's out for you, then?"

"Nope." I give him my best attempt at a wink. "Ditched."

At that, his smile goes crooked and several shades more genuine, like I've pleased him somehow. *God*, that smile. Gideon is good-looking enough it's starting to piss me off. There's something about the way he holds himself, this relaxed half-slouch that keeps drawing my eyes back toward him, and it occurs to me I genuinely don't know if I want to kiss him or *be* him.

"Fascinating." He directs me to turn left.

I want to think of something else clever to say, something to keep that smile right where it is, but as I'm driving, all that's happening in my head is a sustained flatline.

All at once, I realize that I have no idea how to talk to Gideon when I'm not asking for his help.

And then I'm talking before I can think it through. "Hey, do you happen to know anyone local who could help me get into a phone I've locked myself out of?"

Gideon's eyebrows lift at once. "Is it *your* phone?"

"Yes," I say at once, with maybe a touch too much defensiveness, and it doesn't matter anyway, because we're at the school, which means it's time for this interaction to be over.

But when I pull into the parking lot, Gideon doesn't move to get out right away. "So. You're not exactly earning points *against* potentially being on a murder spree."

My smile spreads slowly. "But?"

He grins right back at me. "As it happens, I *do* know someone."

Gideon directs us back to the house that I'd parked outside for all those hours the other day. I have the front of it memorized from the blue shutters to the peeling paint on the white siding, but the backyard is new as he leads me around the house and opens a door without knocking.

I follow him down the back staircase—steep, tall steps—into the basement. It's probably ten degrees cooler down here, and I breathe a sigh of relief as we hit the landing, squinting in the sudden gloom.

"Got a job for you," Gideon says into the dark, instead of hello.

"Yeah, you said," someone calls back from deeper in the room.

I blink rapidly to get my eyes to adjust, and the room takes shape. Wood paneling covers every inch of the walls and the ceiling, and three computer monitors sit on a long plastic folding table. A heavy-duty row of consoles sits off to the side, in front of a whirring fan propped up by an ancient leather saddle.

It's the boy with white hair. He leans back in a battered office chair, frowning over at both of us.

"Think you could break into a phone?" Gideon asks.

He scoffs. "Do I *think*. Yes. Gimme."

Gideon turns to me.

I hold up a hand before I pass it over. "Can you help me *recover* a password? I don't just need to break in, I need to *know* the old password."

The boy tilts his head. "I mean, probably, but there's always a chance it might ruin the phone."

"I don't care. I just need to know it."

He and Gideon exchange a brief glance. Slowly, he asks, "Are you sure? You'd ruin a whole phone just to learn what the passcode *was*?"

"I would," I tell him. "And I will."

"Well, I *was* gonna go get those SD cards." His voice is low and grumbly. "But I'll help you instead. For a fee."

Gideon sighs. "Archer, you—"

"Two hundred dollars." I step forward and pass him the phone. "In cash. Yours, if you can get it done today."

The boy—Archer—considers this. "Are we talking business day, or—"

"Before midnight."

"And how am I supposed to contact you if *I* have your phone?"

"Text me," Gideon says. "I'll keep an eye on Laurie until you're done, how about?"

A warm flush spreads through me.

"And we're still on for later?" Archer asks with a note of suspicion.

"Yeah." Gideon smiles. "I'll just come around later on this evening, depending on how long it takes."

"Wyatt is going to flip shit, you know." Archer eyes Gideon with a pointedness that eludes me. "You promised him all day."

"Wyatt can cope."

Archer's eyebrows lift. "Your funeral, man."

"What SD cards did you need?"

"Don't waste your time on that shit." Archer waves him off, typing a password with one hand.

"It's not a waste," Gideon says. "I'll get them. You're doing me a favor."

"I'm doing *her* a favor," Archer says pointedly, and my stomach twists.

"But—"

"It's not even a favor anymore." He grins. "It's a job."

TWENTY-ONE.

"Thank you." I shield my eyes as we step back into the sunshine. "I appreciate the help."

"Why'd you offer Archer two hundred dollars?" Gideon asks. "He'd have done it for fifty."

I shrug. "I have the money, and I *need* it done today."

With his fingertips still on the door handle, Gideon stares at me. My cheeks flare. "What?"

"Is this some sort of, like, bucket list–type thing?" he starts cautiously. "Like, if you're running off and throwing a bunch of money at strangers because you think you only have so much time left, you should know I'm not going to support you running in front of a semi or something."

I laugh. "No, it's nothing like that."

"What is it, then?"

Well. The truth is out of the question, here. What's left?

I pause, and then I tell him, "Carpe diem."

Gideon groans and lets go of the door. "You sound like my sister."

"Is that a bad thing?"

"*Carpe fucking diem* is always getting her in trouble. She's a *menace*," he says. "Truly, the queen of poor choices."

"Like what?"

"Well, her boyfriend *sucks*. For one."

I can't help the laugh that tears itself out of me, part surprise, part delight. "Tell me everything."

So he does.

"First, she's sixteen, and he's twenty-four," he tells me while we're walking back out to the street.

My eyebrows arch. Jayda did say he'd already graduated, but I guess it's on me that I didn't think to ask *how long* ago. "Okay, that does suck. Isn't that . . . illegal? You could report him, right?"

"Trust me, I did my research. She's sixteen and consenting. There's nothing anyone can do, and he knows it. *And* I'm going away for the summer, so I won't even be around to make sure she's okay."

"Where are you going?"

"Away," he says, with this little smile that *would* set me at ease if I hadn't already seen how worried Tenley seems to be about him. "I've asked some friends to keep an eye on her, but I don't know how well that will go."

"I'm sure she'll be okay." It's a meaningless platitude, but I don't really know what else to say.

Gideon just lifts a shoulder.

I close my fingers around my keys. We're just standing in front of my car now. "So, what do you do around here when you have a couple of hours to kill?"

"Honestly?" Gideon laughs. "I don't very often have *any* hours to kill. But when I do, I go to the museum."

I've seen signs for that around. "That's the airplane one, right?"

He nods. "Bomber Command. It's really cool in there."

I almost mention Vern's, and then I remember that I'm not supposed to know about that. What is *with* this town and planes? Is it a requirement to be a nerd about planes if you live here?

"I'm into the history, mostly," he continues. "I got *really* into everything that happened with the British Commonwealth Air Training Program and the Dambuster Raids a while back, and apparently I don't have an off switch. The planes *are* cool, though."

More Gideon trivia. I grin. "Okay, then show me."

"Really?"

"I want to see," I urge, because it's the truth.

So we go to the command museum. The woman behind the counter raises a hand to Gideon like she's very used to him—is that hot? Oh God. Am I a nerd, just like Val?—and goes straight back to whatever she was doing at her computer. He beckons for me to follow him.

We wander a hallway that's positively *plastered* in plaques and informative posters. The dioramas are cool too, but the real appeal is the enormous room full of life-size planes.

Gideon knows *everything* about every plane in the museum. I'm pretty sure that in my past life—no, in *my* life, I remind myself firmly—World War II isn't my thing, but as Gideon talks about the behind-the-scenes role Canadian pilots played, I'm entranced.

By the time we're finished, it's almost six, and the museum is about to close.

"Christ," he says as we step back out into the evening sunshine. "You should have stopped me. I can get kind of in the zone."

"I enjoyed that," I assure him.

"You know, it's not very often that pretty girls humor me about this kind of thing," he says.

My smile fades as I trail behind him. "Interesting facts are interesting facts."

"Next time," Gideon starts, and then stops on the sidewalk, shielding his eyes.

"Next time?" I prompt.

He's smiling, but there's a bitter cast to the way he shakes his head without finishing the thought. Then he turns, all at once. "Do you want to get dinner with me?"

The way my smile spreads is completely involuntary—all at once, like tearing off a Band-Aid. "Yes, I do."

We go across the street to Zephyr, the cute little drive-in on the corner of the main strip.

Gideon pays and waves a hand when I protest. "My idea, my treat."

Sitting and eating cheeseburgers in the grass at the park with Gideon turns out to be the first *truly* nice moment since I woke up in this hell. It's hard to panic when the sun is a pleasant presence against my skin. The food is good too, and Gideon keeps talking even when I evade all of his questions about my personal life.

I *like* him, is the problem. Even though I have no business feeling the way I do whenever he smiles at me—especially considering he's not even going to remember me tomorrow and that he thinks I'm a completely different person than I really am—I can't help it. There's just something so *easy* about sitting here with him. I wish I *could* answer his questions. I wish I knew if he'd want to be sitting here with me if I looked the way I really do, whatever that might be.

Right when we finish eating, Gideon's phone rings. He fumbles in his pocket and smiles a little ruefully right before he answers. "Yeah?"

He listens for a minute, and I already know by his face who it is, even before he hands the phone to me.

"Yeah, so I cooked the phone," Archer says into my ear. "But I got the passcode."

Eagerly, I ask, "And?"

"0–3–0–4–6–1."

Hastily, I cast around for a pen, patting my pockets.

Gideon hands me a Sharpie.

I toss him a smile in thanks. "Hang on, one more time."

While he repeats the code, I scribble it out on my arm, reading it back to him to confirm.

"Thank you," I tell him, feeling lighter than I have in days. "Seriously."

"Hey, two hundred dollars is two hundred dollars, no matter what shady shit you're up to."

"Who says it's shady shit?"

"Only everything about your actions and also your words," Archer says. "But again. Not my business, and I'm not a snitch. Can you put Gideon on?"

I hand the phone back to Gideon.

He listens for a moment, eyebrows raising with every word. "Nah," he says, at last. Then, lips quirking, he adds, "Yeah. *Yes*, I'm serious. I just . . . don't feel like I need to anymore."

I want to know what he's talking about *so* badly. I want it more than I want to get out of this damn time loop, I'm pretty sure.

"Is Wyatt clawing at the walls right now?" At whatever Archer says, Gideon laughs. "No, put me on speaker." He laughs again, shaking his head with a fond smile. "Wyatt, I will see you before I leave, okay? I'm literally on the way back now. Don't freak out."

I observe him while he's talking. Something swoops low in my gut at the way his eyes crinkle when he smiles.

Oh, help.

He hangs up, that smile fading.

We get back in the car, and I let him direct me back to Archer's house.

As I pull onto the road, I ask, "If you don't mind me asking, why would this Wyatt guy, and I quote, 'flip shit'?"

Gideon grimaces. "I promised him I'd spend today with him and Archer."

"And here you are instead." Another warm wave of satisfaction washes over me, even though I *do* feel bad for Wyatt and Archer.

Only a little bit.

"Listen, you intrigue me," he says. "We've spent all afternoon together and you *still* intrigue me. You almost hit me with your car. You've ditched school and I don't know why. You need to break into a phone that's totally *definitely* yours for reasons unknown. I've always wanted to be famous. If you kill me, I might even make the news."

I give him a wide smile as I pull up next to the curb. "I ditched school because I didn't want to go."

"Atta girl," he says, and an ache twinges in my chest. "Okay, but why did you need the passcode? This whole situation is . . . very weird."

"I'm surprised you haven't found it *too* weird," I confess. "I'm well aware of how it looks, trust me."

"Nothing is too weird," Gideon says. "*Too weird* is for cowards."

I laugh.

"But seriously. Why did you need it?"

"I'll tell you if you tell me what you meant when you said you're going away."

Gideon fixes me with a long, even look. Then he nods. "Okay."

"You first."

He doesn't even protest. "I'm not supposed to know," he admits. "I think they thought they'd have to spring it on me or I'd fight them on it. And they were fucking right."

Dread crackles up my spine. "What's going to happen to you?"

"Are you familiar with the troubled teen industry?"

Instinctively, I nod, horror pooling in my gut as I filter through muddy knowledge. Even though I'm pretty sure I don't have personal memories, the basics flash through my head. Kids getting ripped from their homes, sent away for being more trouble than they're worth. No certainty of when they'll return. Forced to endure the elements, hard labor, no privacy, no life. "What—*you*?"

"Me," he confirms. "According to the emails, I ship out at, like, six a.m."

"But you're—you're so—"

"So what?" His smile is grim.

"So *good*," I finish, helpless.

And Gideon laughs. He almost sounds a little sad when he says, "Oh, Laurie."

"What? You *are*."

"You don't know me." He gives me this smile that's somehow still *dazzling* even though it's tight and bitter. "And honestly, right now, I'm sort of glad for it."

As it turns out, I've already met Wyatt. He was with Archer the night Gideon got arrested.

A little chill runs up my spine as I meet his eyes back in Archer's basement and remember his words, cold with certainty.

He earned it.

Wyatt runs an agitated hand over his buzzed hair as he asks, "Where the hell have you been?"

Archer snorts as he passes me the phone. It looks fine, but I know better than to judge by external appearances. "I told you, Gideon pulled a Gideon."

I huff a laugh as I pull out my wallet and hand over the contents, feeling a little bad that by tomorrow he won't have the money anymore. Then again, tomorrow he won't have helped me. "'Pulled a Gideon'?"

"Good Samaritan bullshit." Archer sounds almost absent as he counts out the bills and then tucks them into his duct-tape wallet. "Not that you're, like, bullshit, that's not what I meant. Or maybe I did."

Gideon rolls his eyes and smiles. "Laurie, this is Wyatt. Wyatt, Laurie."

Wyatt surveys me with apparent displeasure. "Hi."

I offer him a little wave, wondering if Gideon can feel the borderline malevolence rolling off Wyatt.

With a jerk of his chin, Archer asks, "You sure you want that thing back? It's pretty much just a brick now."

I'm not taking any chances. I don't know what the rules are, but I'm not risking waking up tomorrow without the phone in Valerie's backpack, so I slip it into my pocket and nod. "Thanks. Seriously."

"Don't mention it. I love destroying stuff."

I can't tell if he's being sarcastic.

"You're unbelievable," Wyatt's hissing at Gideon. "We had *plans*!"

Gideon is unmoved. "It's my last day. I can do what I want with it, don't you think?"

"It wasn't just *your* last day, though," Wyatt says, heated. "You know, you really can be—"

"It *is* just mine," Gideon shoots back. "You all get to just—well, you don't have to worry about tomorrow, do you?"

"Of *course* we do," he says, distraught, wringing his hands, anguished eyes trained on Gideon's face, and suddenly I wonder if Gideon knows Wyatt is in love with him. "*You're* going to be gone."

"Don't," Gideon says, voice low.

"At least I don't have to talk you out of—"

Gideon makes a low *tsk* sound, and Wyatt falls quiet.

"'Course," he says darkly. "Yeah, wouldn't want you to look bad in front of your new *friend*."

And Gideon's expression turns thunderous. With a last warning look tossed in Wyatt's direction, he turns to Archer. "I'll be right back."

I follow him upstairs when he beckons to me.

Gideon pulls the basement door shut behind him. The sun is setting, the soft evening light gentler to his eye. "Sorry about Wyatt. He's just in a mood. I promise he's really nice, usually."

Oblivious. It's honestly endearing that he hasn't noticed.

"I'll take your word for it," I tell him.

He takes a deep breath. "I just want you to know that I haven't *really* wished tomorrow wasn't happening until now. This has been a really nice day."

"It has." My throat is tight. I'll see him tomorrow, if I want, but I don't want the Gideon who doesn't know who I am.

I want *this* one.

"Why'd you have to turn up now?" he asks, almost reproachfully. "I didn't even get to ask you out for real."

I breathe in deep and let it out. "I wish you could."

Gideon pauses. "Will you have a new phone by the time I get back?"

My heart sinks. "I hope so."

"If I asked for your number, what would you say?"

"I would say yes," I tell him without hesitating.

I know it won't matter that I don't know my own phone number. It's not real. By tomorrow, all of this will be gone. But I want the memory. So I recite random digits, and then I turn to leave before I lose my resolve and try to figure out a reason to stay.

"Wait," Gideon calls after me, and I stop, heart skipping. "You never ended up telling me why you needed the phone's passcode."

"Oh, that's right." I pivot on my heel, and when I meet his eyes, every halfhearted excuse I'd formulated dissolves. What *could* I say that wouldn't sound deeply suspicious? There's nothing of *substance*.

So I tell the truth. "I'm in a time loop. I need the passcode so that I can get into the phone tomorrow when everything resets."

And it's not that I thought he'd believe me. I just didn't think he'd look so *disappointed*.

"Right," he says, with this thin-lipped smile. He just spilled his biggest secret to me, and from his perspective, I totally blew him off with a stupid lie.

"I really wish I had a better explanation."

"You know," he says, and I hate this tone, the quiet disapproval. "So do I."

I force myself to walk away, shame churning in my gut. The weight of his gaze prickles against the back of my neck as I go.

Let Gideon be disappointed in me.

It's not like he's going to remember it.

TWENTY-TWO.

"Bri's mad at me about something," I tell Brett.

He grimaces, closing my locker for me with a bang and pulling me closer so that I'm flush against his side. "Yeah, she mentioned."

"Do you know what it's about?" I ask, slipping my arm around his waist so we can walk down the hallway together. "Because I definitely don't."

"You know the rules," he says easily. "I don't get involved in your shit. She doesn't get involved in our shit."

"Okay, but if it's serious—"

"Seriously, I am impartial," he tells me, pressing a kiss to my temple. "You're my best girls. I can't take sides."

"But I'm your girlfriend." I play up the pout. "You *love* me."

"If you're trying to get me to say that I *don't* love Bri, you are a few sandwiches short of a picnic."

I laugh at that. "I wouldn't dream of tricking you into admitting you love me more, even if it's true."

Brett waggles his eyebrows as he leads me around a corner and then into the auditorium, holding the door open for me as I disentangle from him. "This doesn't count as taking your side, for the record. We just happened to pass through the theater, and whether I knew Bri would be here? That's between me and God."

"And me," I point out.

"I've confirmed nothing." He holds up both hands in surrender.

And anyway, Bri *is* here, standing in a cluster with her drama friends, though when she spots me, her expression turns to granite.

"Yeah, I'm gonna go," Brett says, voice lower. "We're still good for later?"

"'Course." I give him a little smile and let him kiss me goodbye. "Have a good afternoon, okay?"

"You too," he says. "Good luck."

I salute him as I make my way over to Bri, taking the steps up to the stage two at a time.

As if by magic, her friends dissolve like sugar in water the second they see me coming. I can't help a little smile, though I squash it the second Bri turns away and starts walking across the stage without me.

"Really?" I walk extra fast to catch up without breaking the no-running-in-the-auditorium rule, as if it even matters anymore. "Come on, Bri. What did I do?"

"You know what you did." She hoists her tote bag higher on her shoulder, back stiff. Her curls glow bright white under the spotlights.

"Yeah, no, I don't," I tell her.

She turns so fast I almost mow her over, glaring up at me, curls bouncing. "My parents know about Ibha. How could you?"

My mouth drops open as I process her words. "Wait—you think *I* told them?"

"I think you told *your* parents, and then they told my—"

"I would *never*." A spike of fury tears through me all at once, so white-hot I feel it everywhere, in my bones, in my hands, buzzing in my lungs. "Are you serious? I would never in one million years tell *anyone*—"

"But you did, didn't you? It's not like my parents would *lie* about where they heard it."

"My mom doesn't know about you and Ibha," I tell her, nonplussed. "I would swear on literally *anything* that I've never mentioned it around her."

"Ibha called me. She *called* me, because now her parents know too. And guess who told them?" Bri shakes her head, curls swinging. "Do you have *any* idea how humiliating this is?"

Two spots of red have appeared in her cheeks, her eyes bright and glassy.

"Shit, Bri, I'm sorry." I cross my arms over my chest. "That's *not* an admission of guilt, by the way. I didn't and I *wouldn't* tell. You know what my mom is like. I'm not exactly waiting around trying to have heart-to-hearts with her. And what would I stand to gain from telling her? I wouldn't do that to you."

Bri's glare could impale me. And I know this probably isn't real—she's angry with me because she's angry with the world, and deep down she knows it wasn't me, because I only told—

It hits like a slap.

Mom couldn't know. She couldn't have found out from me, because I only told—

I swallow, hard.

"What?" Bri snaps. "Something else you'd like to say? Some other way you'd like to ruin my life?"

At that, I level her with my best unimpressed raised single eyebrow. "Okay, I'm going to let you cool off, I think."

"You're so—" Bri cuts off with a huff.

I put my hands on her shoulders and squeeze. "Hey. I would *never* betray you. I would never betray Ibha like that either. I would not tell my mom that you and Ibha were more than friends if I was being held at literal gunpoint, okay? I know how important that is to you. And if I was involved somehow, I'm sorry, and I mean that."

Then I turn around and leave her there before she can say anything else, nearly tripping on my way down the stairs and skidding around the corner, giving up on rules and bursting into a run up the aisle to the far door in my haste to get outside, fingers fumbling with my phone to make a call.

He doesn't pick up.

"Shit, *shit*," I whisper.

The same voicemail message pleasantly tells me, "Hey, don't do this. Leave me a message and I'll hit you back in five to ten business years. Text me, maybe."

"*Fuck.*" I slow as soon as I burst through the double doors into the courtyard. His message tone beeps. "Fuck, call me. As soon as you can, call me. It's an emergency."

I'm about to hang up—I'll text him a dozen times anyway—when I pause.

On the other side of the courtyard, a group of kids are shouting with laughter.

I take a deep breath, and then I say, "I think Mom knows."

00:93

TWENTY-THREE.

This time, when the nightmare ends, I have a plan.

It seems like on days I interfere, the sirens don't come, and Gideon doesn't get arrested.

So today I won't interfere.

It's not even going to be a chore to stay away, because I have things to do. I'm in and out of the gas station in seconds. This time, I head around the corner and I crouch next to an outdoor outlet, waiting for the phone to charge.

And when it finally powers on, the passcode *works*. I barely even know where to begin, so I scroll through Val's phone. Her messages are functionally useless—she doesn't save full names, only letters with emojis.

Strict parents, I think, and then promptly file that under the folder titled "How Do I Know That?"

Unless there's more hiding where I can't see, Val's only social media app is Instagram. Her most recent notification is from the handle ibhaagarwal.

I click on her profile. It's the girl from the party. Her feed is full of artsy photos. Some are of downtown Calgary, but most are musical. Her most recent post is a shot of a piano with sunlight streaming onto ivory keys, and the one after that is her from behind with a violin held aloft.

Her face isn't anywhere on the profile, but it's definitely Ibha. I click through our mutual friends and then scroll through Val's notifications until I narrow it down to three repeat offenders: therealbriblanchette, _brettlevelmidnight, and yeahlikethe16th.

I click on the first profile next, greeted at once by the girl from the Polaroid in my wallet.

This girl—Bri Blanchette—has, like, a gazillion followers. Her page seems to be a wellspring of body positivity and inspirational captions about following dreams. I'm on her profile too, in her most recent post. Well, Val is. We both have huge goggles on, but that's us all right, in white lab coats, two sets of thumbs-up for the camera. Val's hair is even longer than it was before I let Jayda take heavy artillery to it, curled at the ends. The caption is about a fundraiser we apparently ran last week, raising money for an upcoming mission trip to Nicaragua.

I wrinkle my nose.

The next profile—_brettlevelmidnight—is completely blank. He's in a *lot* of tagged photos, though. Most of them are of indistinguishable figures in hockey gear, but there are a few showing his face, most of them from *my* profile. He has short, sandy-brown hair and a pleasant smile with straight teeth. His square jaw is set over broad shoulders. Val's captions are mostly one-off lines that don't contextualize anything about the posts themselves, but it's just the two of us in most of the photos that feature this Brett guy, which sends a spike of dread through me, especially when I remember what her Mom had said.

Did you talk to Brett yet?

And you have Brett.

Oh boy.

I click off his page.

The last profile—yeahlikethe16th—is sparse, and there are only a few photos of him. In one of them, he's standing cheek to cheek with a guy with a long, straight nose and deep brown skin. In another, he's astride a motorcycle with a helmet under his arm, smile so wide it looks almost painful. None of the photos make any sense of who he is to Val, though, so I click off.

Then I scroll through Val's profile, trying to make sense of her life. A lot of it is hockey or Bri. No selfies unless they're with another person. Some nature photos. Nothing particularly helpful or informative, right up until I see the guy from yeahlikethe16th again. The post is a slideshow from almost exactly a year ago, and in the first picture, he's wearing a graduation robe and has Val—who's wearing a flowing, light-purple sundress—in a headlock. In subsequent photos, she's curated a collection featuring her and this guy in different stages of childhood. I squint at the caption—"okay congrats now get out of my house"—and put together the pieces.

Brother.

The tagged account is different. I tap on elieaton, and several puzzle pieces slot into place. Valerie's brother is Elijah Eaton. This other profile is much like hers, with posts about hockey and some photos with Val. One of a large glowing cross mounted on a wall.

Two accounts, one with no name. The most recent post on the second profile was more than a year ago. I tap back over to the other one—posted three weeks ago. Interesting.

So, Val has a brother. A brother who appears to have *vanished* at home. I didn't see any photos of him on the walls. He has a kind face. Something about the slope of his shoulder reminds me of—

I almost drop my phone, scrambling for the memory, but it's gone. He's just familiar. So familiar it sends suspicion crawling up my spine.

Just one more mystery.

Trinity Christian School isn't hard to find. The sign for it is visible in three of Val's Instagram posts—*honestly*, does she not care about internet safety?—and this time I can follow the route on her phone.

If Val's trapped in *my* body, it makes sense that she'd return to what's familiar, so I will too. I can spend all day here and then maybe even make it back in time to figure out what the hell gets Gideon arrested.

The front doors of the school are more intimidating than I thought they would be. Walking across the grass, I keep my chin high and my shoulders back, trying to look like I belong.

It's not a big school, so I'm not surprised when a few girls standing out on the lawn seem to recognize me, pointing and whispering as I pass. I brush my fingers through my short hair and make sure I've pulled the sleeve of my flannel over my knuckles so nobody sees the tattoo.

At least I'm not the most interesting thing going on by a long shot.

It's your last day, Cheryl had said.

The entire building is a wash of chaos. The second I turn down the hall, I have to duck out of the way of two boys who are running with canisters of silly string, blasting the lockers as they go. I'm pretty sure most high schools don't play music over the speakers, but this one does, at least today.

I'm grateful for the distraction as I scan the hallways. From what I can tell, either school is out for the day, or everyone's got a serious case of last-day senioritis, because the hallways are packed with students and teachers alike, and nobody spares me a second glance.

Well, almost nobody.

"Val!" someone calls.

I turn.

It's the Polaroid girl—Bri. She has her hair pulled back into a large ponytail that bounces as she beckons to me.

Next to her . . .

Oh boy. Brett is staring at me, slack-jawed. He's shorter in person than he'd looked in his photos, and still stands a full head and shoulders taller than Bri.

Apprehension floods through my bloodstream as I approach.

Be cool, I remind myself. *Be Val.*

"Babe," Brett says, and then falters, apparently at a loss for words.

Fucking *yikes*.

"Hi," I murmur.

He blinks at me like he's experiencing the symptoms of a potentially traumatic brain injury. "You cut your hair."

"Yeah," I say, nervous for reasons I can't begin to decipher. "Do you . . . like it?"

It feels like the appropriate question to ask.

And then he says nothing.

Bri looks between us with her bottom lip trapped under her front teeth, then slips away, back toward the lockers.

"It's really short," he says at last.

I touch my hand to the hair at the back of my neck, feeling self-conscious. "Yeah, it is."

"Hey," he says. "I love you. I'll get used to it."

Woof. The whole shebang. The *L word*. I fight the urge to cringe away.

"Great." I don't bother to keep my voice light. "*I'll get used to it*. That's what I want to hear, for sure."

"Sorry, sorry." He scratches his head. "It's . . . cute."

I give him a grim smile and turn away, but he catches my shoulder before I can get very far.

"Hey." His voice drops close to a whisper. "About what I said last night . . ."

I freeze.

Last night. What *else* happened last night besides Val's failed coming out?

"I believe you," he says. "About Lawrence."

I straighten. *Lawrence?* Something goes *ping!* in my chest, like it had about Calgary and about hockey.

Lawrence. *Laurie*. Could it be . . . ?

Breath catching, I ask him, "Oh?"

"I know you. I know you better than that. You'd never do

something like that to me. And I know you didn't mean what you said either."

"Right." I do my best to act like I know what he's talking about.

"I love you," he says, "and I like you too."

Then he pauses, like he's expecting that to be a significant moment, and if I hadn't heard him say it twenty seconds ago, I'd worry this was his first time dropping the L bomb.

"You really love me?" I ask.

"'Course." He slips an arm around me, drawing me closer. "You know that."

I nod, remembering at the last second that I'm probably not supposed to twitch out of his reach. So I force myself to relax into his touch, running my fingertips along my bottom lip.

Brett gives me a squeeze. "What's up? Are we good?"

"You love me . . . unconditionally?"

"Yeah, babe." He laughs. "What's going on? Are you gonna get all existential on me again?"

"Maybe."

"You didn't mean it yesterday, did you? You know I'm crazy about you. Yeah, four years is a long time, but we'll—"

"I didn't mean it," I blurt out, so he'll shut up long enough for me to get to my point. "Obviously. I need to talk to you."

"Okay," he says, all caution.

"Listen, I need your help." I step forward, lowering my voice. "I'm not Val."

He stares.

"I'm just trapped in Val's body," I urge. "We've swapped places. And I know you love her, and you'd want to find her, right? If—"

"Okay." He cuts me off, grabbing me by the shoulders.

I blink up at him.

"I love you." His eyes are wide and serious. "Really, I do, but you are talking crazy right now, and I have to meet the boys in, like, five minutes."

"I—"

"I'll see you after practice?" He gives me what I'm sure is meant to be a reassuring smile. "We can talk about your body-swap thing then, okay?"

Mute, I nod. I don't even have time to register what's going on before he darts in and presses a kiss to my mouth, squeezes my shoulder, and then walks away.

I blink at his back, touching my fingers to my lips.

So that's that. Not that I really thought Brett would be the type to drop everything and believe me, but *still*.

Also, did I just have my first kiss?

It's a sad thought. I don't even know if I've been kissed before.

When I turn, Bri's still at her locker, reapplying mascara in the tiny mirror on the inside of the door, mouth open. Satisfied, she closes the tube, and then when she sees me watching, her smile goes tight and nervous. As I approach, she turns at the last second. "Are you done sucking face with my brother? 'Cause if that's not over, I'm out of here."

Siblings. Okay, I see it, now that I'm looking for it. They both have the same dusty brown-blond hair. If Brett's was longer, it might even curl too.

"We're done," I tell her, letting my hand drop. "I—"

"I'm really sorry," she blurts out. "I slept on it again, and I was acting like a total maniac yesterday, and I know you wouldn't snitch."

Val? What the fuck, man. How is your life *this* insane?

"It's okay," I say cautiously.

"No, it's not." She shakes her head.

"Also, for the record, I wasn't sucking face with your brother," I point out. "I think he's kinda mad at me."

"Nope!" She holds a hand up. "Okay. You know how I feel about this."

I do not, but fortunately, Bri seems to be the type who enjoys talking. "I love you, and you know I love you, but I can't hear details about you two."

I shut my mouth and nod.

"*I* like the hair, by the way," she says, a bit sourly. "You could have told me you were going to cut it."

"It was a spur-of-the-moment thing," I tell her. Technically true. Then I remember I have something to ask her. "Also, you know Ibha?"

Bri startles like I slapped her. "Excuse me—are you serious? Do I *know* Ibha?"

I swallow hard. "Just, I ran into her the other day, in Nanton."

She squeaks. "You were in *Nanton*? Without me? What the fuck, Val?"

And whatever this is, it seems like it's a *much* bigger deal than I was anticipating. "Um—"

"You saw her?" She slams her locker shut and whirls around to me. "How did she look? Did she ask about me? I can't believe you didn't tell me *immediately*. And, you know, that's not a funny way to bring her up."

Slowly, the pieces click together.

Valerie and Ibha aren't exes. *Bri* and Ibha are.

Fascinating.

"Sorry," I say slowly, feeling at once quite pleased that I'm inevitably going to get a redo on this whole interaction. "I . . . wasn't sure how to start, but that wasn't the way."

"It wasn't." She sighs and presses a hand to her forehead. "Seriously, did she ask about me?"

"She asked how you were."

Bri presses her lips together. "I bet she did. Bitch."

My eyebrows arch.

"What else? How did *she* look? Wait, no, I don't want to know."

Christ.

"I know I *just* forgave you, but I think I'm mad at you again." She snaps her locker shut, then links her arm through mine, so she can't be *that* mad. "Okay, I know I've already asked you this, like, a hundred times, but will you reconsider tonight?"

"What's tonight?"

"Val, are you *serious*?" Bri laughs. "We've been over this, like, forty-hundred times. Grad party. Party to end all parties. You said you couldn't come because your parents said no, because, well, you know."

I try to look like I do, in fact, know. Hopeful, I ask, "Is Lawrence going?"

"Who?" Bri frowns, but her expression clears only moments later. "Oh. Yeah, probably. It would be *so* good if you could be there. I don't want to have a grad party without you."

And, like, what the hell.

TWENTY-FOUR.

"Brett's going to lose his *mind*." Bri gets up on her toes to hand me a piece of tape so I can affix a streamer to the crown molding. "I promised him I wouldn't tell you how many times he's talked about how much he wants you to be here, but I was crossing my fingers that you'd change your mind, and he knows I tell you everything anyway."

Late-afternoon sunshine streams through the skylight into the hallway. Even up on the fourth rung of a ladder, I can barely reach the ceiling.

The Blanchette house is, frankly, enormous. I'd thought Val's house was over-the-top, but this is next-level. There are three stories before we even factor in the basement, which I haven't seen yet.

"Okay. Well, here I am." Dubious, I reach up to stick the end of the streamer in place.

"Valerie Eaton!" Bri snatches at my calf from where she's standing below me, eyes enormous. "*Girl*. Is that a *tattoo*?"

"Maybe," I say meekly.

"First everything yesterday, then the hair, now this?" Bri

beckons for me to get down. "Do you have some kind of secret life or something?"

My laughter flutters as I make sure the streamer sticks and then I climb down.

They seem to have a touchy friendship—Bri has no qualms about pulling my sleeve up to run her fingers along the length of the tattoo, turning my arm to see it from every angle. "This is fucking *metal*. Did your parents totally flip?"

"They, uh, don't know."

"Jesus Christ." She shakes her head. "Are you *high*? Do you get high, all of a sudden? Do I know you?"

No, I almost say, but at the last second I just nudge her arm instead. "Hey. High school is over. It's time for new things, right?"

"I've literally never in my life respected you more than I do right this very second. You're so right. Fuck high school." Bri twirls another streamer and hands me the end. "Fuck all of that noise."

I snort a laugh.

The back door slams open.

"Home!" Brett announces.

God, there's *something* about him. I'm honestly a little disappointed—maybe Valerie isn't as gay as I thought. It's like her body reacts to the brassy tenor of his voice and I actually have to resist the urge to dart out into the hallway to see him.

Instead, I walk normally, Bri on my heels. Her Cheshire Cat grin can't possibly bode well, or at least that's what I think until the moment Brett's eyes land on me and light up.

"You came!" Brett flashes a smile so wide that for a second,

I forget we're strangers, and I sort of just want to run straight into his arms. Then that smile falters. "Are you—are you staying?"

"Under duress," I tell him, and then I nod and smile, because I don't think he understands it was supposed to be a joke.

Hours later, the house is full and Brett has me by the hand, leading me through the halls, which are full-to-overflowing. Between them, Brett and Bri must have some serious social pull, because I'm pretty sure there are at least two hundred people here tonight.

Bri is in her element too. She was at the center of a gaggle of girls in the living room when I last saw her, talking and laughing loudly, a flush high in her cheeks.

"Happy graduation to us," Brett says, with this lopsided smile that's kind of cute, actually.

"Happy graduation," I echo. I'm twitchy and on edge—I've been keeping an ear out for this elusive Lawrence all night—but if he notices, he doesn't let on.

"I do like the hair," he says. "Seriously. I know that probably wasn't the reaction you were hoping for. You just surprised me is all."

I've been getting compliments on it all night. Some of them have obviously not been sincere, but the general reaction is at *least* halfway genuinely positive.

I don't drink, but Brett has a beer. There's this charged sort of anticipation that crackles in the way his eyes linger on me as we circle the house, even if I don't know what it's about. If I'm talking less than Valerie usually might, he doesn't call me on it.

"C'mere," Brett says at half past ten. He hasn't let go of my hand for the past hour, and he leads me down the hall, opens a door, and tugs me inside. His room, I'm pretty sure. Surprisingly tidy, though it smells a little musty. I don't get a good look at any of it, because he tucks me into a hug the second the door swings shut behind us. "I'm really proud of you. Seriously."

Tears spring before I even know what's going on. Brett smells *really* nice. "Thank you," I murmur. "You too."

"Does yesterday change everything?" He pulls back and presses a kiss to my forehead. "Are we okay?"

My exhale shudders. "*Are* we?"

"I mean, you know how *I* feel about it."

I consider him. This close, I can feel the warmth of his skin radiating through his shirt. "Re-hash it for me."

"Huh?"

"Tell me again."

"I want to be with you," he says earnestly. "I want everything we talked about. I *do* want to do long-distance. It's not that long of a drive. And I—I meant it. I don't just love you. I do like you, you know. I like lots of things about you."

"Like what?"

"I like how much of a nerd you are." He noses in to kiss my cheek. "I like *you*."

Nerd, okay.

Brett doesn't pull back.

"What else?" I ask.

I don't get to find out. Brett leans in further and kisses my mouth. And it's not like it was earlier. This is a *kiss*.

Even if I don't know what I'm doing, the instincts hardwired into this body seem to have it figured out. I tilt my head, hands coming to rest against his hips, and I kiss him back.

No, I definitely know how to kiss. Brett just does it differently than I like, with a lot more exuberance.

Still, Val aside, if I had questions about my own sexuality, they're gone out the window now. The scrape of stubble against my jaw is turning me *stupid*, actually.

He slips his hands under my shirt, the touch against my skin sending sparks dancing up my spine, and—

This isn't my boyfriend.

I pull back, gasping. He's not *mine*. "I really do want to—"

Brett leans back in and does his best to *actually* swallow the words coming out of my mouth.

The kiss drags me back under. And it doesn't really even matter that he's using too much tongue—too much in general—because it feels so nice to be close to someone, to be touched like I'm wanted. I let him kiss me, and I kiss him back and run my hands through his hair and let him walk me back until my shoulder blades hit the door.

It's not until his hand inches higher up my waist that it starts to feel like a serious transgression. I tug at his wrists. "Hey, I'm not V—"

"Come on," he murmurs, dipping to mouth at the side of my neck. "I wanna touch you. You said when we finish school—"

I put my palms on his chest and push.

Brett makes a low huffing sound, but at least he doesn't resist, just rests his forehead against my shoulder. "Change your mind or something?"

"Hey, man." I'm breathing hard, and not in a fun way anymore. "I'm trying to talk to you about something."

"Okay, okay." As he pulls back, he wipes at his mouth, which I decide is *not* an attractive gesture. "Then talk."

My heart sinks. What could I *possibly* say to him that would help either of us? What do he and Val talk about? If I asked him for help, would he even believe me?

Heaving a sigh, I start, "Brett . . ."

His expression closes off. "So you *did* change your mind."

"Can I just talk to you?"

"You know, you could have said something." He runs a hand through his hair, sinking down on the edge of his bed. "I feel like—you're *always* leading me on, one way or another."

Helplessly, I let my hands hang at my side. "I'm sorry," I tell him softly. "Really, I am."

"Did it ever occur to you to talk to me about this?" Brett gestures to his side table. "I got, like, candles and shit."

There are four tea lights, unlit. He's also scattered wilted rose petals over the bed.

Some of my judgment must be obvious on my face, because Brett scowls. "I didn't have that much time. I thought you weren't coming over until later, when you could sneak out."

And even though I don't know the details of whatever arrangement we've agreed to, I'm not a moron. I can put the pieces together. "Look," I say, irritation rising. "Things obviously aren't super solid with us right now."

"Oh, *obviously*," he says, with such derision that I lose all patience at once.

"Okay, I'm going to go." I pivot on my heel, and I don't realize that I expect him to stop me until he doesn't.

Confusion and dismay whirl as I march down the hallway, rising in a fog that's nearly blinding. How did that go sideways so fast?

A hand snakes around my wrist and drags me to a stop. "Wait—Val."

It's not him. It's Bri. Her eyes are rimmed red and slightly unfocused as she looks up at me from where she's sitting on the ottoman. Happy-tipsy Bri is gone. Her hand is a wrought-iron vise around my arm. Distraught, she asks, "What do I do about Ibha?"

Well, shit.

Cautiously, I try, ". . . Talk to her?"

"I love her." She leans forward and puts her face directly onto my abdomen with a groan. "Val, I love her."

"I know," I say, through faint surprise. "You should tell her that."

"I *did*." Now she's almost wailing. "I already told her, and she said she didn't want to speak to me ever again, and now her family knows, and *my* family knows, and I don't know what to do."

"This shit again?" A hand closes on my shoulder.

Brett.

"Don't touch me," I snap, shrugging out from under his fingers.

"Don't be such a frigid *bitch*," he says, and Bri pulls back with a gasp.

I whirl and stare at him.

He's not my boyfriend but still, humiliation blooms hot behind my eyes.

"Shit, wait." He rubs at his face. "I didn't mean that."

"Yeah," I say, with the nastiest edge I can muster. "I bet you didn't."

Then I walk out the front door and let it slam behind me.

TWENTY-FIVE.

It's nearing midnight by the time I get back to Nanton. I make the drive to the tattoo parlor by memory, stopping a block away, idling for a moment before I cut the engine and get out.

The night air cools my skin as I slip down a side alley, coming to a stop just before the gravel spills out onto the main sidewalk.

At once I see movement, but it's not Gideon.

Jayda and Knox are all over each other. He has her up against the wall by the exit she'd led me out just the other night, and she doesn't seem to be complaining, based on the leg she has hooked around him and the hand she has up his shirt.

Neither of them notice the dark figure advancing on them.

Oh fuck.

The light of the tattoo parlor buzzes and crackles, low neon, illuminating Jayda's hair, Knox's hands where they're knotted in it.

"Get your hands off her," Gideon spits, hauling Knox off her by the back of his jacket.

Jayda shrieks.

My muscles lock against the urge I have to run over there and stop whatever is about to happen.

"Get out of here, Jayda," Gideon says, not sparing her a glance as he whirls Knox around like he's a rag doll. "I mean it. Go."

"Oh, for fuck's sake." Exasperated, Knox raises his hands in surrender. "Back for more?"

"Eye for an eye," Gideon says, and then he rears back and hits him so hard and so fast it's a blur.

Knox's head slams back and hits the brick with a sickening crack.

"What the fuck do you know?" Gideon's voice breaks. "What the *fuck* do you think you know? You don't know anything."

Fumbling to get her phone to her ear, Jayda shrieks, "GIDEON! STOP!"

Staggering, Knox rallies, whipping forward and up with his elbow, connecting with Gideon's nose, but it's the only hit he gets in before Gideon lands another punch, and another, and another, to his jaw, the center of his gut, under his chin so his teeth clack together, and he doesn't resist when Gideon shoves him backward, head cracking against the wall once more.

Knox slumps to the ground.

But Gideon's not done. He kicks him once. And then again, and again, blood pouring from his nose, Jayda dropping her phone on the asphalt as she scrambles to yank him back and pull him off.

This has already happened, I tell myself, hands balled into fists at my sides. *This has already happened, and nothing I do will stop it from happening again.*

But it still takes everything in me to stay hidden.

"GIDEON!" Jayda's hands shake, but she finally gets a good enough grip on his arm that she yanks him back.

"You'll thank me for this one day," he spits, voice a tight snarl.

"What is *wrong* with you?" she begs.

Knox's breathing is jagged.

Gideon staggers backward, turning to face her. When she flinches back, something in his face breaks, crumpling in on itself until he's wearing a vacant mask. "I won't hurt you, Jay. I'm not here for you."

"I don't know you like this," she says tremulously.

Somewhere behind us, sirens cut through the night air.

"Gideon," Archer calls from the alley, a warning as the sirens grow louder.

Run, I want to urge, even though I don't really know why I'm still on his side, after what I just saw.

But Gideon doesn't run.

Knox groans, and Jayda surges forward, sinking to her knees at his side. Her shoulders shake as she turns her face up to Gideon. "Why are you *doing* this?"

Gideon laughs, incredulous, and his voice grows dark with derision. "You really don't know? I knew you were stupid, but I didn't think you were a fucking *moron*."

Jayda's breath hitches and she looks up at Gideon. Tear tracks glisten in the streetlights. "Don't be mean."

Gideon laughs again, cruel this time as a police cruiser skids around the corner, and he doesn't run.

I shrink farther back into the alley.

An officer calls, "What's going on here?"

Jayda points at Gideon. "He attacked my boyfriend."

Gideon stares at her. From this distance, in the dark, it's

impossible to tell what he's thinking, but he's as still as if he's made of granite.

By now, witnesses are trickling out of their houses and out into the street, lured by the noise.

"You're unbelievable," Gideon calls to Jayda as the officer approaches and slaps cuffs on him, this slow smile spreading over his face. He spits onto the sidewalk, a laugh caught in his throat. "*Unbelievable.*"

Jayda hunches over Knox as the officer leads Gideon over to the car, speaking to him in low tones I can't make out. The officer is talking too, but I can't hear him either over the ringing in my ears as he ushers Gideon into the back of the cruiser.

The last thing I see before the door slams shut is Gideon's face in the flickering blue-and-red lights, dark blood streaming from his nose into his mouth, into his teeth.

He's grinning.

00:92-00:82

TWENTY-SIX.

When the nightmare ends and I open my eyes, my hands are shaking so badly I don't even pull over for ten minutes. I just keep driving with a white-knuckle grip of iron around the wheel.

All I can see is that grin. The manic look in Gideon's eye. Blood in his teeth.

I knew you were stupid, but I didn't think you were a fucking moron.

The crack of Knox's skull against the wall.

Who *is* he?

The next loop is a haze. I go back to school and spend the whole afternoon ducking out of the way of students with silly string and kazoos, searching every face for something familiar—*anything* that rings a bell.

Nothing.

I go back again the next loop and follow Bri around, listening to her talk, listening to her forgive me, again, for something I don't remember doing.

I spend a full day tailing Jayda as she goes home from her library job, as she cycles across town to somebody's house in the hours before the party. I watch and wait as she spends *hours* at the barn party, until she leaves and heads to the tattoo parlor, where she meets Knox after work and spends a full half hour making out with him in the back alley, but I leave before Gideon gets there.

This is divine punishment.

Loop after loop, the question echoes: What am I doing here?

There's nobody named Lawrence in Val's phone. I can't find him on Instagram, either in her followers or in Brett's.

Dead ends everywhere.

I wish I knew who I was looking for, but I don't. And Brett's cagey about him, when I go back to ask, to the point where he stops talking to me entirely in a way that screams we might break up. It isn't a huge concern of mine, but still. Interrogating him gets me nowhere, even when I pull out the urgency card. Especially when I start talking about time loops and body swaps.

One night, I charge the phone and stay up late, which is just as miserable as it had been out on the ocean. The last time I see—eyes burning, forcing myself to stay awake on the side of the road while Valerie's phone blows up with call after call from *Mom*—is 6:14 a.m., and then I'm back on the side of the road, blinking in the bright sunlight.

Sometimes I go to Vern's. Every time I do, Gideon comes to talk to me. Every time, he pulls the same lines, smiles when I surprise him, which I can do every day, and I don't even have to think of an original line to do it. And I *know* I shouldn't feel the same way about him, not after what I saw, but I can't help that my stomach flips every time he looks my way.

One day, I follow Archer around.

I stand outside his window and listen to him arguing with his older sister, Melanie, trying to get out of babysitting his nephew so he can spend time with Gideon. I follow him to the gas station where he buys the SD cards, and then back to the house. He and Gideon and Wyatt leave through the back door at half past eight and spend the evening on the edge of town in the back of Wyatt's pickup truck, though they do drive out to the barn party for an hour. Funny that we were there at the same time when I was with Jayda. I just didn't notice.

But I never follow them out to the tattoo parlor.

Instead, I take to walking around town. Sometimes late at night, sometimes during the day. Nanton is sleepy enough that it's almost boring, but it's also large enough that it takes hours to cover the whole thing on foot.

One afternoon, while I'm crossing through the newer residential neighborhood, I see her.

A girl in a floral babydoll dress rounds the corner ahead of me. Her back is to me, but she's carrying a dark box I recognize as an instrument case, and her ponytail is long and glossy black.

"Hey!" I call after her, heartbeat spiking. "Wait, Ibha! *Ibha!*"

She pivots on her heel, catches sight of me, and her eyebrows arch. "Oh my God. *Val?* What are you doing here?"

I reach her moments later, skidding to a stop a few feet away. "I'm—visiting."

"Is—" Ibha's eyes dart around the street. "Is Bri with you?"

"No, she's back home."

Tugging her case close to her chest, she looks down at her feet. White socks bunch around her ankles over the tops of black leather shoes with shiny silver buckles. She tucks a strand of hair over her ear. "What are you doing here, Val?"

"I'm not Val," I tell her, because *please*, God, I need someone to believe me.

She bristles. "What's that supposed to mean?"

I take a deep breath. "What if I told you I don't remember anything at all? I'm stuck in a time loop and I have no idea what's going on or who anybody is."

Her face crumples, and she walks away, chin ducked. Over her shoulder, she says, "This isn't funny."

"No, no, listen, okay, I'm *sorry*." I hold my hands up. "I'm sorry, I just—it's good to see you?"

It's a wild shot in the dark, but she tosses her hair over her shoulder and then gives me a brief look that's not even that angry. Then she nods. "You too. I like your hair."

I touch my hand to the back of my neck. "Thank you. You—you look good."

Ibha stops walking, so fast I have to double back. "Did Bri tell you to say that?"

"What happened with you two?" I ask.

She shoots me a *truly* withering look. "You know what happened, don't you? I'm sure Bri told you *everything*."

I shake my head. "I'd like to hear it from you, if you'll tell me."

"I bet you would," she says bitterly.

"She didn't tell me anything," I tack on, because regardless of whether it's technically true, *I* haven't heard the story from Bri. "I'm sort of in the dark."

"Was it you?" she asks, and there's real reproach in her eyes. "She said it was you."

"Bri still loves you," I blurt out, because I have no idea what she's talking about—story of my life—and I'm not breaking any sort of code when Ibha won't remember I told her.

She takes a full step back from me. "I—did she tell you to say that?"

"No." Helplessly, I step forward to follow. "Honestly, she'd probably be mad at me for it. But she was in tears about it, and I—she still hasn't told me what happened."

"You really want to know? Fine. *Here's* what happened." There's a sudden fierceness in Ibha's tone. "My mom got a job down here, and I told Bri I didn't want to break up even though I'd be moving an hour away, and she said *nothing*."

My throat closes.

"And *don't* make excuses on her behalf," Ibha says, and walks away. Over her shoulder, she adds, "My life is already hellish enough because of you."

00:81

TWENTY-SEVEN.

When the nightmare ends and I've pulled off the road to a place where I can think, I stare at those little numbers on the dashboard and track my stomach as it sinks, slowly.

Nineteen days in a time loop.

Eighty-one to go.

I go to Vern's, because apparently I *like* to suffer. I borrow a book from the library, just so I'll have something to do, and because sometimes when I'm reading, Gideon leaves me alone.

It's been almost ten loops since I saw him fighting Knox, not nearly long enough for the memory to fade, but certainly long enough that curiosity *burns*. Everything I've learned about Gideon goes against what I saw—who *is* he?

"Hi." He leans an elbow against the booth, five minutes before I know he's supposed to leave. "Just to let you know, I'm—"

"Off work now," I finish. "I know."

He blinks.

"And you don't want to keep your friends waiting," I continue with a sigh, because that's what he'd told me the last three times I was in here and we got talking. "Because it's your last day, and you promised it to them. Go. I won't keep you."

Gideon blinks. "How could you *possibly* know that?"

"Oh," I tell him gloomily, flicking my straw. "I'm in a time loop. I know everything."

"Really?"

"Yup."

To my surprise, Gideon slides into the booth across from me. "My friends can hang on for a second. I've *got* to hear more about this."

I give him an amused little smile. As always, Gideon's attention feels like a sudden sunbeam, and I suppose, of all things, having his rapt focus on me isn't the worst-case scenario. "What do you want to know?"

"I love a good time loop," he tells me, with what I'm deciding is my favorite Gideon smile, elastic and easy. "What are the rules?"

"You tell me how you got that shiner and I'll tell you." Leaning forward in my seat, I interlock my fingers, curious whether he'll tell the truth or just a shadow of it.

"Some guy was giving my sister trouble." He gives me a slight grin and a wink that makes my stomach flip-flop. "So I gave him trouble right back."

"Is that the truth?"

"You calling me a liar?" Gideon asks, smile bright. "We just met."

"No, we didn't," I remind him. "I've known you for weeks."

"In that case, you probably already know I'm Gideon," he says, but he reaches a hand across the table, anyway.

I smile, taking it. It's not the first time he's shaken my hand, and it's *definitely* not the first time his warm skin sends a little shiver through me. "Laurie."

"What are the rules of this time loop?"

"Day repeats," I say. "I wake up on the highway. It's kind of shitty."

"Are you a master of many talents now? Like in *Groundhog Day*?"

"Yeah, I've sort of been too preoccupied with finding a paper bag to breathe into every day to really hone my extracurriculars," I say, and he laughs.

"So, how do you escape this time loop?"

"Do you think I would still be here if I knew that?"

Gideon pauses, and then wiggles his eyebrows. "Maybe true love's kiss will get you out."

Dryly, I say, "I really doubt that."

"Hey, I can think of worse experiments."

My cheeks flush with heat. And he's right, technically. I can think of *way* worse things than kissing Gideon.

"Okay, you know what?" Gideon's phone buzzes and for a moment, he's distracted by whatever he sees on the screen.

I spend the pause watching him and hating myself a little. Why does he have to *look* like this? I want to smell his hair. I want to smell his *skin*.

"Sorry. Anyway." Gideon gives his head a little shake. "My friends want to go to this party tonight, but I don't. Like, I *really* don't want to go."

"Then don't."

"I'll do you one better." Gideon taps his index finger against the table's surface. "What say *you* meet me there? Assuming you're still in town tonight."

Gideon's never suggested *this*.

Then again, a kiss has never been dangled in front of him like bait. Just the thought makes my stomach flip with anticipation.

"I'll still be in town," I tell him, and his smile blooms like a wildflower.

"Where are these friends you speak of?" I ask.

Up here in the hayloft, the music is so loud I've had to lean close so he can hear me.

"Ditched." His breath is a hot exhale against the shell of my ear, and all I can think about is kiss, kiss, *kiss, kiss*, like a promise. Then he laughs. "Well, not really. I just told them I'd find them later."

We've been standing here for the better part of forty-five minutes. I've been nursing this iced tea the whole time, trying not to look at Gideon's mouth more than is strictly necessary.

"I'm sure they're thrilled."

"They can cope." He tosses me a coy private smile. "Hey, you want to get out of here?"

I smile right back. "And go where?"

"Out of here," he repeats, which does *not* add further context, but it doesn't matter. I would follow him wherever he went. When I nod, he holds his hand out.

I take it, stomach swooping. So, I should have been talking about kissing this whole time, apparently. Gideon's palm is rough with calluses, grip strong as he leads me down the steps, through the barn, and out into the evening.

The sky is stained lilac, the last remnants of the sunset slipping away over the horizon.

"So." Gideon—regrettably—drops my hand as he walks away from the barn and follows the fence, leading me down a trail cut into the grass over time by wheels finding the same grooves. "Tell me more about this time loop."

"Tell me more about this guy who was giving your sister trouble first," I murmur.

His smile is faintly exasperated. "That's really what you want to know?"

"Maybe I'm into this bad-boy thing you've got going on," I say, rewarded by the way his eyes crinkle. "Sue me. I'm curious."

So he sighs. "All right, all right. There was this bonfire last night. I wasn't going to go, but then Wyatt and Archer—the friends I was telling you about—talked me into it, and I overheard this guy talking about my sister like she was a piece of meat. I lost my shit and tried to hit him. He hit back. That's all."

"Tried to?"

"Believe it or not, I don't have a lot of experience fighting." Gideon gestures to his eye. "I was on my ass in five seconds. Sorry to disappoint, if the bad-boy fantasy *is* your thing."

If anything, I'm a little relieved, but I don't say so.

"Is your curiosity sated?"

I give him an amiable smile. "For now."

"My turn, then. How long have you been trapped in your time loop?"

His light-hearted tone tells me that this is a joke, still. I wish he believed me.

I wish he *could*.

"Three weeks, give or take."

"Fascinating."

"It gets weirder," I tell him. "This isn't my body."

For a second, a flicker of uncertainty crosses his expression, like he's trying to figure out how this factors into the game we're playing.

"I woke up trapped," I tell him. "And I don't know where this girl's consciousness went, or anything."

"Christ," he says, and I vaguely regret dropping that last tidbit, because it looks like he's lost his footing.

So I lift a shoulder. "All the more reason to get out of it, right?"

"Right." He surveys me as we walk.

The path is lovely in the evening light. Wildflowers line the long grass by the fence, yellow buttercups with their petals halfway closed for the night.

"Well, I already gave you my best suggestion." Gideon's back all at once, mischief in every line of his face.

"That you did."

"Might be worth a try." His wide smile sends a swarm of butterflies fluttering through me. "You never know. Maybe you'll kiss a few frogs on the way, but hey, there are much more complicated methods of finding the real deal, and I could think of worse ways to spend a day you get infinite second chances with, couldn't you?"

I tilt my head as I consider this, mostly trying to give myself a second to digest the implications. "You trying to test that theory?" I ask before I can stop myself, and then I regret it, and then I *don't*, because Gideon's smile just grows.

He stops walking. "Is that a trick question?"

"Nope." I flash him what I hope is an affable grin. "I'm just saying, play your cards right, and you never know."

Gideon leans against the fence. "Glad I've got a good hand, then."

Good *God*. Twenty days of this shit and I'm still not used to how smooth he is.

"You know, I feel like that analogy does a real disservice to frogs." I kick at a rock, watching it skitter into the grass. "Frogs are upstanding members of society, and here we are, talking about them like they're the antithesis of princely comportment."

"Antithesis," Gideon echoes, rolling the word around on his tongue. "I mean, would you *really* want to kiss a frog?"

"You don't know my preferences," I point out. "Maybe I do."

"Damn, all right then. Is it going to be a frog or a prince that breaks you out of the time loop?"

"Well, I've just gone to bat for them, so I feel like I'm team frog on this one. And also, down with the monarchy, or whatever."

He grins. "Assuming you *want* to kiss frogs, what would you do with a frog if you caught one?"

I have a feeling we've diverged from the analogy now.

"Dunno," I say with a little smile. "I've only ever been in the business of snaring princes."

"Noted." Gideon turns to look out over the field. "Hey, do you think frogs pay taxes if they're such upstanding members of society?"

"To the frog council, yeah definitely."

"I want to learn more about this whimsical world you live in. I mean, time loops and frog councils. Is Santa Claus real too?"

"No, but the tooth fairy is, and she's a felon."

Gideon *laughs*, this bright and caught-off-guard sound I want to fold up small and put in my pocket. For a second, he's just grinning down at me, and then he shakes his head. "Goddamn, I hope I'm a frog."

"Isn't the whole point of that story that the frog was really a prince in disguise all along?"

"Gonna be fresh out of luck if that's the case," he says. "I'm no prince. I can tell you that much."

For a second, all I can see is that wide, *wide* smile. Bloody teeth. Breathless, I ask, "What makes you say that?"

"I'm not exactly known for . . . What was it you said? Princely comportment?"

"What *are* you known for?"

"Nothing good," he says.

"Doubt it."

"Doubt all you want. Still true."

I shake my head, leaning against the fence next to him. My heartbeat is a wild flutter against my throat.

"Laurie?"

I swallow, and then I turn my head toward him. "Yeah?"

"Can I kiss you?"

My stomach flips. "You've never asked me that before."

"What?" Gideon blinks, momentarily lost, but his smile comes right back. "Oh, right, in the time loop. Well, why not?"

"I don't know," I say. "You tell me."

"See, I've asked you two questions in a row now, and you haven't answered either of them."

"Pick one," I tell him, breathless with anticipation, even though I know how this has to go.

"The first one," Gideon says, eyes darting low and then back up, and all of a sudden, I can't do this.

I *can't*. I want to kiss Gideon, but not like this.

Slowly, I shake my head. "Nothing against you, I swear."

His smile wavers, but he doesn't pull back. Carefully, he asks, "Am I allowed to ask you why?"

"You're allowed."

"Why, Laurie? I feel like I haven't been totally fumbling this, at least. Or do you just not kiss on first dates?"

"Sometimes I do," I tell him. "But we're in a time loop, remember?"

For the first time, Gideon doesn't look like he's having fun with this game. He sighs. "Laurie . . ."

"I want to kiss you," I tell him, and he leans just a little closer. "I promise I *really*, really do, but the thing is, I want it to mean something."

"It would," he says with a little frown, reaching up, trailing fingertips down the side of my cheek. "Is that what you think this is? I'm asking to kiss you just for the hell of it?"

"You might be," I point out, and I can't make myself pull away, even though I know this is a terrible idea. "But that's not—that's not why. I want you to mean it, and I want you to remember it tomorrow."

"As if I could forget," he whispers, leaning even closer. "Like I'd *ever* forget you, Laurie."

I turn my head at the last second, a hand of iron around my heart. "You do," I tell him quietly. "You always do."

TWENTY-EIGHT.

VAL

"So, it's *not* a date," I tease.

Brett's smile is a little bashful as we pull into the parking lot next to Peter's Drive-In. "Did I say it was?"

"Mm, twice." I pull down the sun visor to examine my reflection. "I even got all pretty for you. Did you notice that?"

"This is just the first part."

"Uh-huh, I *knew* you were secretly dating the whole hockey team too," I tell him absently, applying ChapStick. "And here I thought you had your hands full with me."

"You *do* look very pretty," is all Brett has to say about that, apparently. "I'll get us shakes. What do you want?"

"Surprise me." I push open the passenger door to his truck and get out, breathing in the muggy evening air.

"Surprise you," Brett echoes, unimpressed.

"Yeah, surprise me," I repeat. "But if you get it wrong, you'll lose, like, a thousand boyfriend points."

He huffs a laugh and rolls his eyes, stepping out of the truck and stretching. "So, the usual, then."

I nod my confirmation and smile. "And fries, for being the coolest girlfriend ever and not giving you any shit about spending our date night hanging out with your friends."

"Kinda feels like you might give me shit for it later," Brett says, turning to walk toward the order window, and I can't even tell if it's a joke.

I have no intention of following him to the counter. Brett has a specific, clueless way of interacting with cashiers that makes me and my years of food-service experience want to bash my skull in.

Instead, I check my phone for the thousandth time.

Nothing.

Seriously?

I text Krishan—his boyfriend—too, just in case. Krishan's a little more reliable, unless he's been roped into the board game of the month, which was Diplomacy, last time I checked. Twelve-hour run-time. It was a whole ordeal.

I glance over where Brett is greeting the boys with slaps on the back and the usual elaborate bromanship. I scan through who's here, noting that someone's missing—ah.

Matty's across the parking lot, phone pressed to his ear, frowning down at the ground and kicking pebbles across the pavement.

I'm on my way over before I've decided if it's a good idea or not. I only catch the tail end of his conversation, which seems to involve a lot of swearing.

Exclusively swearing, actually.

Matty seems to be on some kind of creative streak, cussing someone out with an originality that's almost poetic before he pulls his phone away from his ear and jabs the screen to end the call. Evening sun catches in his curls as he scowls, sinking down to sit on the curb, putting his face in his hands.

At first, I think he didn't notice me coming, but after a moment, he goes, "Enjoying the show?"

"Yeah, I'm not really sure what's on, is all." I sit down gingerly next to him, a foot and a half away. "You okay?"

"Yeah." He groans, lifting his head and running his hand through his hair. "Just this guy I'm talking to."

I lift my eyebrows. "And?"

"And it's going *shittily*, Eaton," he says pointedly. "Obviously."

"Sorry I asked." I raise both hands. "Wanna talk about it?"

"Aren't you busy?" Matty's gaze drifts to where Brett's still surrounded by the team, mouth ticking up into a smile.

"He told me it was a date, believe it or not."

"How are you enjoying eleventh-wheeling?" he asks, and then squawks when I shove my elbow into his arm.

Matty and I were better friends when we were younger. Don't get me wrong, we're friends now too, but it's a halting, stumbling sort of friendship. The kind that revolves around one life-altering moment, and a secret so big I don't know what to do with it except keep it close, tucked between my ribs where tender flesh will keep it safe.

Except—

"My parents know," I tell him.

"Shit," Matty says, idly. "How much?"

"All of it. Maybe. I'm not actually sure. All I know is there's only one person I told about Bri and Ibha, and it was in written correspondence where I said . . . a lot of other stuff."

Matty's eyes dart back to Brett and he winces. "Stuff like . . . ?"

"Yeah," I confirm, and he grimaces.

"You *have* to tell him. It's not fair to either of you if you don't."

"Is it going to matter?" I ask bitterly. "It's not like—well, he doesn't strike me as the long-distance type."

"Would it matter if he was?"

I don't answer, which is an answer, and I know it, and so does he, and I've never come this close to admitting this, even to myself.

Guilt rises like bile. I pick at a hangnail and keep my eyes on the ground, tracking a beetle's iridescent shell as it trundles across the asphalt.

"Oh," he says, softly. "Shit. That's why you haven't told him."

"After grad, maybe. I just don't want to upset things."

"Are you okay?" He lowers his voice. "About your parents?"

"Remains to be seen." I give him a tight, grim smile. "Shit hasn't really hit the fan yet."

Gravel crunches at Brett's approach.

"You good?" Brett asks Matty, something strange and almost closed-off in his expression.

Matty just waves him off.

I stand automatically, dusting off my legs and taking his outstretched hand. He hands me a milkshake—straight blackberry, like always, with a boyfriend-tax inch already gone off the top—and I dutifully do not mention that he forgot the fries.

00:80-00:75

TWENTY-NINE.

When the nightmare ends and I open my eyes, tears sting at once, hot and blinding. The slow-down is bumpier than usual, and I swipe at my cheeks.

I keep looping.

I go back to school. I hang out with Bri and Brett, and I go to the stupid party.

Brett tries to kiss me, and I duck out of the way.

This is a fucking *nightmare*, and not just because the day repeats. It's a nightmare because I can't stay away from Gideon, and the more time I spend with him, the worse it feels the next time I see him. I've never met anyone who so easily talks about the deep stuff. Who *likes* it. Prefers it to the regular minutiae of small talk.

Over and over, I tell myself I'm going to keep my distance, and then I don't.

"Are you sure we've never met before?" Gideon asks the next time he's across from me in the booth at Vern's. "I swear, you look so familiar."

If it weren't so completely devastating, I'd laugh. I hold up a hand. "Scout's honor. You and I have never met before today."

This time, he's brought us both coffees, lingering even after his shift has ended, and it feels even more like a date than our dinner or our almost-kiss had.

"I have a question for you," I start, all caution.

"Shoot," he says easily.

"Do you believe the universe is looking out for us?"

Gideon's eyebrows spike. "Like, do I believe in God?"

"No, like, I mean—I guess God could be a flavor of what I'm talking about, but—if you messed something up, do you think the universe would course-correct for you?"

"No." Gideon laughs, shaking his head. "No, definitely not."

"You sound pretty certain."

"You have no idea how many times I've messed up. And shit just *keeps* going wrong. No course-correcting here."

"Sorry, I meant—what if you got a do-over?"

At that, he knocks his foot against mine under the table. "The hell are you talking about?"

"Say you missed an opportunity or chickened out of doing something important. Do you think the universe would let you try again?"

"Like time travel?"

"In a way."

"I feel like you're talking around something," Gideon says, and the suspicion hits me—as it often has over the last little while—that somehow, even though he keeps resetting, he *knows* me.

"Do you think if you fuck up bad enough it could trigger a time loop?"

Gideon's smile brightens. "Are you in a time loop?"

Something in my chest deflates like a sad balloon. "No. I guess I'm just feeling existential."

"Me too."

"How come?"

"I'm going away tomorrow." By the way he waves his hand, I'd think he meant he was going on vacation if I didn't know better.

"Where are you going?" I ask, like always.

"Away," he answers, like always. "What brings you to Nanton, anyway?"

I invent a lie. I've been trying a new one every day, so that I'll get new responses out of him instead of following the formulaic pattern our conversations take otherwise. "I'm on my way to Lethbridge. Taking a joyride."

"I was going to move there," he tells me thoughtfully.

My eyebrows lift. "Oh? Going to?"

"Change of plans."

"What's in Lethbridge?"

Gideon hesitates. "School. And my mom lives down there."

I perk up. This is the first time Gideon's mentioned his mother. "You don't sound thrilled."

"She's . . . complicated. But she said I could live with her, and—hey, who am I to turn down free housing?"

"What sort of complicated?"

"Unreliable. She turns up every year or so, promises to do better. Gets my sister's hopes up, which—" Gideon's smile is grim. "Well. It's the one thing I can't forgive her for."

"And you're planning to live with her?"

"I was," he says. "But . . . like I said, I'm leaving town tomorrow. And I don't actually know when I'm coming back."

"Oh."

"Sorry." He gives his head a shake. "I don't know why I told you that."

"It's okay," I assure him. "I don't mind."

"It's just . . ." He rubs his face with his hand. "This is going to sound a little crazy."

"Try me."

Gideon lets his hands drop and offers me a wan smile. "I feel like I've known you for—"

"Ages?" I finish, a sad, sick pit forming in my gut.

His smile widens. "Yeah."

00:74

THIRTY.

00:74, the clock reads, and it's a taunt.

What the hell am I supposed to do with seventy-four days besides torture myself? I circle the town, caught between boredom and frustration as the minutes tick past. I park on the side of the road exactly thirty seconds before the rain starts, and then I sit there and watch the world blur, feeling listless even after the storm fades to a drizzle and the sun sends tentative rays through the clouds.

That's when I spot Wyatt.

He's walking along the main strip, overlarge white T-shirt billowing in the post-storm breeze.

Either I haven't been paying attention, or I've never been here at this exact moment, because I've never seen him walking this way. I haven't seen what he does before he meets up with Gideon and Archer.

So I park the car and I follow him on foot, staying a block behind all the way to the edge of town and then beyond as he walks out to a large shed, though I flatten myself against the fence around the corner and out of sight when I catch a familiar flash of lime-green vest.

"Wyatt," Ricky says, like the word is an accusation and not a name. He sounds almost teasing when he says, "Gideon's already gone, you know."

"Shut *up*, Ricky. That's not why I'm here."

"Why are you here, then?"

"I'm here for you."

"I don't swing that way. I don't think I need to tell you that."

Wyatt sucks in a breath. "Do you *ever* get sick of being an obnoxious, inbred homophobe?"

I cover my mouth with my hand so that no one hears my gasping laughter.

"I'm not *fucking* homophobic, dude," Ricky retorts. "I don't care who you like. I'm just telling you, I don't swing that way."

"And I don't care how you swing." Wyatt lets out a huff, and there's a low scrape of shoe against the ground. Gravel scatters. "I'm here because—it's not too late. You can still tell the truth."

"It *wasn't* me," Ricky insists. "I'm telling you. Gideon and I aren't best friends forever or anything, but do you think I *want* him in trouble?"

"I think you'd do anything to save your own hide." Wyatt sounds out of breath now. "I think your mom knows it's you. I think you're both letting him take the fall for it."

"I think you should let your boyfriend fight his own battles," Ricky counters.

There's a long, stretching pause. The sun beats down on me, sending a rivulet of sweat down my spine.

"He's not my boyfriend," Wyatt says, after an eternity.

"It wasn't me, anyway," Ricky repeats, like he either doesn't notice or doesn't care how wounded Wyatt sounds. "If it was? You guys are so annoying that I'd have fucking admitted it by now. Archer stole my phone and found nothing. None of that shit was mine. And if it was, I'd pick a better hiding spot than the one in the fucking wall that Mom already knows about."

"Ricky—"

"Has it ever occurred to you that maybe he's not innocent?" Ricky hisses. "He's not a fucking *saint*, dude, and I know that might be hard to hear because you lick the ground he walks on, but he's got some serious issues."

"*Ricky—*"

"You know he only found all that old shit in the wall because *he* punched a hole in it." There's a sneer in his tone now. "His mommy didn't show up for him, and he punched a hole in the wall like some psychotic—"

"Shut up," Wyatt explodes. "Stop it. I don't believe you."

Ricky's grin is audible, even though his voice is cold. "That's not my problem."

It's easy enough to monitor Wyatt after that. He goes to what I can only presume is his house. Then, an hour later, he leaves for Archer's in the same battered gray pickup truck they always drive to the party.

This time, like the last few times, I follow them out to the barn as the sun sinks over the horizon.

This time, unlike the last few times, I follow them inside.

I don't have to worry about being recognized by anyone but

Ibha, so I just do my best to blend in, following Wyatt as he and Gideon and Archer watch a game of poker, following them farther up into the barn after Wyatt leans in to whisper something to Gideon. Even once it's becoming obvious Wyatt's pulling him away for a private conversation, I don't stop. I keep following all the way up into the loft, though I stay behind the hay bales, crouched out of sight.

"Gideon," Wyatt says, voice hushed. I can't see either of them from here, but that doesn't matter.

"What did you need to tell me?"

"You're leaving." Wyatt sounds abruptly out of breath, distraught about something. "You're leaving, and we don't know how long you'll be gone, and I just—I need to tell you this."

There's a pronounced pause. Then Gideon says, "Wyatt, I—"

"I really care about you," he bursts out. "I really like you, Gid. I—I *love* you. And not just as a friend."

There's an *eternal* silence.

"Oh, man." Gideon sounds a little sad. "Wyatt."

"I figured you probably already knew that." A resolute edge creeps into Wyatt's tone. "But I wanted to tell you."

"I really care about you too," Gideon says softly. "Really, I do. Just . . . not like that."

"I know." Wyatt sounds so miserable, I feel like a terrible person for even being here to witness it. "I know that. I didn't think you'd—I just wanted you to know."

"Okay," Gideon says.

It leaves a bittersweet ache in the pit of my stomach. Every day, Wyatt confesses. Every day, Gideon turns him down. Every day, neither of them remembers it.

"Can I hug you?" Gideon asks. "You don't have to say yes."

Wyatt says nothing at all, so for a second, I don't know what's going on. Then—

"You are *so* important to me, man." Gideon's voice is muffled, and even if I can't see it, I can imagine how they're standing. "Please know that."

"Yeah." Wyatt sounds strangled.

I don't want to be here anymore. But I'm wedged between two walls of hay, so the only way to escape without revealing myself is to go farther into the loft.

I do, creeping softly, stepping carefully so that I don't make the floor creak.

"Come on." Wyatt is far enough away now that I can barely hear him. Voice tight, he says, "Let's go."

I lose him after that.

The barn is big enough that by the time I get my bearings, the boys are gone.

After a few minutes of wandering, the only familiar face I find is Ibha's. She's standing alone, frowning down at her phone. Her hair falls in a sleek sheet, caught in the glow of her screen.

Like this, she looks terribly sad. Maybe if I really *were* Val, I'd know what to say. Maybe she'd want me to say it.

What happened between her and Bri? And why does at least some of it seem to be Val's fault?

I only catch up with the guys again right before the fight.

I stand in the alley in those last few moments before midnight, eyes trained on the back door of the tattoo studio.

"Who are you?" someone asks from directly behind me.

I whirl.

It's Wyatt, almost invisible in the black hoodie and jeans. "What are you doing here?"

"I'm just—" I falter. How did I *miss* him? "I'm just walking."

"Get out of here," he tells me, with an urgency that's surprising right up until it hits me.

He knows.

My breath catches. The exchange he and Gideon had in Archer's basement echoes in my head.

At least I don't have to talk you out of—

They *planned* this. It's never been a spur-of-the-moment decision. Gideon attacks Knox every night on purpose.

Somehow, I knew this, but to have the confirmation of it so clearly makes me feel a bit sick.

"It doesn't have to go like this," I tell him, a bit desperately.

"What are you talking about?"

"He doesn't have to do it," I go on. "He'll get arrested."

"Who *are* you?" Wyatt asks again. In the dark, the whites of his eyes look like they're glowing.

I don't answer him. "Gideon doesn't deserve this."

Wyatt stares at me for a long time. Long enough that when Jayda screams, we both jump.

I whirl right in time to see Gideon throw the first punch.

"Maybe he does," Wyatt whispers.

Knox's head hits the wall, and I turn around and I stalk away. No point in sticking around. I already know how this ends.

I think about Ibha, standing there by herself. Bri's eyes glassy with unshed tears. The secret box of books in Val's bedroom. Brett's insistent hands.

The way my loneliness curls into a tight fist in my chest.

I can't keep following Gideon around like a lost puppy. I can't keep hoping for a different outcome—talk about the *definition* of insanity—and wasting time.

Gideon's life is Gideon's.

I have my own hell to wrangle.

00:69

THIRTY-ONE.

And since my own hell is being stuck in the body of a teenage girl, I need to focus on finding her.

Determined to ignore the memory of Gideon standing over Knox, I turn around the second I reset and drive into the city. I can't shake the lingering suspicion that the answer to that question is hiding in that big, empty house. In that big, empty life.

Who are you, Valerie Eaton?

It doesn't take much detective work to figure out where Valerie's dad works.

The Wildwood church auditorium is large with vaulting ceilings, walls paneled in cherry wood. Pews frame the stage in a tri-section semicircle.

I'm the only one in here.

I walk up the aisle and then down one of the rows, letting my fingers run along the wooden spine of the pew, dread forming a cold, sick knot in my stomach.

Sinking into the center of the pew, I sit and look up at the glowing cross. It's the same one on Eli Eaton's profile—the one that's been neglected for a year—but that photo didn't really do it justice. It's so enormous I have to tip my head back to see the top.

Empty like this, the auditorium feels like a liminal space.

I let my eyes fall shut.

Does Valerie believe in all of this? Do *I*, whoever I am? There are ties to the church in my blood—not this one specifically, but the capital C Church—but I don't know how strong they are or how deep they go.

I don't know what I believe.

I don't know if it matters.

A memory tickles, a feather-light touch. Something about being very small and hiding behind pews just like these.

Playing with a sibling. Playing after church, waiting for our parents, out of breath, laughing, *knees scuffing on the carpet—*

Wait.

I have a sibling.

I press a hand over my heart. I know it the way I knew about hockey. Gut-level.

"Val?"

At the voice behind me, I startle so badly my teeth clack.

It's Val's dad. I recognize him from the pictures in the office, tall and lanky, with a full head of neatly combed graying hair. He's picture-perfect approachable authority in faded blue denim, gray flannel rolled up to his elbows.

"Hey." I turn in my seat.

"What's going—oh, wow." He stops, taking me in, eyes lingering at the top of my head.

I wait, nerves dripping down my spine like egg yolk as he stares at me.

"You cut your hair."

"Yeah." I swallow hard.

He pauses. He's carrying a Bible—a bit on the nose for my tastes—and as I watch, he tucks it under his arm and shifts his weight. When he finally speaks, all he says is, "Are you sure?"

I manage a tight laugh. "It's not like I can put it back, can I?"

"Do you like it?" he asks, after another significant silence.

"I do."

He nods. "Then if you're happy, I'm happy."

I almost believe him. "Do *you* like it?"

"I think it's . . . modern."

Choking on a snort, I shake my head. Yeah, that sounds about right. A true diplomat's answer. I feel a stab of sympathy for Valerie.

"Has Mom seen it yet?"

"No."

"Oh boy. Do you want moral support?"

"I'm good," I tell him dryly, and I *don't* add that I have absolutely no intention of letting her get eyes on it anytime soon.

He joins me on the pew, setting the Bible down next to him. "This doesn't have anything to do with what we talked about last night, does it?"

His words send a heavy weight sinking through me. "I just wanted to, Dad."

It feels so normal to call him Dad. He just *looks* like a dad. His words are so kind. His *face* looks so kind.

"How does Brett feel about it?"

And we're back to the hair again. Slowly, I nod. "He likes it, I think. Just took some getting used to."

"I bet."

Curiosity rears its head. "What do you think of Brett?"

He gives me a small smile. "Where's this coming from?"

"I just want to know."

"You know what I think. He's a lovely young man. I really appreciated that he took the time to talk to me before he asked you out. I can't think of many other young men that would do that."

Well. That feels a bit gross, but I guess I don't know the whole story. Maybe it *was* a romantic gesture. Maybe Val asked him to.

I'm tired of not knowing.

"Speaking of Brett, have you talked to that friend of his recently?"

"Which one?"

"The Lawrence kid."

Oh, *right*.

My heartbeat skips. Lawrence.

"Is he okay?"

"I think so," I try cautiously. "Why wouldn't he be?"

"I don't think there are very many of your friends that you'd be out past midnight for, no matter how much of a crisis they were in," he says.

I can't meet his eyes. *Valerie, what the hell were you* doing?

"Did he say if he was going to come around some Sunday?"

"Not yet."

"Keep working on him," he says, and claps my shoulder.

There's a brief silence.

Then he sighs. "Honey, you don't seem yourself." He takes my hands, first my right, then my left. "Something's troubling you, isn't it?"

A lump solidifies in my throat. "You could say that."

"Okay." He bows his head. "Let's pray."

THIRTY-TWO.

It just doesn't end. From the moment I wake up—with the dream clinging to me like a film—to the way the days repeat, this whole fucking *thing* is the stuff of nightmares.

At first, I stay away from Nanton. I stay the *hell* away from Gideon and whatever mess he's getting himself into in favor of trying to blend into Valerie's life. I stand in the Blanchette kitchen late one night watching Brett joke around with his hockey friends at the grad party. Loud bass sends tremors through the floorboards, the occasional splash in the pool outside barely audible over the shouts and hoots of laughter.

"You good, babe?" Brett asks, snaking an arm around my waist, and I jump.

"I'm good." I give him what I hope is a reassuring smile. "Hey, is Lawrence here?"

Brett shoots me a funny look. "You mean—Didn't you see him? He just left."

"Like, *left*, left?"

"Yeah. Something about that guy he was seeing."

His name is Lawrence, *and* he's queer. My heartbeat trips and thuds, heavy in my wrist.

"What do you want with him, anyway?" There's a slightly sour edge to Brett's tone that I don't like.

"My dad was asking about him. Ministry stuff, I think. I didn't ask."

I don't think Brett buys that. His eyes linger on me as I turn back to the kitchen island, examining my fingernails.

My skin crawls.

Every second it gets worse. Every second in this body I feel more out of place, off-balance, *wrong*. I can still feel Val's dad's hands holding mine. I can still hear the cadence of his voice while he prayed over me.

When Brett catches my hand and leads me upstairs, I'm ready this time.

"I changed my mind," I tell him, all in a rush the second the door closes behind us, and then I brace myself.

But Brett just looks at me for a minute, and then nods. "I know."

And, yeah, he looks disappointed, but only just.

I blink. "You . . . do?"

"I mean, I'm not surprised. It's not like yesterday inspired a lot of confidence, and then you've been all weird tonight." He catches my shoulder and squeezes. "Thank you for telling me before anything happened."

Wow. Clear communication for the win. "You're . . . welcome?"

"Look." He sighs heavily. "I know I haven't been the best boyfriend recently."

"Oh?"

"I haven't been making you feel like a high-value woman."

Oh, Christ. What the hell kind of cult shit is this? I eye him through my lashes. "And?"

"And it wasn't cool of me to suggest that you'd ever cheat on me."

Well. Confirmation of a suspicion, I guess.

"It wasn't." I nod. Then, even if I don't know if it's true, I add, "I wouldn't. I would never."

Maybe Valerie would. But on some level I know *I* wouldn't. I'm not a cheater.

Brett sinks down onto the bed, leaning against the wall. He pats the spot next to him, so I join him, drawing my knees to my chest.

I wish he was less of a stranger. I wish his arm pressed to mine didn't make me feel like I'm about to jump out of my skin.

"I don't want to be fighting," he says, "and I don't want to break up."

A lump forms in my throat, and I nod.

"We've been together too long to throw it away on one stupid argument," he says. "And don't tell me it wasn't just one argument. I know it wasn't. I know it's more than that. But I—I've loved you since the moment we first kissed, and I'm not ready to give up on that."

Oh no. Oh, I hate that I'm feeling so much about this. Eyes burning, I ask, "Since that moment, huh?"

"You know the story," he says.

"Tell me anyway," I whisper. "I want to remember it through your eyes."

"Again?" Brett tosses me this sideways smile and for a split second, I almost get the appeal all over again. He has a *really* lovely smile, all straight teeth and dimples that I almost want to put my fingers in.

I nudge his arm. "Humor me."

"Okay," he says. "So. At first, you were just Bri's friend. Like my sister."

"Oh, good." I smile down at my knees. "Sibling-zoned, that's what everyone wants to hear."

"I said at *first*!" he protests. "And then one day you were over here after school, and Bri wouldn't help me with my trig homework, so you offered to."

I nod sagely. "Ah, yes. Tutor to girlfriend: the classic pipeline."

Brett laughs. "Exactly. And then we started pairing up in class, because you were—are—so smart, and one day I just thought, Oh, *wow*. She's beautiful."

I smile despite myself.

"I mean, you remember the rest."

"No, keep going." I close my eyes, letting my head fall back against the wall. "I'm living vicariously through you."

"Okay, Greg and I were messing around on the field a few weeks after that, and he accidentally elbowed me in the face."

I grimace.

"I broke my nose. Got blood *everywhere*. It was nasty. Greg passed out, but you got right in there like it didn't even bother you." Brett's smile is audible. "And you were so gentle. You knew exactly what to do, and you didn't take any of my bull about being fine when I obviously wasn't, and you checked to make sure I wasn't concussed."

I nod along as though this isn't brand-new information.

"I still think you thought I *was* concussed when I tried to kiss you." There's a strange, weighted beat, like I've missed a line in the script. Brett clears his throat. "Even though you keep denying it."

"Can you blame me?"

"I'd wanted to kiss you for weeks," he says softly. "I still do."

I open my eyes just as Brett touches my face to turn my chin.

"It doesn't have to mean anything more right now," he whispers.

When I nod, Brett kisses me. *This* is more like the way I like to be kissed. Soft, almost hesitant. Gentle fingers against my jaw.

And I feel *nothing*.

00:65

THIRTY-THREE.

"Tell me about your fight with Knox," I say, keeping my voice casual.

Gideon sucks in a breath and gives me a long, lingering glance.

We're sitting out on the grass behind the barn party. In the evening light, all the tiny white flowers have closed their petals, and dew soaks through my shorts and the flannel around my waist, but I don't care.

I caved. I'm telling myself it doesn't count, because I'm here with an agenda, but even so, I know it was giving in to weakness that I've spent most of today with Gideon. Every second he's asked for, which have been a lot of collective seconds.

It's just easy. Being with him is so much easier than being alone, but racking guilt still claws at my insides. I know I have other things to focus on—namely, finding Val and whatever links us together—but I can't help that *this* is what I want.

To be with Gideon.

"What do you want to know?" he asks.

I've spent today talking around the fight, finding out information I already know: that Gideon and Knox fought, that Gideon's still angry. That Jayda is—presumably—none the wiser.

"Whatever you're willing to tell me." I nudge him with my elbow. "I'm curious about you."

At least that gets me a smile. "It's not a cute story."

"Don't care. Tell me anyway."

"All right. I'd just found out that I'm being sent away." His voice is colorless. "My friends were trying to get me out of my head, so they dragged me to this bonfire. Knox was there with his buddies, and he was bragging about the things he'd got Jay to do for him. Not all of it was like you're probably thinking—but some of it was. I'd been warning her off him for weeks, and here he was, proving he was exactly the sort of douchebag I thought he was. Obviously, he didn't see that I was there, and I just . . . snapped. I didn't know I *could* get that angry. I didn't know what I was doing—I didn't even get to hit him before I was laid out in the grass. I thought Wyatt was going to blow a gasket."

I stare.

"I can't believe I just told you that." He laughs, pushing flyaways out of his face. "Fuck, you're easy to talk to."

I flash him a smile. "I'd say sorry, but I'd be lying."

For a long time, Gideon just looks at me.

"What?"

Softly, gaze steady, he says, "I wish I met you earlier."

I surprise myself when I have to turn away to breathe deep.

"You okay?" Gideon's mostly a silhouette in the moonlight, wisps of hair catching silver, expression a blur.

"Sorry." I swipe at a tear. "No, it's just . . . me too."

"I've never met a girl like you before."

And I just *can't*.

"I'm not a girl," I whisper, so soft I'm not sure he even hears it under the cool breeze coming off the plains. From where we're sitting, the crest of the hill blocks anything beyond but scattered stars.

But he leans closer. "Sorry? You're not?"

Wearily, I tell him, "I'm a guy."

"Oh," he says on an exhale.

"I'm just trapped in a girl's body." It won't mean the same thing to him that it does to me, but it's a close enough analogy.

Gideon blinks once, then leans back on his hands to survey me. Then, with a little smile, he says, "Yeah, dude."

I slump back into the grass, eyes burning. "Yeah?"

He offers me a fist-bump. "I'm glad you told me. Sorry for assuming."

I shake my head as I lift my hand to bump my knuckles against his.

"Is it weird if I say I wondered?"

Hope surges to the surface. Gideon's been flirting with me every day, hasn't he?

"Did you?" I hate how it comes out, all breathy and desperate.

He lifts a shoulder. "There's just something about you, I guess."

My eyes sting. "You're pretty much perfect, you know that?"

"Laurie, I *promise* you I'm not perfect."

"I know what you didn't do tonight," I whisper, at once desperate for him to know, to understand that I've seen the dark side of him and I'm not scared of it.

Gideon's eyes snap to mine. "What?"

"I know what you were planning to do. Get revenge against Knox."

"How'd you know that?" Gideon asks, aghast.

"Because I've watched you do it," I whisper. "I've watched you almost kill him."

"*What?*"

"This is going to sound crazy," I say, and then before he can react, I just keep going, words ripping out of me. "We've met before tonight. But you don't remember."

His eyes—already wide—go even wider.

"I've been stuck in a time loop for more than a month," I tell him. "I've met you almost every day."

"That's not," he starts, and then just shakes his head without saying anything else.

"You always help me when I need it. *Always*."

"Oh."

"You fight him," I tell him. "Every night, you go and you fight Knox. You get your revenge."

"I do?"

"Except on the days you talk to me." I keep my voice light, trying not to let on how important that feels even as a tear falls and I swipe it away. "And I still think you're perfect."

I can't tell if he believes me, and I honestly don't care.

My chest hurts.

I whisper, "And it doesn't matter what I think, because you won't even remember me tomorrow."

He blinks.

"It won't matter." I scrub away more tears. "It won't matter how insane I sound to you right now, because it'll all be gone, and I think—this would all be so much easier if I didn't love you."

Gideon's expression freezes.

"Sorry. *Fuck*." Why am I doing this? Gideon already has to let Wyatt down every day, and now he'll have to let me down too. I'm just adding myself to the list without stopping to think—and it's Gideon, so of course there's a list. *God*. Why'd I have to say that? "That's probably the last thing you need right now."

"Laurie . . ."

"It's okay," I tell him wearily. "Obviously, I don't expect you to say it back, or to even feel—you know what? Forget I said anything."

He laughs. "What—*forget*?"

I can't help laughing too, still wiping away the last of the tears, but then I can't *stop* laughing, and Gideon just sits there. "That's what's so funny about this, right?" I gasp, holding a hand to my rib cage. "You *will* forget."

"I—won't." He sounds bewildered and wary and a little sad and a half-dozen other things that make me feel like I'm asphyxiating on my own misery.

"I'm sorry," I tell him. "I've made you uncomfortable. I shouldn't have said that."

"I just don't understand," he says weakly. "I—do you seriously believe you're in a time loop?"

Defeated, my shoulders slump. I scramble to my feet.

"Laurie," Gideon says, a little reproachfully. "Don't go."

But it's not like I can *stay*. Tears sting. I swipe at them as I walk away.

"Wait, Laurie!"

I don't stop.

00:64 dawns with me behind the wheel, heartbeat wild.

Just the same as always.

And just like always, I drive to the next road to turn around, whipping past Gideon in his tractor, heading back into town.

The ache of last night is enough to puncture through the usual exhaustion, and I groan. I just *had* to say that, didn't I? Never mind that it's true. I *am* falling in love with Gideon, I just—if I could have kept my big mouth shut, I wouldn't have had to see the look on his face.

I pull off the highway onto a side street in a random neighborhood, where I stop and get out, exhale shuddering.

I can't do this again.

I *can't*. I can't keep hanging around Gideon. It's getting too painful.

Sitting down on the hood of the car, I press the heels of my palms to my eyes, and I sit there for a long, long time. For the first time, I let myself just sit. I go nowhere. The phone is dead, so there's no way to track the time, but it has to be at least an hour that I sit there in a dissociative trance while the hum of a lawn mower sends a rippling numbness through me.

I'm just *done*. I can't do this anymore. I can't believe I said that to Gideon.

"Hey!"

I let my hands drop.

It's Gideon.

Gideon, eyes wide, Gideon, stumbling along the sidewalk, Gideon, a hand in his hair, panic stretching thin over his expression, Gideon, looking at *me*, like he *knows* me.

Like he *recognizes* me.

I watch him approach, dread pooling low in my gut.

He crosses the street, eyes wild. When he gets to me, he stumbles to a stop. "What the hell is going on, Laurie?"

00:64

THIRTY-FOUR.

"Oh my God." I cover my face with my hands. "Oh my *God*. No. This isn't real."

"Laurie," Gideon repeats, hoarsely. "What is going on?"

"This isn't real," I repeat, because this is the nightmare, except it isn't. "This isn't real, this isn't—this *isn't real.*"

"I've got to be dreaming." Gideon shakes his head and bends at the waist, hands on his grass-stained knees. "I can't—I don't believe it."

"What . . . happened?"

"We were talking," he says slowly. "Last night. And you ran away, and I went to look for you."

Mortification creeps in slowly. Christ. Last night I cried myself to sleep in the back of my car, and I'd be lying if I said it was the first time I've done it.

"I couldn't find you anywhere." Gideon straightens with a little groan. "I even left the party, I think—or—or *did* I? I don't know. And then I blinked, and I was sitting in my tractor, which was, like, *seriously* trippy, and I was just trying to figure out what the hell is going on, and then . . ."

"And then?"

"And I've been looking for you *everywhere*."

I bite my lip.

"I don't normally drink very much." He presses a hand to his forehead. "I feel—I just don't get why I'm *here*, and not—"

"Gideon." I hold up a hand. "Stop."

"What?"

"Just—look at your phone. Look at the date."

At least he does it. His eyebrows arch.

"June twenty-sixth," I tell him. "You're not being sent away yet."

His gaze snaps up to mine. "What?"

"I know about that," I tell him, for what feels like the hundredth time, except this time I have to be careful about it, because *Gideon remembers the last loop. What the fuck is going on?* "I know about it the same way I knew about Knox. I've lived it before."

Gideon just stares.

"I've lived this day a *lot* of times. I know your June twenty-sixth inside and out, Gideon, because I'm stuck in a time loop."

"A time loop," he says slowly, gingerly, testing it out like it's the first time he's ever said it.

And it's definitely the first time I've ever heard him say it like *this*, with so much dawning horror and comprehension.

"You were serious? You're pranking me, right?" He peers over his shoulder, like he's searching for onlookers, or maybe a camera crew. "This is a prank."

"Yeah, that would make it easier, wouldn't it?"

Gideon sinks down right there into a squat. "Sorry, I need a second."

"Take all the time you need," I say faintly.

"This isn't real," Gideon mumbles. "I'm dreaming."

There is significant commentary I could provide here, but I think I can *hear* his critical-thinking skills grinding to a slow halt, so I just stand there awkwardly, letting my head go anywhere *but* to the fact that Gideon remembers me, he *remembers me* making a total ass of myself and confessing my love like this is the climax of a low-budget rom-com.

Gideon stays down there in the grass as clouds gather and a cool breeze works its way under my shirt.

"Come on. It's going to rain," I tell him.

Overhead, thunder rumbles.

He just makes a tiny high-pitched noise and stays right where he is.

"No, I mean, it's going to rain in about forty seconds, and it's going to rain *hard*. So unless you want to get caught in it, you should come with me."

He looks like an approximation of the guy I've been getting to know as he lifts himself off the ground.

Right on cue, a raindrop hits my nose.

"Come on." I jerk my head toward my car. "We can wait it out in there."

I don't wait to see if Gideon's going to follow me. I just climb back into the car and put my hands on the wheel, breathing deep, and it's a relief when the passenger door opens and Gideon slides inside.

His shock is nearly electric—there's a faintly stunned edge to his expression and his hands tremble where they rest on his knees.

"The storm ends at 1:54," I tell him over the low drumroll as the clouds burst and spatter raindrops over the windshield, and

I try not to sound *too* sympathetic, even though I am. I know exactly how confusing this is.

"Oh hell." Gideon puts his face in his hands, sinking low in the seat. "What the *fuck*?"

"I know," I tell him. "It's a lot to get your head around."

"But you did it."

"I think that's relative." I heave a sigh. "I also have no idea who I am, so my baseline is a lot more *and* a lot less complicated."

Gideon frowns. Then, slowly, he says, "Start at the beginning."

So I do, starting at the beginning—the confusion, waking up with no memories. The way he'd helped me. Tenley. Waking up all over again. Then I work my way forward, stopping only to point it out when the rain stops—Gideon's phone confirms it's 1:54, as if that's going to prove this is all true—and I tell him everything, only leaving out the details about Wyatt's confession, the fact that Gideon's been flirting with me for more than a month straight and, worse, that it's been *working* and now I sort of want to kiss him stupid.

It's surprisingly refreshing to tell him all of it. By the time I'm finished, the afternoon is well under way.

Faintly, tugging at his bracelets, Gideon says, "I forgot about the tractor."

I lean forward and rest my forehead against the wheel.

"I just left it there," he says, like *that's* the priority. "I saw you driving past and I just left it there."

"It won't matter," I remind him.

He just makes a tiny sound of distress. "Wait—so we met *every day*?"

"Most of them."

"You must know a lot about me, then."

"A bit," I admit, which is, you know, underselling the truth by a significant stretch. But it's better than admitting to Gideon exactly how much I know, or he might start thinking about what I said last night, and I sort of need him to not do that or my life is *over*.

"And I hardly know anything about you."

I wave a hand. "Join the fucking club, man."

Gideon gives his head a little shake. Then he opens the car door and steps out.

Uncertain, I follow. Today is exactly the same as it always is—those dark clouds dissipating, sun beating down again—but it feels brand-new to me.

"I need a minute," he says, face turned away from me, then, almost lamely, he adds, "Sorry."

"By all means." I give him a little wave.

Still, I'm not expecting him to walk *away*. He just turns on his heel, like that's that. Even the way he walks looks different. Dazed.

Fuck.

For a moment, I stand there. Do I chase after him? *Should* I? I almost want to. But I said I'd give him a second, so I will.

I watch as he disappears around the corner. Without turning back. Even once.

Well, shit.

I guess . . . I just have to wait for him to come back?

But waiting is a fruitless effort, in the end.

I stay right where I am all afternoon and into the evening, except for when I have to stop and feed myself and chase down a bathroom. It's *worse* than the stakeouts, because this time Gideon *knows* I'm waiting for him.

He knows I'm waiting for him, and he doesn't come back.

00:63

THIRTY-FIVE.

When the nightmare ends, I brace myself for another.

Morning sunshine streams through the windshield, dust kicking up behind me as I slow down and pull off the highway.

Rejected.

Gideon left me yesterday—and didn't come back.

Anxiety rolls in, a simmering storm cloud as my heartbeat kicks up, a frantic rattle. What do I do if he wants nothing to do with me now? Is there even a point in trying to win him back, or is he just going to run away again? *Could* I win him back if I never really had him in the first place?

I stop across the road from Gideon's tractor, but it takes several moments of deep breathing before I can summon the courage to look over.

When I do, he's jogging across the highway.

I fumble to get out of the car.

"Laurie," he gasps, as soon as he's within earshot. "Hi. I'm sorry."

Relief bursts between my lungs and bleeds through my shuddering exhale as I shake my head. "Don't be."

"I am," he insists. "It was shitty of me to run off like that."

The acknowledgment is a balm to my raw nerves. "Maybe a little."

"I had no idea how to get ahold of you."

"There isn't really a way." I cross my arms and lean against the car, and I don't point out that I stayed right where he'd left me. "Every day I wake up with a dead phone."

"That fucking sucks, a little bit."

"I mean, it's not the height of convenience." I shake my head. "Anyway—where did you go yesterday?"

"Tenley. I was—" A frown flashes across his expression. "I was—it was the same as the other night. We were in the middle of talking about something, and I just—then I was back in my tractor."

A stab of guilt twists. My fault. This is all my fault. "You must reset when I do."

"And you reset when you sleep, right?"

"Yeah, sort of."

"We were talking about time," Gideon says. "Me and Tenley." His eyes flicker to the road, a spark of intention. "They were going to say something, we should go back and—"

"Gideon." I stop him with a hand to his elbow. "Tenley won't remember that conversation. They won't remember anything about yesterday."

"Oh." He falters. "Right."

"At least they'll remember you exist." Dropping my hand, I wish I'd tried to make it sound less pathetic.

Gideon looks me right in the eye, as if he's just now realized I'm here, and what it means. "What do you do every day?"

"Survive," I tell him, and I don't really mean it as a joke, but he laughs anyway.

I tail Gideon to Vern's. I don't know why he's so insistent on going—it doesn't matter—but it's endearing that he is, and he asks me to come with him, so I do.

It turns out the motivation is primarily free food.

I sit at the counter as far from him as it's possible to be without being obvious, humming my approval at the smoothie he's just handed me, feeling so awkward about accepting anything from him that I almost forget to say thank you.

Even though I want to, I don't ask questions. Gideon already looks like he's on the verge of some kind of nervous breakdown, so I just stay quiet and let him think and ask questions as they occur to him.

"What do you know about this girl you've swapped bodies with so far?" Gideon's standing in the dead center of Vern's little kitchen, hands in his hair, his own smoothie abandoned in the blender.

I count off on my fingers. "She likes hockey, her best friend is mad at her, she might be gay, she has a boyfriend—"

"Wait, she might be gay, and she has a boyfriend?"

"She's very religious. She owns four Bibles. And who knows—sexuality is fluid, you know."

Gideon's mouth quirks. "Yes, I do."

I comb through that response—what does that *mean*? Is he saying he knows because he *knows*, or just because he gets the idea?

"And what about you?" Gideon asks after a moment. "The *real* you, I mean."

I blink at him. Is he asking—*is* my sexuality fluid? Do I even know the answer to that?

"What do you know about *you*?" he clarifies.

Oh. I lift a shoulder. "Not much. I have a sibling, and I think I'm pretty good on skates."

"And?"

"That's it," I tell him, feeling a bit lame. "I told you, I remember nothing."

"How'd you know about the sibling?"

I pause. "I remember *one* thing."

He snorts a laugh.

The flush of victory stings. "No, but seriously. I occasionally catch, like, *half* of a memory. Concepts. But it's nothing to go off of. I've tried."

"Wait, can you die in this time loop?" Gideon asks, hand hovering over the blender button. "Could *I*?"

"No idea. I guess I'd find out if I was in some sort of horrible accident, but it's not like I'm gonna go *chasing* that, right?"

"You could," Gideon counters.

"Yeah, and I absolutely won't, so—"

Gideon cuts me off by hitting the button, grinning at me while it roars. After, he asks, "But if we die, do we come back?"

"I told you, I don't know, and we are not testing that. Also, no more death questions." I shiver. "You're going to put me off this smoothie."

He laughs, pouring the contents of the blender into a mason jar and then rinsing and disassembling the parts, wiping the blade off on a towel. "Okay, all right. What have we done so far in these loops?"

"Like, you and me? Sometimes we walked," I tell him. "Sometimes we'd go to the party. Sometimes we went to the museum."

"Okay." He squints at me, like he knows I'm holding back. "What else?"

Because I'm feeling bolder, I add, "Sometimes you'd flirt with me."

Gideon flips the towel over his shoulder and leans his hip against the counter. "Did I, now?"

"More than sometimes."

He tilts his head to consider me.

"Sometimes you'd try to kiss me," I tell him, and then regret it immediately, because something fucking *weird* happens in the distant edges of his expression.

"Well." When he looks back down, there's an oddly bashful cast to the corner of his smile. "That's interesting."

It hits me all over again: I get no more second chances with Gideon. If I put my foot in my mouth, I don't get to take it back out tomorrow.

"What else?" Gideon's tone is casual, but also it isn't.

"Nothing's ever happened," I rush to assure him. "I know how weird that would be, and I'm—I'm not a creep."

"I didn't say you were." He doesn't look at me, though, and I can't tell if that's a good or a bad sign.

It's half past three when Archer finally calls.

Gideon looks at the caller ID, considers for a moment, and then powers his phone off.

"They'll probably come looking for you if you don't answer," I point out.

Gideon just smiles. "Let them."

We spend the rest of the day the same way we often do, and it's all the same, except none of it is. I keep having to remind myself: *Gideon will remember, so this time it's permanent. The way he sees you today will stick.*

At just after ten, we return to Gideon's house.

A middle-aged woman with Ricky's wild curls and blue eyes is in the kitchen. She doesn't spare me a glance as Gideon leads me up the stairs without a word, which makes me laugh. "She used to you bringing strangers home?"

Up on the landing, Gideon grins. "Wouldn't *you* like to know?"

It seems to occur to him at the same moment it occurs to me that I have, in fact, played *all* of my cards, and he knows exactly how much I definitely would like to know.

That amiable smile slips, just a little, and he clears his throat and changes the subject. "Where do you usually sleep?"

"In my car," I tell him, and he shakes his head.

"Fuck that, you're not sleeping in your car. I don't care if I get in trouble for having you in my room. They can't—" Gideon cuts off, mouth hanging open.

"What?"

"They can't do anything," he says, sounding awed. "Sorry, it's just sort of . . . hitting me all over again."

"Yeah, it's a bit of a shock at first," I tell him. "You'll get used to it."

"I guess I will."

"Anyway, it doesn't matter where I fall asleep. It's not like I get to *stay* asleep. I just drift off and have a nightmare and wake up on the road again."

"A nightmare?" Gideon asks. "About what?"

"Honestly?" I give my head a little shake. "I don't know."

Every time, I try to hang on to it after waking, but it never lingers. All I know for sure is that it leaves a sick, swooping sensation in my gut, leaves me breathless, leaves me feeling all at once like I don't know what I'm chasing, only that I am.

Gideon pushes open a door at the end of the hallway and pauses. "I don't," he says. "For the record. I don't bring strangers home."

I wish I wasn't so pathetically relieved to hear that.

"I think she's just given up on me." He heaves a sigh, then steps forward into the room and beckons. "Come on. There's even an empty bed."

"I couldn't—"

"Yeah, you could," he says, a low edge to his voice, "and you will."

Okay, so, fuck *me*. If he's going to use that tone, I'll do whatever he tells me to forever.

The aforementioned empty bed turns out to be about a foot

away from the ceiling. Gideon's bedroom is sparsely decorated, but not like the other half of Jayda's room. This looks more like he doesn't spend time here unless he absolutely has to. There are no photos, and the corkboard against the wall is empty except for a pamphlet for the Bomber Command Museum pinned haphazardly in the corner. Glow-in-the-dark stars litter the ceiling.

"Someone forgot to tell the Perrigans that bunk beds aren't fun after you're six," Gideon says. "Top one's yours. Don't say no."

"Gideon—"

"Shut up," he says. "Seriously."

So that's how I end up lying awake in Ricky Perrigan's old bed.

I hadn't realized how much of a distinctive smell Gideon has. His whole room is infused with it, this warm, earthy scent. Leather, maybe.

"I like the stars," I say, staring up at the one directly overhead that's close enough to touch.

Beneath me, Gideon sighs. "I didn't put them up there."

"Who did?"

"Fuck if I know." He lapses into silence.

I didn't bother changing out of my clothes. The one mercy is that they always reset to how clean they were the first moment I woke up, no matter what happens to them, which means I didn't have to navigate changing in front of Gideon. Not that I think he would have looked or even stayed in the room, but still.

"Laurie?"

"Yeah?"

"What happens when I go after Knox?"

I pause, thinking hard. Is it cheating to tell him? It's not like Gideon is really a part of this endless loop anymore. Would admitting the truth mean I'm interfering with, like, space-time or something?

Screw it. Space-time has interfered with *us*.

I make up my mind all at once, and I tell him the truth, plain and simple. "You get arrested."

"Who calls the police?"

"Jayda."

He stays silent for a long time. It's impossible to tell whether this surprises him. Is he disappointed, or was he expecting her to favor Knox over him this whole time? Then he sighs. "You said I always do it. Except on days where I talked to you."

"As far as I know."

He sucks in a slow, deep breath. "Laurie?"

I bite my lip and squeeze my eyes shut before I answer. "Yes?"

"Why am *I* here?"

Letting out a gust of air, I tell the truth. "I don't know."

"You said you love me," Gideon says quietly, and my stomach drops. "Was that real?"

"I only said it because I thought you'd forget."

"But you still said it."

"What do you want me to say?" I turn onto my side so that I can see the corner of his knuckles on the edge of the mattress. When he shifts, the dark leather of his bracelets stands stark against his skin. "What are you really asking?"

And Gideon says nothing at all after that.

The silence falls thick, like a blanket of snow through the summer evening warmth.

I stare at those little stars for a *long* time before I fall asleep.

00:62

THIRTY-SIX.

When the nightmare ends and I open my eyes, my first thought is: *It's really nice not to be alone.*

And it is.

On the side of the highway, Gideon smiles at me. "What do you want to do today?"

Guilt rises at once. Again, that little voice in my head murmurs, *Your fault.*

"I don't want you to feel like—" I swallow. "I mean, I'm the reason you're stuck here in the first place. I already feel bad enough as is. Don't feel like you *have* to spend every loop with me. I'm sure there's got to be unfinished business you want to take care of."

But Gideon just gives me a blank look. "I already took care of my unfinished business. *Dozens* of times, if you're telling the truth."

That Knox is Gideon's unfinished business leaves a nasty aftertaste in my mouth.

"What's *your* unfinished business, then?" Gideon asks.

I have to laugh. "Your guess is as good as mine. I'm solving a jigsaw puzzle, except I don't know what the final picture is supposed to be, and also all the pieces are made of slime."

"Do you ever just . . . drive?"

"Sometimes." I shrug. "It gets old when you're doing it alone."

"I've never been to the ocean," Gideon says thoughtfully, and a smile creeps across my face despite myself.

"We wouldn't get there until the middle of the night," I point out.

And he grins. "So?"

"It'll be cloudy," I warn. "Not much to see."

"Well, yeah." He doesn't look at all deterred. "Who said the point of it was the view?"

It turns out road-tripping is *way* more fun with Gideon in the seat next to me, and because this time it's a planned trip and I have a navigator and someone to talk to, the hours fly by.

"What does this mean?" he asks, running his fingers along the dashboard clock as the bald faces of the Rocky Mountains whip past us. "That first day it was a 64. Today is a 62. I thought it was just broken, but . . ."

I clear my throat. "I, uh . . . I don't really know. It feels like a countdown."

Gideon's hand stills. There's a scar below his knuckle I've never noticed, a tiny pale slash interrupting the dark tan. "A countdown to what? The end?"

I lift a shoulder. "It's not like this time-loop shit came with a manual."

"That you know of." Gideon pushes open the glove-box compartment and starts thumbing through it. He pulls out a sheet of paper, but it's not a manual. Slowly, he says, "Valerie Eaton."

A sick pit sinks in my gut.

It doesn't feel good, is all. I haven't heard that name out of his mouth since I told it to him, all of those loops ago, and it just feels *wrong*.

"That's her, isn't it? The girl whose body you're trapped in?"

"Sure is." I press my lips into a thin line.

"What's she like?" he asks. "I mean, besides what you've already told me."

"How would I know?"

"Well, you've been in her skin."

"Exactly. *I've* been in her skin. Her boyfriend called her a frigid bitch, but that was with *me* in the pilot's seat."

Gideon's whole face shifts when he smiles. It's the first genuine smile I've seen out of him since he got dragged into this, and it lights something up inside of me, this ember secret I wish I could douse. "Were you?"

"*Was* I being a frigid bitch?" I burst out laughing. "Technically, I guess. I didn't put out, if that's what you're wondering."

"I *was* sort of wondering," he says, and there's this devilish edge to his tone that makes my cheeks flare with heat. "He sounds like a piece of work, by the way."

"He's an interesting guy," I start, and then I have to amend it, because I can't actually think of anything particularly interesting about Brett. "He's a . . . nice enough guy, most of the time."

"Definitely boyfriend material." Gideon clears his throat. "Speaking of—how much do you know about Knox?"

"The basics," I say. "Tall, kind of rude, too old for your sister, Catholic parents, folds like a rag doll when you hit him."

Gideon grins, apparently despite himself, because the next second he clears his throat, gives his head a little shake, and wipes the smile off his face. "Anything else?"

"I don't like him much," I admit, "but that's more opinion than fact."

"*Correct* opinion," he says, and then he doesn't even tell me why he asked in the first place.

Thanks to a nearly two-hour detour through the Okanagan during golden hour—Gideon got *strange* when we drove past the orchards and made us stop and reroute to see more of it—it's almost six in the morning by the time we arrive.

Even though it's just a dark blur, Gideon is enthralled by the ocean. We sit side by side on the edge of a pier, not talking. We're definitely trespassing—Gideon talked me into hopping a fence—but I can't bring myself to care.

I might not care even if there *were* lasting consequences.

Maybe it's just the glow of the single light at the end of this dock, but the bruising around Gideon's eye looks softer.

He catches me staring. The corners of his mouth tick upward. "What?"

"Your eye," I whisper.

"What about it?"

"It's healing, I think."

Frowning slightly, he brushes fingertips against the edge of the bruise. Then he rolls out his shoulder with a nod. "I *do* feel a lot less like I just took a beating. I mean, look at your tattoo."

The firm edges of the ink have receded. I'd barely noticed.

"Everything else resets," he muses. "We don't."

Everything else *but* us is on a permanent, whirling cycle. If we can heal, we can get hurt too. I feel certain, all at once, that if one of us died, we'd stay dead. The thought comes with a shiver of dread, and I shove it away with a flippant "Think there's a lesson in there somewhere?"

He grins, but it devolves into a yawn. "You've been acting extraordinarily blasé about this whole thing, you know that? Weren't you scared? Lonely?"

I huff a little laugh, then catch the yawn, turn, and find myself with my cheek against his shoulder. "Oh, desperately."

Gideon doesn't push me off, not even gently, even though I know it's probably weird for him, because I'm barely more than a stranger. He just goes still underneath me, skin warm through his shirt. "If I was trapped for a month and a half by myself and nobody remembered me, I'd have snapped by now."

"I think I'm used to it," I say, before I mean to. My eyes drift shut. "From before."

For a long time after that, Gideon stays quiet. Then he asks, "If something happened once and then the rest of the world resets, do you think it really happened?"

I manage a laugh, but I can't force my eyes open. "Who knew sleep deprivation would make you existential?"

He laughs too, the sound snagging on the wind, carried away. "Everyone."

"I guess it depends if you remember it. If a tree falls, and all that. Do you think it happened?"

"I think if *you* remember it, then it happened." Gideon's voice is gentle and soft, as though he can tell I'm about to fall asleep. "Which I recognize is a bit of a mind-fuck, considering how much I don't remember of all the times we've met."

I nod.

"I wish I did," he adds, after a moment's pause, and through the haze of sleep, I feel his chin rest on the top of my head. "I really do."

00:61

THIRTY-SEVEN.

Neither of us breathes a word about finding a concrete way to break the loop. I'm not even sure Gideon wants to. Now that the initial shock has worn off, he seems almost *cheerful* to be here.

We go straight back to the farmhouse.

It must be a little earlier than Gideon usually arrives, because when we walk in, Jayda's coming down the stairs and they both freeze, wearing identical expressions of surprise.

"Jay." Gideon frowns. "Aren't you at the library today?"

"I'm skipping," she says, which—

Either isn't true, or all Gideon had to do to change her mind—and her timeline—was ask a single question.

"Anyway, good morning to you too." Jayda doesn't miss a beat, though I can't help thinking there's *something* shifty in her eyes, like she's nervous. "And hello, random chick I've never met before. Gideon, who is this?"

"This is Laurie," Gideon says. "Notably, not a chick. Don't assume."

"Sorry," she says, and seems to genuinely mean it, at least. "Nice hair."

I stifle a smile. "Thanks."

"What are you doing tonight?" Gideon asks her.

"I'm going to the McDonnell party."

"With?"

"Who do you *think*?" Jayda asks. "Me, myself, and I."

"Not Knox?"

"I have a life outside of having a boyfriend."

"Could've fooled me," Gideon mutters darkly.

Jayda flips him off on her way out of the kitchen.

"I take it she knows you don't approve," I murmur as soon as she's out of earshot.

"I've tried to talk her out of it at *every* stage, I promise you." Gideon shakes his head. "She's freaking me out."

"I think she might be *trying* to get a rise out of you," I tell him. "She doesn't usually ditch the library. That's where I first met her, actually."

Gideon watches me for a second. Then he gives his head a little shake. "This whole deal? *Bizarre*."

"What, you don't like how much I know about the people in your life?" I quirk a smile. "Tough shit, dude. I don't know about *anything* else."

"We should follow her," he says.

"What, to the party?"

"Yes," he says. "And then after."

"I'm going to go with *don't* do that," I advise. "Speaking as someone who has seen how this day plays out, that route doesn't usually end well."

I'm not expecting the third degree at the party, but then again, I've never attended *with* Gideon in this capacity.

"So, how do you and Gideon know each other?" Wyatt asks. He's leaning against the wall, nursing a plastic cup and doing a terrible job of pretending he's not analyzing and judging everything about me.

"We met through hockey stuff a while back," I tell him, because that's the lie that's been working the best, so far. "I'm just passing through."

"He's never mentioned you."

Despite myself, I smile. Wyatt's possessiveness is so obvious it's a little astonishing that Gideon doesn't see it. And because I'm feeling petty, I lie right to his face. "He's never mentioned you either."

"*Burn*," Archer says from where he's standing next to us, texting rapidly. "Get got, jackass."

"I'm not a jackass," Wyatt protests.

"Definitely." Archer keeps typing. "Because jackasses are known for being self-aware. Jackassery is reserved for those who've completed the five stages of therapy and gotten a gold star in emotional regulation."

Wyatt gives him a cold look that is entirely wasted, considering Archer hasn't looked up from his phone in the whole fifteen-minute stretch we've been standing here. "You should have been socialized more in your infancy."

"Who's socializing with infants?" Gideon asks as he reappears at my elbow.

"Gideon," Wyatt says, relief washing over his expression. "Can we talk?"

I take that as my cue. I touch Gideon's elbow, aware of the way Wyatt's eyes are boring holes into me as I do it. "I'll be right back."

"Sure," Gideon says amiably. "Keep an eye out for Jayda, will you?"

I already know where to find her, but I don't tell Gideon that. Besides, I'm not looking for Jayda anyway.

I circle the party, keeping my eyes peeled.

When I finally find her, my first thought is that Ibha looks like a Disney princess. She's dainty all over; slender wrists and ankles; waist-length, glorious, shiny hair; enormous dark eyes. The lantern light catches her long eyelashes and bronzes her brown skin to a shimmer. She blinks at me. "*Val?*"

"Hi." I feel suddenly out of breath. "Ibha."

"What are you *doing* here?" she asks. Then her eyes dart around the space behind me. "Is Bri—"

"Not here," I tell her, and then I swallow, hard. "I want to say that I'm sorry."

Her eyes fill with tears at once and she pulls away. "It *was* you?"

"No," I add hurriedly, and *God*, I hope it's true. "I didn't do it. I just—I think you should know that Bri's *beside* herself."

"Maybe she should be."

"What would you say if I told you she loves you?" I whisper. "Like, *really* loves you. Never stopped."

Ibha's eyes go glassy. Then, to my surprise, she flings her arms around my neck. "I *miss* you," she whispers. "I miss her, but I miss you too. I miss being friends."

"I . . . miss you too." I pat her back. And the thing is, I do. It feels like there are certain things that are hardwired into this body, straight into muscle memory, and this is one of those things.

I can almost *remember* missing Ibha. "You'd talk to Bri, if you got the chance?"

"I would." She wipes her eyes as she pulls back, smearing mascara. "Of course I would. I love her. I always have."

Well. Maybe *this* is my purpose. Get these two idiots in the same room. How hard could it be?

"You should talk to her," I say.

Her expression shutters, and she shakes her head. "That's not my—I don't want that to be on me. I already said how I feel, and if she—if she *does* love me, I think she should prove it."

From what I know, I privately agree with her, but I don't say so. "I'm going to talk to her," I tell her, and I mean it. "We'll figure this out, I promise."

I find Gideon standing in the loft with a beer bottle hanging loosely from one hand, fingertips to his lips.

"How's it going?" I ask, mildly amused by the slack-jawed look on his face.

"Well, Wyatt just kissed me, so," Gideon says.

My eyebrows arch. Who knew a little petty snark could provoke a whole kiss? "I beg your pardon?"

"Yeah, I was as surprised as you are," Gideon says, and then narrows his eyes. "Wait, how surprised *are* you?"

My silence must speak for itself.

Gideon socks my shoulder, exasperated. "Were you ever

planning on warning me that one of my best friends *kisses* me every day in this time loop?"

"He doesn't," I rush to assure him. "From what I heard one time, he only *tells* you how he feels, usually."

"Every time?"

"Unless something happens to change the original day."

"Like how you said that I leave Knox alone on the days when I talk to you."

My cheeks sizzle with heat. "Yeah. Why do you think that is anyway?"

"I don't know." Gideon's eyes on me are intense, expression intent and analytical, and I've never been so sure that he's lying.

00:60

THIRTY-EIGHT.

On 00:60, the first thing Gideon says to me is "I don't think we've been taking advantage of this whole deal."

I blink over at him as he gets in the passenger seat. "Good morning to you too."

He pulls out his phone and says, "Drive."

"Christ," I mutter, but I follow his directions all the way out to the farmhouse.

He's only inside for a few minutes, returning with a duffel bag hoisted over his shoulder.

"I knew it," I tell him as he's getting back into the car. "You're going to murder me at long last."

"If I murdered you, you might come back tomorrow," Gideon points out. "Except then you'd probably be a little pissed off."

"Probably," I agree, though privately I can't help thinking that dead is *dead*. But I don't say that, mostly because, *major bummer*, partly because curiosity is a blazing crackle under my skin. "So . . . where are we going?"

"You'll see," he says with this little good-natured smile.

Gideon guides me back north up the highway, directing me to turn off at the exit for High River.

I've never stopped here before on my own, which means I have absolutely no idea where we're going until he points me into the parking lot of a recreation center. There are a few letters on the reader board missing, and the "K" in "skate" has been dislodged so that it's hanging diagonally, but I still get the picture.

"Oh," I gasp, pulling into a parking spot near the front.

"You *said* hockey was the one thing you and Valerie have in common, right?"

"I did." A knot at the base of my throat is growing, leaving me feeling a little light-headed. "*Gideon.*"

"What?" He turns in his seat, frowning. "Was this a bad idea?"

"No, no. Tenley even suggested it. I just can't believe I *forgot*."

"Hey, it's not your fault you only have original ideas every ten days," Gideon says, then squawks when I smack his arm.

"That's so rude." I can't even stay annoyed, because suddenly it's imperative that I get inside the building *right* this second.

I have to root around in the trunk to find what I need, but Valerie has everything. The second I'm on the bench inside the change room, something in my chest twinges and relaxes. Once I have the skates laced up, I let out a shaky exhale. For the first time since I woke up behind the wheel, I feel settled. Not like this is my body, but like it *could* be. Like I'm not fighting the urge to crawl out of my skin.

I don't put on most of my gear—just the skates for now—but I bring Valerie's hockey bag out with me.

There's nobody else out on the ice.

I take a step out onto the rink, hoping desperately that I'm right, and this will be easy.

It is.

Right from the moment I glide onto the ice, a snag unhooks between my lungs and I have to stop and stand there with my hand against the board.

"Wanna race?" Gideon asks from just behind me.

"I'll win," I tell him, and I don't even know where the confidence comes from, just that I'm *sure* of it.

"Oh, you are *so* on," Gideon says, and then he's off like a shot, the cheater that he is.

It doesn't matter. I catch up. The muscles in my legs burn as I skate, but it's the best kind of burn. I pass him, and it's *easy*, staying ahead even as he works hard to keep up, taking the lead, hair blowing off my face.

"Christ." Gideon gasps for breath as he collides with the boards where I've stopped. "Uncle, uncle! I give up."

"That's on you for not setting parameters." Winded, I grin like the Cheshire Cat. "Did you think I was lying to you?"

"I thought you might be exaggerating a little, yeah."

"Eat my snow," I tell him, and then I take off again.

Gideon doesn't even bother chasing me this time, just leans back against the boards and watches.

So maybe I show off a little. Maybe I let myself *fly*. Maybe I pivot at the sharpest angles, skating so fast the lines underneath me blur. Then, when I've had enough, I take Valerie's hockey stick, switching it back and forth between my hands, trying to find a grip that feels right, grinning when it locks in.

"Gear up, Norris." My smile widens. "I heard you're a half-decent goalkeeper."

I chase the puck around the rink while Gideon's putting on his equipment, and the thrill of it sends a warm flush through me.

I'm *good* at this. Oh, I missed being *certain*. It feels so good to *know* something about myself, finally. Even having no one else to compare myself to, I know that this is where I excel.

Gideon excels too. Right from the second he gets in front of the goal, I can tell that he knows what he's doing.

I haven't had honest-to-God *fun* since this shit started. I score on him easily at first. This is like second nature, like *breathing*. I'm in the middle of thinking that I would *destroy* him in an actual game, and then he figures me out.

He blocks a shot, and it's *not* just luck. I feint, and then *he* feints, and sends the puck ricocheting back toward me.

Even through the grate, I can see his smile.

"You've got eight moves, Eaton," he says. "Eight *good* moves, but still."

I would still crush him in a game, but only the first time. And honestly, only for the first two periods. He's a quick study.

"Who told you I play goalie?" he asks when we've both exhausted ourselves and are sitting on the bench.

"Tenley. First day." I spray Valerie's water bottle onto my face. "Hockey was the first thing I remembered about myself. I think it's, like, *the* thing Valerie and I have in common."

"Not owning four Bibles?" Gideon asks, and then yelps when I elbow him in the side. "I'm *kidding*, Jesus, you're sharp."

I grin, all teeth.

00:55

THIRTY-NINE.

I'd have never thought there would be a *routine* in a time loop, but we fall into one like it's second nature.

I wake up on the side of the road, turn around, and stop. Gideon gets in the car. We go—somewhere. One day, we drive north, all the way to Edmonton, just because we can, and spend the afternoon on the banks of the North Saskatchewan River.

Every day, Gideon powers his phone off. "I mean, does it matter?" he asks when I point out that his friends and family are probably worried. "Let them worry. By tomorrow, it will never have happened."

Gideon, as it seems, is immune to existential guilt.

Twice, we drive out west. Once, we even make it as far as the ocean again.

On the afternoon of 00:55, we end up at the gas station.

Gideon's been avoiding it. He hasn't said so, but I can tell. Every time we drive past it, he averts his eyes, so when he brought it up today, I didn't even ask why.

"Gideon!" Tenley smiles wide when he walks into the store.

I linger a few steps behind.

"Hey, Tenley." His smile is so wide that suspicion flashes across their face, followed by hope.

"Have they changed their minds?" they ask.

Gideon's smile wavers. Then he catches a breath and says, "Yes."

My eyebrows arch, and I step into the next aisle so Tenley won't see my face.

"*Really?*" they ask, and I've never heard them sound so hopeful.

"Yeah. I get to stick around."

"C'mere." Tenley grabs him by the face and pulls him down, smacking a dry kiss on his cheek. "Oh, that makes me so happy."

Gideon's smile down at them is a fond, private thing. "Hey, I have a question for you."

They pat his cheeks and release him. "Anything."

"What would you do if you were trapped in a time loop?"

"Do you need to break out of it?" Tenley asks, all business yet again. "Are you happy in this time loop? There are philosophical considerations here."

"I'm not *unhappy*," Gideon says, and then seems to remember all at once that I'm there. "Oh, yeah. Tenley, I'd like you to meet my friend Laurie."

"Any friend of Gideon's is a friend of mine. Lovely to make your acquaintance," they say when I creep out from behind the aisle, and just like usual, there's no recognition in their eyes.

My heart twinges, but I manage a smile anyway. "Hey, Tenley. Nice to meet you."

Next, we go to Vern's.

"You know, I only got into World War II stuff because of these old journals I found in my house." Gideon picks up one of the model planes off the shelf. "Did I already tell you about that in one of the loops?"

"I know about the journals." I consider. *Jayda* told me, I'm pretty sure. At least, she mentioned them first. "Is it true that you found them because you punched a hole in the wall?"

Gideon makes a face. "Who told you that?"

"Ricky."

Technically, that's the truth, even if he wasn't strictly telling *me*.

"Well, it's true."

"Why'd you do it?"

"Are you asking me because you don't know, or because you *do* know, and you're curious about what I'm going to say?"

A little shiver runs up my spine, the way it always does when Gideon says something so on-the-nose. "I don't *know*," I clarify. "Depends how reliable you think Ricky is."

"Probably not very. What did he say?"

"Something not very nice about your mom."

Gideon's expression shutters. "I was upset. I didn't know he knew about that."

So I don't ask, even though I badly want to. "How do they connect with World War II?"

At that, he smiles. "Okay, so the journals span, like, a decade. The guy who wrote in them—his name was Andrew Fletcher—basically chronicled his experience of falling in love with his best friend. I got into researching history in the first place because I was trying to figure out what happened to him."

"And?"

"Well, he died in 2010."

"I think you know that's not what I was asking."

"I actually got in touch with his great-great-grandson a while back," Gideon says. "He told me they did get their happy ending."

I swallow, hard.

"He sent me some photos. Apparently, they got married as soon as it was legalized. It was a whole thing because apparently Andrew had been married for most of his life to Finley's sister."

"Messy."

"Lavender marriage," he corrects me.

"I see."

"Anyway, you asked how it connects to the war. Both Finch—that's how Andrew referred to Finley in the journals; it took me *ages* to figure out who he was talking about—and Andrew were in the RCAF. Royal Canadian Air Force," he adds hastily at the look on my face. "I'm trying to put together a timeline of their life. Well, two timelines. One will be for an exhibit in the museum, which will be really cool. Tenley's the one overseeing it."

"And the other?"

"The other's just for me," he says, smiling. "I don't know. There was something really healing about reading through this queer kid's story as he tried to figure out who he was. I got a little obsessive about it, actually."

"I'm glad they got their happy ending."

"Me too." Gideon's smile fades, expression settling as he

stares out the window, still turning the airplane around between his fingers. I could listen to him talk about this for *ages*. Then he catches me staring at him, and the corners of his mouth tick upward. "What?"

I blurt out, "Your eye's almost better."

It's true. The yellowing has almost entirely smudged out.

"Is it?" Gideon touches fingertips to the bridge of his nose. "I hadn't noticed."

Neither had I, which is disconcerting. I guess I just spent so much time looking at him, I was blind to the gradual changes.

Gideon seems unconcerned. "Anyway, how are we going to help *you* find yourself?"

"Well, I need to look for Val," I tell him, after a moment to think. Even though I'd like to keep killing time with Gideon indefinitely, I know there's a countdown to think about. My stomach flips. "Wherever she is. I've got no idea how we connect yet, and I only really have one lead."

"Which is?"

"Some guy Val knows named Lawrence."

Gideon's eyebrows spike. "There's a guy with *your* name wandering around, and we *haven't* been looking for him?"

"I've been busy," I say, and I wish he'd stop looking at me so he wouldn't notice that my ears are flushing hot.

00:54

FORTY.

"This is a terrible idea," I mutter.

Gideon snorts a laugh. "This was *your* idea."

"Don't remind me." I groan and slump forward against the steering wheel. "Why are we doing this again?"

"We can still leave," he points out. "But for the record, I do think it's worth a shot. You look for this Lawrence guy, and I'll see if I can make a scene and get Valerie's attention, if she's here."

I nod, but I still feel a little queasy, even if I don't really get why.

The Blanchettes' house is no less intimidating now that it's familiar. I'm earlier than I was last time, and still, the party is in full swing.

I find Bri completely by accident, because she's sitting on the front steps.

Even this early, she's still definitely been drinking by the time I get there. "Val!" she bursts out at the sight of me, eyes shining. "You came! Your *hair*!"

I fight the urge to wince. I was actually hoping to avoid her, if only because tonight I have a mission, and also because I don't want to explain Gideon.

Too late.

Bri goggles at him from her perch on the steps.

"This is Gideon," I say after a pause. "Gideon, this is Bri."

"Good to meet you," Gideon says. I've told him about Bri, and I can see it in his eyes, that curious glint, like he's trying to figure out what I could have done to make her upset.

"Likewise." Mad at me or not, Bri still catches my eye and without an ounce of subtlety mouths, *Holy shit.*

My cheeks flare with heat. Admittedly, he *does* cut a striking figure. Even halfway healed, the bruise around his eye lends him a dangerous edge, and that's *before* you factor in the ripped jeans and leather jacket, which I *didn't* stare at the entire drive up here, thank you very much.

"I'll meet you back here in an hour?" Gideon asks, and when I nod, he turns and disappears into the house.

"Who the *fuck* is *Gideon*?" Bri asks me, breathless, the second he's gone.

"Hockey friend."

"Has Brett met him?"

The thought of Brett and Gideon in the same room makes me feel like I'm covered in hives. I shake my head.

"I don't even like men, but I might make an exception for him," Bri says, and mimes fanning herself as she stares down the hallway where he'd gone.

I clear my throat. "*Anyway.* Speaking of hockey friends—have you seen Lawrence anywhere?"

Bri gives me a blank stare. Then she laughs. "What—you mean Matty?"

I fucking guess so. Is Lawrence a last name? "Yes."

"I haven't seen him yet."

Okay, *too* early.

"What do you need him for?"

"I just do," I tell her, distracted, and then I wander off without really meaning to, listening hard.

I don't make it ten steps before I'm accosted.

"Val?"

I crane my neck, trying to spot where Gideon's gotten to.

"*Val.*"

"What?" I snap, turning to face Brett at last.

I only catch the tail end of his expression as it shifts into shock.

His lips press together. "*Hi*," he says, pointedly. "Where have you been today?"

"Busy," I tell him absently, and I only feel a little bad, because this isn't real, and tomorrow he'll have forgotten it, and he is *not* my priority tonight.

"You cut your hair."

Terse, I say, "Yes."

"Can we talk?" He honestly sounds a bit pathetic. "Please?"

"Fine." I don't let Brett drag me to his bedroom. Instead, I take him by the hand and lead him out into their backyard, until we're around a corner and out of earshot of everyone else. "What's going on?"

"I love you," he says. "And I—I just wanted to say that I believe you. I'm sorry I ever insinuated there was something going on between you and Lawrence."

Okay, *now* we're getting somewhere. "Why did you think there was something going on?"

"I mean, I know you two have *some* kind of secret."

Brett can't *know*, right? There's *no* way Val told him the truth.

Then it all goes to shit, like, *instantly*.

"VALERIE EATON!" Gideon bellows from somewhere closer to the house. "THE REAL ONE! YOU KNOW WHO YOU ARE!"

Brett's head swivels. Derision coats his tone. "Who is *that*?"

"No one important," I lie, worn out. Gideon's still yelling, but not so loud, so I can't hear exactly what he's saying.

"So it's *not* Matty." Brett's jaw hardens.

"What are you talking about?"

"You're keeping something from me, and he knows what it is." Brett glowers. "I fucking *knew* there was someone."

"You *just* said you believed me that there wasn't."

"Yeah, because I'm looking for literally any proof that you're not a slut for anyone except me."

I have to blink for several seconds to parse meaning from that clusterfuck of a statement, and then I glare at him. "Hey Brett?"

"*What?*" he snaps.

My heart is hammering. "It's over. It's *so* over."

His mouth hangs open. "I—what's over?"

"You and me. We're done."

"I—what?"

"I don't want to do this anymore."

Brett stares at me, and then he shakes his head. "No."

"*No?*"

"Yeah, no." He keeps shaking his head.

"You just called me a *slut*."

"I didn't mean it. All couples go through rough patches. This is just—God is testing us."

"You *believe* in that shit?" I throw my arms up in the air. "Are you serious? It's not a front?"

"You *don't* believe in it?" Brett shakes his head like he's trying to rid his ears of water. "What is going *on* with you?"

"I'm gay," I burst out.

Technically, not a lie.

Brett goggles at me. "Who *are* you?"

"Not your girlfriend," I toss back, chest heaving, and then I have to whirl around and leave right that second, before I say anything I'm seriously not proud of.

The second I'm out of his sight, I stop and cover my mouth with my hand, breathing hard, bent at the waist. It's not my breakup—it's not my *life*, but actually coming out—even if it's Val's truth, and only mine in an inside-out way—makes me feel like I just ran a race.

Then, on my way back around the house, I nearly run straight into somebody.

"Are you okay?"

Yet another fucking person I don't know. This guy is tall and blond—he has a serious Achilles vibe going on—and he puts both hands on my shoulders. "Eaton? You good?"

I snap out of it, blinking rapidly. "Uh, yeah. I have to go."

Turning, I pull out of this stranger's grasp, and I don't make it another three steps before I hear someone call after me—no, after the *stranger*—jovially, "What's up, Lawrence?"

Oh shit.

My stomach swoops, and I whip back around just as his hand closes around my wrist.

"Listen, I've been looking for you," he says, voice low and urgent. "We need to talk."

FORTY-ONE.

VAL

"What were you and Lawrence talking about?" Brett asks as he pulls into Centennial Park, breaking the silence in the truck that's been stretching ever since we pulled out of the drive-in ten minutes ago.

"Graduation." It's barely a half-truth, and I'm not even sure I feel bad. It's not like I can tell him what we were *actually* talking about, which only leaves Matty's boy problems, and Brett gets a little weird whenever it occurs to him that Matty isn't straight as an arrow.

Don't get me wrong, Brett's not a homophobe, obviously. He's always been great about Bri. It's just that I think the *bisexual* thing confuses him. Not in that outdated *pick a side* way either, but it's just another thing that sets Matty apart and makes him a little different. A little unreachable.

If you're not willing to reach very far.

"Told you it was a date," Brett says with a soft little smile as he cuts the engine.

I take his hand in the parking lot and trail after him as we walk in silence down the cement path, veering off the grass. Kicking off my shoes, I let go of his hand to pick them up, relishing the soft grass underfoot.

After a long while, Brett stops. "I need to ask you something."

"Okay." Trepidation churns in my stomach as I shield my eyes from the setting sun.

"I heard what Lawrence asked you."

My chest tightens. "What do you mean?"

"At school this morning. *Did you tell him yet?*" Brett traces air quotes around the words. "You weren't really talking about the car, and you weren't talking about your dad."

Is there a point in protesting?

"I'm *him*, right?"

I stay silent, because it's true.

"What did that mean, exactly?" Brett takes a deep breath. "If something happened between you and Matty, you can tell me."

I stare at him for several seconds before his words compute. "I'm sorry—are you asking me if I *cheated* on you?"

Brett's jaw tightens. "I didn't want to say it like *that*."

But, yeah.

"Matty and I are just friends," I tell him, tone brittle.

"You kissed him," Brett points out.

"We were twelve!" I laugh, this sharp sound I hate even as I make it.

He seems to hate it too, if the way his expression twists is anything to go by. "I don't know, maybe feelings linger!"

"I do not have feelings for Matty," I snap, and it's true.

"But—"

"I kissed Matty *once*, when we were twelve, and nothing has happened between us since then." That's also true. Helpless, frustrated, I run a hand through my hair, wincing as my fingers catch in a tangle. "Where is this even coming from?"

"I found it," he says, voice low. "Or, I mean, I *saw* it in your closet last time I was over."

Matty's sweatshirt.

Fucking hell. My stomach drops. Okay, yeah, I can see how that might look—he gave it to me, is all, and I just kept it. I *should* have given it back, but he never asked, and it's been this little reminder ever since of why self-control is important. *Essential.*

Plus, it's really comfortable. And it makes me feel a little like . . .

Well, that doesn't matter right now.

"It's not like that," I insist. "Matty gave me his sweatshirt one time, and I keep forgetting to return it. It means nothing."

"What could you *possibly* have been talking about, then? If that's not it?" Brett asks, voice raised, and to my horror and total mortification, my eyes sting and my heart starts pounding.

I turn away to cover my face with my hands.

Get it together. You cannot fall apart every time someone yells at you.

"Oh shit." Brett sounds exasperated more than anything else. "Don't cry, Val. I'm sorry, I shouldn't have—I'm sorry, let's talk about this rationally."

I blink furiously until I'm certain I won't cry. "Why would you accuse me of something like that?" I look up slowly. "Do you *want* it to be true?"

His mouth drops. "*What?*"

"Do you?"

"Why the hell would I want it to be true?"

"It might be nice," I say, heart pounding, "if you had an *actual* reason to end it, right? Something that no one could possibly fault you for."

"What are you—I have *no* idea what you mean."

"I'm not a *moron*." I shake my head. All at once it feels stupid that I'm holding this milkshake, stupid that I'm standing barefoot in the grass, and Brett's looking at me like he *does* think I'm a moron. "All we ever do is fight, or talk about *nothing*, or hang out with your friends, and I just—what's the point?"

Brett swallows, hard. A muscle works in his jaw. "What's the point of *what*?"

"Don't pretend like you're excited about four years apart," I say. "I know I'm not."

"Of course I'm not excited," Brett says slowly, "but that doesn't mean I want to *break up*."

"Don't you? Do you even like me?"

"I *love* you," he says urgently, taking my milkshake and setting it down on the grass along with his, straightening to take my face in both of his hands. "Val, I love you."

"That's not what I asked."

Cutting through the thick silence, my phone rings.

FORTY-TWO.

For just a moment, the nightmare isn't real.

This stranger—*Lawrence*—is sort of dazzling. At once, I have the same impression I did of Gideon when we were still virtually strangers, where I'm not sure if I want him to like me or if I want to look like he does.

Either way, the surge of longing is so powerful that for a second I just stare at him, mouth half-open. "*You're* Lawrence."

"Well, to some." He looks so disarmed that my heart sinks.

"And to others?" I ask, on edge, begging, *Say it, say you're Valerie, please.*

Lawrence doesn't. He just gives me a sharp look. "I mean, Matty, mostly." I must look crestfallen, because he takes me by the shoulder. "Hey, are you okay?"

"I've been hoping for something," I tell him. "It didn't pan out."

"Do you mind if I ask you what?"

I stare at him, and then I shake my head. "What did you need to talk to me about?"

"Brett." He sinks down onto the steps leading up to the back garage. He pats the concrete next to him. "Come on. Sit with me a minute?"

I sit. "What about Brett?"

"It's not been very cool of me to be so intense about telling him," he says. "It's your relationship. Therefore, it's your business."

Valerie, you messy bitch.

"We broke up," I blurt out.

"Good," he says, and then freezes.

I laugh despite myself.

"Yeah, good. Fuck, I know as his best friend I'm probably not supposed to say that. But as *your* friend, I just—you haven't seemed happy in a while. Neither of you have."

"Has he said something to you?"

"I just know him. And I know you." He nudges my knee. "I'm happy for you, for the record."

I nod. "Thanks."

"What did you mean, *I'm* Lawrence?" he asks. "You sounded . . . confused."

I give him a wan smile. "I'm just sorting through some stuff."

"Aren't we all?" Lawrence sighs, and the smile he gives me is so brilliant I can't help but smile back. "But you'll figure it out. You always do."

When I find Gideon by the pool, he's surrounded by a group of girls.

"What do you want with Val, anyway?" one of them is saying. "She's taken, you know."

"So I've heard." Gideon sees me coming and hides a grin in his shoulder.

"Did you see her hair?" one of them whispers to another. "It's like, what kind of statement is she trying to make, you know? I just feel bad for Brett. She looks like a—"

I clear my throat, gratified when they both whirl and jump.

"Val!" one of them says, way too brightly. She has sleek, long brown hair and freckles, one of those perfect princess noses set over heart-shaped lips. A silver cross dangles from a chain around her neck. Her voice takes on a nervous, sing-song cast. "*Hey!*"

"You can go now," Gideon says to the girls, eyes locked on me, and I'm sort of obsessed with him. "Also, consider being less rude. It's not cute."

The freckled girl flushes scarlet as she and her friends turn tail.

Gideon grins at me. "You ready to go?"

"You look like you're having fun." I could *eat* him right now. It's not even that those girls were actually bothering me, but it's the fact that I think he might say that for *anyone*.

He gives me a brief look, smile wavering. "You look like you . . . aren't."

I've *got* to start paying attention to what my face is doing. At least I *have* a good excuse. Wryly, I tell him, "Yeah, well, your little stunt just lost Val a boyfriend, so thanks for that."

"That bad, huh?"

I shrug.

"Yikes," he says. Then, as he walks past, Gideon hip-checks me into the pool.

Sound vanishes. The world mutes as cool water surrounds

me, flooding my mouth and nose, and I emerge, spluttering and gasping. "*Gideon!*"

"You looked like you could use it," he says, looking so pleased with himself that I *laugh*, still spitting water.

"You're such an asshole!" I tell him, but then we've started a chain reaction, and a half-dozen kids follow suit and jump into the pool after me.

I haul myself out of the water onto my stomach, up over the edge, but it's like now that laughter has taken root, it's rippling through me, this breathless mirth that I have no control over, and Gideon's laughing too.

He holds out a hand to let me up. I take it, ignoring the rush that sings through me at the contact, and then I try to use my leverage to yank him off balance, but he's too strong.

"Nice try." Gideon smiles down at me, and then lets go of my hand, blinking up at somebody past my field of vision.

"Valerie Eaton," Bri says, from above me, hands on her hips. She *sounds* mad, but there's a quirk in her lips that I recognize somehow. "You are *wasted*."

There are pictures of the three girls plastered all over Bri's room.

There are pictures of her and Ibha alone, and some of the two of us, but mostly it's the three of us, arms around each other.

Like we were a trio. Like we were a trio for *years*, I think, examining one from when both Ibha and I had braces. Bri's whole room is painted a soft yellow, and she takes the hand towel from me. I'm wearing her sweatpants now, so short on me they leave two inches of exposed leg above my ankle. I've told her twice that I'm stone-cold sober, and maybe it's because she's definitely *not*, but my protests have fallen on deaf ears.

"Who the hell was that?" Brett asks from the doorway. "First I heard someone shouting for you, and now there's this fucking guy from *Nanton* in my yard and he's pushing you in the pool or some shit?"

Oh Christ. Did Brett talk to Gideon?

"You know, you could have just said there was someone else," he says, scowling. "I'm not a moron, Val."

"Go away, Brett." Bri shuts the door in his face, then whips around to face me. "Excuse me, *Valerie*. Is this how I'm finding out that you two *broke up*?"

"Maybe?" I wince. Bri's a wildcard. I have no idea how she's going to react. "Are you mad?"

"Are you *kidding*? I pitched a *fit* when you told me he kissed you, because I thought you were going to be awful together. And I was right, by the way! You *are* awful together. He's too—too—like, don't get me wrong, I love him to death, but he has *no* idea what to do with you."

I cover my mouth with my hand so she won't see me laugh, but it doesn't matter. She's grinning at me.

"God, I'm *so* relieved. I would have continued to support you guys, but I'm *so* glad I don't have to." Then she straightens. "Wait. Are you sad?"

When I shake my head, her smile takes on a mischievous cast.

"What?"

"It *does* have something to do with Gideon, doesn't it?"

"Absolutely not."

"You are *such* a liar." Bri swats me with the end of the towel, shaking her head, but she doesn't push it.

And somehow, I know she's holding back something important. Suspiciously, I add, "Say whatever it is you're not saying."

Bri shakes her head. "It's nothing."

"It's not nothing."

She bites her lip. "It's just been a long time since I've seen you laugh like that. Maybe since Eli left."

My smile fades. "Bri . . ."

"What?"

I don't even know what triggers the thought. It's like something in my head—in the deep recesses of the part of my brain I can't access—yanks an emergency ripcord. I blurt out, "What happened with you and Ibha?"

Bri's expression shutters. She turns away from me, balling up the towel in her hands.

Carefully, I probe deeper. "Why didn't you say anything when she said she didn't want to break up?"

"You talked to her?" Bri frowns. "Look, she acted like I should be *happy* that she was moving. It felt like she was trying to get rid of me."

"What if she wasn't?" I press. "Bri, do you still love her?"

"I've loved her since I first saw her," she snaps, like it's supposed to be obvious. "What do you know? Did she call you too?"

Too? I've lost the plot.

I shake my head. "I don't know anything. I guess I just... tonight's got me thinking, is all."

"No kidding," Bri says. "You know, I didn't think you were going to come."

"Neither did I." I don't even know if I'm speaking for me or for Valerie.

00:50

FORTY-THREE.

"Do you think you'll die?" Gideon asks me one evening.

We're walking back to the farmhouse across the neighbor's field. I don't even *know* where my car is. It's been that kind of day—a wanderer's day, trying to make up for the chaos of inserting ourselves into Val's life. We've walked so much there are hotspots on my heels, and I'm still not ready for the day to be over.

"Jeez." I shoot Gideon a glance out of the corner of my eye. "That came out of nowhere."

"Sorry. I can find a smooth segue into it, if you want."

I laugh. "I don't mind. Do you mean, like, at the end of the loop? Or just generally? Because I *don't* think this time loop solves immortality, unless the fountain of youth is in Nanton."

Gideon laughs. "You *know* what I meant."

"I don't know what will happen when we get to zero." A nasty lurch in the pit of my stomach sends bile searing up the back of my throat. "Maybe."

"Maybe," he echoes.

I don't want to talk about this. "Want to go to that party?"

He shakes his head. "There's only so many times we can go to the same party before it gets old."

"You're telling me." I shoot him a little smile. We've actually only been to the barn party twice together, but both times I spent the whole time wishing we were alone somewhere else. Plus, I could do without Wyatt glowering at me from the corner.

Usually, we steer clear of the Perrigan house until it's unavoidable.

But today we just sort of naturally find our way inside. Mrs. Perrigan is home, but she's up in her sewing room, and one of the girls passes us wearing enormous headphones and doesn't spare me so much as a double-take.

Gideon makes us sandwiches. I lean against the counter and watch him while the overhead light reflects off the shiny linoleum. The kitchen is clearly the most recently updated part of the house: sleek chrome fixtures shine, and the appliances are just as nice as the ones in Valerie's kitchen.

We eat cross-legged on the living-room floor, and when I get crumbs on the carpet, Gideon grinds them in with his thumb and a wide grin.

"This house," I start, fingertips resting on the well-worn floor. "Do you like it here?"

"It's not always so bad." Gideon looks up at the mantel, where there's an enormous family photo that he and Jayda are notably absent from. "I mean, the Perrigans are fine. So long as I'm not myself, like, ever, and keep quiet and keep Jayda out of trouble."

"Sounds like paradise," I say dryly.

"If something is a *big* deal, they don't actually make that much of a fuss about it. Like when Ricky drove their new car into the front sign of the church, *nobody* knew about it. I only knew it was him because I was listening through the vents when they were talking about it."

"I guess that's good parenting."

"I think it's more like embarrassment." Gideon shakes his head. "I think they hate the idea of anyone knowing—"

A loud banging on the front door interrupts him mid-thought. He frowns up at the entrance to the mudroom.

Then a woman calls, "Gideon!"

All traces of amusement and curiosity drain from his expression as he stills.

The banging starts up again.

Gideon swears under his breath and gets to his feet. "One second."

I stay on the floor for all of thirty seconds after the door opens before I get up and follow.

From where I am behind Gideon, I can't make out more than a silhouette and the left arm of the woman standing on the porch outside the mudroom.

"You're a good boy," she's whispering by the time I get within earshot. Her voice is a low smoker's rasp. Traditional American tattoos blur under sun-browned, leathery skin, and her frizz of hair is a brassy blond, blue eyes under drooping eyelids smudged with dark kohl liner. When she touches a hand to his cheek he doesn't flinch exactly, but a muscle works in his jaw and the line of his shoulder tightens so that I have to resist the urge to step forward and tell her to back off.

Gideon's shoulders are a tense line. "I said not to come here again."

"Gideon—"

"I *told* you," he says. "There's a reason we live here and not with you, remember?"

She doesn't even flinch. "Where's Jay?"

"You already know I'm not telling you that," Gideon says, and then he shuts the door in her face.

I step back the second he does, but not so fast that I don't see the look on his face in the split second before he turns to face me entirely. Crushed like flimsy aluminum.

He looks through the peephole in the door for a full two minutes before he sighs. "My mom."

And even though I'd pieced that together, it sends a little jolt through me.

Gideon runs a thumb along his bottom lip, lost in thought. "She must have been coming here every night, and we never knew."

"What does she want?"

"What does she ever want?" His tone is wry and bitter. "Access to Jay, mostly. And if I give it to her, Jay will talk me into giving her whatever it is she's asking for, because she's *always* trying to get her shit together so we can be a family. Always. Once, she even almost got there."

"Oh, Gideon."

"She's been writing me," he says, slowly. "She's been writing Jay too. But Jay doesn't know. I can't let her see those letters. It would break her heart, and I can't—I can't put her through that again."

I hesitate. "Are you okay?"

"I don't really want to talk about it," he says. "Nothing personal. It's just—"

"I get it, I promise." I hold both hands up. "No need to justify."

Gideon sits back down in the living room, glowering at his half-finished sandwich. "Did I ever tell you why they're sending me away?"

"No. I asked once, but you didn't want to tell me, so I didn't ask again."

"It's Ricky's fault."

My eyebrows lift.

"Drugs," Gideon says darkly. "They found a brick of weed in the wall. Which, first, even if I *was* hiding a brick of weed, I would never put it there. That's a dumb hiding spot. Second, I don't even smoke."

"Right. How do you know it was Ricky?"

"Who else would it be?" He gestures wide, sounding weary. "Ricky's in with Knox. I know it was him."

Interesting.

"I *know* it," Gideon says, and it almost sounds like he's trying to convince himself. "I just do."

00:45

FORTY-FOUR.

"Oh, for fuck's sake." I huff. "Budge over. *You* wanted to do this, remember?"

Sunshine beats down on my back. The rubber raft lurches as we pivot around a sharp corner.

"Well, I *did*, but now I feel like I might be sick." Gideon's knuckles are white around the rubber handle.

"If you're going to throw up, do it outside of the raft," I tell him, and the woman next to him scoots over with a nervous little laugh.

"M'not going to throw up," Gideon mumbles, but he does look a bit green.

"Cross rafting off your bucket list."

"Put it on my 'fuck it' list instead."

At least he's still coherent enough to make jokes.

"It's almost over," I assure him.

We're two hours west today, rafting in Banff. *I'm* enjoying it, but Gideon's been pale and peaky for most of the afternoon.

"Well?" he asks afterward, toweling his hair dry at the edge of the river. "Ring any bells?"

"Nope." I shake my head. "I have no idea whether I've even been on a raft before."

He wrinkles his nose.

"It was a good suggestion, though," I add. "We'll find something else that was muscle memory like skating was one of these days."

"It's not a good day unless you learn something new about yourself," Gideon says, and then he yanks his wet shirt off over his head and collapses onto the grass.

It's not ogling, exactly.

Okay, it is. I'm just not sure what *else* I'm supposed to do. I've never seen anything as magnetic as the way muscle shifts under Gideon's skin as he moves.

I'm way too self-conscious to remove my own shirt, so I just sit down in the damp fabric, hoping the sun will be enough to dry me off. I ask, "Can't it be a good day even if all we did was have fun?"

He cracks an eye, squinting at me suspiciously.

"What?" I cross my arms across my chest.

"I think you are possibly the most anxious person I've ever met in my life."

"Is that related or are you just being kind of a dick?"

The suspicion melts off his face as he grins. "No, I just mean, who the hell is speaking right now? You're halfway through a time loop that's *going* to run out, you don't know what happens at the end, and you're talking about *having fun* being all you'd need to call a good day good."

My face flares with heat. "Uh, c'est la vie?"

Gideon laughs, then shakes his head. "I will *never* understand you."

"I'm not sorry," Gideon whispers. He's so close I can make out flecks of green in his eyes.

I've never noticed them before. They're sort of beautiful. *He's* sort of beautiful.

We're sitting cross-legged on the roof of the car. Stars spread over us, though the darkest part of the night is over. In the east, the light purple of dawn threatens to bring another day. Another reset. If I moved forward an inch, my knees would touch Gideon's.

Gideon's wearing the sweatshirt from Val's go-bag. It even fits him—I think it's a guy's to begin with—and every time I look at him, something lurches in my gut.

"What are you not sorry about?" I ask.

"I'm not sorry I made you and that Brett guy break up."

"Technically, you made *Val* and 'that Brett guy' break up, so I'm not the one you owe an apology to."

"Oh, come on. You know he sucks. Didn't you say he called you a frigid bitch?"

"He did say that, yes."

"So, point proven."

"But why aren't you sorry?"

Gideon picks at his bracelets. All he says is, "He sucks."

After a moment, I ask, "And?"

"You deserve better."

"What makes you think you know what I deserve?"

"I just do."

I shake my head with a little smile as the sky behind Gideon shifts, pink to pale yellow, purple edges pushing toward the indigo above us and swallowing the stars one by one. "You seem to have a strong sense of justice."

"How do you mean?"

I stifle a yawn and gesture at his eye, even though the bruise is gone now.

"That's different." Gideon grimaces. "He hit first, for the record. And hardest. I found out he was sleeping with her, and not even because he *likes* her," he bursts out. "The way he talked about it made it sound like he was only doing it to get to me. And he's *eight* years older than her. It's not okay. You get why I said something, right?"

"Of course," I murmur. "I'm not judging you."

"She deserves better." His tone slides, colorless. "I couldn't do *nothing*."

I swallow down a lump in my throat.

"Laurie." Gideon's voice is unbearably gentle.

All of a sudden, I can't breathe. There's just *something* about his tone. My voice is a rasp. "Yes?"

"*You* deserve better too. Forget Val for a minute."

"Brett's not *my* boyfriend, though."

"I know." Gideon rests his hands on his knees, staring down at his fingers.

Sitting like this, his knuckles are only a half inch from mine.

When he finally speaks, it's not what I think he's going to say. "When did the looping get old for you?"

I have to blink down at the car.

It . . . hasn't. Has it gotten old for *Gideon*?

Slowly, I ask, "Why?"

"No reason," Gideon says, and it doesn't sound true at all. Then he heaves a sigh and shifts, farther from me. "What do we do next?"

I recognize a change of subject when I hear one, but I decide not to push it. Heaving a sigh, I shake my head. "I don't know. I get that her life is kind of stressful, and I get why she'd want to stay away from it, but I just keep wondering . . . why isn't Val looking for me?"

"Maybe she is," Gideon points out. "You don't know that she isn't."

I make a noncommittal noise.

"Maybe you just keep missing each other," he adds. "Like ships in the—"

00:44

FORTY-FIVE.

I blink rapidly, hands on the steering wheel.

Christ. Hello?

The field whips past me, the low rumble of asphalt an accompaniment to my confusion.

"Did you fall asleep?" Gideon asks when I find him on the side of the road, tractor abandoned. "I didn't think I was being *that* dull."

I smile despite myself. "No. I forgot to pay attention to the time. I reset a little after six."

Gideon kicks the wheel. "Well, that sucks."

"Does it?"

"I mean, sort of. What if you really wanted to get to tomorrow?"

"Yeah, I think wanting it isn't enough. You think I'm still here because I didn't *wish* hard enough?" I ask dryly.

Gideon's the one to suggest going back to Valerie's house. As if we might glean more clues there. I'm starting to think that if Gideon had been the one stuck in the time loop, he'd have figured it out within a matter of days. I'll admit, having someone around constantly reminding me of the countdown *is* adding to the overall sense of urgency.

Forty-four days to go.

The second the door opens, the Devil is at my ankles.

"Oh, *fuck* off," I snarl, batting at her. "Sorry, I should have warned you. Evil dog."

"Evil," Gideon echoes, clearly bemused at the sight of the Devil's rhinestone collar.

"Oh, just you wait."

There's a flashing light on the answering machine. A voicemail, probably from the school. I press the button to delete it.

A voice echoes through the house. "Valerie?"

Oh, for fuck's sake.

Gideon's eyebrows lift, but I don't have time to warn him about *anything* before Cheryl is rounding the corner.

"Mom." I swallow. "Hey."

The moment she sees me, Cheryl freezes. Her mouth opens and closes like a fish, and after *several* seconds, all she manages is, "Your—your *hair*. What did you *do*?"

"I cut it." I don't even add *duh*, even though it takes a Herculean effort.

That's when she notices Gideon. Her whole expression shifts, a wide, false smile. "Oh, hello!"

"Hi," Gideon says as the Devil sniffs his shoes with aggressive attention.

"This is Gideon," I tell Cheryl.

"Valerie." That false smile widens. "Can I speak with you a moment?"

I let her drag me into the kitchen.

"What is going *on*?" She whirls on me the second we're alone. "Your hair, and—and you've never mentioned a Gideon before."

"He's a new friend," I tell her.

"A church friend?"

"Yeah," I say, because, *whatever*. "Listen, we're just going to go upstairs, I'm—"

"You absolutely may not have a boy in your bedroom. I don't care *who* he is."

I whip around to face her. "Cheryl?"

Her mouth drops open, that nearly comical *my daughter might as well have just slapped me* look on her face.

"I don't have to listen to you," I say. "There's not going to be any *funny* business, if that's what you're worried about. This is important. We'll be up in my room."

"Do not—" Her voice narrows to a choked rasp. "Do *not* take that tone with me, young lady."

"I'll take whatever tone I want," I tell her, and then I turn on my heel and walk away.

When I come back into the hallway, I find Gideon still by the door, but now he's crouched low.

The Devil has her front paws up on his knee, tail wagging at a million kilometers an hour as she strains to try to reach his face, covering his hands with little kisses.

His tone shifts into a croon. "*Hi*, baby. Oh, you're a good girl, aren't you? You're so pretty."

I stare at him, slack-jawed.

"Yes, you are." He scratches her between the ears, then picks her up. She goes without complaint, snuffling at his ear. "Yes, you *are*. Oh, you're a little sweetheart, aren't you?"

"Honestly, this is a colossal betrayal," I tell him. Then, with a wince, I ask, "Did you hear any of that?"

"Every word," he tells me solemnly. Then he offers his knuckles for a fist bump with his free hand.

"Come on," I say, "before she recovers too much."

"I feel like she might *actually* put you in a straitjacket," Gideon whispers, and I stifle a laugh.

We scour Valerie's bedroom. I spend more time watching Gideon while he looks—I've seen everything already, after all—but he doesn't have to know that. He can't put the Devil down or she starts barking down by his ankles, so he carts her around the room tucked under his arm as he inspects Valerie's belongings, looking increasingly amused.

"You weren't kidding about the Bibles." Gideon runs his fingers along the spines. "Yeesh."

"I wonder how much she really believes it." I step forward, a little closer. "Do you?"

"Do I believe in *God*?" Gideon laughs. "No. Do you?"

"I don't know. I don't think so. I also don't think it matters."

He gives me a little smile, lingering by an encyclopedia of car-engine types with well-worn pages, like she actually *uses* it as a reference book, *God*, Valerie. "Respectable approach."

"What do you think of Cheryl?"

He purses his lips, clearly trying not to laugh. "She sure is . . . something."

"You don't have to be polite," I point out. "She's not *my* mom."

"I hate her," he says immediately, and I burst out laughing. "Could you *imagine* growing up with her?"

I shake my head, still smiling. "Honestly, I don't know how Val hasn't psychologically snapped and driven into oncoming traffic by now."

Gideon pulls out the encyclopedia with distinct amusement.

"I've *been* telling you she's a loser," I say.

"Everyone has their coping mechanisms." He flips it open, thumbing through the pages one-handed. "It's kind of cute."

I raise both eyebrows and shake my head, staying out of his field of vision as he moves to put the book down, sucking in a sharp breath as something flutters out from between the pages.

It's another Polaroid, of the very same car I've been driving around in. On the back of it, someone—Valerie, presumably—wrote *Lincoln Bought a Car* in looping cursive, which makes very little sense.

Looking at it makes my stomach lurch.

"Who's Lincoln?" Gideon asks, looking over my shoulder.

I stare down at the name. *Lincoln*. It's the only other name that makes as much sense to me as *Laurie* had, right from the beginning. Instinctual. Important. I'm aware of how dazed I sound when I say, "Someone that matters."

"Are you remembering something?" Gideon's on high alert at once.

My head throbs. I squeeze my eyes shut, and I'm on the verge of something enormous, I can feel it.

But it fades like a lost sneeze.

I groan, knocking my head against the bookshelf. "I really wish I was."

FORTY-SIX.

Time moves differently with Gideon stuck here too.

It's slipperier, somehow. I keep forgetting urgency, and every time I remember that eventually we'll run out of days, my stomach lurches like I've just realized I left the house and didn't turn off the stove.

"I come up here sometimes when I need to think," Gideon says one evening. He's been quiet all day, and now he leads me up onto the roof from the balcony at his house, like it's something we've done already a dozen times before.

And I do need to think. All day, I've been turning the name *Lincoln* around in my head and hoping something sticks.

No luck.

From where I'm perched next to him, I can see past the trees that encircle the farmhouse, looking out over the fields toward the rolling foothills. "It's lovely."

He smiles, and it's almost grim.

We're quiet for a long time. Clouds pass overhead, swallows flashing silhouettes above us as the sun sinks toward the mountains.

"Why do you think you're here?"

I manage a laugh. "Is there any point in speculating?"

"Speculate," Gideon urges, and knocks his knee against mine.

"Okay, well, I'm pretty sure Val tried to come out to her parents," I tell him, shifting my feet on the gritty shingles. "She tried to, and she couldn't. Didn't. Maybe—maybe the universe *is* trying to give her a second chance. Maybe somewhere out there, I need one too."

Overhead, the sky blossoms, orange and pink fading through purple to a twilight blue.

I sigh, leaning back on my arms. "Damn. That's a sunset if I've ever seen one."

"And it happens every night." This time, his smile looks real, even if it fades right away. "Isn't that crazy? We've never seen it from up here."

And here we are, sixty-six days in. It took us that long to see the sky like this, and that's a comfort, of sorts. Even in a day that repeats, there are new little pockets of delight. Something beautiful hiding around the corner.

"You said you come up here when you need to think," I say. "What are you thinking about?"

He stays quiet.

Cautiously, I ask, "Gideon?"

"You think we could break the loop?" he asks, leaning to the side just enough that his shoulder bumps against mine for a moment. "Or will it break by itself when we hit zero?"

"I don't have the answer to either of those questions, and you know it," I tell him.

"Well." His voice is matter-of-fact. "We *have* to break it. Before zero."

A twinge in my chest pulls like a finger on a harp string, so swift and subtle that it hurts. "Got bored with me so fast?"

"No," he says firmly. "Stop that. It's not like that."

"Then what is it like?"

"We *have* to figure it out," he insists, and there's a bite to his tone I don't recognize, a resoluteness that tears along my skin, a painful jagged edge. "I want *out*."

"Why are you being so intense about this all of a sudden?" I ask. "I know it's not—it's not *excellent*, exactly, but you never have to—if we break the loop, they're going to send you *away*."

"I know," he says, infuriatingly calm. "Laurie, I—"

"So you—you *want* to leave?" I blink rapidly. "Is it really so miserable to—"

I can't even finish the sentence, my chest is too tight. Aching. I turn my face away, tucking my knees to my chest. *Be with me.*

"Laurie," he repeats. "*Look* at me."

I do, reluctantly, blinking over at him and hoping he can't tell that I'm about to cry.

Gideon touches two fingers to the side of my face, and there's something in his expression that leaves me breathless.

"What?"

"Laurie," he says softly, a third time. He takes a breath, and then just *looks*.

Wonderingly, I stare at him. It's all I can do while he's looking at me like this, like he's pinning me in place with the force of his gaze.

I swallow, skin burning where he's touching it. "Gideon?"

"I'm going to say it back now, okay?" he murmurs, running his thumb along my cheek.

My mouth drops open. "You're . . . *what*?"

Gideon laughs, and then he leans forward and presses a kiss between my eyebrows, pulling away to rest his forehead against mine.

My heart pounds fast and high at the back of my throat.

"I have to be sent away," he murmurs. "You get that, right? I *have* to go, so that I can come back, because I—I'm falling in love with you, Laurie, and I want to come back, and I want to have—I want a *life*, you know? One that has tomorrows. I want tomorrows, and I want you in them."

Eyes smarting, my breath quivers. "You—you do?"

"Yeah," he murmurs. "Yeah, I really do."

I can't breathe. I can't *move*. I feel like—maybe I'm dreaming or something.

But I'm not dreaming. The breeze against the back of my neck is very, *very* real. There are the shingles under my bare feet and Gideon's forehead against mine, and somehow I'm not touching him and I think, probably, that's criminal.

So I reach for him, trembling.

"You know, I keep almost asking you about something," he whispers, when my hand finds his shoulder.

I swallow hard. "What?"

"We had all of those loops before I was in it with you."

I nod.

"You said sometimes I tried to kiss you. Did I ever actually do it?"

"One time," I say, a little tremulously, "you asked if you could, and I said no."

He brushes a strand of hair out of my eyes. "Why?"

"Because I wanted you to remember it," I whisper, dangerously close to tears.

"I'm going to remember this for the rest of my life," Gideon tells me, and then he lifts my chin and leans in to kiss me.

It's the sort of kiss that knocks the wind out of me.

Gideon kisses me, and everything in the world narrows down to this. He kisses me, and for just a moment I forget that we've never done this before, because his lips against mine feel so *right*.

At *last*, I wind my fingers through his hair to pull him closer, deepening the kiss, and then it's over way sooner than I'd like.

I stay perfectly still when he pulls away to rest his forehead against mine again. My heart is still hammering, the loudest thing in the evening air. Exhale trembling, I ask, "You mean it?"

"I couldn't keep not saying it back," Gideon whispers, pressing feather-light kisses to my cheek, my jaw, the tip of my nose.

"Don't say that," I tell him. "Don't, I might cry."

"Well, *that* would be a deal-breaker," he says, smiling, and then when I let out a wet laugh, he kisses away the tear that escapes.

"The rest of my life," he repeats, a promise. "I'll never forget this. I'll never forget *you*."

And this time I believe it.

00:33

FORTY-SEVEN.

The nightmare is an afterthought.

I open my eyes and slam on the brakes, pulling off onto the side of the road, kicking up gravel and dust in my wake, just like every other time I've stopped too quickly.

It's not a dream.

Gideon laughs breathlessly when I get out of my car to greet him, smiling so widely the echo of it burns in my cheeks, and when I fling my arms around his neck, he lifts me straight off the ground. I wrap my legs around his waist, and it feels like *this* is the moment I've already lived seventy times.

"Hi," he whispers, right in my ear.

I can't stop grinning. "Hi."

"I'm almost glad that didn't break the loop," he tells me.

"No *almost*," I tell him as he lets me down, and I'd kiss him if he wasn't already stepping away. "I'm just glad."

"'Course you are," he says, and I'm too happy to snark back, *What's that supposed to mean?* so I just smile wide.

The urgency of the loop evades me all day. I can't make myself think about anything but this moment as we sit side by side in the grass behind the farmhouse, tucked out of sight, ankles a tangle.

Gideon's thinking about it though. I can see it in his face. We're cycling through fruitless thumb wars—he keeps winning, and I don't even care, I just like that I get to touch his hands now—and he's been quiet for the last half an hour.

"What?" I ask at last.

He heaves a sigh and traps my thumb. "I'm trying to decide if I should be offended that I'm not your true love."

I splutter a laugh, indignant until I catch the edge of the smirk that means he's joking. Only making a halfhearted effort to escape from under his thumb, I remind him, "That was *your* theory, not mine."

Gideon smiles agreeably. "It's not that I *thought* saying how I felt would break the loop, but it's got me wondering. It changed things when you did it, right?"

My face burns. "We still don't know if that was what looped you in."

"It was a theory."

I yank my thumb out from under his, daring a glance up at him. He's watching me from under his lashes, a soft smile playing at the corners of his mouth. "Have you decided whether you're offended yet?"

"Immensely," he says gravely, and lets me trap his thumb. "I have a lot riding on this, you know."

"Oh?"

"Well, it all hinges on getting out of this time loop, so. You can get on that now, thanks." He winks. "How *do* you think you'll fix it?"

"I think when Val and I meet, we'll swap," I tell him, as confidently as I can. "Wherever Valerie is, I think we'll *know* when we find each other and everything will set back to normal."

He stills. "You think?"

"Yeah. Like, on sight."

"That's not how it worked in *Freaky Friday*. They were together all the time."

"Well, I don't think Valerie is my mother."

"Maybe you're her dad."

"Yeah, you *do* realize you have no idea what I look like, right? I could be totally off-putting."

"Maybe I don't care." Gideon traps my thumb again. "Ever thought of that?"

"You can't just *not* care." Laughing, I try to wriggle out from under the pressure, but I can't.

"Why would I care?"

"Maybe I smell bad."

"Oh yeah, and that's a problem that can't be solved in about five minutes."

"Maybe you'll think I'm ugly."

"You are *full* of potential disasters, aren't you?" He prods my shoulder with his index finger. "What are you *really* worried about here?"

"It's just—you *always* flirted with me," I point out. "*Every* time we met. That was based on how I looked, wasn't it?"

"I mean, I can't speak for me of, like, forty-odd yesterdays, but I think that was only at *first* because of how you looked." He tilts his head. "And then I was just, like, blown away by your showstopper personality."

"Maybe I *am* Valerie's dad, and I'm, like, fifty. Did you think of that?"

"I bet you'd be a DILF," he says with a little grin.

I burst out laughing. "You don't think there's something potentially problematic about that?"

"I don't think you're fifty."

"No?"

"I think you're my age. Don't you?"

"But what if I'm not?"

"Laurie, I mean this in the kindest and most gentle way possible, but you have *got* to chill."

I pretend to consider it.

"Also, you can't base anything on the fact that I flirted with you," he adds. "I'm a *huge* flirt. Ask Jay. It's one of my many flaws."

"Nuh-uh." I shake my head, leaning closer, so that my nose almost brushes against his. "You have no flaws, actually."

He grins. "You are the *only* person on planet Earth who thinks that."

"I'm the only one who's properly unbiased. I'm the only one who knows that you'd help a complete stranger, over and over, when it was of no benefit to you."

Gideon groans, tipping his head back. "Stop, you're soiling my reputation with every word."

"You don't give a shit about your reputation," I say softly.

"No," he agrees, even softer.

When his eyes drop, I lean closer, but he pulls away and puts a hand on my shoulder. Heat rushes to my cheeks, and I'm already embarrassed even before he says, "I shouldn't have kissed you."

Yikes.

I swallow hard and pull away entirely, but he grabs my shoulder.

"No, Laurie, not like that. I just mean—think about it."

I raise my eyebrows and gesture wide. *What am I supposed to think?*

"How would you feel if the situation was reversed? If you got dropped into your body and found out someone else had been taking the reins?"

I hadn't even *thought* of that.

I lie back in the grass and groan, running my hand along the side of my face. "No, I know. I know, I know. You're right."

"It's nice that you want to though." He laughs.

I glare at him through my fingers. "You're such an asshole."

He just grins. "So they say."

00:25

FORTY-EIGHT.

"Absolutely not." Bri doesn't stop as I slow to a crawl on the road next to her.

At least I know her routine well enough now to have intercepted her on the walk home from school.

"I know you're sort of still mad at me." Again, I urge, "Please get in the car."

"Fuck you," she says, but there's not really any heat in it. "First everything yesterday, then you ditch me without warning today. Now you show up like nothing is wrong with *some guy* and *short hair* and you tell me to *get in the car*?"

I tilt my head.

"I have to prepare for the party," she says, which isn't a *no*.

"Please?"

She gets in the car.

"I'm pretty sure this is illegal," Bri huffs as she puts her seat belt on. "I'm pretty sure this is abduction of a minor, and I could press charges. Also, who the hell are you?"

From behind us, Gideon says, "Please don't mind me."

"Yeah, I'll just *not* mind the stranger in my best friend's backseat." Bri whips around to glare at him. Then her expression does something complicated, and somehow I *know* what she's thinking, because it's the same thing I thought when I first saw Gideon, which is: *Holy Christ.*

It was Gideon's idea to bring Bri back to Nanton. Yep, Gideon is a *lot* more mission-oriented than I am—whereas, if it were up to me, we'd continue to live in our happy little bubble, pretending time will never run out.

"Where the *hell* are we going?" Bri shoots me a private little look that I'm pretty sure means *Who is this guy?* or *Why is he beautiful?* or maybe both.

"I'd blindfold you if it didn't feel like you might kill me."

"You're right, I *would* kill you," she says. "What the hell is this?"

"Chill." I shake my head. "Just trust me."

"Absolutely not," she says, but at least she doesn't stop me from getting on the highway.

I've never been more glad that Gideon is an excellent conversationalist. Once he gets Bri talking, she doesn't stop. I had no idea Gideon was interested in musicals—actually, I'm pretty sure he *isn't* and he's doing an admirable job of faking—but he keeps her talking, right up until she makes a joke, there's an awkward pause, and I realize that I've missed my line in a familiar routine.

"Okay, what is going on with you?" Bri asks. "You're not yourself. Like, at all. Have you been possessed?"

It hits me like a slap. *This* is what's always missing with Brett. Does he even know me well enough to know that something isn't right?

"Sorry." I give my head a little shake. "Zoned out."

And that's when we see a sign for Nanton.

"Let me out of this car," Bri says, tone cold as ice.

I laugh. "Yeah, no."

"I know where we're going. And I *won't* do it."

I raise both eyebrows. "Yeah, you will."

"Oh my God," Bri whispers incredulously the second we get to the party and Gideon leaves us alone. "Who *is* he?"

"Gideon," I tell her simply, and it doesn't even matter that it's obviously not the answer she's looking for, because she's still goggling at his retreating figure.

"I don't even like men, but I might make an exception for him." Bri tucks her bottom lip under her teeth, clearly appreciating the way he walks.

I nudge her arm. "Hey. Do you know someone named Lincoln?"

"Like, the American president?" Bri huffs an exasperated laugh, and she's joking, but a homing beacon lights up in my head anyway, which makes *no* sense. At my blank expression, she rolls her eyes. "Come *on*, Val. Can you knock it off for, like, *two* seconds?"

"I don't—"

"You're being a real freak today. Like, what the *hell*, Val? Why did you bring me down here?"

"You know why," I say, and right on cue, Ibha comes around the corner.

Bri's breath catches. "I'm not talking to her."

"Yes, you are."

"Am *not*."

"You miss her," I tell Bri simply. "You regret how things went down."

Whether she agrees with me, it's too late. Ibha spots us. Across the room, eyes wide, her mouth makes the shape of a word. *Bri*.

And everything in Bri's face goes soft.

I figure that's my cue to leave.

Gideon's in the middle of a discussion with Wyatt and Archer when I find him, ten minutes later.

Neither of them looks particularly pleased to make my acquaintance. They never do when Gideon's already told them he's ditching them to hang out with me, but Wyatt in particular glowers at me the whole time we're standing in a cluster, until I can lure Gideon away.

"How was it?" I ask as he follows me up the barn stairs.

"I didn't let him say it. I feel kind of bad, but I just . . . you know."

I do know. Every time I think about Wyatt potentially trying to kiss Gideon, I feel like I could spit fire, even though I know it's not really my business.

"How did it go with Bri?"

"Pretty well, I think. I should check on them," I say, as we're rounding the corner, and Gideon snorts.

"Yeah, I really don't think you need to."

He's right. If I'd had any doubts, they're *certainly* gone now. In a corner over by the speakers, Bri has Ibha pressed up against a bale of hay, Ibha's hands around her neck.

Gideon gives me a fist bump. "Nice work, Cupid."

"Now to wait and see if *that* was Valerie's unresolved business," I say, and even as Gideon smiles at me, I can tell that neither of us thinks this was it.

We stay at the party later than we ever have, because of Bri.

It's almost nice to pretend that we're a normal couple, at a normal party.

A normal couple who can't kiss. Or *shouldn't*.

I want to. *God*, I want to.

"This is really cool." Gideon traces the contour of my tattoo with his index finger, following the scales down to the fangs before his hand comes to rest. His fingertips stop against my wrist, just above the flickering tongue of the snake, right where my pulse flutters.

I look up.

He's so close. Gideon's eyes are mesmerizing.

"Don't do that," he whispers. "Stop it."

"I'm not doing anything," I protest. "I'm *literally* not doing anything. You're the one who should stop."

"Your eyes," he says on an exhale.

God, I hope he likes *my* eyes, whatever they look like.

"This isn't kissing you," I point out, because he's still watching me like I'm causing him some kind of pain.

"You have to stop looking at me like that." He *has* to know that I would if I could.

"You're one to talk." I feel light-headed. Up close, I can almost feel how warm he is. But I do drop my gaze, even though it's the last thing I want to do.

Gideon's fingers trail along my open palm, and then he

interlocks our fingers. When I pull him out of this dangerous little corner, he doesn't let go.

It's after midnight now. The music isn't quite so loud, and the crowd has shifted. Older kids, like—

"Ricky," Gideon says when we pass him, nodding in greeting.

"Who's this?" Ricky asks, nodding at our hands.

Gideon stops. A muscle ticks in his jaw, and I can almost see what he's thinking, because I'm thinking it too: *You can't have this*. "What do you want?"

Ricky heaves a sigh. "Am I not allowed to be curious?"

Gideon doesn't answer him. At first I think that's going to be it, but after a moment, he shakes his head. "No, you know what? Fuck this. *Fuck* this. No, you're *not* allowed to be curious. I know what you did to me."

I squeeze his hand once, a warning.

Ricky rolls his eyes. "*Dude*, it—"

"You know they wouldn't do this to *you*, right?" Gideon's almost pleading with him. "If you just owned up to it, they wouldn't—"

"But it *wasn't* me," Ricky says, exasperated. "I've told you a hundred times, it wasn't—I didn't even tell them, I swear. Mom found out all on her own."

"Why are you doing this?" Gideon asks, helpless and frustrated. "What have I *ever* done to you?"

"Fuck you, man." Ricky shakes his head. "I'm telling the truth."

"So am I," Gideon says, and regardless if either of them believes the other, the unspoken question curdles in the air between them.

Then who isn't?

00:19

FORTY-NINE.

The nightmares are eons away.

On 00:19, in the evening, Gideon takes me skating again. This time it's a free skate, and we're not the only ones on the ice. I don't care, though. I'm not here to race anyone or to play hockey. I'm content to hold Gideon's hand—even if I do have to glare him into submission about it, *Everyone holds hands, Norris, this isn't going to shatter your moral compass, is it?*—and glide across the ice and imagine, for just a few hours, that tomorrow the rest of the world will go on.

I don't want to think about what happens when the clock hits zero. I just want to live in this moment forever. *Forever.*

"Slow down," he says. "Okay?"

"Okay," I whisper.

"Do you trust me?"

I nod, and he pulls me into a twirl.

"Slick moves," he comments, but then I've spun right into him, and my palm rests against his chest, and we're inches apart, like this.

"I think Valerie did some figure skating," I whisper, and I'm not really even tracking what I'm saying.

"That makes sense," he says. "If you both did hockey."

Then he spins me away, pulling me across the ice with him.

"You know, I sort of thought you might have when I first saw you skate. You skate like a dancer. So fluid."

"Really?"

"It's mesmerizing," he murmurs, pulling me into another spin where we're both turning together. "You're mesmerizing."

"Stop," I tell him, out of breath.

He grins. "Or what?"

"I've never felt like this," I whisper. "Never, never."

"Neither have I." Gideon's so close his nose brushes against mine. "I don't think I ever want to again."

I pull away, just enough. "What do you mean?"

"I mean, I don't . . ." he trails off, and our spin peters out slowly, until we're standing still on the ice. "I don't want to feel like this about anyone else."

"You don't mean that," I say, a low whisper.

"I mean it."

I shake my head. "You don't even know who I am."

"I don't have to." And he's so *stubborn*. He looks completely resolute as he says it, like he really believes that, and when I shake my head, he scoffs. "What, do you really think I'm that shallow?"

"Nobody doesn't *care*," I say. "What if I'm hideous?"

"Been over this," he reminds me, and taps the side of my head lightly with his index finger. "You wouldn't be, to me."

"You are so full of shit," I tell him, but my eyes are burning as I blink away tears, and I think he knows it.

"For the record, I can't wait to meet you," Gideon says. "Whoever you are."

We step out of the ice rink and into a summer evening so warm I'm shuddering with it.

Gideon waits all of ten seconds before he pushes me up against the brick wall, hands at my hips, and then he doesn't even kiss me.

I knew he wouldn't, but the flush of proximity goes to my head in half a second flat, and I can't stop looking at his mouth, the bow of his upper lip, I want to put *mine* on it so bad it's difficult to remember why I'm not supposed to.

And at least it's obvious that Gideon's not holding back because he doesn't *want* it. "I love you," he whispers, like it's an urgent secret. "How you are right now, and how you will be, one day."

"What the fuck?" I whisper, choking back tears. "What the fuck, Gideon? You can't say that."

"Can," Gideon murmurs. "Can, did, will again, probably."

"You're perfect," I whisper, tracing the shape of his face with my fingers. "How are you this perfect?"

"I'm not perfect," he says, like clockwork.

"To me," I insist, and to my surprise, he concedes.

"To you," he whispers with a brief nod, blinking quickly, like it's not just me fighting back tears.

"I wish this wasn't how we met," I whisper. "I wish I met you as me."

Gideon leans forward, and it's almost a kiss; he brushes his nose against mine. "I wish that too."

"I wish there was, like, *any* certainty of a tomorrow. Like some kind of light at the end of the tunnel."

"Maybe that's just life," he says. "Isn't that how it always is? Nobody has a guarantee that their life will go on past the exact moment they're living in."

"I don't care," I burst out, desperation breaking open inside of me. "I want to be able to pretend."

Gideon touches his forehead to mine, and everything goes quiet. "Then pretend."

00:10

FIFTY.

On 00:10, we find Jayda where she doesn't belong.

"What are you doing in my room?" Gideon demands.

Jayda scowls at him from where she's standing next to his desk. One drawer is open, and the closet door is ajar. "Nothing."

"Are you looking for something?" he asks.

For a moment, a note of real panic flashes behind her eyes. Then her expression hardens, steely with resolve. "What'd you do with the letters?"

Gideon blinks.

"Yeah, I know Mom's been writing to me. I know you've been hiding it from me too."

It's like all the fight goes out of Gideon at once. He takes a step back. "You know that was for your own good, right?"

"Oh, *fuck* you," she says. "You're always saying that, but who are you to be the judge of that?"

"I'm your brother." He sounds genuinely wounded. "Why are—why are you *so* determined to think the worst of me?"

"Because you do shit like *this*?" She gestures wide in the room. "You *lie* to me!"

"I never lied," he says, but it falls on deaf ears.

"You can't decide things like this for me!" Jayda throws her arms up. "First the letters, and then Knox said you started shit with him *again*."

A flash of incredulity breaks through Gideon's frustration. "Yeah, *obviously*. You won't listen to me when I—"

"I'm not *five*!"

"He's a *bad guy*, Jay!"

"Oh, and I'm just supposed to take you at your word, am I?"

"Yes!"

"How? How could I possibly trust you?" Blinking away tears, Jayda folds her arms tight. "You say you're looking out for me, but you're hiding letters from Mom, and it's not like *you* have your shit together, do you?"

Gideon squeezes his eyes shut, hands balled into his fists at his sides. When he speaks, his voice is level and soft. "How'd you even find the letters anyway?"

"Don't put things in your stupid wall hiding place unless you *want* it to be found," Jayda snarls. "Everyone knows about it."

Then she stalks out of the room.

"I did," Gideon says, later that night. He sounds almost hollow from below me.

I'm not anywhere close to asleep. I stare up at the little green glowing stars. "You did what?"

"I did keep the letters from her." The bunk bed creaks as he sits up.

"I know. You told me." Quietly, I get up. Less quietly, I climb down, sinking onto the mattress next to him.

"Mom was sort of off the rails even before I was in the picture." It sounds like he's reciting the story, completely detached. "Like, I have *no* idea who my dad is, and I'm not sure she does either. Her parents were both racist fucks who kicked her out once it was obvious I was part Indigenous, and that was right before Jay was born."

Aghast, I cover my mouth with my hand. "Seriously?"

"Racist fucks," Gideon repeats, and then he leans to the side and rests his cheek on my shoulder. "I don't remember them much. I *do* remember the apartment we lived in after that. It was the three of us for a while. We lived with her until I was nine, and then she just couldn't keep it together enough to be a fit guardian."

I rest my cheek on the top of his head. "Gideon. I'm so sorry."

"I'm not. We got to stay together, didn't we?"

"I mean, I'm glad you can see a silver lining, but *still*."

"When I was twelve, she got her shit together for a while. We all lived together for about nine months, and then she fell off the wagon again. Jay took it really hard."

Staying silent, I press a kiss to the top of his head.

"It scares me," he says. "I hate feeling like it doesn't matter what I do. She's just going to end up living the same life."

I nod.

"I'm not destined for greatness or anything, Laurie." Gideon shakes his head, pulling back. He doesn't even look sad, just tired. "Sometimes it feels like that's all my life is. Trying to make it better for Jay. Like, what else am I good for? I *just* want to keep her out of trouble, and I can't even do that. Look at Knox."

"You're good for lots of things."

"Like what?"

"You love history," I point out. "You're super smart. You're great with people."

Gideon stares at me like I've grown a second head.

"What?"

He shakes his head. "Sometimes I forget you don't seem to see what everyone else does."

"And what do you think they see?"

"I'm a mixed kid with a deadbeat mom and abandonment issues," he says without hesitating. "They think I'm harder than I am. They think I'm going to be meaner than I am. Sometimes it feels like it doesn't even matter what I actually *do*."

My heart breaks for him. "I don't see any of that. You know what I saw when I first met you?"

Gideon says nothing.

"I saw someone kind enough to stop and help," I tell him. "Sweet enough to help a *stranger*. They just don't know you."

"I don't want to talk about this anymore," he whispers sadly.

"Okay." I tuck my arm around him. Quietly, because it still freaks me out to say it, I tell him, "I love you."

Gideon deflates like a balloon with a little groan, sliding down so that his head rests against my knee. "I love you."

"I'd kiss you right now," I tell him.

He smiles up at me. "Yeah. Me too."

And it *kills* me that I can't.

"You're a really good big brother."

Slowly, his expression shifts, wan and tired. "Thanks."

"If I had a brother," I tell him, "I'd want him to be like you."

Gideon squints. "Well—I don't know if I *love* that, conceptually. I don't feel very brotherly about you."

"Okay, that's not what I mean," I say, and then I freeze.

If I had a brother. The phrase evokes the same elusive frustration that the name *Lincoln* still brings. Which doesn't make any sense, I don't remember specifics—

"Oh my God." I straighten all at once. "You know how we've been talking about muscle memory?"

To Gideon, this has nothing to do with *anything* we've been discussing, but he takes it in stride, eyebrows raised, looking up at me. "I . . . yes?"

All at once, I'm shaking all over. "What if some of the things I've remembered aren't from my head? What if they're memories from this *body*? Like, I knew how to skate, right? Valerie knows how to skate."

Gideon looks doubtful.

"Do you understand what this means?" I ask. "We know I'm not a girl, right? So I couldn't be Valerie, which means maybe some of these memories I've been having aren't *mine*."

"Okay, but—"

"Listen. When I was first going through Val's social media—fuck, I didn't charge the phone today, I can't show you, goddammit, anyway—I saw her brother's profile, right? And it reminded me of something, but I didn't know what."

"Right," he says, wary.

"I've already figured out I have a sibling. And just now,

I was *certain* that I have a brother." My heart races, adrenaline pounding. "Seeing Valerie's brother triggered something, but what if—what if he wasn't reminding me of my brother?"

"What if?" Gideon asks, clearly not quite following.

"What if he reminded me of *me*?"

FIFTY-ONE.

Nightmares bleed from every sharp angle of the Eaton house. It's barely noon when I darken the doorstep once more, trepidation building with every breath.

This is the earliest in the day I've ever been here, so I'm halfway hopeful that I'll have the house to myself while I do my detective work.

But when I round the corner, Cheryl is in the kitchen with the landline phone in one hand, a ceramic bowl in the other.

I jump, slapping a hand to my chest. "Oh, sorry. I didn't know you'd be home."

"Last day over already?" she asks, then looks up and gasps.

"Yes, I cut my hair. You hate it. Can we skip the theatrics?"

"Please—" She sucks in a breath. "I don't care for the lip."

"It's hair," I tell her. "It'll grow."

"I know you stole your phone back." Her tone is casual, but I can hear the note of danger. "That'll be another conversation with Dad, by the way."

Okay, Valerie. What the hell happened?

"You could have told me he changed his number," she says,

reproachful. "When I asked you a few weeks ago, you lied to my face. I don't appreciate that."

"... Who changed his number?"

"*Elijah*," she says, exasperated. "Don't tell me he's asking you to gaslight me now."

Convenient for today's purposes. My mouth opens and shuts. "Why would he do that?"

She sets the bowl down, so hard I'm afraid it's going to break.

I flinch, a shiver running up my spine.

The bowl stays intact.

Would I ask my little sister to gaslight our mother? *Fuck*, is Cheryl my actual mother?

"We're going to talk about all of this tonight," she says. "I think it's high time we all spoke as a family, don't you? He might answer, if you were the one calling."

I don't think so, I almost say, but then I manage to squash it down at the last second. I wish I just *knew*. I wish I could remember how I feel about Valerie. We're close, that much I can tell, but *how* close?

"Tonight," I confirm, because Cheryl's still watching me expectantly. "Sure."

Then I turn and walk down the hall. Closed doors stare me down. Which one is mine? There's only one left to try.

The room past Valerie's is the only one I haven't touched.

Does that mean something? Have I been subconsciously avoiding it?

Caution between every heartbeat, I push open the door.

At once, it's like a crypt.

A layer of dust coats the desk, as if it hasn't been touched at all since he—I—left. There's nothing on the walls—*nothing*. No posters. No photos.

It looks like it belongs to nobody.

The bookshelf is mostly empty, except for a few textbooks, some spiral notebooks, and a battered leather book that's lying on its side, face-up.

It's chance that the golden embossed letters catch my eye.

I step closer.

Three words. A name. His name.

Elijah Lincoln Eaton.

Not mine.

No.

I'm in motion before I know what I'm doing, carrying the book with me. My feet take me to Val's room—to *my*—

A fragile thread in my chest snaps. Lincoln is Elijah's middle name. I push open the bedroom door.

My bedroom door.

Valerie's Bible is in the exact same place I found it the first time. I turn the Bible and stare down at it. I've had this information since the second loop—it's on her fucking *license*, it's been right there the whole time—and I didn't know.

Maybe I didn't want to.

The matching embossed letters glitter golden.

Valerie Lauren Eaton.

I know it all at once: I was wrong.

The memory is thick like syrup, dragging with the weight and ache of panic and sorrow.

This voice, this body's voice, the one I hadn't recognized

when I'd first used it, *my* voice, begging, *Please don't. Lincoln, please don't go.*

I'm coming back eventually, he said, voice taut, like he was going to cry. *I'm going to come back, okay? I'm not going to leave you with them forever. I'm coming back.*

I can't breathe all of a sudden.

Slowly, I slide down the wall to the floor, book clutched to my chest, wheezing.

I'm coming back.

Lincoln and Laurie. *Lincoln and Laurie.* Nicknames.

The first thing I'd known about myself, even if it hadn't felt like it meant anything. Gideon on the highway, all of those loops ago, when I was even more clueless than I am now. He'd asked, and I'd told him.

It's been here the whole time.

I run my fingers over the letters, as the truth sinks in, a slow ripple of dread, frost up my spine. There is no real Laurie. There *is* no Valerie somewhere else out there for me to find, trapped in a body that's mine that I can come home to, because I *am* in my own body.

I'm Valerie.

FIFTY-TWO.

VAL

I can't help it. I whip out my phone, heart thumping wildly.

The caller ID reads: L♥.

"Who the fuck is L?" Brett asks as relief floods through me.

"I have to take this," I tell him. "Sorry."

He catches me by the wrist. "No."

I blink up at him. "Excuse me?"

"No," he repeats. "We're having this conversation, and you can't go all Val on me and run away to whoever this L guy is."

"It's *Lincoln*," I snap, "and I'm not running away, I have to talk to him about whether my mom read through our private emails and subsequently, whether I actually *am* responsible for the hell Bri's currently stuck in, so thanks, I *will* be taking this."

"Val—"

I've already hit Accept, snatching my shoes off the ground, and I'm pressing my phone to my ear when I call over my shoulder, "I'll find my own way home."

"Jeez," Lincoln says in my ear. "Hi."

"Sorry, that was for Brett."

"Ooh, are you fighting?" he asks, voice perking up as if I've given him a prize.

"Is now the part where you tell me you think I should?" I ask. "Because today is *not* the day."

"You know what I think," Lincoln says idly, sounding *way* too chill.

"You saw my texts, right?" I march away across the dry grass barefoot, shoes swinging. I crest the hill, Brett falling out of sight. With a stab of regret, I realize that I've left my milkshake behind. "You know what's going on?"

"I do." He still sounds like we're discussing the weather.

"Sorry, are you under duress?"

"Why would I be under duress?"

"I told you, I think Mom got into my email." The full impact of it hits me for the first time. I stop dead still, a lead weight forming in the pit of my stomach. "I'm *sorry*, Linc, I have no idea how it happened, but I—she can probably read everything we said."

"Yes," he says, still calm.

"I don't know what she knows," I tell him, eyes smarting. "I don't know how far she got, but she could have read *all* of it. She could know about Krishan, she could know—" I choke on a sob. "She could have your address, Lincoln. I'm *so* sorry."

Lincoln pauses to digest this, and when he finally speaks, his voice is infuriatingly calm. "Laurie?"

I sink down into the grass, pressing a hand to my mouth. I curl into myself, knees to chest, lungs tight.

"Laurie?" Lincoln repeats.

I gasp, "Yeah?"

"Hey," he says, voice softer. "Buddy. It's *okay*."

"No, it's not," I say, strangled. "It's not okay, I fucked up your whole life—"

"You did *not*. I knew something like this would happen, at some point."

Air vanishes.

Lincoln's always been more even-keeled than I am—when we moved from Vancouver in third grade, he put down roots like he'd always been here while I floundered for months before I met Bri—but this is *too* far.

"What?" I gasp.

"Mom is Mom," he says simply. "She was going to snoop, one way or another."

"No." I swallow hard. "You can't just be so chill about—*no*."

"I can't just be the only person not giving you a shit time right now?" Lincoln almost sounds *amused*. "Laurie, I told you—hang on."

There's a muffled voice on the other end of the line.

I hear Lincoln say, "Yeah, it's Laurie. Yeah, it's not—no, I know. He's just—he needs me, okay?"

At that, the tears come. I've only ever heard Lincoln talk *about* me once before, and I felt the similar head-rush of overwhelm then, too, a straight shot through my whole body like an electric shock.

"Sorry," Lincoln says, close to my ear again. "Okay, listen to me. You cannot worry about how this affects me, all right?"

I swipe at my eyes. "How could I not—"

"I'm ready for this," he says gently. "They *can't* hurt me."

All I can do is sit there, fresh tears spilling down my cheeks, chest concave.

"What we have to worry about is you," he says. "What are you going to do?"

"I don't know."

"Do they know you're trans? Are you safe?"

"I don't know," I say again, tight and miserable. "I don't know what they know."

"What are you going to tell them if they ask?"

"I don't know," I repeat, frustrated. "I feel like I don't know *anything*. I just want—"

"I know. And you're *so* close. You are. Did you tell Brett just now? Is that what that was about?"

"No." Salty tears run into my mouth. "He thinks I'm cheating on him."

At least Lincoln sounds genuinely bewildered when he asks, "*What?*"

"With Matty," I say, "because *Matty* knows, and he keeps telling me it's not fair to not tell Brett, and I just—I don't know what to do."

"Does Matty know?"

"What, that he was the one who made me realize I'm not a girl?" I laugh bitterly. "Sort of. I don't know. Maybe."

"Is he cool?" Lincoln's tone takes on this *edge*, like we're back in elementary school and I'm being teased about my freckles all over again.

"He's cool," I assure him, and I even manage a little smile.

"Are you going to tell Mom and Dad?"

"Should I?"

"If you want to," he says. "Sometimes I wish I had, just so I could have known what they'd say. But I know the gender stuff is a lot more complicated."

"I miss you," I blurt out.

"Yeah, dude." He huffs a sigh. "I miss you, too. Get down here soon, okay?"

I close my eyes and envision it. Me and Lincoln in Lethbridge. A fresh start. It's been my lifeline for months. It's my lifeline right now. "What if I tell them," I whisper, "and it goes badly?"

"Then you say *fuck it* and come down here early," he says. "And we'll figure it out."

FIFTY-THREE.

I'm Valerie.

I'm Valerie. The one thing I thought I knew for sure, that *I'm not a girl*, isn't even true. Or—and my stomach twists at the thought—it *is* true. It's still true, I'm just in even deeper shit than I thought.

I stare down at the Bible.

Lincoln and Laurie.

It comes back slowly, in fits and starts.

It's like whatever prompted this hell has released me all at once, and discovering this one thing has started the rest of it unraveling like thread from a spool. Lincoln's face is clearer in my head than it has been since this hell started.

I snatch my laptop—*my laptop*—from my backpack—*my* backpack; everything in this room is mine—and my fingers fly over the keyboard, typing in the passcode on muscle memory.

I know where to look. I know where to find the locked document with my passwords saved, the handles for accounts that I've been logged out of this whole time. A whole life kept hidden.

My whole life kept a secret, even from me.

There's only one place to go.

I don't even need directions.

I rip past Nanton without stopping, and the way clears itself. I know this route, I've driven it before. Gideon occurs to me when I'm already forty-five minutes away, and I don't turn back.

Not for this.

This, like the journey back home, I have to tackle on my own.

It's late afternoon by the time I arrive.

Lincoln's apartment is on the edge of town, on the second level of a squat building with outdated orange stucco. I know to park across the street against the curb, because I've done it before. I know the way up the winding wrought-iron staircase with the wisteria climbing the railing, because I've already walked it.

I'm trembling all over when I knock on the door.

It takes a while, but eventually, it opens.

My brother looks out at me, eyebrows raised. Faint surprise, but pleasure too, until he fully takes in the energy I'm radiating and falters.

"Holy shit, your hair," he whispers. "Did Mom *kill* you?"

The same essential puzzle pieces that make up my face are in his somewhere too. Those shocking blue eyes. Lincoln's freckles dust the tops of his arms and not his nose, which is broader than mine, but not as long—Mom's side of the family, I remember—and that's when it's real.

"Laurie?" he asks when I say nothing, and I burst into tears.

"Oh shit." He ushers me inside, pulling me into a hug.

I'm a little taller than he is, but he's broad, wide-shouldered and strong, his hair closely cropped, and he smells just like he always has.

This is the nightmare, I think, and then I can't *stop* crying, and Lincoln holds me tight and rubs my back until the deluge slows to a hiccupping drizzle.

"The hair's not the worst of it," I tell him at last, shrugging out of the shirt and putting the tattoo on full display.

"*Sick.*" He turns my arm this way and that. Heavy calluses line his palms. I *know* his hands. "Badass. Also, do you need a lawyer?"

I manage a laugh despite myself, wiping my nose with my sleeve. "It's good to see you."

"It's good to see you too." Lincoln draws me in by the arm.

Every step ushers in familiarity, like the world is loading around me in a lagging video game.

I can't stop staring. At the apartment, at the plant in the corner, at Lincoln, who leads me into the kitchen. At the cat—black and sleek with large, inquisitive green eyes—who looks at me from around the corner and then sprints away down the hallway.

It's almost warm enough out to cook an egg on the pavement. Lincoln makes tea anyway, and I watch him and a hundred versions of him in the past repeat the same movements. The same soothing ritual.

Neither of us speaks until he hands me a mug and leans against the counter.

"What's going on, Laurie?" Lincoln asks. "What happened?"

"I fell in love," I whisper, and it's not what I meant to say, but it *is* true.

Lincoln squeezes my shoulder. "Oh?"

"Not with Brett," I clarify, and he laughs.

"Yeah, I could have seen that one coming."

"*Hey.*"

"No offense to Brett. But you know how I feel about him."

And I do. I smile despite myself, wrapping my hands around the mug. It's too hot for tea, but the warmth is soothing, anyway. Lincoln never liked Brett, even before we started dating. "Well, we broke up."

Not *strictly* honest, but, hey. Baby steps. If you break up with someone enough times, maybe eventually it'll stick.

"Good." Lincoln nods. "How'd he take it?"

"Mostly fine." I shrug, and then I remember what Lincoln used to call him and I have to smile into my mug all over again.

"Tell me about this new person."

So I tell him about Gideon. I leave out most of the details, because I don't—I don't *want* to get into the time-loop thing. I don't want to have to explain all that. I just want my brother. I tell him the basics, and I invent a few things, like how we met—through hockey, my most reliable lie—but the important things would bleed through any façade. How kind he is, unfailingly. How much he loves Jayda. How he's so nice to look at it makes me feel like I need to do sprints just to get it out of my system.

How he loves me, somehow.

"I'd like to meet him," Lincoln says when I've finished, and then I'm crying all over again.

"I *want* to introduce you," I tell him. "Problem is—"

The turning of the deadbolt makes us both jump.

"Oh shit." Lincoln straightens at once. "Krish's home. I didn't warn him you were here."

I struggle through the sludge of memories to locate—*Krishan*. Yes. Lincoln's boyfriend.

I'm not coming back, Laurie.

Don't say that.

I can't stay here. I'm—we got a place. An apartment.

Please don't go.

I remember it now. I'd *begged* him.

Lincoln, please don't go.

A guy nearly as tall as Knox slips into the apartment, letting his backpack hit the ground with a thunk. It's the guy from Lincoln's Instagram.

And as soon as I see his face, I remember him. I remember sitting on the edge of Lincoln's bed when he'd first told me about him, *Okay, you know that guy I've been talking to? He only lives a three-hour drive away. I know. We didn't even realize for ages, but that's drivable, right?*

"Oh, hey, Laurie," Krishan says with a little wave. "I didn't know you were visiting."

"Neither did I," I tell him, still a little tearful.

His smile falters. "Shit, are you okay?"

"Give us a second," Lincoln says to me, getting up and leading Krishan down the hall. From here, I can hear only lowered voices, indistinguishable murmuring.

I've never been so scared to be alone. The jitters snatch at me and my hands are shaking before I can stop them, breath coming in shallow gasps.

I force myself to still.

Breathe.

It's too crowded in my head. There's too much going on. Memories skate by: Lincoln building us a fort out of blankets, Lincoln taking me out on our first drive alone the day after he got his permit, Lincoln holding me down and threatening to spit on me but grinning too wide to mean it, Lincoln showing me how to shoot a puck, Lincoln coming out haltingly when we were thirteen and fourteen like he was afraid of what I'd say, Lincoln taking me out at the knees on the neighbor's trampoline, Lincoln tearing up his own shirt when I split my lip on the trampoline's springs and begging me not to tell, Lincoln showing me how to flip pancakes perfectly, Lincoln driving away.

Lincoln. His nickname became his screen name.

He comes back down the hallway alone.

I look up, resisting the urge to cry all over again. "Can I ask you something?"

Lincoln nudges my knee as he sits down. "Anything."

The real question almost meets the air: *Was leaving worth it?*

But I don't let it out. Instead, I ask, "How did you deal with it? You and Krishan were already dating by the time you met in person."

"Yes," Lincoln says, cautious. "How'd I deal with what?"

"Did you ever worry you wouldn't be . . . what he expected? Like, physically?"

Lincoln squeezes my arm. "Yeah, but that went away as soon as we met up. The right person doesn't care about things like that."

"What if . . . you *weren't* what he expected?"

"Laurie." Lincoln gets suddenly *solemn*. Way too solemn to be actually serious. "Please tell me you didn't catfish someone."

"No, it's not that," I tell him, smiling despite myself. "Nothing like that. I meant, what if he expects something else?"

"Then there's nothing you can do about that," he tells me.

I nod.

"But he's going to react better than you expect," he tells me. "You know how I know that?"

"How?"

"Because he's not Brett *Fucking Wonder Bread* Blanchette."

This time when I start to laugh, I don't stop.

FIFTY-FOUR.

Gravel sprays when I skid to a stop on the edge of the highway. Morning light splays warm fingers through the windshield and I sit for just a moment before I get out.

One last moment to live in before I have to face the truth for real.

I can do this.

"Sorry," I blurt out, first thing, when I get out of the car and find Gideon jogging across the highway, expression harried.

"*Laurie.*" Gideon tugs a hand through his hair. "You can't just—I had no idea where you were, or if you were okay, what the hell happened?"

The sight of Gideon in front of me is a sudden reality check. Gone is the warmth of Lincoln's apartment, the relief of our laughter. Gideon is real and expectant and I've worried him and I'm not who he thought I was and I *can't* do this, actually.

"Sorry," I repeat numbly, and then I turn on my heel and march off the side of the highway into the long grass. I vault over the low wire fence and keep going, ignoring Gideon calling after me.

But it doesn't take him long to catch up.

"Laurie," he repeats, exasperated, and catches my shoulder.

I burst into tears.

I drop low to the ground and bury my face in my hands and I wish, I *wish*, that figuring out who I am could involve less crying. Humiliation burns the back of my throat as the first few sobs rip through me.

I don't hear Gideon sit down next to me, but I do feel him pull me against his chest, and I let him do it. I let myself fall against him and I cry until I'm a hiccupping mess, and then I cry a little bit longer, because at this point, the difference between ugly crying on Gideon's shoulder for five minutes versus for half an hour is negligible, probably.

At last, I pull back, wiping at my eyes.

"You don't have to talk about it," he tells me gently. "You know that, right?"

Tears threaten to choke me all over again. I do, though. I *do* have to. Gideon deserves to know. I have to tell him, but if I say it out loud and the truth becomes a part of this for real, what then?

I still can't do it.

My tears dry. The wind whispers through the long grass in ripples of gold and the sun beats down on my shoulders and every time I open my mouth, the words dry up.

Fortunately, Gideon is patient. He leans back in the grass, uncharacteristically quiet, and doesn't push me, even as the minutes crawl by, even when I can see on his watch that we have been here for hours and it's past one o'clock. As always, every time I look at him, longing opens up inside of me, yawning and cavernous.

"You don't have to talk about it," he repeats, after an eternity, every word slow and carefully considered. "But if—"

I bolt to my feet, shaking my head. "I don't know *how*," I cry, but I don't take off again.

Gideon stands and nudges my elbow.

"It's just me," he says. "What are you afraid of?"

Everything.

In my head, Lincoln says, *The right person won't care about things like that.*

So I say, "I went back home."

I told Gideon that much of the plan. I *didn't* say that I was going to go cry myself to sleep on my brother's couch, but to be fair, that *wasn't* the plan.

"And?" he asks. "Were you right?"

I shake my head.

"Something else?" Gideon prompts.

I nod. "I have to tell you something."

"Okay. I'm ready."

There's nothing else for it. I take a deep breath, and I say, "I'm Valerie."

He nods.

I try again. "No, I mean I *am* Valerie. When I went home, I went into Lincoln's room, and I remembered. All kinds of things. I'm—there isn't anyone else out there."

"I know." Gideon's expression is unreadable when he turns to me.

"You . . . know?"

"Do you remember what you said to me the first night we met? I mean, the first night *I* remember?"

My cheeks burn.

"Not that thing." Gideon gives me a small smile. "The other thing, before that. You told me you weren't a girl."

I'd forgotten all about that.

"I know we haven't talked about it," Gideon says slowly. "But are you really telling me it never crossed your mind?"

"This isn't what I wanted." It doesn't come close to conveying the hopelessness dragging me down. "This whole time I thought I felt so out of place in my body because my real self was out there waiting for me. Of course I didn't want—"

I can't say the rest. This body that's all wrong stretches skin over my bones like a glove made for somebody else, one that's never fit.

Softly, Gideon asks, "Are you okay?"

"No." My voice comes out a rasp. "This isn't fair."

"I know."

Throat tightening, nausea rises. "Especially to you."

He frowns. "How do you mean?"

I kick at a rock, staring at it as it skitters over the yellow line onto the highway. Then I mumble, "You went into this thinking you were going to get something different at the end."

"No, I didn't."

"You *did*."

"Laurie." Gideon's voice is quiet. "I've known this for a while."

My gaze snaps up to his. "Excuse me?"

"I mean, not a *while*, but I think I figured it out properly when I saw you with Bri the night we brought her here. I don't even know what it was. It just—clicked."

He might as well have pulled the ground out from under me. "Why didn't you say anything?"

"Wasn't my truth," he says. "If you threw something like that at *me,* I think I would freak out. I've *never* doubted that I'm not a girl. From the sounds of it, that's been the only constant in this whole thing for you, right?"

During those first loops, it had been the only thing I was sure of. *This body is wrong.*

This body isn't mine.

I stare down at my fingers. Those brown-sugar freckles.

It *is* mine, is the thing.

Mine, and still wrong.

Tears well up, and I shake my head. "I want to wake up. I don't want—I don't want this. This isn't what I promised you."

Then he gives me a little smile. "Laurie, you are *so* in your head." He pushes my hair out of my eyes, fingertips dragging along my scalp, and it's been so long since he's touched me that the contact sends arcs of electricity coursing through me. "What do you think it means that I flirted with you *every* time we met? Do you think I'm not as stupid for you as you are for me?"

I gape at him.

"I *am* excited to meet you," he says. "I meant it when I said it, and it's still true. I'm excited to meet all the versions of you. We're going to get out of this, and then you're going to do whatever the hell you like with this body, and I'm going to keep loving you."

All I can do is stare at him. Breathless, I whisper, "What the fuck is wrong with you?"

Gideon beams.

"Why are you being so perfect?" I demand. "Where do you get off on this shit?"

He laughs, and then I can't fucking take another second of this.

"Will you *please*," I start, snatching the front of his shirt and making a fist in the fabric, "kiss me now?"

"Shit, you're right, I *can* do that, finally," Gideon says, and catches me by the jaw and just does it, kisses me with a force that knocks the breath out of me.

The snarling, desperate creature that's been lashing out with claws every ten seconds goes perfectly still and then evaporates. I let go of Gideon's shirt, because he's so close that I have better things to do with my hands, like snaking them around him, fingertips on his spine.

Hands at my waist, he backs me up against the car. I could dissolve like this, sugar in water, the drag of Gideon's lips against mine a tether. I twine my fingers through his hair, pulling him down, pulling him closer.

"Silver linings everywhere if you look for them," he murmurs against my mouth, and I *laugh*, and some distant part of me is bleeding relief that I get to keep this body because it's the one that Gideon's got his hands on.

We kiss until I can't breathe, and we don't stop then either. I *have* to touch every inch of bare skin I can reach—his arms, the back of his neck, the stretch of rib cage his shirt doesn't cover—and Gideon seems intent on turning me into a puddle against the driver's-side door.

I'm not paying attention to the time. I don't *care* what time it is. I'm not thinking about *anything* when the storm hits.

Rain washes over us, and it's *not* romantic like it would be in the movies, it's *wet*; my hair is stuck to my forehead and dripping in my eyes and my clothes cling to my skin, and none of it matters, because I don't want to stop.

It's a semi-truck blaring past that forces us apart, spraying us with droplets that sting against my bare legs, and Gideon gasps and starts to laugh into my mouth.

Water runs off of him in rivulets when he pulls back, dripping from his hair.

My fingers fumble with the door handle as I wrench it open, getting back inside, out of the storm.

Gideon circles the car to join me.

I shiver as the leather sticks to my wet clothing, and I *can't* look at him as he slides into the passenger seat, and then I do anyway, and all I can see is the way his shirt is stuck to him and how *good* he looks like this.

"We should find somewhere to dry off." My voice is a ragged rasp.

"Yeah." Gideon sounds equally off his game. He pushes his wet hair back and slumps against the seat.

My hands are shaking.

"Start driving before I do something stupid and impulsive," he says, and then when I turn the keys and start the engine, he swears. "Oh my God, I can't fucking *look* at you. That's *illegal*."

"What am I doing?" I protest as I pull onto the highway.

"Every day I sit in this car and I watch you drive and I have to remind myself why I said I'd stay away from you."

I can't go without touch for a single second longer, so I reach over and place my palm on his knee, bare skin under shredded, soaked-through denim.

"Don't," he says, strangled. "*Don't.*"

I let out a trembling laugh and pull my hand back. The windshield wipers work at triple speed, and still I have to squint to see through the blur.

At least it gives me something to focus on, at least until I turn off at the first road—the one with the tractor shed where Ricky works—and when I glance over, Gideon's staring at me.

A shiver runs down my spine. I see it in his eyes, the same helpless want that's had hooks in me for *weeks*.

I drive until I see a building—an old shed with a tin roof, half filled by a car on a block with weeds growing through the open hood—and I pull inside and slow to a stop.

"We can't," Gideon says. "Not here."

I don't say anything, but the question—*Why not?*—must be obvious anyway, because he shakes his head.

"It's not how I pictured this," he says. "And we could get caught."

I ignore the last bit, stomach flipping. "You pictured it?"

"Oh, I have been driving myself fucking *crazy*," he says breathlessly, still staring, and I snap.

"What would it take?" I ask him, and I touch my palm to the side of his face, and it's like he was just waiting for it; he leans into me at once, meeting me halfway until our noses are nearly touching over the gearshift. "You *know* it wouldn't matter if we got caught, right? It won't matter tomorrow."

"You don't know that," he says, like he *always* does when

I say something to a similar effect. He sounds several degrees less certain when he adds, "We can't."

"Fine." I lean in closer, not quite the whole way. "Don't kiss me then."

I don't pull back.

Gideon lets out a fluttering exhale and makes a low, pinched, helpless sound in the back of his throat. "You're the *devil*."

"I'm not doing anything," I remind him. "All you have to do is not kiss me."

"Oh, is that all?" he asks, and I can't help smiling widely.

"What did you imagine?" A flush of victory sends a thrill through me as Gideon leans closer, lips ghosting against mine.

I never get an answer. Gideon kisses me, and it's every kiss we haven't had, it's everything all at once: rain on the tin roof, Gideon's hands, his mouth, the way that I forget everything but the square inches of skin he's touching, like it doesn't matter that this body is still a stranger's and always has been, because his calluses feel like a promise.

This is my *body*, I think, and it's true. *This is* my *blood under your hands.*

Take it and remember me.

FIFTY-FIVE.

When the nightmare ends and I open my eyes, I know three things only: first, I never asked for these freckles to be mine; second, the radio station blowing static works just fine in my room at home; and third, I'm going a hundred and twenty clicks in the wrong direction.

I miss my best friend.

At least Gideon understands that this is something I need for *me*.

I'm alone this time when I pull up next to Bri.

"Oh my God." Her mouth drops open at the sight of me, and she stops walking. "Your *hair*. And is that a *tattoo*? Val, what the hell?"

"Please get in the car," I urge as I stop too.

"Are you having a manic episode?" she asks. "I've heard that sometimes impulse decisions are symptoms of a manic episode."

"I'm not having an episode. Get in the car."

She does, but not without a little huff. "I'm pretty sure this is illegal. I'm pretty sure this is abduction of a minor, and I could press charges."

The corners of my lips twitch. "Then do it."

We go back to her house and sit in her bedroom, cross-legged on her bed.

I've sat right here hundreds of times before. I've spent most of my *life* with Bri, and each moment crashes into the next, a slow collision.

Volunteering together at Vacation Bible School. Secret handshakes in fourth grade. Being camp counselors together. Sitting and practicing braiding, winding her curls into even plaits. How scared she'd sounded when she'd come out, falteringly, like she'd thought I'd condemn her for it. The summer of friendship bracelets and the way her face had lit up when I suggested we make a third in our matching set so Ibha could have one too. The way she'd *screamed* when I told her Brett had kissed me, how she'd gone scarlet in the face, how she hadn't spoken to me for three weeks, she'd been so upset. Throwing dolls off the third-floor balcony for the plot. Watching the first musical theatre show she'd starred in, beaming in the front row. Walking through the halls at school arm in arm with matching scrunchies. The first time I'd snuck out and across the neighborhood at night because I couldn't take the shouting, how she'd snuck me into her bedroom without question.

Bri's been my best friend for as long as it's mattered.

"I love you," I blurt out. "You're really, really important to me."

Bri's eyes go wide. "What is this? Did you abduct me for a murder-suicide?"

"What—*no*! Why is that everyone's first thought when I'm trying to be sincere?" I shake my head, but at least now the tension is broken. "Also, this isn't an abduction. We're in *your* room."

"What is going on, Val?"

"I love you," I tell her again. "I need to tell you something."

"God, just do it. You're freaking me out."

"I'm not a girl," I tell her, steadily at first, then wavering. "I think. And my name isn't Val."

"Oh," she says, uncertainly, and then, "*oh*."

I swallow. "Yeah."

"Are you trans?"

Slowly, I nod.

"Yeah." She nods too. "Yeah, you are. Wow."

I blink. "Yeah?"

"You've been . . . different this year." Then her eyes go wide. "Oh my God. I didn't even support you yet. *Yes*. One hundred percent. I have your back, no matter what."

I could cry. I *might*. "Wait, you knew?"

"You remember New York?" Bri asks, and it feels so, *so* good to know what she's talking about.

I *remember* it. It's my life, and I remember it. I remember the senior-year trip we took over spring break; I remember running through Times Square hand in hand with Bri the night after we saw *Cats* on Broadway. I remember how hard we laughed, and then the way I cried, in our hotel room trying not to wake up the other two girls sleeping in the other queen bed. Bri had just held on to me while I cried, even when I wasn't able to articulate what was wrong.

I nod.

"I think I knew *something* was up then. I just didn't know what it was."

I want to crush her in a hug.

"Does anyone else know?"

I shake my head. "So far, just Lincoln. Do you remember when my mom found out you were queer?"

"Fuck, that was at Eli's grad, wasn't it?" Bri sighs. "I'm still sorry about that, by the way. I didn't know she'd recognize the flag colors, or I never would have worn the stupid bracelet in the first place."

"Hey," I object. "That bracelet wasn't stupid. I gave you that."

"You know what I mean."

And I do. I *do* know, and it feels so good. I want to luxuriate in this moment forever. "Anyway. I told him that day."

She nods.

"And—you're going to be really pissed about this."

"Did you—"

"*Not* Ibha," I assure her. "I had a breakdown in Matty's car last fall and told him everything."

"*Matthew Lawrence* knew before I did?" Bri screeches, and I let out a belly laugh.

"I'm sorry, I'm sorry!"

"You are *dead* to me." Bri grabs her pillow to smack me with it.

I hold my arms up to shield myself, squawking laughter. Then, when she sits back, shaking her head with faux disapproval, I let out a breath that releases *months* of tension.

Softer, she asks, "Does Brett know?"

I shake my head. "I'm going to tell him though."

Bri bites her lip.

"And I know that's going to mean it's over. It's okay."

"Wow." Slowly, she nods. "Big changes."

"*Big* changes." I let out a shuddering sigh. "I really love you."

"I love you too," she says, eyes glassy. "*Stop*, you're going to make me cry."

"I'm not done. I want you to know that I would never intentionally jeopardize your privacy," I whisper. "Never."

"I know." Bri wipes her cheeks. "I'm sorry that I was such a shit about it."

"Yeah, you really were, weren't you?"

"It's Ibha. She makes me crazy."

I roll my eyes, but I'm smiling.

"I'm so glad you told me," she whispers. "Thank you. I'm really sorry if you felt like you couldn't say it earlier."

"I was just . . . processing."

Bri nods. "I remember what that was like. What do I call you?"

With a little smile, I tell her, "Laurie."

00:05

FIFTY-SIX.

The church auditorium feels smaller, somehow.

I sit in the pew and wait. My heartbeat thuds, steadier than it has in weeks.

But knowing what I'm bracing for doesn't lessen the impact.

"Val?"

Slowly, I turn to face my dad.

"What's going—oh, wow." His eyebrows lift as he takes me in.

"Can we put the talk about the hair on hold?" I ask. "I know it's a shock. I just—Please?"

He looks a little hesitant, but he nods.

"You love me, right?"

Dad nods. "Val, of *course* I do."

Dad. *My* dad. I can't keep thinking about him as Valerie's dad, because this is the man who raised me. This is the man who held me when I was sick, who used to play-wrestle with me on the floor, who taught me how to read.

Memories flood through me, a constant threat of overflow. Picking apples in the backyard. Building Marbleworks courses in the basement. Sitting with my chin against his shoulder while he read aloud to me and Lincoln, acting out the voices to *The*

Chronicles of Narnia. Friday-night pizza after swimming lessons. Him teaching me and Lincoln how to set up a tent. Sitting at the dinner table and learning what he really thought of people like me.

"You'd love me no matter what, right?"

He sucks in a breath as he tucks his Bible under his arm. "Val—"

"Last night," I start. "I didn't get to tell you the whole truth."

"Honey." It sounds like a warning. Carefully, he sinks into the pew next to me.

"What if I wasn't me?"

"I think this is a conversation we should be having with your mother here."

"You won't even hear me out?" I whisper.

He frowns at me. Then, just like last time, he takes one of my hands and then the other. "Let's pray."

Dismay courses through me. Why is that *always* the solution? Why does it feel like a replacement for anything *real*? The sort of deflection that's almost a dismissal?

I don't want to talk to the Lord. I want to talk to my dad.

"*Heavenly Father*," he starts, with a little squeeze to both of my hands, and I can't help it.

A tear escapes, running down my cheek.

"*You know her struggle better than I ever could.*" He squeezes my hands again. "*You understand the weight of temptation. You know what she needs. I pray that you give her strength. Guide her through this maze and help her to divine what is real and true, and what isn't.*"

It just all feels so *pointed*. The weight of everything I said and didn't say last night hangs between us, a suspension bridge set to snap, cables taut, and he won't even talk to me.

"*Be with her in Spirit,*" he continues, and when my shoulders shake, he must take that as a sign of encouragement. "*You are the source of all beautiful things, Lord. I pray you'd light the way for Valerie and build a hedge of protection around her. In your name, Amen.*"

"Amen," I echo.

"You're gonna be okay, kiddo." He pulls me into a hug and kisses the crown of my head.

It's a sense of loss that feels like rage.

"See?" He squeezes my shoulder. "Better already."

But I *don't* feel better.

I just feel hollow.

FIFTY-SEVEN.

On the tail end of 00:04, we creep back into the farmhouse and find the last piece of the puzzle completely by accident.

Gideon's door is ajar, lamp light casting a glow under the door and onto the hallway floorboards. There's someone moving around inside, and even before I catch a flash of Jayda's jaw, I know it's her.

"She's never been here before," Gideon murmurs to me. "Did we do something different to change the timeline?"

"We've never *seen* her here before," I point out.

"But we've been in my bedroom before at this time," he says. "I think we've even been awake this late before."

"Exactly. We've only ever been in the room or out of the house," I say. "Maybe she's only in there because *we're* not."

Gideon pauses to digest this, then sucks in a breath. "*Everyone knows about it*," he says. "Oh my God."

"What?"

Gideon doesn't respond. He steps forward into the room and flips the overhead light on. There's a mean edge to his tone when he asks, "Looking for something?"

Jayda jumps at the sudden blinding light and scrambles back

from the wall. Hand to her heart, she whispers, "Oh my God, *Gideon*. Don't do that."

"I'll do whatever I want when you're snooping through my room." Gideon speaks at normal volume. "Ricky was telling the fucking *truth*. It wasn't him."

"What wasn't him?" Jayda's frantic gaze darts to the wall.

"Where do you fucking *think* I'm going tomorrow?" Gideon demands, stepping toward her.

She shakes her head. "I don't know what you're talking about."

"They're sending me to fucking *rehab*," he spits. "You *set me up!*"

"I was just keeping it there until we could move it," she says, tearful. "I wasn't trying to set you up."

"Keeping it there for Knox, right?" Gideon shakes his head. "He's a *moron*. You know that, right?"

"I—" Jayda's breath catches.

"And don't play dumb either. *Everyone knows about it*, you said. You told me not to put shit in my wall hiding place, and that's where they found it, because you *put it there*, and you *knew* they'd find it."

"Gideon—"

"Let me guess." His voice is deadly. "Knox needed someone to get caught so they wouldn't suspect *him*."

"It was supposed to be Ricky," Jayda says tremulously. "But they didn't check the car when he crashed it."

Gideon runs a hand through his hair. "Ricky drove into the church sign on *purpose*?"

"They were going to find the drugs. Nothing bad would happen to him, but at least the pressure would be off Knox, right?"

"And nothing happened, so you tried to pin it on *me*? Because you were *pissed*? Jayda, what the *fuck* is wrong with you?"

"I'm sorry," she says, and the first tear falls.

He must read something in her expression that I don't, because his eyes go wide and he sucks in a breath. "You could prove it," he says, comprehension dawning. "You *could*, couldn't you? There's a paper trail."

"No." Jayda shakes her head, but even I can see it now, that cornered-animal edge to her expression.

"You have proof that he asked you to do it," Gideon says, a low demand. "Why wouldn't you give it?"

"I don't want him to go to jail."

"But you'd let them send me away." Gideon's tone is steely. "Right. I see."

"Gideon—"

"Get the fuck out of my room."

Jayda tosses me a frightened look on her way out.

FIFTY-EIGHT. THE NIGHTMARE

In the nightmare, tears run hot down my face.

There's a pressure constricting my ribs; this dress is too tight. I can't breathe like this, and shame makes a mess of every heartbeat.

"You are my *daughter*," Mom snarls, her grip a vise around my arm, and her eyes crackle with a rage that sends a whip-crack of fear up my spine. "You are a direct reflection of this family. I can't believe you would have kept this from me. Why did I have to find this out through Bri's *mother* when you've clearly known all along?"

The murmured hum of conversation carries on the breeze over the garden behind the church. Sunshine blazes down on both of us; a bead of sweat drags a fingertip down my spine under the choking fabric.

"Bri is my best friend," I choke. "There's nothing wrong with who she is."

"Nothing—" She laughs, high-pitched incredulity. "Do you have *any* idea how it would look if people knew?"

"I don't *care*," I burst out. "You're saying I should cut her off because she's different? Because of the optics?"

"I'm not saying that," she says, and then doesn't offer me a different meaning.

My chest heaves. "What if it was me? What if *I* was different?"

"Are *you* gay?" she demands. "Is that what you're saying?"

"*No*." I shake my head, loose curls swinging.

"You're ruining your makeup." She releases my arm to drag a thumb under my eye, and I fight the urge to twitch away from her. All business again, she says, "Pull yourself together. We still have to take family photos before Elijah takes his robe off. You and I will talk more about this later."

When she walks away, I sit down hard on a wooden bench, fighting the urge to scream. Then I lean forward and put my face in my hands.

Fuck. I ruined it. I ruined Lincoln's graduation day by breaking down when Mom found out Bri was gay; this is what she'll always remember, isn't it?

I sit there until I can get my breathing under control, and then I sit there some more.

Footsteps crackle, dry grass crunching.

If this is Brett, I really *am* going to scream.

But it's not.

"Are you okay?"

I recognize the glinting leather of Lincoln's shoes as they stop in front of me and my exhale quivers. "Do I look okay?"

"I mean, not particularly."

"I don't really want to talk right now." I keep my voice low, and

I keep my face buried in my hands. "Have fun on your trip. Tell Krishan I say hi."

"I will." Lincoln sinks down onto the bench next to me.

A cricket chirps somewhere in the bushes.

You are my daughter.

I let my hands drop and I ball them into fists. "When you come back, I need to tell you something."

He's quiet for a long time.

So long that I look up.

He's biting his lip, sunlight caught in his fine golden hair and the collar of his nice blue dress shirt. He's taken his robe off, I realize.

"Lincoln?" I ask, and somehow I already know what he's going to say before he even says it.

"I'm not coming back, Laurie."

My stomach drops. I shake my head. "Don't say that."

"I can't stay here." He looks down at his hands. "I'm—we got a place. An apartment."

"But you're—"

"I'm eighteen now," he reminds me. "I *can't* stay. I can't come back here. If I leave, it's got to be—it's got to be for good."

"Please don't." I clutch at his arm, and I hate myself for this. For how selfish it is. "Lincoln, please don't go."

"I'm coming back eventually." His chest heaves and he puts an arm around me, tugging me close. "I'm going to come back, okay? I won't leave you with them forever. I'm coming back."

I press my face into his shoulder. All at once, I feel incredibly small. Too young for this.

"I'll come get you," he assures me. "I don't *want* to leave you.

I just can't stay here anymore. I always feel like they know who I really am, somehow."

"Do you think *I* don't know what that's like?" I pull away, standing up, motions jerky, skirt fabric fluttering in the wind, clinging to my legs. I want to claw this too-tight dress off my body. I want to claw this *skin* off. I want to let myself dissolve into something else, some other shape. "I'm not who they think I am either."

"I know," he says gently, standing too.

"No, you *don't*," I snap. "Nobody does. I don't even—it doesn't *matter*. It's not like I could ever do anything about it."

"You'll get out of here too."

"It's not the same." I'm sniffling all over again, wiping at my eyes. "I'm never going to get to be who I really am. Don't you understand that I'd be losing everything?"

"You'd—" Lincoln cuts off, bewildered. "What do you mean?"

"What do you *think* I mean?" I fling my arms out. "I've been trying to tell you for months. I'm not—I'm not who everyone thinks I am."

"What are you saying?"

"I'm not a girl," I spit, heartbeat hammering in my ears; that's the first time I've ever said it out loud, and I wish I hadn't, because now it's real.

"Oh," Lincoln says, and blinks.

My chest heaves.

"You're not, are you?" He reaches for me.

I step backward.

"I'm sorry." He catches me by the arm and pulls me into a hug. "I didn't know. I wasn't—I wasn't looking."

Gasping, I squeeze my eyes shut and I cling to him.

"I see you." His grip tightens around me. "I'm sorry, I see you now."

I press my cheek against his shoulder so hard it's a grind of bone against bone, and then I pull back. "I'm very happy for you," I tell him, and I mean it, but I hate that I still sound like a petulant child.

"I'm sorry," he whispers.

It doesn't even matter if he means it. He's *leaving*.

In the distance, Mom calls, "*ELIJAH!* Where did you go?"

I feel his sigh leach through his whole body, quiet resignation.

Then he steps back, catching my hand. "We'd better get back to them. I just—you know I'm not leaving you forever, right?"

Yes, you are.

I swipe at my eyes. "I know that you have to do this."

"I do," he tells me sadly. "And it'll be your turn before you know it."

Then he squeezes my hand. "I'm really glad you told me. We'll talk about it more, I promise."

As he lets go, I nod.

"Come on," he says. "Only a few more hours of torture."

For you, I think, but I don't say it aloud.

I watch his retreating back, and then I carefully dab at my under-eyes and rearrange my curls, and I follow.

This is not a nightmare.

It's my life.

FIFTY-NINE.

The nightmare ends.

I open my eyes, shaking all over, and tears pour down my cheeks.

Instead of turning around and stopping right by Gideon's tractor like I usually do, I pull off the side of the road and heave sobs into my hands, forehead pressed to the steering wheel.

I don't know how much longer it is before there's a tentative knocking on my window.

Not a nightmare. Never a nightmare. My heartbeat still rattles with the same adrenaline of the last ninety-seven days, but this time I know why. This time, it sticks with me after I open my eyes.

Blindly, I fumble for the locks, flipping the switch to let Gideon in.

He sinks into the seat, frowning at me before I've even had the chance to say anything. "What's the matter?"

"I keep remembering things," I tell him, not bothering with any preamble, forehead still pressed to the wheel. "I *have* access to all of her—my—memories, but sometimes specifics jump out at me."

He nods. "What did you remember?"

"The nightmare." My voice quivers.

Gideon places his hand on my back, between my shoulder blades, a gentle reassurance, and that's enough.

All day, Gideon's not saying something. We're both subdued after I tell him about Lincoln, but it runs deeper than that. He's pensive, watching me when he thinks I'm not looking, until it's driving me crazy.

"*What?*" I ask, finally, when we're walking back from Tenley's.

Twilight settles around us. Crickets hum in the grass lining the pathway.

Neither of us had fun today. I know everyone in Gideon's life, and to all of them, I'm a stranger, and I feel it, the thing Gideon was talking about all of those loops ago when we were sitting on the top of my car.

It's getting old.

I want Tenley to remember me.

Gideon wants tomorrows. I can feel it radiating off him.

Quietly, he says, "There's something we're not trying."

My stomach lurches. Dread spreads like ice, frosty fingers crawling over my skin. "What?"

"I've been hoping it wouldn't come to this," Gideon says. "But there's something we haven't tried. One thing you haven't done."

And *instantly*, I know what he's talking about.

"No." I shake my head. "I don't want to. Please. I don't—I don't want to tell them. I'm not ready."

"You've had a hundred days to get ready," Gideon counters, and I flinch away.

It stings like he slapped me.

"Laurie, that's not—that came out wrong." He sighs. "I just mean—you said it yourself, right? Ages ago. You were the one that said you tried to come out to your parents, and that it didn't work. You said you thought maybe the universe was trying to give you a second chance."

His words ring in the empty space between us.

I stare down at my shoes, at the dusty ground. Voice low, I say, "You don't get to tell me how my own story goes."

"I know that." He scuffs a hand across his forehead. "I *know*. I'm not trying to force you. I'm just *saying*."

"It's going to end if we figure it out," I say, miserable.

"It's going to end anyway. Isn't it important to *try*?"

"Am I not enough?" I burst out. "Fuck, I'm not enough for you, am I? I'm *never* enough."

He balks. "That's not what this is about."

"I wasn't enough for Lincoln to want to stay," I burst out, and I didn't even know that's what I was so desperately hurt about, even still, a year later.

"What are you *talking* about?" Gideon demands. "I would never think you're not enough. I *love* you."

I blink back tears. "You *seriously* want me to bring my parents into this?"

"That's not what I'm saying. It's not about them. It's about—there's magic in honesty."

"That is *such* bullshit."

"What if, at the end of this, you die?" he bursts out. "What if you're meant to—I don't know—figure this out, and then you'll get out, but if you don't—what if you—don't you ever wonder what triggered this in the first place?"

I glare at him, pulse racing, chest heaving.

"Laurie," Gideon starts, and he sounds desperate and sad and more than that, *afraid*. "What if you're already dead?"

SIXTY. VAL

By the time I get back to the house, my eyes are dry, and my conviction is a steel mass in my chest.

Mom is waiting up for me. I find her at the kitchen table, looking over her day planner and holding a wineglass aloft, swirling the dregs of crimson left at the bottom.

She doesn't look up when the door closes behind me.

I clear my throat. "We should talk."

"Yes," she says, in that flat, emotionless voice that means trouble is coming. "I think we should."

"You read my email," I say, not a question.

Mom sighs and sets the wineglass down with a soft click, pushing her chair back. She doesn't acknowledge what I've just said. "You lied to me."

"Are we not going to talk about how that was an *incredible* violation of privacy?" I keep my voice even, because if I show my cards now, everything I say will get dismissed without consideration. "I'm almost eighteen years old. Why are you reading my emails?"

"You live under this roof," Mom reminds me. "We pay for

everything you own, we pay for your phone, for your computer, we have the *right* to go through them to find out what you're using them for!"

"What I'm—" I choke on a laugh. "Okay, so ... I have no privacy, then?"

"You'll get privacy when you pay for it yourself," she says, voice still flat. Empty. Deadly quiet, she adds, "You lied to me. You lied to both of us. You told us that Elijah wasn't speaking to you either."

"I'm not the PROBLEM!" I shout, and then I just stand there with horror dripping down my spine as it sinks in that I said that out loud.

Raised voices must have alerted Dad that something is going on, because he's standing in the doorway now.

"Why were you signing your emails as Laurie?" Mom asks, ignoring him.

"Code names," I mumble. A half-truth. Middle names. *Lincoln and Lauren.* "It's just what he calls me."

There's no way to tell if she buys the surface-level truth.

Dad steps into the room, brow furrowed. Carefully, he asks, "What's going on out here?"

"I think Valerie has something she'd like to tell us," Mom says.

Dread turns the pit of my stomach to ice. "Don't I deserve the chance to tell you on my own terms?"

"You lost that chance when you lied to us," she says.

"Because I *had* to. You see that, right?"

"You didn't *have* to do anything. You chose to do that. You chose to lie." Mom pins me in place with her gaze like I'm a dead insect she's sticking down forever. "Are you going to admit it?"

I know Mom. I know that tight, near-murderous look in her eye. She knows.

She *knows*.

"I do," I say tremulously. "I do have something to tell you."

And then I burst into tears again.

Dad moves like he's going to step forward and then doesn't.

"You're going to know," I whisper miserably. "I feel like you might have already figured it out."

Dad glances at Mom, who just stares at me, and I see the first flicker of uncertainty in her steely gaze.

"I . . ."

All at once, I can't do this. My palms are clammy, breath hitching as my mouth opens and shuts.

"It's okay," Dad says, stepping toward me. "Hey, honey, whatever this is, we can work it out."

"We won't," I tell him miserably, swiping at my cheeks. "You're going to hate it. You're going to hate *me*."

"I could *never* hate you," he says. "Val, I'd never hate you, even if—"

"Even if I was gay?" I blurt out, and it's not even the whole truth, but it's a damn good place to start.

The tears keep falling.

He blinks. I can see the wheels turning behind his abruptly blank expression as he struggles to catch up with what I just said.

And somehow, I've surprised Mom too. This isn't what she meant. Whatever she read in those emails—whatever she was ready to confront me about—it wasn't this.

Her eyebrows rise so high her whole hairline shifts, and she shakes her head. "I don't—this isn't the time for this conversation.

You graduate this weekend, and then your internship starts on Monday."

She says it like it's final. Like there's no room for discussion.

"I don't *want* the internship," I tell her helplessly, *finally*. "I don't want the stupid internship, I don't even—"

But I can't say the rest of it out loud, so I don't. I just swallow it down and breathe in, slowly.

"Valerie, listen to me." Mom's entire expression is tight lines, a tangle of puppet strings pulled taut. "You're going to be wonderful. You're already such an asset to the church, and I know you're going to grow leaps and bounds in your faith over the next few months, just like I did when I was your age. Don't throw that away."

She's not even *acknowledging* it. This is about the internship now.

"You can't pretend what I just said is not real," I say carefully. "It's real whether you like it or not."

"Whether I—" She cuts off with a sharp, exasperated laugh. "Valerie, listen to me. Do not ruin your life over something that doesn't define you."

"You are a beautiful blessing," Dad interjects, placing hands on both of my shoulders and squeezing lightly. "You are *our* beautiful blessing. You are always going to be our daughter, no matter what. We will *always* love you."

I'm not your daughter. I haven't been your daughter in a long, long time. I only cry harder, which they both seem to take as encouragement.

"You are held in the palm of His hand," Dad tells me, pulling me closer into a hug. "I know this must be really confusing, but it's okay. You'll get through this."

Mom starts to pray out loud a moment later. I last about five words before I start to tune her out, gray static rising.

I couldn't even *do* it. I didn't even get to say it.

I stand there, limbs numb. Dad holds me and Mom drones on, and I feel like I'm about to throw up.

At last, they both release me.

"We'll talk further consequences on the weekend," Mom says. "For now, I'll take your phone, and let's—let's not let this incident overshadow what a tremendous achievement graduation is, okay?"

Incident.

Bile rises, throat burning.

I nod robotically, handing over my phone. Fortunately, on the way home, I already thought to change the passwords for everything, so hopefully Mom can't keep reading.

None of it hits me until I'm sitting on my bed, still feeling numb.

I just ruined my life.

I *ruined* my life, and for what? I ruined my life, and I ruined Bri's and I ruined Lincoln's life too, the life he so carefully put together, the one he's guarded like the precious, fragile thing it is.

But I didn't.

The thought is a lightning strike to my nervous system.

I *didn't*.

I didn't ruin anybody's life. All I did was talk to my brother, in private, the way I've been doing for years. All I did was *dare* to be myself.

Why is it my fault that nobody in my life is ready for me?

00:02

SIXTY-ONE.

The nightmare lurks inside my own house. It doesn't have claws or rows of teeth. It's just two people; my heroes who have no idea who I really am.

We wait until later, when we know Dad will be home. The evening air feels like a heavy blanket, suffocating.

"You don't have to do this," Gideon reminds me for the fifth time in the last hour, voice low.

"Yes, I do." Misery coats my lungs. "I have to try, right? You were the one who said it."

"Do you want me to come in with you?" Gideon asks.

"Honestly, it's probably better if you stay outside." I take the keys out of the ignition and hand them over. "You can be my getaway driver."

Gideon doesn't laugh.

"I have to do this," I remind him and myself. "Second chances, right?"

"Right," he echoes. Then he reaches over and touches my cheekbone. "Are you ready?"

"No," I tell him. "Would you be?"

"No," he admits. He catches my hand and threads his fingers through mine.

I suck in a deep breath. "It's time, though."

It doesn't feel like time.

I don't want to do this.

But I will. If it'll get me out of here and into a real tomorrow with Gideon, I'll do anything.

Mom's spitting fire before I've even set foot in the house. The door isn't all the way closed before she rounds the corner, all systems go. "You have got *some* nerve, you—"

I'm ready for the gasp even before it comes.

"Oh." She freezes in place. "Valerie. Your *hair*."

"Yes, it's short, I know," I say, impatient. "And yes, it *is* because of what we talked about last night, and what we didn't talk about, because you wouldn't let me."

"Don't." Her nostrils flare. "Valerie, be careful."

"Careful of *what*?"

It's different to see her, the way it had been different to see Dad, knowing he really *was* my dad.

This is my mother.

She's a stranger.

I know her better than I know anyone in the world. She's imprinted on my DNA. The way she smells, those Mom hugs that no one else can give. Hearing the car door slam and flinching.

Her teaching me how to tie my skates. Being on my best behavior, always, *what if Mom finds out?* The way she'd put my art up on the fridge with such a pleased, proud smile. The omnipresent harried edge to her expression, those pursed lips. Her raised voice freezing my blood.

"Sit with me," I say stiffly. Louder, I call, "Dad?"

He's already in the living room.

I feel three steps detached from my own body as I walk to the ottoman and sit, spine ramrod straight.

This could be it, I remind myself. *This could break the loop. No do-overs.*

I wait for them to sit across from me, and then start cautiously. "I need to tell you something."

Dad gives me a swift nod. It's not encouraging, exactly, but it prompts me to start, and I do.

"I've done the best I could to be the perfect daughter," I tell them, slowly, choosing each word carefully.

Mom starts to cry before I've even said anything of note.

My throat closes, so I have to force the rest of it out. "But I'm not. I wish I was. I wish I *could* be, but I can't, because I'm not your daughter at all."

They both stare. There's not even a flicker of recognition in their eyes.

"I'm not a girl. I can't keep going like this, or I'll—" My throat closes. "I can't."

"I don't understand." Mom's voice is thick with tears.

"Yes, you do," I tell her. "Maybe it's a bit of a shock, but I hope you can get your head around it someday."

She's already shaking her head. "Why would you choose this?"

"I'm not choosing it," I remind her, as patiently as I can.

"Val," Dad says, slowly. "Honey, come on. This isn't you."

No, I think bitterly. *No, it's not, and that's the point.*

"I know you better than this," he urges. "Come on, you're my little girl. You've always been—you're so—"

"I'm so what?"

He settles on "God doesn't make mistakes."

"So I'm a mistake now?"

"No!" He runs a hand over his bald spot. "Honey, no, of course not. I'm trying to help *you* see that. You're young. You don't know what you want. You don't know what you *need* or who you are. None of this is going to be important to you five years from now."

"How could you know that?"

"I *know* you."

"You don't. My name is Laurie," I tell him, surprised by how my voice shakes. "That's what Lin—Elijah calls me, because it's my name. I know you'll probably never see me as your son, but that's what I am."

Mom snaps, "So Elijah knows about this, then?"

She didn't know.

My heart sinks. Somehow, she didn't know. Somehow, she read through everything we wrote to each other and willfully didn't see it. All that registered was the first betrayal: that I'd kept him a secret this whole year.

"He's poisoning you against us," she says tearfully, and I want to *laugh*.

"Is that seriously your takeaway from this?"

"He up and left without warning, and now—"

"Don't pretend like that was a surprise." I scramble to my feet.

You'll get out of here too.

It's not the same. I'm never going to get to be who I really am. Don't you understand that I'd be losing everything?

This is losing everything, I realize. I look at them both looking up at me, and I realize I was right to be afraid.

I was also right that I'm not ready. I'm not ready for this part. I'm not ready to stand here and see the way they're looking at me, disappointment intermingling with hardened resolve.

"You know *exactly* why he left," I tell them. "You bullied him out of the house and you've done it to me too, and you won't know either of your children because you are *so far* into your shit that you'll pick your faith over your *family*. Are you proud of that?"

Mom blinks at me, mouth half open.

I stand there, fists clenched so tight my nails dig into my palms, chest heaving. "I'm done," I say. "He did it; so can I."

No do-overs, I remind myself, and a wave of terror washes over me. I pivot on my heel and practically *run* out of the room, flinging the front door open and slamming it shut behind me so hard it just bounces right back open on its hinges.

"Come back here!" Mom shouts, and I can't tell if she's following.

I scramble down the steps and out to the car.

Gideon's in the driver's seat, and he looks up as I come barreling down the driveway, scrambling to start the engine.

"Go," I tell him, the second I have the passenger door open, before I've even sat down. "Go, *go*."

"I'm going," Gideon says hastily, and the second I have my seat belt on, he floors it in reverse out of the driveway, peeling down the road.

When I chance a look over my shoulder, right before we turn the corner, the front door is still open.

There's nobody in the doorway.

It's dead silent except for the rumble of the road underneath us for several blocks. I have no idea where we're going, and I'm not sure Gideon does either, but there's nothing I can say, because the rush of blood in my ears is louder than anything else.

"I'm sorry," he says, at last. "I take it that didn't go well."

I can't—

"Come on." Gideon pulls off onto the side of the road.

I can't make myself look at him. Whatever's there, I can't face it.

"Did you . . . get to say what you wanted to say?"

"I didn't want to say any of it," I manage.

"Oh, Laurie." He touches my cheek, brushing away a tear I hadn't even registered. "I'm really sorry. I should never have asked you to do that."

"I'm glad I did it." I swipe at my eyes. "I think."

Gideon says nothing.

"I hope it worked," I whisper, and it feels like all I ever do is lie, lie, lie.

SIXTY-TWO.

When the nightmare ends and I open my eyes, I know three things only: first, freckles spatter the backs of my hands where they rest on the steering wheel; second, the radio is blowing static; and third, I'm going a hundred and twenty clicks on a highway I know by heart.

I slow to a stop, maybe for the last time.

The fourth thought comes slow, like the lurch after a fall: *It didn't work.*

Gideon's waiting for me by the side of the road. He doesn't look surprised, just resigned.

"So much for magical honesty," I say, and I wish I couldn't see the pity in his expression.

"I really thought that was the solution." He follows me to the car.

We drive into town in silence. I don't know where I'm going, and I'm not sure I care. Gideon tunes the radio to a local station and we drive, winding a pathway through the back streets of Nanton. They're all familiar by now. I know every front door, even if I don't know who they belong to.

A covert glance at Gideon's watch shows me it's nearly two by the time I finally stop the car on the edge of town, looking out at the blue haze of the mountains.

"I knew it wouldn't work," I say at last.

Bone-deep truth. It's a relief to say it, even if it stings on the way out.

"I just . . ." I heave a sigh. "I already knew how they were going to react. I've known that for a long, long time."

"I'm really sorry," he says, voice soft.

Overhead, thunder rumbles.

"How do we break the loop?"

I stay silent.

"We *have* to break it. We have to try. We can't give up now. I can't lose you," he says. "I'm not good at losing people."

My laughter is tight and bitter. "Is anyone?"

"This can't be it," he whispers. "It *can't* be."

The first raindrop hits the windshield.

I slump back in my seat. All I can see is Dad's face. Defeated, I ask, "Does it matter?"

"It *matters*," he says. "It matters. All of it. Everything we've done *has* to matter, doesn't it?"

"Maybe it doesn't. Maybe none of it matters. Maybe we'll get to the end and nothing will have meant anything real."

"Don't say that," he says with a swift shake of his head. "Laurie, don't."

"What was the point?" I ask, and my chest feels raw. "We've tried everything. I've made up with Bri. I've broken up with Brett. I got Bri and Ibha back together. I came out to my family. What else is there?"

Rain spatters on the windshield, a steady torrent.

What else is there?

It hits me all at once.

A gasp stutters in my chest. I sit straight up in my seat.

"What?"

"It wasn't me coming out to you that brought you into the loop," I tell him. "That wasn't the only thing I told you for the first time."

"What do you mean?"

"I trapped you here," I whisper, mind whirling. I've told Bri that I love her, and it didn't bring her into the loop, but that was different. I've already told her that dozens of times. She already knows it.

At least, I hope she does.

"I told you I love you." My heart trips, and all at once it feels like I'm running a race. "I *wanted* you to be with me. I was so—I was so fucking *lonely*. I wanted you with me, even if I didn't know that's what I wanted, and—"

"What?" Gideon asks, after a moment, when I don't keep talking.

"I know how to break it," I whisper, and misery coats my lungs.

Gideon goes very still.

"I just figured it out."

It settles, easy.

An ache, the scrape of concrete against skin, ragged breathing. I know it the way I'd known who I was when I finally got there.

The simplicity of it sends revulsion crawling up my spine.

All at once, I can't breathe. I push open the car door and step out into the rain.

"Laurie, where—"

I don't mean to cut him off, but the door closes before I can hear whatever Gideon's about to say.

He gets out of the car, shielding his face with his hand. "What are you doing?"

"You know, I've never really wanted to leave?" I wipe at my eyes, and I don't know if I'm wiping away tears or the rain that's soaking through my shirt and making my hair cling to the back of my neck. "I might have wanted to know how to break it, and I might have even wanted to get out, but I never *wanted* what was on the other side."

Gideon lowers his hand. "What are you saying?"

"This whole thing started with me running away," I tell him, and I'm spitting water now. "I was running away from my life."

"Oh," he says, a gust.

"That's what I remember more than anything else," I whisper. "How hopeless it felt. I didn't want—I *don't* want to have to face what it would mean to stop living that lie."

"You don't want it to end," Gideon says.

I swallow, hard. "Do you?"

"I—" Gideon cuts off. He sounds a little wounded when he says, "I told you I do. I told you why."

"I said it a long time ago, didn't I?" My voice is a ghost. "Maybe the universe is giving me a second chance."

"But not at coming out."

I shake my head. "I don't think that's the important part. I *know* it's not."

Gideon shivers.

"It's a second chance at being *me*," I say.

"Which means that when the clock runs out . . ." Gideon trails off. "If you don't *want* it . . ."

It's almost too dreadful to think about. And it's almost lovely, in a way.

It's almost a relief.

Slowly, I tell him, "I think when the clock hits zero, so do I."

"Do you want that?" It's the most devastated he's ever sounded.

"I don't know," I say, because it's the truth.

Gideon watches me for a long time. I see him in my peripherals, gaze intent, and all the while, my heart pounds in my throat.

There's a strange sort of serenity to it. If it was just over, I wouldn't ever have to face the rest of this life. I wouldn't have to figure it out.

"Let's do it right," he says, suddenly. "It's the last day. We should do it like we mean it."

And I don't have to ask what he means.

SIXTY-THREE.

My perfect last day would involve a lot of things.

Breaking up with Brett—*Fucking Wonder Bread*, Lincoln's voice adds in my head—Blanchette isn't one of them.

I don't wait for the party—I don't have time for that. Instead, I catch him in the parking lot at school.

His eyebrows arch at the sight of me. It's the same look he always gives me when he first sees my hair, and today I can't be bothered.

It hurts worse than it has before, though, because I remember him.

Brett.

My first boyfriend. Maybe even my first love, but not the way I'd always thought that would feel. Everything he's meant to me rushes to the surface, threatening to boil over. I'd been *so* happy when he kissed me, and that was real. When we were younger, sometimes he'd be throwing dolls off the balcony too. It had felt so nice to hold his hand. I do remember those study dates before they were dates, when I'd had to force myself to stop staring at his dimples. Skating together was easier than anything else, exhilarating, something like love. When he would laugh until he cried, it always felt like I'd done something right. Maybe I had.

"You cut your hair," he says dubiously, like if he makes it sound like a question instead of a fact then it might not be true.

"I did," I say. Then I clear my throat. "Brett, can I ask you something?"

"Anything." When his eyes finally drift from my hair to my face, something softens behind his expression.

"Why do you love me?"

That softness vanishes, replaced by fear. "Why?"

"I want to know," I tell him, and the simplicity of it must be enough.

"Okay, well, I love how passionate you are," he says. "I love how much you care about your family. Even when they're difficult."

Difficult is one word for it.

"I love that you're . . ." Brett gestures wide. "I mean, we were friends first, right? I love that we have hockey in common. I love that you like being involved in ministry. I love how good we are together."

I want to ask, *Are we?*

Instead, I catch a breath. "Would you still love me if I wasn't a girl?"

He cocks his head. "But . . . you *are* a girl."

"What if I wasn't?" I ask. "What if my body was different? Would you still love me?"

"I'd . . ." he starts, and then I see him *really* think about it.

That's all I needed.

Instead of answering, he steps toward me. "What are you really asking?"

"I think you already know that." I'm surprised by the complete and total overwhelm. "Matty kept saying that it wasn't fair not to tell you, and he was right. I'm not the perfect girlfriend."

It hasn't quite fully registered yet, I can tell. Blankly, Brett asks, "Matty knows?"

"That's the secret," I tell him, exasperated. "I didn't cheat on you. I just told him that I'm not a girl. I didn't mean to tell him. It just happened, and I'm not sorry, but I *am* sorry I let this go on so long without being honest with you too."

"Wait." Brett's voice is tight with emotion. "What's happening right now?"

I give him a sad smile, and then I step forward and I wrap my arms around him. It's honestly a surprise when tears burn. How many times have I hugged Brett and only felt guilt? "I think you already know that, too."

"I'm pretty sure this is illegal," Bri tells me as she's getting into the car, after she's done freaking out about my hair. "I'm pretty sure this is abduction of a minor, and I could press charges."

I tell her, "I love you."

"The *fuck*?" Bri shakes her head. "If you're only doing this to kill both of us, I want out."

My eyes water. "You're really important to me, you know that?"

She *actually* takes hold of the door handle.

I laugh. "Okay, okay, you're an awful bitch. Is that better?"

Suspiciously, she squints at me. "Marginally."

It's no less of a relief to tell her the truth on the way—almost the whole truth, anyway. I tell her about the emails, and my parents, and Lincoln, and when I apologize she starts crying. I tell her about me. I tell her who I am. It's no less difficult to just say it, even though I know how she's going to react.

And it's no less difficult to get her to actually do the damn thing and talk to the girl she's still in love with.

"Just giving you a push," I tell her as I nudge her across the barn.

"Oh, *hell* no."

"What if I told you that you've done this before?"

Bri turns and stares at me.

"What if I told you it's all going to be okay?" I say, softer. "What if I told you she'll forgive you?"

"How could you know that?" Bri asks, but her voice quivers, and then she looks over her shoulder, and I see the exact moment she catches sight of Ibha.

I'm startled by the rush I feel when I see her. Ibha. One of my best friends in the world, and I've spent all of this time not remembering that I love her too.

Ibha, ever soft-spoken. The voice of reason. One of the most beautiful people I've ever met, inside and out. How she can make a violin sing. It's imprinted into my bones, the way she and Bri would belt show tunes in the car on the way to school at half past seven in the morning. That smile she'd given me when I'd bought her that dainty bracelet with tiny gems in oranges and pinks and white, even before she'd told me she was the sort of person who would wear it. Dutiful big sister, loyal friend, right up until she wasn't there anymore.

She'd belonged so instantly, even if she hadn't believed it. Well—that was mostly Bri's fault, for being so hostile in eighth grade before she'd figured out she was down *bad* for her doe eyes and not just enraged by her presence for no reason.

Her mouth falls open at the sight of us. "Bri?"

"Go," I whisper to Bri, nudging her forward.

"Hey, Ibha," Bri says, nearly stumbling.

"I don't want to see you," Ibha says, voice tiny and tremulous. "I don't—you have *no* idea—I can't see you right now."

"I'm sorry," Bri says. "I know, and I'm so sorry this is happening, but mostly I'm sorry for being such a moron."

"Go away," Ibha counters, and thank God Bri doesn't listen.

"I love you," Bri says, simply. "I've been an ass."

"Yes you *have*," Ibha snaps, and then her resolve shatters and she throws her arms around Bri.

I watch them with a sad, soft smile.

Perfect day.

And then it's Gideon's turn.

"I'm really sorry I didn't tell you about Mom's letters," he says. There's something soft and subdued about his tone. "I know you know about them."

Jayda's eyes are wide in the lamplight outside the barn. I'm standing out of sight, watching, because Gideon asked me to.

"I didn't keep them from you to hurt you," he says, and that's how easy it is.

Jayda's face crumples. "I know."

Still quiet, still gentle, Gideon says, "I know what you did."

She sucks in a breath. "What?"

"I know you planted drugs in my room," he tells her. "And

I know what you don't know, which is that the Perrigans did find them. And I'm in a lot of trouble now."

Her eyes are enormous and glassy. "You are?"

"I'm not going somewhere nice tomorrow," he tells her. "They think the drugs were mine, just like you hoped. But now they're basically sending me to rehab, and it's an *awful*, awful place, Jay."

"But you're not—"

"*I* know that," Gideon says patiently. "And *you* know that. But *they* don't know that."

"I can't sabotage him," she says. "I love him."

Gideon sucks in a shuddering breath. When he lets it out, he swipes at his eyes. Quietly, he asks, "More than me?"

With a little sob, Jayda shakes her head.

"You could make it right," he tells her. "You'd get into trouble, but only a little."

She nods, wiping at her eyes.

"I love you," he tells her. "No matter what you decide."

"I love you too." Jayda turns and flings her arms around him.

"I'm not going to make you do it," he whispers as he presses his cheek to the top of her head. "I just hope you will."

"What do we do if the loop ends and time keeps going?" Gideon asks when he's done talking to Wyatt and Archer and it's all been done, and there's nothing left to do but wait.

I give Gideon a sad little smile. "I don't think it will."

From up here on the roof, the stars are beautiful.

I watch the same clouds form the same patterns they've made for a hundred days as they pass over the moon and swallow down the lump in my throat.

"But if it does?" he asks. "What then?"

"Then we get to keep going."

He's quiet for a long moment, staring down at where our fingers are laced together. "If it worked."

Crickets hum in the grass far below.

"If it worked, and Mrs. Perrigan believed Jayda, then tomorrow they won't come for me."

My lips twitch into a smile. "They *definitely* won't."

"You sound confident."

"Oh, believe me. If I have anything to do with it, you're not going anywhere. If need be, *I'll* abduct you myself. You could come to Lethbridge early. Lincoln would love you." I feel a stab of regret that I never introduced them. All this time, and I never brought them together.

Maybe that was on purpose. It would have hurt like hell.

"You think?"

I nod. "I know."

Gideon squeezes my hand. "For the record, whatever happens, I think you're going to be okay."

The breeze pushes my hair off of my forehead. I lean my head against his shoulder and let out a breath, long and slow. "For the record," I tell him as the moon shines over us, "I hope you're right."

SIXTY-FOUR.

VAL

I don't start out with any kind of plan.

It comes down to this: me and my go-bag sneaking out through the garage door, contraband phone clutched in my hand, morning dew dampening my shoes as I duck around the side of the house to the car.

My phone is dead after a night in the top-left drawer of Mom's bureau, but that's fine. I know the way down to Lincoln's—mostly—and I can charge it when I get there.

At least the car is mine. At least I bought it from Lincoln with my own money, and even if they come after me, I'll give it up.

I just won't come back.

I get in, fingers trembling. My hands shake so badly that for a second I have to brace myself against the steering wheel, looking up at the house. I have a childhood of memories here, and right this second, none of them feel important somehow.

The last time I sat here like this it was the middle of the night.

I'd been out walking alone at half past two a.m. on a Friday when Matty had found me and insisted on driving me home.

We'd barely spoken until he parked in the driveway and turned the car off.

We sat in silence for a while before he quietly asked, "Where were you going, Val?"

How could I tell him that I didn't know? That I just needed—out?

"I just... wanted to clear my head." I shivered, and Matty handed me his sweatshirt. Too tired—and too cold—to protest, I tugged it over my head.

"Do you..." Matty paused before he asked, "Do you want to talk about it?"

"I can't," I told him, swallowing hard. "I can't tell you."

"Can't or won't?"

When I didn't respond, he sighed. "Look, I'm not going to prod, but I know how fucking miserable your house can be. Eli talked about it all the time."

I nodded.

"And I might not get it, but I know how hard it is to feel like you don't have anyone to talk to."

I almost commented on the hidden implications—that we both knew Brett didn't count as someone I could talk to—but at the last moment, shook my head. "I—can't."

"Why not?"

"Because I'm a coward," I whispered.

"I think you're a lot of things, Val, but I don't think you're a coward."

"You would if you knew."

"Try me," he said. "I might understand."

That was the worst of it. He *might* understand, and if he did, then what? I rubbed the sleeve of his sweatshirt between my index finger and thumb and stared out the windshield at my house in the dark, windows all empty eyes staring straight back.

I could get out. This could be over right now.

"Sometimes, I wonder . . ." I trailed off.

Matty just waited.

After an agonizing silence, I shifted in my seat toward him. "How do you know who you are?"

His eyebrows lifted.

"Like, *really* who you are. What makes you . . . *you*?"

"Shit," he said. "I guess that's kind of complicated. Can you add on to that at all?"

"Do your insides match your outsides?" I asked, voice scraped raw as though I'd been screaming the question over and over.

Matty breathed in, slow. Then he sat back in his seat and nodded, once. "Tell me the whole truth, okay? See how it feels. I'm a locked vault, I promise. I won't tell a soul."

"What if I wasn't a girl?" I asked, all in a rush. "What if I'm not the person I look like I am?"

For a moment, we sat in the silence.

Matty's brow pinched, like he was thinking hard. Then, as casually as if I'd asked about the weather, he asked, "What if?"

"What if I hate—what if I *hate* this person?"

"Which one?"

"Both," I said miserably. "I don't know."

"You don't hate yourself," Matty said gently. "It might feel like it, but you don't. You're just stuck right now, is all."

"And I'll never get unstuck."

"Never's a pretty powerful word." Matty shifted, bending his knee as he turned to face me completely. "How did you know? Like, what prompted it? If I can ask—don't feel like you have to tell me."

"You sort of helped me figure it out, actually," I told him, because what the hell. I was already spilling all of my secrets. Why not this one too?

"How do you mean?"

"I've been jealous of you as long as I can remember," I admitted. "And I couldn't figure out why. I just—I wanted to be you so bad it made me hate you sometimes. And one day we were at practice, and you were showing us how to run a drill, and it just hit me like this lightning strike. I *wasn't* jealous because I wanted to do what you do. I was jealous because I'd never ever get to do it the *way* you do. I'd never get to be—*like* you."

For a moment, Matty sat in the quiet and digested everything. Then he smiled, just enough. "So you're saying I cracked your egg a little bit?"

I gave him my best smile in return, even though misery made my face heavy. "Recognition of the self in the other, or something."

"Well, I'm honored."

I choked on a laugh. "You should be."

"What should I call you?" he asked. "Are you still Valerie, or do you want to go by something else?"

"Lincoln calls me Laurie," I told him. "But nobody else knows, so maybe—I guess, stick with Val for now."

He nodded. Then, mostly to himself, he said, "I'm going to use your last name. I mean, shit, everyone calls me Lawrence even though I hate it, don't they? It won't even be weird."

I burst into tears.

"Oh, shit, hey." Matty put a hand on my back as I bent forward and put my face in my hands.

Matty let me cry, and he didn't say anything when I definitely got snot and tears on the sleeve of his sweatshirt either.

"God." I wiped at my eyes when the tears finally slowed. "Sorry."

"No," he said. "No *sorry*. Don't do that. You just told me something huge, okay? That was really brave."

I sniffled. "Don't feel very brave."

"I don't think we ever feel very brave when it counts the most." Matty rubbed a little circle on my back.

"You're amazing," I told him. "Seriously. Brett's lucky to have you as a friend."

"Thanks. I try." Matty's little smile faded. "He doesn't know?"

I just laughed, tight and bitter. "God, could you imagine?"

"Thank you for telling me," he said quietly. Then, even quieter, he added, "Laurie."

By the time I get out of the city, it's midmorning.

The drive is numbing, in a good way. Pasture flits by me as I drive, faster than I've ever driven before in my life. The sky stretches out, endless horizon to my left, the familiar surge of mountains to my right, snowcapped even in June.

I drive through Nanton, barely curbing a half-hysterical urge to stop and see Ibha. I'd say sorry, I think, as the town disappears in my rearview.

The road in front of me blurs.

I tighten my grip around the steering wheel, turning the volume up on the radio just as the signal fades to static, loud white noise to match the frantic buzz in my veins.

You're just stuck, is all.

And I'll never get unstuck.

Never's a pretty powerful word.

If I admit it to myself—those words poised with venomous fangs: *I can't do this anymore*—then that means everything has to change. It means I lose everything.

What is there for me? Lincoln made a fresh start, but he had something to cling on to. He had Krishan waiting for him; a whole *life* waiting for him.

What do I have? I'd have to start over at zero. I'd lose my home, if you can call it that. My parents aren't safe, but they've always been *there*.

A tear slips down my cheek.

I don't know if I'm brave enough for that.

A blast of sound jerks me out of my reverie. A semi-truck is laying on the horn—I'm drifting into the wrong lane—and I go to jerk the wheel, and then I just—

And then I just don't.

I can't do it.

It's a mistake the second I make the choice. The second it's too late.

Yeah, my life is going to be a total nightmare for a while, but I don't want it to end, not really, and I can't believe I'm only realizing it now that

DO YOU WANT IT?

SIXTY-FIVE.

"Do you think it'll matter?" Gideon asks, voice quiet in the gloom.

I swallow hard. "I don't know."

It's well past five in the morning. We're ending the loop where it starts, but I had to get out of the car to pace a half hour ago, circling the spot on the road where I wake up.

I could draw the skyline from this patch of asphalt with my eyes closed. It would make a pretty painting, especially like this, with the clouds muddying the horizon.

Just after six, it starts to rain.

It feels fitting, though. I turn my face up and let droplets mist against my face, and when tears well, I don't stop them.

"There are so many things I still want to say," I whisper, a croak in the dark.

"Say them," Gideon tells me. He's leaning against the car with his arms folded, subdued. Watching me.

I shake my head. "Too many."

He pushes off the car and takes my hand, forcing me to stop walking. With a little sigh, he draws me closer, tucking an arm around my waist.

I knock my forehead against his sternum. "At least I got you out of all of this."

He laughs. "Silver linings."

"You're big on the silver linings now, huh?"

"I'm a changed man." It starts out as a joke, but then his smile fades. "Because of you."

"Gideon . . ."

"You changed my life, Laurie," he whispers. "You know that, right?"

I swallow hard.

"I was close to giving up. I was ready to just let it happen."

"I know. I think—" I swallow. "At the beginning of this, if I had known, and you told me that when the time ran out, I might just be *done*, I would have been relieved."

"And now?"

My exhale shakes.

Around us, the calls of morning birds fill the air. The breeze whispers through the long grasses, the sun dragging slow, sweet dawn across the horizon.

Gideon's watch beeps.

"It's time," he tells me, as if I don't *know*, as if the sound doesn't send my heart racing. "You ready?"

"I'd better be," I say. "It's—you and me, okay?"

"Every day," he murmurs. "Every damn day, Laurie."

"And there will be so many tomorrows," I murmur, because it *has* to be true.

He nods. "And you'll be in all of them."

"I'll *never* forget you," I promise, heart pounding. "No matter what."

"No matter what," he agrees.

"You'll fight for it, right?" I ask. "You won't let them walk all over you?"

"Fuck, I'll try." His arms tighten around me, and then his watch beeps again. I suck in a shuddering sob.

"I love you," he whispers, shaky.

I cling to him tighter, face turned into his neck. "I love you. I'll see you tomorrow, okay?"

It has to be real, and it *is*.

I want out. I want a shot at figuring out who I could become.

I *want* this life.

With a deep breath, I squeeze my eyes shut tight and cast a last, helpless wish out into the universe.

I want to live.

I want to live.

I want to live.

EPILOGUE.

Here's the thing.

All the corny shit about self-love is true. People say it to you, and it makes you laugh, because *yikes*. And then, after you've done all your scoffing, they have the audacity to be *right*.

Beauty creeps in slowly, but you have to make space for it on purpose.

You have to water your own garden. And for a long time, it feels like you're standing there watering dead earth, but then it's there. All of a sudden that first green shoot unfurls, and it makes you get on your hands and knees to marvel at it.

All of a sudden you're standing in line at the grocery store with your brother and you love him so much it feels like you're going to puke. All of a sudden you're on your first day at a new job and you realize you're only, like, regular levels of anxious about it. All of a sudden you're watching your friend's dog hurtle across a field to bring a ball back to you and his ears are flapping in a way that makes your friend laugh like she's dying and your chest *aches* with how happy you are that you're still around to see it.

All of a sudden you're moving into dorms for your first year of university, and it occurs to you that you have an entire lifetime stretching out in front of you, and it doesn't scare the shit out of you anymore.

Okay, it does.

But it's the good kind of scary.

"I probably should have made sure my roommate's going to be cool before we lugged all this stuff up here, right?" I say, surveying the mess of boxes and bags. I definitely have a lot less stuff than I would have if I'd come from home, but this is more than enough for me.

"No." Lincoln sets down the last of the boxes to point at me. "No *should*. Come on."

I trail after him back into the hallway.

Whatever he's about to say gets swallowed as someone calls Lincoln's name and his head snaps up. "Hang on. Wait here. I'll be right back."

I nod, touching a hand to my pocket as I stop next to a bulletin board so covered in paper fliers that I can't even read most of them. Mom will want to know that I'm moved in, even if I don't really want to tell her. "I should probably—"

"Ah!" Lincoln whips around to stop me, like he's reading my mind. "*Enough*. No more."

I give him a sheepish little grin.

Lincoln—my big brother—is trying to train me out of my *should-haves*. It's a real challenge too, because recently my life is *made* of a collection of *should-haves* that are piling so high they're outgrowing their foundation.

I *should have* stayed home this summer for the church internship my mom was obsessed with me doing, but I didn't. I *should have* given long-distance a shot with my ex-boyfriend,

Brett, but I didn't. I *should have* come out to my best friends Bri and Ibha way earlier, like, *months* ago, but I didn't.

Instead of all that, I had a little breakdown, skipped the last day of school, drove down to Lethbridge the day before graduation to see Lincoln, and then didn't come back, not even to walk across the stage. I cut all my hair off—Mom was *pissed*—and came out to Bri and Ibha on FaceTime the same day, back-to-back. Brett and I broke up when I went back to get some of my stuff, and then I spent the next two weeks driving Lincoln up the wall agonizing over whether I was a bad person for not feeling that sad about it.

"Nice tattoo," someone says to my right.

"Thanks." Instinctively, I touch my wrist where my new tattoo is still bumpy against my skin. It's just a little thing—Lincoln and I got matching two-inch snakes—but I can't help smiling whenever I see it.

I look up to—*Christ.*

One of the best-looking guys I've ever seen in my life is at my elbow. His long black hair is up in a loose bun, dark eyebrows framing equally dark eyes. The collection of intense features—striking cheekbones, long straight nose, strong jaw, heavy brow bone—should be too much, but he just looks sort of like a walking heart attack that spent all summer outside, skin warmed to a golden brown.

"I'm Gideon," he says.

I hold my hand out. "Laurie."

"Good to meet you, Laurie." He takes my hand to shake it, and I have to hold back an audible gasp.

I'm *certain* I've met him before, all at once. The memory is frustratingly elusive, but it's there, and I—I kind of want to go on holding his hand for as long as I possibly can, but I don't want to be a freak, so I let go, and I nod. "Likewise."

"Have we met before?" He tilts his head to consider me. "I swear, you look so familiar."

"I was *just* thinking that! Did you ever play hockey in Calgary?" I ask. "Or—wait, did your family ever go to Wildwood United?"

He shakes his head. "Nah, I'm from Nanton."

I brighten. "Oh, I have a friend there! Do you know Ibha Agarwal?"

Gideon laughs. "Wait, *you* know Ibha?"

"Yeah, she's dating my best friend." I hold up my phone. My lock screen is a picture of the three of us, taken when I came back for Stampede this summer. It's not the best picture of me, because I'm laughing so hard I'm a little blurry, and you can't even see Bri's face because she's got her lips pressed to Ibha's cheek, but every time I look at it I feel warm all over.

"She's friends with my sister," he says. "Small world, I guess."

"I guess," I echo, smiling at him. He's right—it really *does* feel like we've met before, somewhere. I don't get the chance to think about it too hard, though, before Lincoln's returned and is on me, gripping both of my shoulders.

"Oh, good! You've met." Lincoln grins, slapping Gideon's back. "Laurie, this is the guy I was telling you about."

"Oh shit, *you're* the new goalie?" I grin, extending a closed fist. "Nice. Way to go, dude."

Gideon knocks his knuckles against mine. "Looks that way."

"This is Laurie, my little brother," Lincoln says, clapping a hand to my shoulder. He says it proudly, just like he's said it about forty billion times in the last several days, as though being as intense an ally as possible will make up for the way Mom and Dad are going to react, whenever I get around to telling them.

And honestly? It sort of does.

"We're still fighting with admin to get Laurie transferred to *our* team," Lincoln explains to Gideon. "They're giving us a bit of grief about fairness and athletic ability, as *if* Laurie couldn't outskate every single one of us."

My cheeks warm.

"Oh shit." Lincoln fumbles with his phone. "Hang on, Krish is locked out. I'll be right back, okay?"

"Okay." I smile at him as he goes.

"Well, I hope they approve your transfer," Gideon says once Lincoln is out of earshot. "Now I really want to see you skate."

I grin. "I'll race you, if you want."

"Hell no," he says. "I'm all rusty. I haven't properly played in months."

"Why not?"

"Just working a lot. And I was up here visiting my—Well." Gideon waves a hand. "That's a story for another day."

"Okay," I say, and then, surprised at my own boldness, I keep going. "Guess you can tell it to me another day, then."

He laughs, clearly surprised and a little pleased. "Shit, I guess so. Are you going to be at the mixer tomorrow night?"

"I think Lincoln would scalp me if I didn't go," I tell him. "Even though parties aren't really my thing. What about you?"

"I wasn't particularly looking forward to it, but I'm glad that now I have a real reason to show up," he says.

Then he drops me a little wink.

Christ, he's smooth. I fight the urge to touch my hands to my cheeks, where I'm sure I've gone red all over.

"I'll see you tomorrow, then." Gideon grins, like he knows full well that I've been totally and *completely* struck dumb, and like he's pleased with himself about it.

"Yeah," I echo, lifting a hand in farewell as he turns away. There's this strange, overwhelming warmth that feels like it's about to burst out of me, and even though I don't know where it's coming from, I don't hate it. I watch him go, and under my breath, I murmur, "See you tomorrow."

ACKNOWLEDGMENTS

This book was born from an unusual place of confidence, and naturally as such gave me more trouble than any other book I've ever written. I tore open some old wounds to get this one out onto the page, so to anyone who had the misfortune of being around me during this most wretched of drafting processes—thank you, and I owe you basically forever.

It's very much intentional that the secret sauce to breaking the time loop had nothing to do with coming out. This was never a "coming out" story. In a lot of ways it's about "coming in" instead. The innate bravery of living as a queer person doesn't necessarily map directly onto transparency—for many of us, that isn't safe. This is about the first step—deciding this life is worth it—and committing to living it.

That said, I have to thank every trans person who lives their lives openly and without shame. You're invaluable, and I owe my own journey to every one of you who showed me it was possible. Thank you, thank you, thank you.

I also owe a bigger-than-usual thank-you to my parents: beyond my gratitude that you fostered a love of writing in me early on, for so many reasons, this book wouldn't exist without you.

My brilliant miracle of an agent, Jenna: I still think you might be a witch. I owe so much hope to you—thank you for believing in this story, championing it far beyond what I thought it deserved, and coaxing me back out of my shell to commit deviances.

ACKNOWLEDGMENTS

To Kristin—this brilliant whirlwind began with you, and it's been both an honor and a privilege to be able to work with you. I'm still astonished by your wholehearted love for Laurie and the way your discerning eye sharpened this book and pulled the magic to the forefront.

To the rest of the brilliant team at Norton—Rebecca Munro, Rachelle Mandik, and Delaney Adams; Hana Anouk Nakamura and Dion MBD for the stunning cover; and Naomi Duttweiler for marketing to the heaves—thank you.

My fabulous readers: Bugs, Jack, Jamie, Jules, Mikala, Noa, Teddy, and Theo. You sustain me and encourage me, and most important, you met me where I am with this one and took the time to fall in love with it. Thank you.

Mairead, for all of your enthusiasm and encouragement during the initial chaos of this book—thank you. Jules, your brilliant advice and steady presence encouraged me through the crisis of faith that nearly stalled this book for good. I owe you one forever. Mikala, I would be utterly lost without your relentless belief in me.

Jamie, for stabilizing the ecosystem of the half-manic creative process both on a literal level—by stopping me from eating deli meat over the sink—and on a metaphorical level through your invaluable feedback and unwavering confidence at every stage.

To everyone who reads this: All my tomorrows, and all my love.